Huldah:
PROPHETESS

SHARON DOW

A historical novel

HULDAH: PROPHETESS
Copyright © 2014 by Sharon Dow

ISBN: 978-1-4866-0382-4

Word Alive Press
131 Cordite Road, Winnipeg, MB R3W 1S1
www.wordalivepress.ca

WORD ALIVE
—P R E S S—

Library and Archives Canada Cataloguing in Publication

Dow, Sharon, 1966-, author
        Huldah : prophetess / Sharon Dow.

Issued in print and electronic formats.
ISBN 978-1-4866-0382-4 (pbk.).--ISBN 978-1-4866-0383-1 (pdf).--
ISBN 978-1-4866-0384-8 (html).--ISBN 978-1-4866-0385-5 (epub)

        1. Huldah (Biblical prophetess)--Fiction. I. Title.

PS8607.O987335H84 2014   C813'.6   C2013-908462-2
                                             C2013-908463-0

Sharon Dow is a storyteller of the first order. My wife Adrienne and I have read her first historical novels out loud to each other with great fascination. And having read the first chapters of her third, we eagerly welcome *Huldah: Prophetess*.

Sharon's significant historical research, combined with her vivid imagination and facility with language, animate the lives of little-known Bible characters with credibility and give an enriched understanding of the epochs in which they lived.

—Rev. Dr. Jim Reese
Pastor Emeritus of Benton St. Baptist Church, Kitchener, ON
Founder of *Jim Reese Ministries*
Author of *Courtship Chronicles*

The stories of the Bible are true, but they give us only a brief glimpse into the lives of their characters. We need to remember that those names represent real persons, and the use of some sanctified imagination can help us think about what it might have been like to play their parts in history. In this book, Sharon Dow helps us imagine the life of a prophet who was both young and female—that is, someone who's not exactly the typical biblical character. What would it be like to be Huldah at a strategic point in Jewish history? Read with your imagination in gear.

—Dr. Stanley K. Fowler
Professor of Theological Studies
Heritage Theological Seminary
Author of *More Than a Symbol*

Sharon Dow's books seem to get better and better. This book will grip the reader's attention! As in all of the author's books, the portrayal of life in biblical times is rich and will make Scripture come alive for the reader.

—Heather McKenzie
Communications Coordinator
Former Director of Connected Women
Women's Ministry FEBCentral

Dedication

To my three daughters-in-law, I dedicate *Huldah: Prophetess*. Meghan, Amy, and Melanie, you have added new perspectives to our family. My sons have chosen well. I appreciate your willingness to gather the family in your homes and to spend time with your mother-in law. You are dedicated wives and mothers, and my life has been enriched because of you.

acknowledgements

To read a book is a rapid exercise; to write a book is a long process. There are many obstacles along the way. Because many people in my life have taken 1 Thessalonians 5:11 to heart, I have overcome the obstacles and moved forward.

> *Therefore encourage one another and build each other up, just as in fact you are doing.*
>
> 1 Thessalonians 5:11

Thank you to the many people who took the time to encourage me on this journey. You are truly appreciated.

I especially wish to thank the team who read my manuscript when I entered it in the Word Alive Press Free Publishing Contest. You saw potential in my work and encouraged me immensely when you chose my story as the contest winner!

The team at Word Alive Press has been an encouragement to me. Amy Groening and Jen Jandavs-Hedlin have patiently answered my questions. Evan Braun, my editor, took great care with my manuscript. I know I have a stronger book because of his attention to detail. He is talented and patient, and I was happy to accept his suggestions with confidence in his expertise.

Once again I want to acknowledge my prayer partners, The Pergamum Prayer Team. These ten individuals faithfully pray for specific requests during my writing and publishing journey. I can never fully thank them for their faithfulness.

My family has always supported me in whatever path I have chosen. Their faith in me, their love and support, has made it possible to indulge myself in my writing.

Sharon Dow

My husband, George, deserves my greatest thanks. He faithfully reads all that I write, marks errors to repair, always loves what I write, lifts me up when the road is rough, and even cheerfully does the laundry! Thank you for believing in me!

And to you, my dear readers, without you there would be no purpose in producing books. You have made my heart sing with your praise of *Antipas: Martyr* and *Pergamum: Satan's Throne*. Your enthusiasm for my stories has given me the desire to keep writing. I trust you will enjoy *Huldah: Prophetess* as much as you did the first two.

May God pour out his blessings on you!

Hilkiah the priest, Ahikam, Acbor, Shaphan and Asaiah went to speak to the prophetess Huldah, who was the wife of Shallum son of Tikvah, the son of Harhas, keeper of the wardrobe. She lived in Jerusalem, in the Second District.

2 Kings 22:14

part one

*H*ot sun beat down on the streets and alleyways of the Second District of Jerusalem. No cooling breeze swept through the narrow laneways or disturbed the debris gathering along the edges of the dirt. A small woman struggled with a cloth bundle, pulling it behind her. The bundle was untidy and awkward, having been tied loosely with a thin cord. Up ahead, she could see the entrance to her home. A few more tugs and she would be there.

She paused to wipe her brow with her headscarf. A lock of dark hair slipped from under the covering. She didn't care. With one sandaled foot, she pushed the door open and entered the cool house. Thick mud walls kept out the worst of the oppressive heat.

"Huldah, is that you?"

Her mother's voice.

"Yes, Mother, I'm back."

Huldah dropped the bundle on the dirt floor and flexed her shoulders, working out the tightness. She paused for a moment to let her eyes adjust, then slipped in behind the curtain separating the main room from the sleeping area. Her mother, Salome, smiled at Huldah from where she was propped up in bed.

"Are you feeling any better?" Huldah stood as tall as her fourteen years would allow and clasped her hands.

"Yes, yes, much better," Salome said.

Huldah drew her lips together and her shoulder muscles bunched.

"Did the baby live?" Salome lifted her face toward Huldah and squinted her dark eyes.

Huldah stamped her foot and rammed her hands under her arms. She drew her brows together and lowered her eyes. "No, of course the baby didn't live." She tossed her head back, releasing strands of dark hair. "I told you it wouldn't live. Why did you send me?"

"Child, I sent you because I was sick and couldn't go. You know that." Salome struggled to sit up. "Come here, child." She reached out her hand to Huldah.

"No, no, no. I won't be consoled. You can't make it better. The baby died. Can't you understand? The baby died and now I'm to be blamed for that." She flung her arms wide, glared at her mother, then ran from the room.

"Huldah, come back."

Huldah, who had inherited her mother's fine features and small frame, heard the words but ignored them. In her haste to leave the house, she kicked aside her bundle.

Outside, she climbed the rough steps at the side of the house. Reaching the roof, she collapsed on the mattress under the shelter her father had built for her. She slept here in good weather, preferring it to the close quarters of the house.

Tears came, but only briefly. She had known the baby would die and so had been prepared when the little body was born dead. How she knew these things, she could never explain to anyone. It was just a feeling she got, and so far she was always right.

She slept deeply for some time. When she opened her eyes, the sun was still bright, but the rays were slanted, making shadows on her rooftop. The aroma of roasting lamb curled up over the roof. The tempting smell came from the house next door.

Shallum's mother must be cooking today. I wonder if she'll bring some to our house. My mother won't be preparing the meal this night.

Huldah stretched to her full length, lifting her arms high over her head. When she was on her feet, she moved to the edge of the roof to look over the laneway in front of the house. Her body slumped down on the rough ledge, leaning on the low wall surrounding the roof. With her face cradled in her hands, she stared at the familiar sights: baked earth, ragged children darting in the lane, an abandoned cart across the way, and dirt, dirt, dirt. Her thoughts whirled away to the private place in her mind, the place where she was somebody—somebody important.

I'm fourteen and nobody. She shook her head and came back to the present. Shouts and bleatings came her way. *Oh no, the flocks are coming in. Father will soon be home from the temple, and I've not started the meal or put away the things from the birthing.*

She scrambled from her perch, using her hands to press down her robe while adjusting her headscarf and trying to shove her hair under it, but without much success. Her feet slipped on the steep steps as she arrived at the bottom, out of breath and frantic to reach the indoors before her father arrived.

When she pushed through the door, she heard her mother's sobs from behind the curtain. No time to check on her. She grabbed the bundle she had kicked aside earlier and pulled it to the corner, where her mattress was pressed against the wall. Rolling the bundle onto the blanket, Huldah opened it, dumping the contents: long strips of cloth from the birthing, towels soiled and wet, the unwashed basin, her mother's cutting tools, plus herbs and spices used for dressings and teas. She scooped up the wet towels and cloths and dumped them in the tub next to the door. Next, she tucked away the basin and utensils to wash later. When she finished, she heard a knock on the door.

"Huldah, are you in there?" The door eased open and Esther's friendly, smiling face appeared.

"Yes, Esther, I'm here." Huldah smiled to herself as Esther carried in a tray laden with food.

"I can't stay, but here's some lamb and vegetables for your meal." Esther shoved the tray into Huldah's waiting arms. She leaned her head around Huldah, looking toward the curtain. "Is your mother any better today?"

Huldah nodded and placed the tray on the table. She knew Esther liked to keep up on village gossip. Reluctant to give out more information, Huldah watched silently as Esther's eyebrows rose.

"Well, I'll be going. I need to feed my family." Esther backed from the room, arms folded over her chest.

Remembering just in time, Huldah said, "Thanks for the food, Esther. It smells wonderful."

Esther bowed her way out, closing the door behind her.

Huldah's lips curved up, almost meeting her wide eyes. She rubbed her hands over her face. *Thank you, Lord. This means I won't be in trouble with Father.*

The low table was soon set with clay bowls, cups, and wooden spoons. When Huldah finished, she heard her father approach. He always cleared his throat before entering the house; she didn't know if it was just a habit or a signal to the family that he was home.

She looked up when his shadow darkened the doorway.

Amaziah was a big man, towering over her. His dark beard had streaks of grey, matching the bushy eyebrows overhanging deep-set eyes. But it was his nose that drew attention—large and humped where it had been broken in a fight in his younger days. It seemed to dominate his face and took on a life of its own when he talked.

When he entered, his eyes roved up and down her body.

"Well girl, is my meal prepared?" his deep voice rumbled. His lips pressed together in a straight line when he hung his cloak on a wooden peg just inside the door.

Huldah hated to admit it, but she was afraid of him. She nervously moved the plates around on the table.

"Yes, Father. Esther was good enough to bring us a fine meal."

"Esther?" Amaziah swung his massive head toward her. "What did that gossip want?"

"She was just trying to be kind, Father. She knows Mother is sick." Huldah could feel her stomach begin to tremble. He always had that effect on her.

"Sick? Lazy, more like it." He glanced at the curtain, then moved toward it. Pushing it aside with a wide hand, he looked down at his wife. "Well, are you going to sleep all day?"

Huldah heard her mother whimper.

"Woman, get up and eat with the family." Amaziah let the curtain fall into place, moving to take the low seat at the head of the table.

The door opened again and her brothers arrived—Jairus, the youngest, and closest to Huldah's age; Malachi, the middle son; and Lot, the oldest. Two older sisters were married and lived in the homes of their in-laws.

Her brothers were laughing and talking among themselves when they entered. Lot and Malachi were large like their father, but Jairus was small and delicate.

They removed their cloaks just as Salome peered around the curtain, her hands trembling. Her usually ruddy face was pale. Huldah rushed to her side and put her arm around her. Together they walked to the table.

Jairus pushed two pillows in place and helped ease their mother down on them.

Amaziah stretched out his hand over the family table. "Lord Almighty, the mighty one of Israel, we invoke Your blessing on the food we are about to receive. Hear our prayer..."

Huldah stopped listening. She knew the prayer would continue for several minutes, as always.

How can he be a priest of the Lord and be so mean to all of us? It was a question she asked herself day after day. The priestly image he portrayed in the temple was not the man her family lived with. Her mother refused to talk about it, so Huldah lived without answers, in fear of him. Sometimes she feared for her life—and for her mother's life.

two

H uldah… know-it-all.
Huldah… sorcerer.
Huldah… liar.
Huldah… dreamer.
Huldah… baby-killer.

Taunts followed her while she hurried past the boys who hurled them. Wild, cruel laughter mingled with the chant until she wanted to put her hands over her ears, wanted to spit in their leering faces, wanted to kick their dirty bare legs. Word had spread that the baby had died, and that Huldah had predicted it.

Once she was out of sight of the boys, she rounded the corner of her laneway, leaned against the trunk of a tree, and let her body slide to the earth. She dashed at the tears hovering on her eyelids, tears of anger, not sorrow.

"I didn't kill that baby. I know I didn't." Her fists pounded her knees. She continued to pound and shout until a face appeared near her own.

"Huldah, what's wrong?" Her best friend, Sara, knelt beside her, peering into her face. "Stop, Huldah. Talk to me."

"Sorry, Sara." She sat up, grinding her fists into her sides. "It's those boys again. I'd like to—"

Sara laid her hand on Huldah's shoulder. "You know you wouldn't do anything."

"I know. You're right, but it makes me so angry." Huldah stood and brushed the dirt off the back of her tunic. A lopsided grin replaced her drawn features. "Where did you come from? I thought you had to watch your little brother today."

Sara laughed, a musical sound. "My aunt came by and wanted to take him to her house for the day."

"I'm so glad. I hate going to the market by myself." She linked arms with Sara and the two girls strolled off in the direction of the market.

They chatted about everything under the sun until Sara stopped and swung Huldah around.

"Did you really know that baby was going to die?" Sara was so close that her breath grazed Huldah's face.

"Yes, I knew." Huldah closed her eyes and lowered her head. Shame filled her. She didn't know why it should; she hadn't done anything wrong. Her hands clung to her face until Sara pried them away.

"I know you didn't do anything wrong. You couldn't." Sara squeezed Huldah's arms gently. "You're just a whole lot smarter than the rest of us. You're full of goodness."

Huldah jumped as though struck, her brows puckering together. "No. Don't say that. I'm not good."

"Come on, let's get going. We'll talk about this later."

The two girls walked the beaten path in a silence broken only by the call of a raven and the murmurings of doves. High overhead, a hawk circled, intent on his search for a midday meal.

When they neared the market, the pungent smell of spices permeated the air and the din of bartering assaulted their ears.

Huldah never tired of the market: the lowing of cattle mingled with the bleats of sheep and goats. Hens routed through the dirt around the stalls, in search of kernels of grains dropped by farmers. Spices, freshly baked bread, honey-laden dates, and pastries watered the tongue. Throughout the area, colourful turbans and robes made a feast for the eyes.

Angry voices haggled over prices. Sara pointed to where an old woman was shaking her fist in the face of a young stall worker. The worker's face turned red as he shouted, hands on hips, body leaning toward her until their noses almost touched. He threw his hands in the air and the old lady grabbed her bit of cloth and disappeared among the crowd.

Sara laughed behind her hand. "I think she got the better of him that time."

"I don't know," Huldah said, laughing with her. "He looks quite pleased with himself. Now, I need to purchase cinnamon and cumin, as well as dates. Let's visit Levi's stall. His dates are always fresh."

She pulled Sara along with her as she moved through the crowds.

Once her purchases were made, Huldah turned to leave—then stopped abruptly. Her face paled.

"What's wrong?" Sara asked.

"I see my father with a group of priests. If he sees me, I'm in trouble." She pushed past Sara and started running. Sara hurried after her.

Once they were through the market, they dropped down in a shady area, panting for breath.

"Why... why will... you be... in trouble?" Sara wiped her forehead with the back of her hand, gasping out the words.

"The priests are meeting to decide if I did something wrong with the baby. Father told me to stay in the house." Huldah rested her chin in her hand and sighed.

"But Huldah, you didn't kill that baby—"

"Of course I didn't. But how do I convince a bunch of arrogant priests who won't even let me speak?"

Sara's hand flew over her mouth. "Huldah, be careful what you say. I've heard they have spies everywhere." She reached out her hand and tried to pull Huldah down beside her, but Huldah shrugged her off.

"I'll call them arrogant and worse." She stopped in front of Sara, hands on hips. "I defy them to find me guilty of anything."

"You frighten me. Let's go home before you get caught out here." Sara rose from the ground.

"You're right. If my father catches me, I don't even want to think about the consequences."

three

"I tell you, we can't let this continue." Broden cleared his throat and pounded on the table, eliciting stern looks from the older priests.

Baz raised his hand. "I can't see what harm has been done…"

Broden silenced him with an angry glance.

Wiry and strong, Broden cut a fine figure. His blue robe swished when he rose and strode around the room. His hands were long and narrow, with tapered fingers that made him look more like a harpist than a priest. A twisted gold ring circled the third finger of his right hand.

"No harm done?" Broden hunched his shoulders, clipping the words off one by one. "The baby is dead. I'd say that's harm enough. But that's not all, not even the main thing. We can't have this young girl telling us what's going to happen."

Broden leaned forward and pounded the table.

"Now we come to the crux of the matter." Judah leaned forward and shook a finger at the others. "I agree with Broden. This can't continue. The people will become superstitious."

"And we'll lose our power. Isn't that what this is really all about?" Ahiram looked from one priest to the next. "Let's not fool ourselves, brothers. Without the support of the people, we're nothing." His gaze swept the group, lingering on Baz. "What say you to that, Baz?"

Baz shrunk in his seat, lowering his head. He answered not a word. He was the youngest, and known for his liberal ideas. The older priests viewed him with suspicion.

"It's time we heard from Amaziah." Broden turned to the big man. "Will you speak to the matter? After all, she's your daughter."

Amaziah sat up straighter. He gnawed at a fingernail and heaved a deep sigh. "Fellow priests, this matter gives me great pain. I'm loath to claim the relationship, but we have all known her since she was at her mother's breast.

But Ahiram is right; we can't afford to lose our power. The people must stay under our influence. Do with her what you must."

Amaziah's shoulders slumped and he sat back in his seat.

Baz jumped up from the table. "This is insane. You must see that the baby would have died anyway." His brows pulled together, deep lines creasing his forehead and lodging above his nose. "I say leave her alone and see what the future will bring."

Broden stood slowly, a look of arrogance frozen on his face. "Fellow priests, before we deal with the girl, we must deal with this aberrant priest."

"Here, here," echoed around the table. Hands slapped out a rhythm on the hard surface.

Deep red suffused Baz's face as he looked at his fellow priests. "You're wrong about all of this. This is not how we've been trained to act. Where is compassion? Where is justice? Where is love?"

With one last look at them, Baz stood and left the room.

As the curtain swept back into place, Broden sat again, and in the shocked silence he gathered his thoughts. "He's young. He doesn't understand what we need to do. We can talk with him later, but for now, back to the girl. What is your pleasure?"

"She must be sent away," Ahiram spoke softly, with the weight of authority. "The people will forget about her and we can carry on."

"What say the rest of you?" Broden asked.

Agreement was soon reached. She would be sent away.

Even Amaziah agreed with the decision and promised to have her out of Jerusalem by sunset.

"I have relatives in Joppa who owe me a favour," Amaziah said. "They will take her in."

And so was made a decision that would disastrously affect so many of their futures.

"One further thing." Broden's eyes made contact with each priest around the table. "No word of this decision must reach Hilkiah. The High Priest has some strange ideas and would thwart our plans."

"What about Baz?" Ahiram's words hung in the air. Not a sound could be heard, not a muscle stirred.

Broden leaned in to search their faces. "Leave it with me. I promise that word will not reach the High Priest through him."

H

Baz walked the path from the temple to the Second District, his head down and hands folded behind his back. He wasn't sure what he was going to do, but felt compelled to do something. Occasionally he kicked a pebble in his path, trying to contain his frustration.

As a nation, we're in serious trouble and no one can see it. The priests are the worst. They're so afraid of losing power over the people that they keep blinders over their eyes.

A slight breeze ruffled his hair and he realized that in his haste he had left his turban at the meeting. He ran one hand over his head and enjoyed the freedom.

"I really am becoming a rebel." Baz smiled to himself when he thought about the looks that would freeze on the faces of the others if they could see him now.

He became aware of eyes watching him. Stopping, he scanned the area. Under a tree to his left sat a young girl with her scarf covering most of her face. Her large, frightened eyes stared at him.

"Huldah?" He swung his head around to check for others. No one was in sight.

She shrank against the trunk of the tree and put her hands over her eyes, her shoulders shaking.

"Huldah, don't be afraid. I'm not going to hurt you." Her wide eyes appeared again over her hands. "Yes, I was at the meeting with the priests, but I don't agree with them. You're safe talking to me." He straightened and stood back, as though giving her room to assess the situation in her own way.

Slowly, she lowered her hands to the ground. Wet with her tears, they soaked up dirt from the foot of the tree.

"Are they going to stone me?" she asked in a quiet voice. A tiny tear slipped down her face, piercing his heart.

He rubbed his hand over his cheeks. "I really don't know. I left the meeting before they decided. All I know is that you're in danger."

Huldah rose and he reached out to touch her shoulder.

"Whatever their decision," he continued, searching her eyes, "I think you need to be away from here, at least for a while. Is there somewhere you can go?"

"I'm only a girl. I have no way to leave and nowhere to go."

Her composure surprised him. He had expected hysterics.

"What about your mother? Would she know of somewhere you could go?" He wrung his hands together, lines appearing between his brows.

"Do you know my mother?" Her wide eyes seemed to stretch even farther. "She's virtually useless at present, so afraid of my father that she'll go along with whatever the priests decide."

Baz walked away a pace, his chin dropping to his chest. He turned and approached her again. "What about a neighbour?"

"Esther. She lives next door. There's no love lost between her and my father."

"Then go quickly. There's no time to waste. Once they make a decision, they'll carry it out before the day is over." He gave her a little shove in the direction of home. "Wait. If there's any way you can get word to me of where you are, I can keep you informed of their decision and when it's safe to return."

She nodded, then disappeared down the path. He watched her go. Shaking his head, he wondered what the future held for this young girl who obviously had talents given by God, but rejected by men.

four

*A*maziah trudged along the pathways to his home. He was in complete agreement with the other priests, though he dreaded the encounter with his wife, daughter, and son Jairus. His other two sons would be with him. In fact, they would probably want to know why she wasn't being stoned. He knew he would have gone along with a decision of stoning, but he was secretly glad for the lesser punishment.

The heat penetrated his consciousness. Sweat pooled at the base of his neck and ran down his back. Insects buzzed around his head, forcing him to swipe at his face again and again. Dust lay thick along the laneway, adding to his discomfort. His pace gradually slowed in his reluctance to face the coming ordeal.

Huldah was different from his other children. They were all afraid of him; she was, too, but she had spunk and stood up to him. He chastised her for it, but also took a certain pride in her stubbornness.

I think she picked up some of my traits. That would make any father proud, but she must never know; it would rob my influence over her. I'm glad she'll be spared a more severe punishment.

Salome looked up when he entered the house. Jairus and the others were lounging about, waiting for his return.

"Is the meal prepared, woman?" he asked curtly.

"It's ready, husband. We only await your presence and Huldah's." Salome continued stirring a pot over the fire. Steam drifted from the cooking pot, filling the room with a spicy aroma.

"What do you mean, awaiting Huldah? Where is she?" He removed his outer cloak and wiped his face with a damp towel his wife had prepared for him.

"I don't really know." A look that he decided was fear flicked over her countenance.

"What do you mean, you don't know?" He spit the words out at her, grinding his teeth.

"The girl's touched in the head, if you ask me," Lot said, rising and approaching the table.

"She is not." Jairus jumped up, fists bunched.

"Go ahead, weakling. Hit me. I dare you." Laughter spilled from Lot's lips. He shot out an arm and spun Jairus around so that he fell to the floor, sputtering. Blood spouted from Jairus's split lip.

"Enough," thundered Amaziah. "Jairus, go wash at the well. Lot, sit down and listen."

Lot returned to his seat, his face still creased with laughter. Malachi punched him on the arm, grinning.

Amaziah turned toward his wife again. His bushy brows pulled together and his chin jutted out. "Wife, you haven't explained yourself. Where is my daughter?"

Salome cowered by the fire. The blood drained from her face. She clasped her hands together, but the tremble in them was still visible.

"Answer me, woman." Amaziah took a step toward her, which seemed to loosen her tongue.

"She went to the rooftop after finishing her chores. When I called her to help prepare the meal, she wasn't there."

"Did you not hear her come down the stairs, woman?" Amaziah grasped his beard and snorted. His red face contrasted sharply with Salome's.

She straightened her back and faced him. "No, I was sleeping. You know I'm still weak from the sickness."

"Sickness?" The word roared from his mouth. "I think you meant weakness, did you not?"

Amaziah turned from her, grabbed his cloak with a swish, then beckoned to Lot and Malachi to follow him. The men swung out the door.

"Lot, go north along the lane. Ask everyone you see if they've seen her."

He then pointed up the lane to the many houses clustered in haphazard fashion along the dirt byway. Horse-drawn carts trundled along the packed earth, stirring up dust with each plod of a hoof.

"Malachi, check the roadway to the east. I'll head south toward the market. The foolish girl seems to like it there." He shook his head and spit on the ground. "She's almost as feebleminded as her mother."

Both boys grinned at him.

"Go, and meet me back here before the sun sets."

H

At the crossroads, Huldah veered off the path that led home, circling to the north, passing close to the Garden of the Tombs. She rarely came this way, because the tombs made her feel uneasy. The Garden was silent at this time of day. No one was in sight, so she slipped by her home in the adjacent lane. Once past this point, she took a narrow path that wound behind the houses and came out just above Esther's house.

Esther had been her neighbour ever since she could remember. Esther's husband, Tikvah, was a steward in the king's palace. Old King Manasseh had been king even before she was born. Talk around the city was that he would soon die, and his son Amon would be king. But today, she cared not who was king.

Please be home, Esther, she mouthed as she approached the back of the house. *And please be alone. I don't want to see Tikvah, and I don't want Shallum to see me.*

Thoughts of Shallum brought a blush to her cheeks. Her parents had long ago completed all the necessary bargaining to pledge her to be Shallum's wife.

I can't think about that now. I won't be anyone's wife if the priests find me.

There was a small entrance on the north side of Esther's house, hidden from view of her own house. She stepped up to the door and knocked softly. She wrung her hands together, licking her lips which had gone dry with her fear.

"Huldah, how nice to see you."

The words startled her and she looked up into Esther's eyes.

"What's wrong?" Esther reached out and grabbed her arm, pulling her into the dim interior of the house. "Huldah, tell me. Is it your mother?"

Huldah took a deep breath. "Esther, I'm in trouble. Bad trouble."

"Come into my room where we can talk undisturbed." Esther pushed her through the doorway and arranged the curtain in place. "Now, tell me everything."

And Huldah did.

"I don't know what to do," Huldah said, coming to the end of the tale. "My mother is weak, and if I go home, she will give in to my father. Even if she knows where I am, she'll tell him." Tears dribbled over her cheeks. She swiped at them with the back of her hand. "What will I do?"

"I'll think of something, Huldah," Esther said. "We need to get you away for a while. Let things calm down. If we give it some time, something bigger will come along to catch the priests' attention and they'll forget about you." Sitting down beside Huldah, Esther put her arm around the girl and rubbed her back. "Whatever we do, it will cause pain to you, to Shallum, to your father, and especially to your mother. You realize that, don't you?"

"Yes, I've thought of that. But it would cause my mother more pain if I were to be sent away, or even stoned." Huldah raised her tear-streaked face. "I'll do whatever you think is best."

"Good. Because I have a plan." Esther stood and paced the room once. "You are now fourteen, isn't that correct?'

"Yes, almost fifteen." Huldah drew her eyebrows together and tilted her head.

Esther smiled down into the girl's questioning face. "Then you're almost old enough to be married."

"Yes, I suppose I am." Huldah's hands were clasped tightly; the knuckles gleamed white.

"If you were married to Shallum, the priests wouldn't be able to touch you. You would no longer be a maiden, but a married woman. And not only a married woman, but one whose husband works in the palace every day and has the ear of the king."

"I see." Huldah smiled and felt her body relax for the first time since she had left Baz. "But how can we do this? My father will want to carry out the punishment. He'd look bad to the other priests if he didn't. Appearances are everything to him."

"No, no, Huldah. Don't you worry about that. My Tikvah will look after your father. He'll make him see the benefits." She leaned in close to Huldah's ear. "He'll make it worth his while, and you know your father can't refuse a good bargain."

Huldah's face clouded when she thought of her predicament. "But what will I do now? Today?"

"Stay here, for now. No one comes in except me. The men of the household know never to enter unless they're invited." Esther grinned. "Once it's dark, I'll come back with the rest of the plan."

She slipped out through the curtain, leaving Huldah to ponder the next steps in her life.

five

"There's someone at the door," Esther said, looking up at her husband. A frown creased her forehead. "Who could it be?"

"I'll check." Tikvah rose from the low couch where he had been enjoying the evening meal with his family. Shallum stood to accompany him, but his father waved at him to remain seated.

Voices could be heard coming from the front entrance.

"Greetings to you, Lot." Tikvah stood tall and straight, looming in the doorway. "What brings you to my door at the evening meal hour?"

Lot shuffled his feet and looked at the ground. "My father has sent me to inquire if you've seen my sister, Huldah."

"Look at me when you speak." Tikvah folded his arms over his bulging chest. His eyes seemed to bore into Lot's head. "Why would I have seen your sister? Is she not at home, where all respectable girls are at this time?"

"She's not at home. We must find her." Lot's lips clamped together, stretching into a thin line.

"Be on your way. You'll not find her in my house." Tikvah closed the door in the boy's face.

Esther and Shallum turned their heads toward him when he resumed his place at the table. Breathing deeply, he picked up his piece of bread and dipped it in the stew before him. He raised it to his lips.

"Well, who was there?" Easter sat very still, raising her eyebrows.

Tikvah lowered the bread to the side of his bowl. "It was Lot, from next door." He lifted the bread again.

Shallum's head snapped up. "What did he want at this hour?"

"Yes, what did he want?" Esther echoed.

"You two are certainly curious. Apparently I'm not to be allowed to continue my meal until your curiosity is quelled." Tikvah replaced the bread and wiped his fingers on the small towel by his bowl. "It appears Huldah is missing."

Shallum jumped from his seat, his face suffused with red. "Missing? How could she be missing?"

"Sit down, son." Tikvah gestured to Shallum. "I can't talk to you when you're on your feet. Lot didn't give any details, just that she was missing and they had to find her." He signalled for the meal to continue. "She's probably home by now."

Shallum sat, but only pushed the food around in his bowl. His eyes were downcast and his shoulders hunched.

Esther folded her hands in her lap, and she, too, lowered her eyes. The room became very quiet.

Tikvah looked up from his meal. "What is the matter with the two of you?"

Esther ran her hands over her face. "I have a terrible secret."

"A what? A secret? From me?" Tikvah almost choked on his last bite.

Shallum lifted his widened eyes to his mother's face.

"Yes." Esther clasped her hands together and nodded. "And I can only tell you if you both promise to keep what I say confidential."

Tikvah gave a gruff laugh. "How can we decide that before we hear what it is?"

"This is serious, Tikvah." She reached out her hand and laid it on her husband's arm. "Please."

He patted her hand in a familiar gesture and smiled. "You're a good wife, Esther. I'll keep your confidence. Shallum will, too."

Shallum merely nodded.

"I know where Huldah is." Esther's voice was barely a whisper when she leaned in to speak to her husband and son. The words dropped on the table between them.

"Now, how would you know that? You're talking foolishness, and you know I don't like foolishness." Tikvah scooped up another spoonful of his supper.

"She's here, in this house, at this moment."

Tikvah's eyes popped open. He scrambled up from his reclining position, knocking over his bowl.

"Are you crazy?" he sputtered. Heat crept up his neck and face. "How can she be here? What are you trying to do, get us all in trouble?"

Esther seemed to regain her composure while Tikvah lost his. "Sit down, Tikvah, and I'll tell you the whole story. You, too, Shallum."

When she had finished the story, silence reigned. Shallum sat with his head bowed and hands folded in his lap. His lips were in constant motion, but no sound could be heard.

Tikvah recovered first, took a deep breath, and shrugged his shoulders. "What, dear wife, are we to do about this?"

"I have a plan. I'll need both of you to help, or it won't work." Esther reached out to her son, gently placing her hand on his shoulder. "Shallum, are you with me?"

Shallum looked up, his face a mask of pain, lips pulled down and eyes squinted. "I'll do whatever I can to help." He sat back with his arms crossed, rubbing them. "Will this have any effect on our marriage plans?"

Tikvah raised his head sharply. "I hadn't thought of that."

"Listen to me, both of you." Esther shook her finger at them and drew in a deep breath. There was a smugness about her when she faced her men. "Shallum, you will take her to my sister's house tonight. I'll send with you a small scroll explaining the situation." She nodded at him. "She'll keep her as long as needed."

"Wife, are you..."

She raised her hand to stop him. "Tikvah, your job will be to convince Amaziah that Huldah's marriage to Shallum should take place right away. Once she is married and her husband has the king's ear, the priests will have no alternative but to drop their charges."

"I see you have it all worked out." Tikvah's folded arms seemed to challenge her. "And just how am I to convince Amaziah to go against the priests?"

Esther leaned over the table, placing her hands on the cloth spread between them. "Perhaps it's time to arrange the transfer of that piece of land he covets," she whispered. Both sets of eyes rose abruptly.

After pulling on his beard a number of times, Tikvah said, "That just might work."

"Then you'll both do it?" Esther's face lit up.

"Yes, I'm convinced."

Shallum seemed in a daze. "I, too, will do what you suggest."

H

Two figures traversed the back alleys and laneways of the Second District of Jerusalem. A heavy cloud cover hid the moon, a brisk wind ruffling the dust into little eddies around their feet. From time to time, the larger figure paused to assist the other over rough ground. No words were spoken, but the couple seemed to be of one mind.

The Second District gave way to the other sections of the city, and still the two toiled on. At last they stopped before a house set back from the laneway. A light could be seen coming from a window near the door. Upon knocking, the door was quickly opened.

"Uncle, it is I, Shallum. Is my aunt at home?" Shallum stepped into the ray of light escaping from the house.

"Yes, yes, come in." His uncle Joseph stood back and they entered. "I'll get her. She's involved with one of the children at present, but will want to see you right away."

When his footsteps faded, Shallum glanced at his companion. Only Huldah's dark eyes were visible. The rest of her face was circled with her headscarf, a delicate blue which contrasted sharply with her eyes. Not a hair escaped tonight. Her breathing was audible in the quiet house.

"You'll like my aunt Abigail," Shallum said. "She's a very loving person. I promise you'll be safe here."

Huldah indicated her understanding with a nod, but remained silent.

A swish of a robe preceded Abigail's entrance. "My nephew, how unexpected and lovely." She held out her hands to him and greeted him with a kiss on both cheeks.

Abigail then turned to his companion, seeming to only now become aware of her. "And who is with you?"

Huldah's head lowered so that nothing other than headscarf and robe was visible. A slight tremor shivered across her shoulders.

"Aunt, if you would be so kind and first read the message from your sister, I'll answer all your questions." Shallum withdrew the small scroll from beneath his cloak and handed it to her. She tilted her head at him but accepted the scroll, unrolling it and scanning the contents. The array of expressions that crossed her face might have been humorous had the situation not been so serious. Finally, she looked up.

"This must be Huldah." Abigail covered the space between them and took the girl into her ample arms. Huldah's head rested on her shoulder.

"Nephew, say goodbye to Huldah and be gone. You must retrace your steps across the city before the guards begin their patrol." She waved her hand at him. "Tell my sister I'll do everything she says and wait for word from her. Not to worry, we'll be fine." She gave Shallum a final push out the door and closed it firmly behind him.

Huldah stared at the closed door, her former life ended with the final slam. The future loomed before her like a dark menace.

six

The lamp burned long into the night while Amaziah sat hunched over the table. Salome had long since retired, weeping, to her bed. Gasping coughs came from behind the curtain. Lot and Malachi had disappeared into the night, and only Jairus sat with his father.

With head bowed, Jairus sniffed repeatedly. His hands were restless in his lap, wringing each other again and again. Deep heaving breaths punctuated the air.

A fist dropped onto the table with a startling thump.

"If you can't stop that vile sniffing, leave me in peace." Amaziah snarled the words from pressed lips. His big head shook from side to side while glaring at his youngest son.

Jairus leaped from his place at the table, wiped his arm across the bowls and baskets still in place, and scattered the remains of supper onto the floor and down the front of his father's robe. Amaziah's eyes widened, his mouth fell open, and his bushy brows threatened to cover his eyes. He, too, jumped from his place, hands tightened into fists.

With one last look over his shoulder, Jairus rushed to the door, flung it open, and stormed out. His father rushed behind him, but when he opened the door, there was no sign of his son.

"Who cares? Let him go," Amaziah flung the words to the darkened sky.

Again he slumped down at the table, and this time he put his head in his hands. Brooding thoughts crowded his mind: *Where is Huldah? This is an affront to me. When the other priests find out, I'll be disgraced. My own daughter has defied me.*

He struggled to his feet and paced the small space around the table. *She knows I'll find her, and when I do, she'll wish she only had the priests' punishment to deal with.*

A soft knock interrupted his tirade. He watched the door. The knock came again. He shuffled softly to the door and opened it.

He stared at his neighbour. "Tikvah, what brings you here tonight?"

"May I come in? I wish to speak with you on an urgent matter." Tikvah put his hand on his neighbour's arm.

"Come in." The reply was surly but Amaziah stood back and let the other enter.

Once they had taken their places on the cushions around the table, there was a moment of silence. Amaziah noted that Tikvah didn't mention the remnants of the meal strewn over the table and floor. He waited for Tikvah to speak.

"I have reason to believe there is grief in your house tonight." Tikvah raised his eyes until they were on a level with Amaziah's. His look was intense.

"What brings you to that conclusion?" Amaziah folded his arms over his ample chest but lowered his eyes from the gaze of the other. This was followed by a snort and a humph.

"I have news of your daughter." Tikvah leaned forward and grasped Amaziah's arm.

Amaziah repelled him. "I'd like to know how you have news when I can't find a trace of her." He shifted his position and placed both hands on the table. "You speak lies. Lies to your neighbour. Disgusting."

"Amaziah, please listen." Tikvah folded his hands before him in an attitude of supplication. "I know of the priests' gathering today."

Amaziah's head snapped up and his jaw dropped.

"It's all right, my friend," Tikvah said. "I'm not a gossip. What you and your fellow priests do will not be relayed to Hilkiah by me. However, he is the High Priest and should be aware of what goes on in and around the temple."

"Mere conjecture on your part." Brave words, but Amaziah's hand trembled, betraying his agitation.

"No, my friend, do not deny it. Word is out and has circulated around the city."

A flash of fear widened Amaziah's eyes. He wiped a hand over his face and continued to stare at Tikvah.

"I know you were to remove her from Jerusalem tonight," Tikvah said.

"Someone has talked. It was Baz, wasn't it?" Amaziah stood and placed his hands on his hips. His mouth opened, but no words came out.

"Sit down, friend. I have further news and, I think, a good solution to your problem. I know where Huldah is and I can assure you that she is safe."

Amaziah sat like one in a daze. "Safe? What do you consider safe? And where does that leave me? If she isn't out of the city by dawn, my reputation will be ruined. I'll lose everything." He was almost in tears when he leaned toward Tikvah. "Tell me where she is."

"No, I'll not tell you." Tikvah sat back. "You may tell people she has gone, and that will be the truth."

He wiped his damp hands on his robe. "But how can I be sure?"

"You will need to trust me." Tikvah leaned forward again. "Listen to me, Amaziah. Huldah's marriage must take place as soon as possible."

"Ha. That's a good joke." Amaziah slapped the table with the palm of his hand. "Who'll marry her now?"

Tikvah's eyes never left Amaziah's face. "My son, Shallum. I have the king's ear and no one will dare touch her once they are wed."

"And how would I get a priest to marry them when she is supposed to be under discipline and in another city? Answer me that."

Tikvah leaned very close and spoke in a low voice. "There is a piece of land behind our houses that you have coveted for many years. What if I were to tell you that I would make all the arrangements for the marriage and that the deed to that land would fall into your hands?"

Amaziah rubbed his beard. His jaw worked back and forth with vigour. "What would I tell the priests?"

"Once the marriage is accomplished, you won't need to tell them anything. Just mention the ear of the king. That should stop all talk."

H

Swirls of darkness inundated the air before Huldah's eyes. It was alive and writhed before her. She was not afraid; only curious. Her head tilted to one side, her left ear probing her surroundings. She squinted, seeing shapes emerge from the fogginess before her. Her hand tried to touch the shapes, but they withdrew from her. She let her hand drop in her lap, content to watch.

In the midst of the mass, a face formed. Light gathered around it and eyes and lips took form. Whether it was male or female, she couldn't tell. It didn't seem to matter. The shape of the head fluctuated in the swirls, but the eyes fastened on hers and the lips moved.

Huldah struggled to hear the words escaping from those lips, but the force of the eyes held her back.

She breathed deeply, the cool air refreshing her. She knew it was a message for her, a message she was unable to hear or comprehend—but that didn't seem to matter. What mattered was the peace that invaded her being. She knew she could look into those eyes forever.

The vision faded, darkness returned, and at this point, Huldah slept.

When she awoke several hours later, the dream stayed with her.

She sat up in her borrowed bed, staring out the small window overlooking a field of ripened wheat. With the backs of her hands, she rubbed her eyes and shook her head.

Was that a dream or a vision? A vision, I think; dreams are never so vivid and personal.

Her feet dangled over the side of the bed and she could hear sounds coming from the other areas of the house. Someone would soon be coming to awaken her.

I've got to get up and face the day, but I know this vision means something. Something important. But what?

A knock came at her door.

The day stretched out before her, frightening in all its intensity. This was the day when her life began anew—or ended. She pulled on a rough homespun robe, ran her fingers through her hair, opened the door, and took her first step into the unknown.

seven

*W*eeping, weeping, constant weeping. Wails circled the walls and settled on the furniture, permeated the cooking pots, wrapped the inmates in layers of tears. On and on it went until Amaziah could stand it no longer.

"Out, you fools." He heaved himself from the stool by the fire where he had sought refuge. His face burned from the heat of the fire, or from the rage that swelled within. He knew not which. He clutched his robe in one hand, and with the other he flung open the door and pointed out.

Several women had gathered around the table, their arms around Salome. Eight pairs of startled eyes took in his form and scurried for cloaks and sandals. One by one, they eased by him, eyes downcast, scarves pulled over their chins. When the last one exited and the door was firmly shut, Amaziah turned his wrathful eye on his wife.

"Woman, there will be no more weeping in this house." His brows hung over his eyes and his chin jutted out. "Your daughter is not dead. You must weep for her no more."

Salome, eyes closed, lips clamped together, spoke not a word. Her head lowered until her chin rested on her chest. Her shoulders heaved several times until a sigh escaped her lips.

Wrath grew inside Amaziah until it exploded with a force unknown even to him. With one leap, he reached across the table, grabbed her scarf, and ripped it from her hair. His hands found deep layers of hair and pulled her to her feet. With one mighty thrust, he threw her across the room and roared his rage. Her head hit the edge of the hearth, stilling her body and spilling her blood.

The shock of the blood seemed to snap him from his anger. In one step, he reached her side, lifted her, and carried the limp form to the bed, where she opened her eyes. Ragged and sticky, the edges of the cut lay open just above her ear. Amaziah grabbed a damp cloth, sponged the spot, then bound it with a clean bandage he'd found in her midwife's bundle. He once more laid her down on the bed, left the room, and then the house.

The cool night air should have calmed his nerves, but instead his anger rose again.

It was her fault. He shook his fist at the stars above him and roared his displeasure. *I would never have thrown her if I hadn't been driven to it. All those wailing women are enough to put a man off his food for a week.*

The more he walked, the better he felt. His shoulders straightened and he threw back his head.

It certainly wasn't my fault. Why am I plagued with foolish women?

With one last thrust of his fist, he gathered his robe around him, reversed his direction, and headed back the way he had come.

H

"But how can we do this?" Shallum's plaintive cry roused his father from his reverie.

Tikvah raised bleary eyes to study his son. What he saw pleased him. Shallum's dark hair curled around shoulders usually straight and strong, but now bent over the table. But it was the boy's eyes that caught Tikvah's attention. Such clear, honest eyes. Compassion spilled from them. Pride swelled in Tikvah's soul.

"My son." Tikvah reached out with one hand and grasped Shallum's. "Our God will show us the way. One day, one step at a time."

"It's almost the new day." Shallum rose from his place at the table and gazed through the window at the lightening sky. Puffs of purple clouds mingled with the rose colours that stained the horizon. "What will today bring for us, for Huldah?"

A shudder ran down Shallum's body.

"My son, come sit." Tikvah gestured to the empty seat. "You and I will break our fast and then seek an audience with the High Priest."

Fear flicked over Shallum's face. Half-hooded eyes hung under tightened brows; the line of his mouth spoke tension.

"What if he says no?" Shallum asked. "Or won't even see us? What will happen if this gets back to the other priests, the ones who handed out the discipline…?"

"Enough, Shallum. You forget yourself. We will trust in God. We will trust that Hilkiah does the right thing. If God is in it, it will work out." Tikvah stood and gently put his arms around his son. "Come, we must begin our day. The sun has topped the horizon."

ℋ

That same morning, sun hit the doors of the temple. Hilkiah strode toward them, glancing at the outer court that was already filled with people milling about; some purchased doves for sacrifice, others were intent on the various objects that graced the tables, and still others talked in small groups. Mixed with the people was the noise of animals held for sale. Sheep and goats butted each other in their excitement, innocently welcoming the morning.

Groups parted when Hilkiah approached. Sunlight glinted off the gold band on his forehead. His robe's fringe of tinkling bells and pomegranates stopped just short of the ground and exposed gnarled feet shod with leather sandals. He adjusted his breastplate, adorned with twelve precious stones, conscious of eyes that darted looks at him.

His mind was in a muddle. Word had reached him that the rogue priests were restless again, holding secret meetings.

I've lost control of them. They hold the power, but I must never let them know that.

A frown deepened his forehead, but no other signs of distress were visible on his face. He had long ago learned to keep his expression calm and aloof. He swept through a pair of doors which had been quickly opened by doorkeepers when he approached.

Inside was bustle and noise. Hilkiah ignored it and proceeded to his own room, which was away from the others. His scribe, an old man named Benjamin, scrambled to his feet when Hilkiah entered, spilling ink and a scroll onto the floor. While he stooped to retrieve his possessions, Hilkiah sank onto a low couch at an ornate table.

The table had been carved many years before by an artisan of the tribe of Dan. The work was intricate, and displayed a scene of the escape from Egypt. The wood was worn smooth from years of elbows leaning on it while their owners debated deep questions. Today, Hilkiah didn't even notice the depiction, too weary with the heavy burdens he had to bear on his aged shoulders.

He watched Benjamin from the corner of his eye, but made no attempt to help or even comment on the mess. The scroll was retrieved quickly; the ink took longer to deal with, but it, too, was eventually cleaned.

Hilkiah looked up when the last of the ink disappeared. "I have a meeting soon and will need your services. Please meet my guests and bring them to me."

Old Benjamin scurried away to do his master's bidding. Meanwhile, Hilkiah continued his stare at nothing. On the outside, he looked calm; inside, his brain churned with questions.

So many things to ponder, so many people far from God, so many priests far from God. Some days, I feel far from God. His head slumped into his hands. *So discouraging. Some days I feel like the only one who even knows God exists. And now these priests are forming little groups, power groups. I've lost control.*

He raised his head, straightening his face into calmness again.

A moment later, Benjamin returned, holding aside the curtain while Tikvah and Shallum bowed their way into the room. Hilkiah watched them with lids half-closed, then rose to greet them.

"Please be seated." Hilkiah extended his hand to indicate places at the table.

Tikvah took the place opposite Hilkiah, while Shallum slipped into a seat farther down.

"I will not need you at present," Hilkiah said to Benjamin, "but stay close for my call."

Once the men were settled, Hilkiah nodded at Tikvah.

"We have come on a very unusual matter." Tikvah sat back on the low cushions, folded his arms, and fixed his eyes on the priest.

Hilkiah nodded again. "Please continue."

H

The voices swirled around Shallum and he sank deeper into his own thoughts. His hunched shoulders and bowed head were stiff with the tension that spread through his body. *What will Hilkiah decide? If he decides no, what will happen to Huldah? To me? Please God, remember your children. Remember that we need you.*

"Let me ask you some questions." Hilkiah leaned his head to one side and turned his eyes on Shallum. "Shallum, you are a respected member of our community and the king values you as one of the keepers of his wardrobe. Why do you wish to protect this young girl, not even a relative?"

With a deep breath, Shallum slowly nodded. He folded his hands together to still the tremble, resting them on his deep blue robe. "Yes, you could say I hold an important place in Jerusalem, but if the importance of the role becomes greater than my compassion, I will have failed as a member of this community."

"Well said, well said." For the first time since they'd arrived, Hilkiah smiled. The skin around his eyes crinkled which gave his face a younger appearance. "Yours is not a popular opinion, I would venture to say."

"From what I hear, that is so." A smile crept over Tikvah's face, too.

"I am well aware of the group of priests who arrived at this unfortunate decision," Hilkiah said, his smile fading as he stroked his white beard. "They are not in charge, but have wrested power from me by appealing to the people. Son, are you prepared to make this great sacrifice and jeopardize your position at the palace?"

Hilkiah stretched out his arm from his white sleeve and pointed one finger at Shallum. Light from the doorway glanced across the High Priest's breastplate; its twelve precious stones blinked into Shallum's eyes. For a moment, he lost track of his thoughts but slowly raised his eyes to meet the priest's.

"I, like my father, believe compassion comes above all." Shallum's mask-like face looked like it might crumble at any moment.

"Very noble." Hilkiah pursed his lips, then turned back to Tikvah. "What reason do you give for wanting this marriage to take place?"

Tikvah threw his shoulders back. "I've had an understanding with Huldah's father for many years, and it is my wish to honour that promise."

"And you, Shallum, what reason do you give for this marriage?"

The room became silent. Shallum could sense the thoughts of the other two while he contemplated his answer. Finally, he lifted his face to both men. "I love her."

"Then I am satisfied." The smile lit up the priest's face again. "I am not so old that I don't understand the ways of love."

Shallum released his shoulders. His arms stretched out to touch his father's. "Thank you" was his simple reply.

"Now, let's get down to business and arrange the matter." Hilkiah turned toward the curtain and called for his scribe. "Benjamin!"

The scribe's eager face appeared inside the curtain. "Yes, master." He bent low and nearly lost his balance. He grabbed the curtain for support and soon righted himself.

No irritation or amusement showed on Hilkiah's face. "Please, sit in your usual place and record the details of our discussion." All-business now, Hilkiah faced Tikvah. "Will her father agree in the end?"

"Our agreement is too advantageous for him to back out." Tikvah grinned widely. "He's in."

Hilkiah's raised eyebrows bespoke disbelief. "He may be in danger if the others find out."

"If our plans are carefully made, there should be no danger," Tikvah said. "Besides, what choice does he have? He's already broken the promise made to have her out of the city last night. He doesn't even know where she is."

Hilkiah shifted his attention to Shallum. "You know this will not be a traditional wedding ceremony, as our culture dictates. Are you prepared for this?"

"Yes," Shallum spoke without hesitation. "If you're in it, it will honour God. That is my only concern."

"Then let's do it." Hilkiah clapped his veined hands together. "Benjamin, I don't need to remind you that everything you've heard is guarded by the strictest secrecy."

Benjamin's pen fell to the floor; ink sprinkled over the area that had been bathed in it earlier. "Fear not, master. I will say nothing. And even if I did say something, no one believes me anyway. But I can assure you that I will remain…"

Hilkiah's hand shot up in the air. "Stop. You've said far too much already."

"So sorry…"

"You will need to see the king," Hilkiah said, turning to Shallum. "One of the rogue priests may decide to approach him with a complaint. They don't support the king, but there is always that danger." He leaned in close over the table, lowering his voice. "The old king is mad, but there are times when he rises and makes his will known."

Tikvah laid his hand on his son's arm in a tight grasp. "We will go directly there at the close of our meeting."

"Can you meet here after the moon has set?" Hilkiah said. "It's very unusual, but these are unusual times and circumstances."

Tikvah nodded. "Yes, we'll be here."

The two men left the palace in silence, Shallum wondering what the night would hold. Would they really be able to arrange the marriage? Would the king give permission? His life seemed to hang in a balance.

eight

"He's dead! He's dead!" The cry rang through the city streets. Citizens stopped to watch while a lone man ran frantically, shouting the words. His turban had fallen off and long, stringy hair stretched out behind him.

A palace guard turned in the direction of the cries, then reached out an arm to halt him.

"What goes here?" The command was sharp and loud. He shook the man to make him stop his cries. A crowd gathered around them. "Here, here, stop that. What's your name?"

"Elah, most noble master." The words came out in a gasp. Sweat beaded on his forehead, ran down his neck, and stained the top of his robe. His mouth hung open and his eyes were wide with terror. He leaned forward and gagged, disgorging his last meal. The amassed press of people quickly backed away.

"Now look what you've done." The guard pulled Elah away from the area and shook him again. "I need answers, and I need them now."

Elah opened and closed his mouth twice. "There's a dead man... on the path... behind the market..."

"How do you know he's dead? How do I know you're not making this up?" The guard shook him a third time. "Talk sense to me."

"He's dead. No question about it." Deep gasps continued to pour from Elah's lips. "Come with me and I'll show you."

A sharp whistle brought three guards running. After a hurried consultation, all five of them moved toward the market.

The throng swarmed a distance behind them; no one wanted to miss the action.

"Stand back," the first guard said as they walked through the laneways.

The crowd pressed forward until swords appeared in the hands of the four guards. They swung them until the message penetrated and the people turned away. They muttered, shouted threats, pushed, and jostled, but they left, a mass of colours undulating under the sweltering sun.

When it was just the four guards and the dishevelled man, the small procession moved on, Elah in the lead. The eyes of the guards remained steadfast on the quest, unresponsive to the many calls from market vendors. Elah never wavered in his path through the stalls, pushing past beggars and housewives alike. Some loiterers moved to fall in behind, but a curt command from the guards discouraged them.

One of the guards moved forward to walk beside Elah. He glanced at him, but his eyes flicked from side to side, saliva spilling from slack lips.

"Where is this body you claimed to have found?" the guard asked.

When he got no response, he touched Elah with a gloved hand. Elah shuddered at the touch, but didn't break his pace.

"I'm thinking this is a useless exercise. There is no body."

Elah stopped along a worn path and raised a shaking arm to point a short distance off the path. The first guard moved ahead, followed by the others.

A corpse was sprawled facedown in a pile of nettles, its robe ripped and sullied. When one of the guards turned the body over with his foot, a gasp escaped his lips.

"It's Baz, the young priest!"

All four leaned over the badly beaten body.

"Don't touch him." The first guard swung out his arm to stop one of the others. "The High Priest will want to see where he fell and cleanse the body."

The cry of a vulture broke the silence. Elah looked up to see them circling overhead.

The first guard glanced at the sky. "The body's not safe to be left alone. One of us should stay while the others go for the High Priest."

"Well, I'm not going to stay. I have a meeting I must attend," said one guard.

"Not me. I don't like dead bodies."

"I'm sure not going to stay here alone. Maybe whoever killed Baz will be back."

"Then what should we do?" asked the first guard. "Someone has to stay."

"Why not Elah?" replied one.

"Great idea," said the first guard.

"Here, Elah, come here."

Elah had backed away from the sight once he'd led the others to the place of the dead. He now held his hand over his mouth and nose, his eyes wide and fixed. His head snapped up at the sound of his name.

"Quickly, come." The leader beckoned him with sharp jabs of his hand.

Elah's feet dragged across the dirt toward the small group huddled around the body. When he approached, the guard grabbed his sleeve and pulled him closer.

"See here, we need you to be quick about it. You must stay with the body and keep the birds and animals away." He pointed to the sky, where the circles grew lower and tighter and the cries louder. "We're going for the High Priest. You stay until he comes."

Elah's eyes widened when he turned his gaze on the guard. His mouth opened and closed a few times before his voice could be heard. "I can't stay here."

The guard grabbed his shoulder and shook him violently. "You'll do what you're told, unless you want to join this one on his way to wherever he's going."

With one last shake, the guard let him go with a shove that sent him sprawling next to the body. Elah scrambled up with a cry of terror only to see the backs of the guards heading toward the market.

The first guard made a full turn. "And if I hear that you deserted your post, I'll hunt you down." He cut the air with his sword, then replaced it at his waist and joined the others.

Alone, Elah scanned the surrounding brush and worn path. In the distance, the sun shone on the grain fields with a golden glow that shimmered under the direction of the light breeze. Raucous cries overhead brought his attention back to the body. He wished they hadn't turned him over; the corpse's glassy eyes made him edgy.

I can't stay here, I can't. But if I leave, that guard will find me. I should have just left the body and not told them.

He turned his back on the corpse and hugged his arms close to his chest, letting his head fall forward. It snapped back up when a whoosh of wings and shrieks from the throats of a dozen birds penetrated his brain. He swung around to see them land on the body.

"Fly, birds, fly!"

Arms flapping, robe flying in the wind, Elah raced toward the invading birds, flailing his arms.

"Shoo, get on with you. Get out of here."

The vultures lifted momentarily with protesting screeches, but settled again amidst a flurry of wings. Opened beaks prepared to feast.

He grabbed a rock from the hard ground, threw it, and connected with one of the larger birds. All lifted into the air. Elah breathed deeply, a curve of the lip betrayed his pleasure at having defeated the birds. They circled in what appeared to be a lazy pattern. He used the lull to gather a pile of rocks and sticks, gathering them at a distance from Baz, but within throwing range.

H

It seemed to take forever before the guards, accompanied by the High Priest, reappeared on the path. Elah stood back from the corpse, a deep sigh escaping his lips when the group approached.

Hilkiah walked with a stoop to his shoulders that reinforced his age. He had donned a dark cloak over his priestly robes. The wind played among the layers shrouding his thin body.

Circling the body, the guards blocked the view of anyone other than Hilkiah, who leaned over the body, not touching it, for that would make him unclean. Straightening his frail shoulders, he looked each guard in the eye, finally turning his gaze on Elah.

"It's definitely Baz." Hilkiah's shoulders hunched, outlining sharp shoulder blades through his robe. With arms outstretched to the sky, he raised his eyes. Words of prayer worked their way through his stretched lips. "Jehovah, Lord God Almighty, may his soul rest with You. Accept him into Your presence, turn not Your face from him."

His arms dropped to his side, gripping the edges of his robe. He turned from the broken body, head held high, arms straight at his sides. Pausing a moment, he looked deeply into Elah's eyes.

"His name must not pass your lips," Hilkiah said. "Retribution will follow if you should talk." He swung to face the guards and repeated the message. "The body must be cleansed before it's moved."

The High Priest snapped his fingers at one of the guards, who quickly moved forward. "The water vessel, if you please."

Hilkiah's hand trembled when he received the skin of water. The lid slid off easily. Moving again to stand beside the body of Baz, Hilkiah poured some of the water into his hand and began sprinkling it over the corpse.

"Blessed are You, O Lord our God, High King of Heaven, the one true Judge."

All around the body he walked, sprinkling water and chanting. Vultures circled high overhead, silent now, but ever-watchful while the sun beat down on the heads of the watchers and the desecrated remains.

When the skin had disgorged most of its water, Hilkiah handed it back to the guard, who poured the remaining drops over the priest's hands. He rubbed them together vigorously, wiped them on a folded white towel carried by a second guard, gathered his robe around him, and without a second glance moved away from the body toward the marketplace.

ℋ

Elah watched him go, wondering how a back could be so stiff. He backed farther away from the body and sank to the dry ground. His eyes followed the movements of the guards while they wrapped the body in white cloths. It was silent work, other than a cough now and then which thinly disguised their choking sounds at seeing the discoloured cloths. At last they moved away, the body carried between two of them.

A deep sigh escaped Elah's lips as his eyes drew to the sky overhead. The vultures screeched again and slowly settled down on the ground where the body had lain, uselessly pecking at the dirt.

ℋ

"I demand an explanation." Hilkiah's eyes roved over the three priests seated at the table in front of him. Folding his arms, he hoped, gave the impression of authority. He swayed slightly on his feet and pain ran up his spine from standing. Shifting his feet eased the pain, and he forced himself to concentrate on the men before him.

"What explanation would you like us to give?" Broden leaned forward, making eye contact. His nose curled up and he pursed his full lips.

Deep lines creased Hilkiah's brow. "Perhaps you could explain why a dead body was found today beyond the market." His eyes never left Broden's face. "Did you think you could meet without my knowledge?"

Hilkiah left his place and moved around the table. When he passed behind Broden, he paused, letting his hand drop to the man's shoulder.

"And do you think I don't know who leads this group?" Hilkiah asked. "Do you think I don't know of your rebellious ideas and plans?"

He stroked his beard with his left hand, thrust out his right, and pointed a finger at each of them in turn.

"You are fools, all of you," he said, his voice rising and gaining power. "This time, you've gone too far. I've left you alone, hoping you would come to your senses, wanting to avoid the painful scene to come." He knew his body trembled, but he couldn't stop yet. "Now justice will be done. The land will be returned to its rightful overseers. Guards, take them away."

The last was a shout and the tramp of feet approached.

Broden jumped from his chair, pulling at his beard and hair. "Wait! You have no proof. You're the fool. No one listens to you."

Judah hadn't moved, but Ahiram was weeping softly.

"Look at these men." Broden gestured toward them. "Good men. Men who have served our country and King Manasseh."

Ahiram slowly shook his head. "It's no use, Broden. It's over. God is not pleased with us." He lowered his face into his hands and wept. Judah remained still.

"It's too late. Your time is up." Hilkiah swept aside the curtain and six guards entered with swords displayed.

The three were tied and led from the room, Broden still shouting his innocence.

The curtain swished back into place and Hilkiah sank to the floor. He stretched out facedown, arms above his head, tears staining the mat.

"What have I done?" Hilkiah pounded the floor with knobby fists. "How did I lose control and allow this to happen?"

He felt rather than heard a form bend down beside him.

"Come, my master, you must rise," he heard the voice of his scribe say, "There is work to be done."

Benjamin patted Hilkiah's back, and it was enough. Hilkiah struggled to a sitting position.

"Here, help me up," Hilkiah said.

Benjamin grasped the old priest's hands. Together, they managed to help each other to their feet, swaying to gain their balance. Hilkiah's once-clean robe was smudged with dust.

"Master, sit down until you're stronger." Benjamin eased Hilkiah onto one of the chairs. "I'll bring you some wine. That will help you recover from the weight of the day."

Hilkiah rested his arms on the table while Benjamin shuffled from the room. Flashes of the day strode across his inner vision, and he shuddered when each scene was replayed.

I know Broden's the killer, but how to prove it? I need a witness. Maybe…

A slow smile spread across his.

I'll need to be sharp to outwit them. They're nothing if not clever.

Another shudder ran down his body, but this time it had a tinge of anticipation.

nine

"Huldah, may I come in?"

When Huldah opened the door, Abigail stood before her. Pushing the hair back from her face, Huldah gulped twice, nodded and stood aside.

Abigail carried a wooden tray with steam rising from the containers. She didn't look at Huldah when she set the tray on a small shelf. "I've brought you some heated goat's milk with a little honey and bread fresh from the oven; it'll make you feel better."

"Th–thank you." Huldah sank down on the edge of the cot and reached for the clay cup with shaky hands. Using both hands to steady the drink, she lifted it to her lips. The warm liquid slid down her throat and brought her some comfort. Its warmth spread through her body.

Abigail pulled an old stool close to the bed and eased her ample frame down beside her. Her bright blue headdress didn't quite hide the curly dark hair beneath it. Today, her smile was absent.

"Huldah, you don't know me, but I'd like to be your friend." She tentatively reached out her work reddened hand to touch Huldah's arm. "I know some of your situation from the note my sister sent me."

Huldah lifted her eyes to meet Esther's. Taking a deep breath, she sighed and lifted both hands to cover her face. The tears came and she wept in gulping sobs. Her small frame rocked back and forth on the narrow cot.

Abigail settled on the bed, her arms wrapped around Huldah's thin shoulders. The two hugged in silence until the sobs subsided and Huldah was still once more. Abigail sat back and wiped the tears from Huldah's face with a damp cloth from the tray.

"Feeling a little better now?" Abigail brushed back the hair from Huldah's eyes.

Huldah tilted her head and curled her lips up in a tiny smile. "I think so," she whispered.

"And do you think we can be friends?"

Huldah nodded twice. "I would like that very much."

"Do you feel you can tell me the whole story? I promise I will hold it in secret for you." Abigail slipped back onto the stool, folded her arms around her body and watched her guest.

"Yes." Huldah's voice faltered, but it was strong. This time, Huldah held out her hand and placed it in Abigail's.

H

The morning sun strengthened while Abigail and Huldah sat on benches around the table. They had moved from the bedroom when Huldah finished her story. Joseph, Abigail's husband, left for the temple, taking their oldest son with him. Shouts and cries of the children came from outside the house.

Huldah nibbled on her bread, dipping it in goat's milk. The lines on her face had relaxed as she shared her story with Abigail.

"You have a wonderful gift." Abigail leaned across the table. "Don't let anyone belittle what you have. Only God gives those kinds of gifts."

"Sometimes it's frightening, like when the baby died." A log shifted in the fireplace, sending up a shower of sparks. "But I know the baby would have died anyway. I didn't kill it." A fresh batch of tears hung on her dark eyelashes.

"Of course you didn't kill the baby. You will learn how to use your gift to help people. Even in this, you were prepared." Abigail turned to check the fire, making sure no sparks fell where they could cause a fire. "Would you like more milk?"

"No, thank you. I'll just finish what I have here." Lifting her cup, Huldah took another sip. "It's peaceful sitting here with you, Abigail. I was so afraid last night, but now I have a new friend."

A smile touched the corners of Abigail's mouth as she marvelled at Huldah's youthful beauty.

"We may soon have a wedding to plan," Abigail said. "Your wedding. Isn't this what every young girl longs for?"

"Yes, but it's frightening, too." Huldah wrapped her arms around her body and shivered, but the smile hung on her lips.

"You have known my nephew for some time, I believe."

"I've known Shallum all my life. He's lived next door since before I was born."

A flash in Huldah's eyes showed a little fear still there.

Abigail saw the look. "Most brides aren't in love with their future husbands, so don't let that worry you. Love comes later." She shook her head gently and heaved a sigh. "Sometimes it's so hard until that happens. But I know my nephew is a good man. I know he'll be kind to you."

A blush rose up Huldah's neck to her face, and she covered her face with her hands. "That's not a problem," she whispered, "I've loved him forever. I only fear that he may not love me, now that he's forced to marry me."

Standing, Abigail reached Huldah and put her arms around the girl. "That will come, little one. Right now, we're going to talk about what you should wear. I have some ideas." She pulled Huldah to her feet. "Come with me."

Abigail led her to the room she shared with Joseph.

"I think you're about the size I was when I wed Joseph." She placed her hands on Huldah's hips and grinned. "You'd never believe it now, but I was once a slim young girl."

Abigail removed a bright cloth from a wooden box resting in the corner. When she lifted the lid, she rummaged through the contents and finally withdrew an exquisite robe. The white cloth was embroidered with delicate flowers around the hem.

Huldah gave a quick intake of breath. "It's beautiful. I couldn't wear that. It's much too fine for me."

"Here, feel the cloth," Abigail said, shoving the garment into Huldah's hands. "Run your fingers over the flowers. My grandmother made this for me." Abigail smiled at the memory.

Huldah's fingers traced the pattern of the fine work. She gathered the fabric to her and hugged it. "I've never seen anything so beautiful. I can't accept, but thank you for offering."

"Nonsense. You're going to wear it." Abigail took it from Huldah's arms and spread it out on the bed. "Look at me. When would I ever be able to wear it again?"

A deep laugh shook through Abigail. She sat down on a wooden stool and continued to laugh.

Finally, Huldah joined her. Her eyes squeezed shut, almost vanishing completely, and her mouth fell open as mirth consumed her. She dropped to the floor at Abigail's feet.

When the laughter subsided, Huldah jumped up, grabbed the material again, hugged it to herself and said, "I'll wear it. I'll wear it with joy."

"Let's try it on you and see where we need to make adjustments."

Abigail was sensible once again and helped drop the garment over Huldah's head. A pull here, a tug there, then she stood back with one hand on her chin and looked it over.

Huldah didn't move. Her eyes roved over the length of the robe. At last she looked up at Abigail, her eyebrows raised in question.

"It's beautiful on you. You are breathtakingly lovely."

ℋ

The palace loomed menacingly before father and son as they approached. Heat shimmered from the exterior, the sun pouring its strength on the earth. Sweat eased down Shallum's back and beaded his forehead. He wiped his face on his sleeve, drawing it across his face.

"You look warm, son." Tikvah peered at the boy's face as they walked.

"It is warm, but the cause is anxiety, not the sun." He wiped his brow again and glanced up. A few lazy clouds drifted over the horizon with no apparent destination in mind.

"Son, you work in the palace daily. Why should you be afraid now?" Deep lines furrowed Tikvah's forehead. He put his hand on Shallum's arm and stopped him. "Why are you worried?"

"It's different when I come here to work," Shallum said. "I almost never see the king, but I hear the reports from those who do. What they say in the market place is true: the king is mad."

"Those are only rumours, son. Lift your eyes to the heavens and see your God." Tikvah's grip tightened on Shallum's arm. "The king is a long way from God, but God hasn't moved. He's right here with us. He'll do what's right for us."

Shallum's shoulder muscles relaxed and he breathed deeply. "You're right, Father. I'll focus on God, not men. King Manasseh is only a man, after all."

A deep chuckle rumbled in Tikvah's throat. "Don't let him hear you say that."

He punched Shallum's arm and the two men moved off again. This time, Shallum's shoulders were back and his head held high.

"Who goes there?" The palace guard stepped from his place in the shade and confronted Tikvah and Shallum. His hand rested on the sword hanging at his waist. Not a smile or a blink moved his face.

Tikvah and Shallum bowed low.

"I am Tikvah, with my son Shallum, and we've come to hold an audience with the king."

"And you have an appointment?" The guard looked at them with motionless eyes.

"No, but it is the right of the people to access their king." Shallum swallowed. He hadn't planned to speak, but he knew this guard and resented his treatment of them.

The guard's eyes and tightened brows flicked to Shallum's face. He pointed to the palace gate. "By all means, gain entrance." The voice was tight, with a hint of sarcasm.

While they moved toward the gate, it was pushed back by two guards dressed in the traditional rough woollen tunic of slaves, lacking embroidery or fringes. An additional drab, colourless strip of cloth served as a belt. The Jews were forbidden to acknowledge these captured victims of the king's latest war efforts.

Shallum felt sorry for them, but he knew he and his father were being watched, and any infraction of the king's law could bring instant death. The smell of their unwashed bodies was overpowering. Their dignity had been stripped from them.

Life is uncertain, Shallum thought to himself, *and perhaps for us, too. The king may not sanction our request.* But time enough to think later; the doors of the palace stretched open before him and he entered its sacred halls.

A servant, this time dressed in the finest linen with a deep crimson fringe, beckoned for them to follow him. His leather sandals made no noise on the smooth tiled floor.

Human voices swirled around them; whispered voices, voices raised in argument, sharp commands. All combined to add vitality to the air of the entrance hall. Torches hung from the walls, even though it was daytime. Smoke from the torches hung in the air.

Once they were out of the steady stream of bodies moving to and fro through the palace, the servant stopped and turned to face them. His thin lips curved back, revealing surprisingly good teeth.

"Tikvah, what brings you to the palace today?" the servant asked. "We don't see you here unless you have business."

"We seek an audience with the king. Will you take us to him?"

With his head to one side, the servant frowned. "Are you expected?"

"No, but it is necessary that we speak to him," Tikvah said.

"I warn you, he has alternated between despair and rage all day. Another day might be better."

Tikvah shook his head. "I'm afraid it must be today. We'll take our chances."

Without another word, the servant turned and moved toward the throne room. Tikvah and Shallum followed quickly, one with determination, the other with fear.

Shallum knew the king would know him. He had been in his presence occasionally for fittings and wardrobe choices. This fact alone might make it more difficult for them. But it must be done. It was too late to turn back.

ten

When they neared the throne room, Shallum slid the edge of his robe over his nose. His lips drew down and he felt himself gagging. Leaning in close to his father, he barely moved his lips.

"What is that awful smell?" Shallum asked. I've been in here before, but I've never smelled anything like this."

"I'm not sure. Just be on your guard." Tikvah held his head high but did not cover his mouth and nose.

Before they reached the curtain which set apart King Manasseh's day rooms, strange noises assaulted their ears. The curtains were thrust aside with the horns of a young goat. It bleated frantically and ran without direction. They stepped aside and it plunged down the hall, saliva streaming from its lips. Close behind came a second, larger goat, its coat damp and matted; it, too, made harsh sounds as it followed the first goat. Next came slaves in hot pursuit, losing ground with each step they took.

Roars of raucous laughter spilled out of the opening.

"We may have chosen a very bad time to approach the king." Tikvah pursed his lips as he looked both ways down the hallway. The laughter from the throne room was becoming hysterical.

With one hand on the curtain, the servant paused, tightening his shoulders as a piercing scream split the air. He glanced at Tikvah before parting the curtains and entering the room. Tikvah and Shallum followed.

Colours and sounds blended in a jarring discord. The room was filled with people: slaves trying to right overturned furniture, servants attempting to calm the king, shepherds herding the remaining animals into pens lined along one wall, women of the court holding cloths over their faces so that only large dark eyes were visible. Each voice jangled and blasted in an attempt to be heard over the harsh din.

The servant conducting Tikvah and Shallum held out his hand to stop their progress. His eyes remained fixed on the king.

"Stay back," the servant commanded, gesturing with his extended arm. His gaze swept the room before he turned to them, eyes wide and brow furrowed. His whisper was almost unintelligible under the shrill racket. "Let's go. Back out slowly, so we don't distract the king."

Tikvah began to shuffle his feet back towards the door, but it was too late.

"Wait." The command flew across the space that divided them. "I say wait!"

King Manasseh shoved aside the servants hovering over him and pulled himself to his feet. Matted hair hung down from a crown perched atop his head. His head swivelled from side to side, spittle dripping from open, protruding lips. The material in his robe had once been fine and fashionable, but now hung in tatters from his emaciated frame. He swayed on his feet and pointed to the three leaving the room.

Silence descended on the room, except for the animals, which continued their rigorous protests, and a few vexatious sniffles from the women.

"I recognize you." The king indicated Shallum. His arm trembled visibly. "Something to do with the wardrobe, am I not right?"

Shallum fell to his knees in a deep bow. "Yes, my Lord."

"Who comes with you?" The strain was too much for the king and he fell back onto his throne.

"My father, Tikvah, my lord." Shallum remained in a prostrate position on the floor. The other two remained very still.

"Servant, you may leave them with me and return to your duties." A flick of the king's wrist was all it took for the servant to turn and glide from the room. "State your business."

Shallum took hope that the madness of a few minutes ago had passed, that they might gain the permission they had come for. He would need the king on his side to protect Huldah.

"We would ask for a private—" Tikvah got no further before the king's arm shot out, his finger pointing.

"You have not been spoken to. I'll deal with only the young man."

Tikvah bowed and wisely remained silent.

"Now," the king said, "what is it you want to say, young man?"

A snicker and giggle broke the human stillness. The disturbance seemed to put the king off-balance. Swinging his head, he searched the room with his eyes. They landed on a group of young women, now huddled on the far side of the room, clinging to each other. Even from a distance, Shallum could see their eyes wide with fear.

"Out, out, out of my sight." The king dashed from his seat, arms flailing, hair flying. "Out! Get them out of here. I will not be meddled with. I will not—"

His foot slipped on the debris on the floor, and he would have fallen if not for the quick attention of two servants who had never removed their gaze from him. They pulled him back and gently eased him into his chair. The king's ravings continued, although more feeble now.

A guard materialized and began to empty the room. The goats were ushered out a side door, along with the rest of the women. He motioned for Tikvah and Shallum to retreat. The last they saw of the king, servants were bending over him, administering a drink to him. His body was limp and easily handled.

Outside, Tikvah turned to Shallum. "We must come back. We still need an audience with him." He shook his head, and Shallum recognized the sorrow in his father's eyes. "I know he's not been a good king, but my heart goes out to an old man who can no longer handle the stresses of the kingship."

"Let's give him an hour and try again," Shallum suggested.

H

Once again, they stood outside the palace gates. Sweat formed on Shallum's spine, and he refrained from wringing his hands together by concentrating on the guards watching them. The peaceful surroundings belied the turmoil within, and a gentle breeze carried the fragrance of pomegranate trees blooming in the palace garden. Although unseen, their sweet scent permeated the air.

This time, it appeared they were expected and no challenge was given when they passed through the gates. The same servant met them, bowed stiffly, and indicated they were to follow. The change in the atmosphere was striking—no goats, no slaves running through the halls, no shrieks from the throne room. All was quiet and serene.

The servant stopped and swept aside the curtain.

"Tikvah and Shallum," he announced in a loud voice, followed by a deep bow. He stepped aside and gestured for them to enter.

Shallum was amazed. The goat smell was gone, the floor had been swept, the women had disappeared, and the king was upright on his throne arrayed in a fresh robe, watching them. Both men bowed deeply, then waited for the king's command.

"Come forward, my friends." King Manasseh's voice was strong and vigorous, contradicting the recent reports of ill health circulating in the city. When they approached, however, his signs of age became visible—sunken cheeks, shoulder blades protruding through the robe, and slack skin on his neck and arms. But a piercing flash still flickered in his eyes.

With heads bowed, the two men knelt before their king.

"Rise, friends." The king extended his arms, thin lips stretched in a smile, revealing gaps in his teeth. "What brings you to the palace?"

They stood, arranging their robes in front of them.

Tikvah stepped forward. "We come on the advice of the High Priest. We have a situation that needs your assent, my lord." Tikvah bowed again.

"Go on, tell your tale." The king leaned back in his seat, his head propped on one hand while he shifted his body. His head tilted to one side.

"I would like Shallum to share in the telling, if that is permissible." Tikvah made his request with back straight and chin firm.

The king merely nodded. Shallum moved in beside his father and made the ritual bow. His stance was relaxed, with feet apart and hands folded at his waist. The relaxation was only a mask; his insides churned with fear. He remained silent for a space, gathering his thoughts. The room was very still, holding only a few servants, all of whom were busy in another section of the large room.

"My lord, I have an unexpected situation that needs conclusion today," Shallum said. "A life is in danger. I come to you, because you hold the power to grant my request."

"Carry on. What is it you need?" The king gestured toward Shallum and leaned forward, eyebrows drawn together and lips parted.

"My lord, I need your consent for a marriage to take place this night."

The king's eyebrows shot up. "I must have misunderstood your comment, young man." He shook his finger at Shallum and tossed the hair back from his face, long, grey hair heralding his advanced years. "Please speak again."

Shallum swallowed and nodded. Warmth spread up his neck. "I'm afraid you did not misunderstand me." He raised his eyes to meet those of his king. "A girl's life is in danger if this does not take place, tonight."

Eyes squinted, the king leaned on his throne, frown lines gathered between his brows. "And this girl is…?" His hands twirled in the air.

"Huldah, my lord."

"Huldah." The king roared out her name, straining to come to his feet. "She deserves to die. She's brought terror to the priests. She killed a baby."

Tikvah stepped forward again, his hand out to the king. "Please, let me explain."

King Manasseh fell back on his seat and closed his eyes. "Yes, explain. I'm weary of the priests and their stories."

Tikvah told the story while the king listened, asked a question now and then, or made a comment. He shook his head several times while Tikvah spoke, and he slumped in his seat until his head rested on the back of the throne.

When the events were told, the king struggled into a sitting position. There was no sound in the room until the king sniffed audibly.

"I've heard rumours that the priests were undermining Hilkiah, but they come in here and convince me that he is wrong and they are right." The king clutched his arms to his chest. "Sometimes I don't know who to believe, but Hilkiah is trustworthy, I know that."

A commotion arose in the outer room. The king raised his eyes to the doorway, where two slaves lay prostrate on the floor.

"Who dares interrupt the king?" King Manasseh demanded.

"My lord," one of the slaves said, rising to his feet, "there's been a murder in the city. A priest has been killed." He fell back into the same position once he finished his message.

"Stand up, both of you." The king's command sped across the room. He snapped his fingers at them. "Who has been murdered? Quickly now, give me your message."

"It's Baz, my lord. The priest Baz."

"It's happening. My kingdom is falling apart." Tears fell from the king's eyes and his body went limp. A servant hurried to his side and called another.

"You'd better leave now," a servant whispered to Tikvah.

They left the throne room to the sound of hysterical weeping and babbled words. Outside, they paused to glance at each other.

Shallum put his hands in the air. "What now?"

eleven

While Huldah fingered the fine material in the garment, the room began to fade from her vision. Abigail's voice deepened and took on a smoother tone until it was no longer her voice, but one unknown to Huldah. Light shimmered around her in iridescent circles, causing her to blink. The circles swelled and retracted, dazzling in their intensity until they parted and Huldah saw outlines and shapes. With narrowed eyes, she tried to determine the picture forming before her. It was hazy and flared, colours quivering just out of sight.

She took a step toward the light, her hand extended to keep her balance. The path beneath her feet was rough and rocky, but she kept going, paying no attention to the way, her eyes focused on the growing outlines of images. A gasp escaped her lips when she recognized the depicted location—the lone hill beyond the market. The scene was foggy, but unmistakable.

What's happening? Something is wrong.

She stepped closer, peering through the shimmering veils expanding and contracting before her eyes. Using her hands, she pushed aside the filmy curtain. Another gasp forced its way through her clenched teeth, for now she saw men surrounding a man on the ground. The faces were unrecognizable, but their actions were clear. A man was being beaten before her eyes. She tried to stop the attack, but her limbs were immobile; no sounds came from her lips when she opened her mouth wide in a scream.

The scene faded, but before it disappeared she caught a glimpse of a twisted gold ring on the third finger of the one beating the turbanless victim. The blue robes of the priesthood flared in the fading vision.

H

"Huldah, are you all right?"

Two strong arms surrounded her and gently placed her on a stool.

"I'll get you a drink," Abigail said. "Stay right here."

Huldah rubbed her eyes and tried to recapture the scene she had so recently left, but it was gone, leaving only the memory. A very vivid memory.

"Here, drink this."

A clay cup was thrust into her hands and Huldah gulped the cool water. Abigail sank down on a seat beside her.

When Huldah regained her perspective of the room, she was alarmed to see that Abigail was flush with worry.

"What happened, Huldah? One minute we were talking about the dress, and the next you were staring straight ahead with your mouth open. You didn't respond to any of my questions." Abigail put her hands on Huldah's arms and squeezed gently. "Tell me what you saw."

Huldah shook her head to clear her thoughts. She needed time to process what she had seen. There was no question in her mind that she had seen a vision, a more vivid one than she had ever seen before. Someone had been badly beaten, maybe even killed, and the priests were responsible, especially the one with the twisted gold ring.

She rubbed her hands over her face again, drawing her shoulders in tightly before turning to answer Abigail.

"I need to get word to Shallum. It's urgent." Huldah jumped from the low seat and paced the small room, wringing her hands in distress. She stopped before Abigail and stared into her eyes. "How can I get word to him? Please, you must help me. What can I do?"

Abigail put both hands over her mouth and closed her eyes. "Yes, I'll help you. We'll send one of the boys to Esther. She'll send Shallum." She swept from the room, Huldah following closely behind.

Huldah's mind was becoming clearer. She began to pick out other details from her vision. She was sure she knew exactly where the attack had taken place.

I know I could take someone to the exact spot.

The boy was soon dispatched and Abigail once more asked her what she had seen.

"I… I can't tell you." Huldah clasped her hands and lifted her shoulders in a shrug. "I'm sorry, Abigail. I'd like to tell you, but I think I must share this only with Shallum. He can decide what happens."

"Let's sit in the garden while we wait for Shallum." Abigail beckoned for her to follow. "Does it have anything to do with the marriage that will take place tonight?"

Tears hovered close to the edge of Huldah's voice. "Please, I must not talk about it. I'm so sorry. You've done so much for me and I must seem ungrateful, but I don't mean to be."

"I'm sorry, too, Huldah. I shouldn't be asking. I know you'd tell me if you could, or if there was danger."

H

Shallum shaded his eyes to better see a figure moving rapidly toward him. It was definitely a woman, and if he didn't know better he'd say it was his mother, but she never ventured to this area of town, unless she was with his father on some special outing. The woman appeared flustered and determined, not slowing for any reason, skirting around anyone in her path. When she drew nearer, the resemblance to his mother increased. He drew his father's attention to the figure.

"That's Esther!" Tikvah said. He folded his arms over his chest, clamped his lips together, and set his jaw firmly in place. "What's she doing coming here? She knows that it's not a woman's place to interfere. I will have words with her about this."

Shallum put his arm around his father's shoulders to calm him. "Why don't we wait to see why she has come? I think she'd need a good reason to follow us here."

When Esther's eyes found them, she raised her head, waved, and approached, chest heaving.

"Tikvah, Shallum." She fell against her husband, her breath coming in gasps.

Tikvah straightened her, gripping her shoulders. "What is it, Esther? It must be important for you to forget yourself like this."

"Yes, yes, it's important. Urgent." She took two deep breaths, her eyelids fluttering and her hands moving restively in front of her.

"Esther, calm yourself and tell us what troubles you," Tikvah said, shaking her shoulder gently. His eyes roved over her face.

"Abigail's boy has come to report that Shallum is needed immediately at their house." Esther exhaled a sigh. "He said it's urgent."

Shallum leaned in toward his mother, brows pulled together and lips turned down. "Is Huldah all right? Is she sick? Did he say what was wrong?"

Tikvah let go of Esther and grabbed Shallum by the arm. "Relax, my son. Don't borrow trouble. Go quickly and do what you can to help. Then return and let us know what has happened."

Shallum eyes widened when he looked at his father. "But what about the king?"

"I'll see the king when it's possible. You go." He gave his son a sharp shove.

Shallum turned on his heel and began to run in the direction of Abigail's house, fearful of what he might find.

ℋ

Shallum entered his aunt's house, swept the curtain aside, and sought Huldah. He found her pacing the inner room, wringing her hands and moaning softly.

"Huldah, I'm here." His voice was pitched higher than normal and he was aware of a tremor of panic in his tone.

She turned to face him, a flush deepening the hues on her face. "Shallum…"

Huldah stretched out her hands to him. Time seemed to stop when their eyes met.

A fly buzzed around the window, seeking a way out. Children's voices filled the background. Huldah opened her mouth, but no sound came.

Shallum scanned her face, looking for a reason for the summons. He observed the flicker in her eye, the flare of her nostrils, the troubled lines on her brow.

"Shallum…" Time clicked into place again and she was before him, clutching his arms.

"What has happened? I can see you're troubled." He took her hands in his, hands cool and clammy. "Tell me how I can help."

"I've seen a vision. A priest is dead and I know who killed him."

Her breathless reply caught him off-guard. "How can you know this? I heard of it before my mother delivered your message."

"I… I saw it." She dropped her eyes to the floor, hands falling limp at her sides.

"Huldah," he said, his hands still gripping her shoulders, "are you telling me you've seen a vision?"

Her eyes sought his again. "I think so."

"Here, let's sit." He led her to a couch and they sat. "Tell me."

The story unfolded accompanied by tears and sniffles. He interrupted from time to time with a question, but the story was finally told. She sat with her hands folded in her lap.

The only sound in the room was the fly, still trying to escape. Shallum was aware of the distraction, but kept his eyes focused on Huldah.

"Huldah, you've been given this by God himself." He took one of her hands, still cold in the warm room. "Hilkiah will need to hear what you've seen."

The eyes she turned on him were large and glassy, shiny with unshed tears. "I can't."

That was all. A simple refusal.

"But don't you see? You must." His tone was urgent, compelling, demanding. "Look at me, Huldah. God has given this knowledge to you. To you alone. I'll be with you; I promise."

She lowered her eyes and tipped her head. She appeared to consider his request.

At last, she looked up, stretched out her hand to him, and parted her lips in a tiny smile.

"You're right." She nodded twice. "I can't keep this information hidden. I'll come with you." As they stood from the couch, she adjusted her robe. "It may be a risk, but it's one I must take."

Lifting her chin, she thrust her shoulders back and moved toward the curtain.

twelve

The holding cells at the back of the temple were filled with a deafening roar. Prisoners snarled threats to the guards; guards barked commands in return. Over the clamour, Broden could distinguish quarrels and harsh disputes.

Broden leaned against the wooden bars. "Cowards, that's what you are. Cowards."

He shook his fist and pounded on the cell bars. *I could say worse; they haven't heard the last of me yet.* Rage built in him until he barely recognized his own voice.

"How dare you arrest the chosen of the Lord!"

A massive guard approached the bars. He roared with laughter. "Chosen of the Lord? Now that's a good one. I've seen you in operation. Hah. You took away my mother's property." He snapped his fingers in Broden's face. "Said she was a prostitute. Lies, lies, all lies."

The guard spat in Broden's face and moved away from him.

"When I get out of here, your life won't be worth the smallest temple coin." Broden ground his teeth and snarled. Heat suffused his face and neck, disappearing below the neckline of his priestly robe.

Judah pulled on his robe. "Come away from the bars, Broden. They're not worth your rage." He managed to get Broden to the wooden bench running along the back of the cell. "Sit. We'll be out of here soon. Hilkiah doesn't have a shred of evidence against us and will be forced to let us go."

He patted Broden's shoulder, which shook beneath his hand.

"This will give us a reason to get rid of the high priest," Judah whispered, leaning close to Broden's ear. "You'll be the next High Priest. Think about that and let these curs rant and bellow. Their time is short."

Broden slumped on the seat and became silent. In the sudden quietness of the cell, the sound of weeping became audible.

Judah swung his head around to face Ahiram. "What's this about?"

Choking sobs met his question. Ahiram was bent over. Hands covered both his eyes and his shoulders trembled. Judah shook him. Broden stayed hunched on the bench, eyes focused on the floor.

"We... we... were wrong." Ahiram's words came out in a raspy whisper.

Judah's hand shot out and covered Ahiram's mouth. "Say one more word like that and you'll be next."

Ahiram swallowed and fell into silence.

Two guards watched the performance of the three priests. "Now, isn't that a pretty sight?" the larger guard jeered. Loud guffaws circulated through the holding cells.

Even Judah sank down on the bench, caught between a sullen priest and a sniffling one.

"When we get out of here, we'll make plans to rid the earth of these guards." Judah raised a clenched fist. "They haven't heard the last of us."

ℋ

Five strides to the corner, turn, six strides to the door, turn, five more strides to the next corner. Round and round the room Hilkiah paced. Benjamin sat at the table and scribbled on his scroll. He raised his eyes occasionally to follow the pacing of his master.

"I need a witness." Hilkiah paused. "Someone must have seen something."

Benjamin nodded.

"Or maybe a prophet." Hilkiah resumed his walk, hands gripped under his chin.

A servant slid his hand inside the curtain and beckoned to Benjamin, who rose and slipped out of the room.

"What is it?" Benjamin asked.

"There's someone here to see the High Priest," the servant said. "A young man with a girl. Shall I bring them to you?"

Benjamin put a finger on his cheek and frowned. "Ask their names."

He waited while the servant did his bidding, all the while hearing the soft shuffle of feet behind the curtain. Hilkiah mumbled, but the words were indistinguishable.

The mumbling stopped and Benjamin eased the curtain aside. Hilkiah was on his knees, with his forehead touching the mat on the floor. Words escaped his lips.

"Father God, give your servant wisdom… and a witness."

Benjamin let the curtain slip back into place, giving Hilkiah privacy for his petitions to God. When he turned back to the open room, the servant returned.

"Shallum and a young woman. He says it's imperative that they see Hilkiah." The servant raised his head but kept his eyes lowered. "Shall I bring them?"

Benjamin stroked his beard, his mind whirling with thoughts. "Yes, bring them."

While the servant turned to do his errand, Benjamin once again slid aside the curtain and leaned into the small enclosure. "My lord, forgive my interruption, but Shallum and a young maiden seek to speak with you."

The words of supplication stopped and slowly Hilkiah rose to his feet. "What do they want?" His voice was irritable.

"They didn't say, my lord." Benjamin's grip tightened on the curtain. He watched Hilkiah draw his brows together in a frown. "I think you need to see them. I feel you must."

"Then let them come." Hilkiah put his hands on his head and sank into his chair, closing his eyes. The lines between his eyes deepened. His eyes opened quickly when Shallum and his companion were led into the room.

"My master." Shallum fell to his knees before Hilkiah, bending deep until his forehead touched the floor.

Benjamin studied the girl—a slim figure, bent slightly at the shoulders, head lowered, and face shrouded with a veil. He couldn't distinguish any features and soon let his gaze wander to Shallum, who had risen to his feet.

H

"This is the second time I've seen you today, Shallum." Hilkiah inclined his head, extending a hand to him. "What can I do for you this time?"

"Master, I think I may be able to be of service to you." Shallum cleared his throat, then took a deep breath. Reaching behind him, he gently pulled Huldah beside him. "This is Huldah, the girl who will be my wife."

She lifted her veil and raised her eyes to Hilkiah's. Lips pressed tightly together, she stood with her hands clasped in front of her.

"My lord," Shallum continued, "Huldah has received a vision that we believe is from the Lord."

Hilkiah rubbed one hand over his beard as he looked from one to the other. "Then let's sit, and you can tell me what she has seen."

The three sat on the benches in front of the table. Huldah tugged at her scarf, covering her face once more.

"Please, master," Shallum said. "I think Huldah should tell the story in her own way."

With raised brows, Hilkiah glanced at Huldah, then back at Shallum. "If this is what you wish, then let her begin."

Her voice was soft and tremulous when she began her tale. Hilkiah leaned forward as she related the vision of the beating and identification of the attackers. When she mentioned the twisted gold ring, his eyebrows shot up and he began to lift from his seat. He dropped down again, shoulders slumped. When she finished her story, one hand covered his mouth.

"Do you know the identity of the man with the gold ring?" Hilkiah spoke the words slowly.

"No, my lord, but I know he is a priest," Huldah said, looking directly at Hilkiah. Her hands were still now, giving the appearance of calm.

The silence stretched out between them while he seemed to process what he had heard.

After a time, he raised his eyes to meet Huldah's. "Would you be willing to tell your story to others?"

Her shoulders slumped and her hands became restless, smoothing the fabric of her robe over and over.

"If I may speak for her…?" Shallum glanced at her. She trembled nervously. He faced Hilkiah again. "With your permission…"

"Yes, yes, speak."

"I believe she is fearful of what may happen to her if these priests find out she has spoken to you of her vision." He paused to swallow and clear his throat. "As you are aware, she is under punishment from them."

"Little they can do to hurt her where they are now. With her witness against them, they'll be the ones under punishment." Setting his jaw firmly, he sat back and folded his arms. "What will it be? I need her to speak out or I'll not be able to prove that the priests murdered Baz."

She jerked her head up. With hands fluttering in front of her, she rose. "I'll do whatever you want me to do. Take me where you will. Let the consequences fall where they may."

thirteen

The palace sounds ebbed and flowed around Tikvah while he stood outside the entrance to the throne room.

Will King Manasseh receive me this time? We soon need an answer. The King could have the prisoners released, or he could have them executed. Either way, Huldah isn't safe.

A steady movement of people passed before his eyes. Tikvah observed the flow of people—slaves tied together with ropes, headed to the stone quarries; peasants who looked for hand-outs from the king; travellers from other courts with their strange speech and outlandishly coloured robes; servants carrying trays with olives, pomegranates, figs, and an assortment of breads; priests trailing behind an important-looking dignitary with a tall headdress trimmed with gold threads.

Tikvah was so absorbed in his musings that he almost missed the signal from the king's servant, who beckoned him to approach. He straightened his robes and followed the servant into the presence of the king.

The king was seated on his throne, but the usual assortment of slaves was absent. No sign could be seen of the ladies from the first interview. King Manasseh had donned a fresh robe of white linen, trimmed with the dark blue that was a favourite of the palace. His hair was neat and he smiled a greeting. Tikvah approached, bowing low.

"This time we can hope for no interruptions." The smile curving King Manasseh's lips even seemed to reach his eyes. "Where is your son?"

"He was called away to another emergency, Your Majesty." Tikvah bowed again. "I am here on his behalf, to await your ruling on the marriage."

"Yes, yes, the marriage." The king rested his head on one hand, elbow propped on the arm of his chair. "You know the priests are guilty, don't you?"

Tikvah managed to keep his jaw from dropping, but his eyes did widen. "If you say it is so, I believe you."

"Oh, it's so. I've been deluded by them too long. They think they can run the country. They forget that I am the king." His fist pounded his chest. "Do you know that? Do you know that I am king?"

"Yes, of course, my lord. You are the king." Tikvah's knees began to tremble. He had to get the king off this dangerous subject and back to the marriage.

"My son, Shallum, also knows you are in charge. He would be very happy if you would approve his marriage."

"Yes, yes, the marriage. Go ahead. Tell him to marry her. I give my permission." The king's voice sounded strong and under control. "But those priests, I need to do something about them."

The servant who had ushered Tikvah in appeared at this side, and in a whisper suggested they leave. Tikvah bowed again before the king, who no longer seemed to be aware of his presence, and backed out of the throne room.

Once outside, he thanked the servant and fled the palace.

H

"Stop crying. It's more than a mortal can bear," Amaziah snarled at his wife, grabbing handfuls of his hair. He was anxious, but he would not admit that to her; not ever. Salome lay prostrate on a mat on the far side of the room. "Get up, woman. Weeping won't solve the problem, nor will it bring Huldah home."

"But where is she?" Salome wept intensely. She beat her fists on the straw pallet, wetting the strands with her tears. "Why won't you tell me where she is?"

"You don't need to know." He kicked the bench beside him, rage building in his body. "I told you she's safe. That's all you need to know."

"But she's my baby. I want her." Her words were punctuated with sniffs and coughs. She vigorously wiped her face with her scarf.

"I've had enough. Get up and go to your bed." He grabbed her arms and forced her to a standing position. "I'm leaving and I don't know when I'll be back."

With one last kick at the bench, he hurled open the door and stormed outside. He strode up the path behind their home.

That woman will be the end of me. It's bad enough that the priests have been arrested and Huldah has fled; now I have to put up with the wailings of a crazed woman. He flailed his clenched fists. Looking at the sky, he shook his fists in that direction as well. *I came close to hitting her. I should have. She deserves it.*

His feet struck the path in a heavy rhythm. One fist smacked the other as he replayed the scene with his wife.

A hand grabbed Amaziah's shoulder, spun him around, and brought him to a halt. His mouth opened to protest until he realized he was staring into the face of his neighbour.

"We need to talk, Amaziah." Tikvah pulled him forward up the path.

In the tense stillness, vibrant birdsong trilled in the air, a dog barked, and the scurry of small animal feet could be heard in the bushes. At length, they came to a large, flat rock.

Tikvah guided Amaziah to sit with him. "I don't like to intrude on a friend and neighbour, but I couldn't help but overhear your discussion with your wife."

Amaziah jumped up from his seat. "Discussion? Hah. Call it what it is—tirade, disagreement, harangue, abuse. Whatever name pleases you." Spittle flew from his mouth and lodged in his beard.

"My friend, I don't want to insult you. I only want to help. Please, sit with me."

Amaziah slumped down on the rock, his face in his hands. "I've really messed up my life."

"Do you want to talk about it? I may not be able to change anything, but I can listen." Tikvah squeezed his arm. "Breathe deeply, my friend. The fresh air will make you feel a little better and help calm you."

Amaziah slid off the rock again, and with folded arms stared down the path. A light breeze could be felt here in the shade, and the fragrance of an unseen flower filled the air. Turning, he glanced at Tikvah, "Please, yes. I would like to unburden myself. There's no one else I can trust."

"Take your time. I'm not in a hurry."

"You know that I've been involved with the priests who want things to change, who want Hilkiah out. I thought it was the right thing to do." He rubbed his forehead. "No, that's not quite true. I knew there was the most to gain by joining them. They were gaining power, and with the power came money." Sweat beaded his brow and he swiped at it with the back of his hand. "You must think I'm disgusting. And you're right. I am."

"Amaziah, I'm not going to judge you. I just want to hear your story. Together, we can figure out how to change things." He put his hand on Amaziah's shoulder. "I want to be a friend."

"You'd actually help me?" Amaziah's eyes went wide and his eyebrows rose to meet his hairline.

"Yes, I'll help. Continue your story."

"It was the power, more than anything. I like the feel of people looking at me with respect, looking to me for authority. It feels good. Everything seemed to be going well until the problem with Huldah." He paused to swallow, his grief threatening to overwhelm him. "She's always been different, from a small child. I pretended she annoyed me and disappointed me, but actually I was proud of her. I never let her know, or my wife, but I could see that she saw things, felt things even I couldn't understand. And she wasn't afraid to stand up to me and state her opinion." His eyes had a faraway look. His lips curled into a smile when he thought about her. "But everything changed when that baby died. I was frightened, because I knew the priests would blame her. They were afraid that if the people knew she had visions, somehow it would undermine their power."

Tikvah joined him, and the two walked along together.

"I was weak. I should have told the priests that I would stand up for my daughter. Instead, I went along with the punishment they doled out. All except Baz." Amaziah stopped and gripped Tikvah's arm. "And now Baz is dead, because he wasn't afraid to stand up to them. Because he let her know." His wild eyes stared into Tikvah's. "I'm afraid I'll be next, because I'm her father. They'll kill me."

"But you know they're under arrest—"

"That won't help. They have power. There are no witnesses. They'll be out by sundown." A tremble shook his body. "I won't last the night."

"Amaziah, you don't know the whole truth."

"What don't I know?"

The grip tightened on Tikvah's arm. "I've just come from the palace. There is a witness."

Amaziah's jaw went slack. "A... a witness? No one would be foolish enough to speak against the priests. Hilkiah is powerless."

"You're wrong. There is a witness, and she's willing to speak out against them."

"Who? Probably someone no one would believe." Scorn laced his voice. His head shook from side to side.

"Huldah is the witness."

Amaziah felt a shock jolt through his body. His knees went weak and he thought they would fail him. He staggered against Tikvah. "What are you saying?"

Tikvah helped Amaziah back along the path to the rock. Power seemed to have left him and he leaned heavily on his friend. Once they were seated, Amaziah held his hands tightly, waiting for the explanation.

fourteen

The room seemed to be filled with priests. Light chatter permeated the air when Hilkiah stiffly entered. He was old. He knew he was old, and yet he still had a job to do. God still wanted him, apparently needed him, to lead the priests of the temple.

The talk ceased while Hilkiah moved across the smooth floor. His priestly robe swished and pomegranates swayed lightly with each step.

Frown lines appeared on the priests' forehead when they became aware of his presence, and then Shallum's. A collective gasp caught in their throats when Huldah slipped into the room, face veiled and head bowed.

Hilkiah turned when he reached the front of the room and faced the assembled priests. His face was pinched and grey; even his eyes looked tired. Silence greeted him and he beckoned Shallum and Huldah to stand beside him. His shoulders slumped and his beard trembled, but he lifted his hands.

"Almighty God, bless these, Your priests. Give them listening ears, open minds, and wisdom that defies human comprehension." His voiced wavered. "Let them hear the words spoken to them and recognize your power."

His hands slipped to his sides as he looked around the room at every eye fastened on him. Nobody moved.

"You have all heard of the tragedy that has befallen us today. It is a disgrace before our God." Stronger now, Hilkiah squared his shoulders and lifted his voice. "Baz is no more. We can only commit him into the hands of our God. But the ones who perpetrated this deed must be punished according to the Law of Moses."

Murmurings rose from the group and heads nodded their agreement.

"Until a short time ago, we were confounded. Without a witness, we were unable to proceed. We knew who had committed this act, but were powerless to do anything about it. Even though I arrested them and they were safely under guard, I knew I'd be forced to let them go." His lips drew into a thin line. "But all that has changed."

The priests glanced at each other, eyes wide with questions. Bodies shifted on the wooden benches and sandals scuffed the floor.

"We have a witness," Hilkiah said.

"Praise be to God," shouted one of the priests. He jumped from his seat and threw his hands in the air. Others followed his lead until the room pulsed with their voices.

Hilkiah raised his hand for silence. "You need to hear what the witness has to say." He glanced at Shallum. "You all know Shallum and his father."

Heads nodded and smiles lit faces.

"But he is not our witness."

Eyebrows raised again. Not a sound ruffled the air in the room.

"The witness is a woman. A young girl, really."

The restlessness started up again, with all eyes turned to face Huldah.

"Not only is she a young girl, she is the daughter of Amaziah."

A clamour broke out through the room. Shocked individual voices penetrated through the disturbance.

"This cannot be!"

"But he's one of them."

"How could we believe anything she says?"

Hilkiah raised his hand. When they were again silent, he lowered his hand. "Please, you must listen, and then decide whether her story is believable. I believe her."

He moved to Huldah's side and took her hand in his. With Shallum at her other side, Hilkiah led her to the place where he had addressed the priests.

"Do not be afraid, my child," Hilkiah said. "Shallum and I will be right beside you. Just tell them what you told me."

With a trembling hand, Huldah adjusted her veil so her face was uncovered. Slowly, she raised her eyes to look at the group. A deep red spread up her neck, staining her cheeks, but her voice was strong.

She recounted the experience of the vision. Ripples of disbelief moved through the crowd of priests, their heads shaking from side to side, shoulders rising and falling. Huldah continued. Gradually, the looks changed. A few heads nodded, and a smug smile or two appeared.

When she finished, she moved back to stand behind the two men.

Hilkiah cleared his throat, covering his mouth with his hand. He let his eyes roam over the priests.

"You have heard the witness," Hilkiah said. "If you have questions, now is the time to ask them."

No one moved.

"Then what is your pleasure? Do you believe her? And if so, how must we proceed?"

Talmar, an elderly priest, struggled to stand, using a smooth stick to assist him. His hand shook when he raised it to Hilkiah. "I believe her. I believe God has sent this vision." He turned his head and glanced at each one sitting near him. "I know her father well. He may be 'one of them,' but he is not corrupt, only led astray. I say we bring these men to justice. I dare not call them priests; that would be an affront to God."

The priests jumped from their seats and stamped their feet in a rhythmic agreement.

"God is good. God is holy. God will not be mocked."

$\mathcal{H}$

The throne room was packed when Amaziah squeezed into a small corner, far removed from where the king was seated. Murmurs filled the empty spaces above the turbaned heads. He furtively glanced through the opening between two heads directly in front of him and a sea of colour swam before him—the bright blues and whites of the priests, crimson robes of the merchants, deep purples indicating royalty, and dirty browns of the common man blended together.

He pulled a sleeve across his forehead, which cooled him for the moment. Others were warm, he knew from the stench of perspiration building up around him. Faces grimaced in anticipation of the trial about to take place, the deed not in keeping with the splendour of the room.

Amaziah breathed deeply, as much from fear as from the need for air. The whispering continued until the heavy blue curtain near the throne was thrust back, revealing the guards and their prisoners.

Amaziah shrunk back from the opening, hoping he wouldn't be seen while one by one the incriminated were led before the king. The guards wore the distinguished robes so familiar to all who visited the palace. Today their heads were bare, their hair tied back with golden circlets.

The three prisoners had been relieved of their priestly robes and were attired in the grey garb of prisoners. They were a pathetic trio.

Judah held his head high and looked only at the king. His hands were tied behind his back. The chains wrapped around his ankles made walking difficult, but he clung to what little arrogant dignity remained to him.

Broden, on the other hand, resisted the guard, jerking his body back and forth. His lips were pulled back, baring his teeth.

"Take your hands off me, you cur." Broden's voice raced across the room. "I can walk by myself."

He gave one final thrust with his body and threw the guard off-balance. Cheers broke out from some of his supporters. Quickly the guard regained a standing position and Broden was once again tightly held.

The last to appear was Ahiram. Those who had known him would have had difficulty recognizing the bent form being escorted behind the others. Limp grey hair hung down his back, partly obscuring a face which seemed to match the hair colour. His eyes were swollen and tears could be seen on his sunken cheeks. Slumped shoulders and bent knees completed the picture of misery.

At last, all three were forced to their knees before the motionless king. King Manasseh leaned forward on his throne and stared at the three before him. Slowly he rose, arms crossed over his chest. Today, his eyes were clear and his posture erect. Gasps circled the room when the king spat at their kneeled bodies.

"You disgust me." The king flung both arms into the air, fingers wide-spread. "And to think I once trusted you. But you must have your trial. It is the law."

Once again, the king slipped into his seat. "Bring the witness."

Amaziah began to tremble uncontrollably. How could they do this to him? He would be marked forever, the father of the girl who had caused judgment to fall on the priests. When his lips, too, began to shake, he clamped his teeth together. Fortunately, no one appeared to be watching him; all eyes were fixed on the scene playing out in front of the throne.

A servant entered the room, leading Shallum and Huldah to the king. Amaziah had to admit that he was proud of her. She was showing more courage than her father had ever done. Her shawl covered all of her face except her eyes, but he could see the determination in the way she carried her body—shoulders back and chin up, just the way he had taught her.

The king beckoned her to stand beside him. When Shallum walked with her, the hand of the king sharply indicated he was to stand back. Alone, she approached the throne.

The king spoke quietly to her, but the whispers didn't reach him. At a flick of the king's wrist, a chair was placed beside the throne and Huldah sat straight, looking out at the mass of faces.

"We are all aware that there is power beyond our human comprehension," the king said. "This young girl has experienced the power and will tell us what she has learned." He turned to her with a thin movement of his lips. "You may begin."

Huldah told her story in a voice that could be heard throughout the room—strong, confident, convincing. When she finished, she laid her hands to rest in her lap and looked to the king.

"I need no further evidence," King Manasseh said. "Guilty! You are guilty of murder and treachery, and the penalty for your errors will be death." He rose again and pointed a long finger at each of them in turn. "Guilty. Guilty. Guilty. Before the sun sets, you will join the fathers who have gone before."

The king beckoned the guards.

"Take them away. I wish to see them no more."

The crowd broke out in excited chatter when the three were led from the room. The king disappeared through a curtain behind the throne, and Shallum took Huldah's hand and followed. The mass of bodies surged through the curtains until only Amaziah remained in his corner. He, too, slipped from the room.

H

The sun was nearing the horizon when the shameful procession wended its way through the gates of Jerusalem. The king had spoken, and the punishment was set: death. People huddled close to buildings along the route and leaned against the walls when the group passed. They were curious, yet afraid; outraged, yet drawn to the sight. The scene was poignant. Death must be punished by death.

The prisoners were indistinguishable from each other in their dark robes with hoods pulled low. All three were bent at the shoulders, the arrogance now gone. The lead guard paused just outside the gate to allow the others passage. At the back, a burly guard brandished a whip, which he used freely. The prisoners remained mute, strung together with thongs, stumbling under the burden of the whip and perhaps their own consciences.

Amaziah and Tikvah were among the watchers close to the gate. Their shoulders touched when they, too, leaned away from the forlorn band that stumbled in the near darkness. When the last prisoner was propelled through the gate, the guards on the gates moved to close and bar them for the night.

"The deed will be done according to the law. A tragic tale." Tikvah shook his head while peering at his companion in the fading light. "It is contemptible when the chosen of God stray from His ways and pursue their own ends. It leaves a bitter taste in my mouth to see such potential end this way."

Tikvah pulled his robe tight around him, more for comfort than to ward off the evening chill. His drawn brows gave his face a desolate look. His eyes were riveted on the closed gate.

"Tikvah, that could have been me," Amaziah said. The harsh words were ground out between clenched teeth; they were laced with fear. "What a fool I've been."

Amaziah fell back against the wall behind him, its mud bricks still warm from the afternoon sun. Both hands covered his face, his chin sinking to his chest.

"God has given you a second chance," Tikvah said. He moved in close to his friend and put his hand on his shoulder. "Take that chance, my friend. Embrace it. Change your heart and serve the Lord."

"I will." He raised his head and Tikvah, in the little light remaining, could just make out the outline of the smile that came.

Tikvah circled his shoulders with one arm. "That's good. That's very good." He squeezed gently. "Now let's go home. You have some work to do there. Your wife needs you."

Amaziah groaned. "This means I need to make things right at home, doesn't it." It was a statement, not a question.

"Yes, neighbour, you need a new beginning."

The two men walked through the streets of the Second District in companionable silence. When they neared the house, Tikvah paused in the street.

"We have a wedding to attend tonight." Tikvah's voice held a note of glee.

"A wedding. Of course. My daughter is getting married." Amaziah shouted the words. "My wife will be beside herself with joy."

"Then let's make haste and gather our wives. Shallum and Huldah deserve our presence." He slapped Amaziah on the back.

H

Silence greeted Amaziah when he pushed open the door to his home. All was dark within. Not even the smallest of candles was lit. He felt his heart sink when he eased his way inside. Where was Salome? He felt his way through the room, arriving at the curtained area to their sleeping quarters without encountering anyone.

"Salome? Are you here?"

Silence.

He brushed the curtain aside and felt for the bed. His hand touched her, but she did not move.

"Salome. Please answer me." His voice pleaded, begged, hoped.

His question was greeted with a sniff. There was still no movement on the bed. He sat beside her and put his hand on her back. "Salome, I need to talk to you. Please turn and face me."

Something in his voice must have touched a deep place in her heart, because she rolled over onto her side. He stroked her face with his rough hand, felt the tears that lay on her cheeks.

"Oh Salome, I'm so sorry."

"Sorry... for... for what?" It was a tiny sound that escaped from her lips, high and almost shrill.

"It will take me a lifetime to tell you." He brushed back her hair from her face and leaned over her, planting a soft kiss on her damp cheek.

She trembled beside him, hesitatingly reaching up to touch his face. "Whatever it is, as long as you stay like this, I will like it." He could hear a smile in her tone.

"Can you believe I still love you after the way I've treated you?" Both her hands were now captured in his and he lifted them to his lips. "I want things to be different between us. Will you forgive me?"

She sat up in bed and wrapped her arms around him. "I don't know what has brought this change, but yes, I will forgive you. Gladly, joyfully, thankfully."

"Then, little one, we have something important to do tonight."

"You haven't called me 'little one' in years." Wonder broke into her voice as she swung her legs over the side of the bed. She laughed, a trembling little laugh. "What has happened, Amaziah?"

His quiet chuckle joined hers. "It's a long story, and you'll have to trust me to tell you in stages. Right now, we have a very important event to attend."

He lifted her gently to her feet, marvelling that she had so readily forgiven him. *What a fool I've been. But no more.*

"An event? But it's late. What could it be?" Salome reached around him in the darkness. She found her small candle and took it to the fire to light.

"You, my dear, are to witness the marriage of your daughter at the temple." With his arm draped around her shoulders, Amaziah twirled her around. "Can you imagine?"

"You've seen her? Oh my girl, you've seen her?" Her mouth fell open and her eyes grew wide.

She still retained much of her youthful beauty when she smiled, he realized. *What a fool I've been. She's had no cause to smile in recent years.*

"No, I've not seen her, but Tikvah has told me. Esther will come to help you dress."

He watched the play of emotions on her face—wonder, joy, excitement.

She clapped her hands together, covered her mouth, then threw them high in the air. "My joy is full to overflowing. God has wrought a miracle in my home."

fifteen

Slowly, Huldah turned in a complete circle while Abigail watched. Light from the kitchen fire spilled on the white dress, causing it to shine. Embroidered flowers around the hem glowed with delicate colours. Pure white linen fell in soft folds from the crown of her head, held in place by a ring of garden flowers in hues of red and gold.

"You are breathtaking." Abigail's eyes shone when Huldah faced her once more. She wiped her eyes on the corner of a cloth that had been carefully concealed beneath her robe. "Lovely only begins to describe you."

"I have no idea how you were able to put all this together," Huldah said, her lips curled up in a bright smile. She blinked twice before glancing down again at the beautiful robe.

A twitch of Abigail's lips sent her eyes dancing. "Oh, I knew someone who knew someone who knew someone… Everyone was willing to help, all the neighbours and their friends. There's nothing like a wedding to make us all a little tender, remembering our own special days."

The bride embraced her. "I could never have done this without you, and I'm scared."

Huldah's lovely face fell and her lips trembled.

"Don't you worry. Once your groom arrives, all your fears will disappear." Abigail patted her face, straightened the flowers, and smoothed back the folds of linen. "All brides feel that way before the wedding. It's only natural. This is a life-changing step for a girl."

"I know. I feel filled with gratitude to have Shallum's love. All I want is to be a good wife to him." Her hands clenched at her sides, but she managed to let her face fall into a calm demeanour.

H

"May I come in?" Esther's cheery voice echoed in the room when she poked her head through the doorway. Amaziah had gone ahead to meet Tikvah and Hilkiah.

"Esther." Salome hurried across the space that separated them and fell into Esther's open arms. "My cup is full, my joy is overflowing. God is gracious to them that fear Him. Praise His name." Her arms tightened around her friend and the two hugged.

Esther pushed gently on Salome's shoulders. "We don't have much time. I need you to come with me, and bring your best robes."

Salome looked into Esther's eyes and pursed her lips. "I don't have any robes suitable for a wedding."

"Salome, this is a night for happiness. You must rally your spirits. Now, take your hands down and listen." She placed her hands on Salome's shoulders and leaned closer so their noses were almost touching. "Don't worry about a robe. I have plenty for both of us. Just come with me and we'll get you ready."

Hand in hand, they left the house and walked next door. Salome's eyes widened when she gazed on the array of robes waiting on Esther's bed. Head scarves in an assortment of colours and fabrics were draped over the robes. Jewels sparkled in the dim light provided by the tall candle close to the bed.

Salome stopped just inside the door. "Esther, what is all this?"

"You, my friend, are the mother of the bride, and as such you must look the part." Esther grabbed her arm and pulled her into the room. "The choice is yours. I cannot wear half of the garments I own. Please, I want you to try on some of these."

Running her fingers over the soft materials, Salome signed. "I've always dreamed of owning clothes like this, but Amaziah has never seen the need."

There didn't seem to be any bitterness in her voice; it was just a fact. She lifted one deep purple robe, covered with fine stitches of white embroidery around the neckline and hem. Burying her face in the cloth, she breathed in the fragrance of the material. With a tiny curve of her lips, she held it to her breast and gazed at Esther.

"May I try this one?" Salome asked.

"My friend, that is a good choice. With your pale skin and dark hair, it should suit you well."

Esther held the robe and helped Salome into it. She straightened the fabric, pulled the lines into place, adjusted the neckline and sleeves, then stood back and looked at Salome.

"What about this white headdress?"

"Do with me what you will," Salome said, drawing her shoulders together. "I am overwhelmed."

Esther added the headdress, then turned to the table. From it she chose a circle of gems on a gold band. She added it to the headdress, to hold it in place.

"Salome, you are lovely. Here, come closer to the light." Esther turned her friend around, continuing to adjust the fabric. "Done. We cannot improve on perfection."

"Oh, you're being foolish." Salome dismissed her friend's comment with a flick of the wrist. A tinge of warmth crept up Salome's neck and blossomed on her cheeks.

Esther hugged her friend, kissing each cheek in turn. "I'm not being foolish; you are beautiful and it's time you started believing in yourself again."

Silence fell between the two women. The only sounds were the birds bidding the world good night. Soft shadows stole into the room; the candle light swayed in the small breeze from the open window.

"Come, Salome. You are about to become a mother-in-law. We mustn't miss the ceremony."

Taking her hand, Esther led her from the house along the darkening path to the temple.

$\mathcal{H}$

On the other side of Jerusalem, the two who were most involved in the night's events hurried through side streets and narrow paths that skirted the temple. Shallum held Huldah's hand as they passed through the darkest part of their walk. She stumbled once, but he quickly steadied her arm and they continued.

The columns of light that outlined the entrance to the temple came into view when they rounded the last twisting turn in the path.

"I'm frightened." Huldah pulled on Shallum's arm and tried to see him in the gathering darkness. "What if some of the supporters of the priests who want to kill me show up? What if we're both in danger?"

"Huldah, once the priests were executed, those who supported them will want to stay out of sight." He patted her hand and pulled her closer. "Don't be afraid. I believe we're doing the right thing, and God will honour our decision."

"As long as you're beside me, I'll be fine." She dropped her hand from his arm.

"I'll be beside you for the rest of our lives. There is no place I would rather be. Come, we must hurry."

They swept past the lighted lamps and into the interior of the temple. There was mystery here in the semi-darkness. Strange shapes loomed in the outer court, made larger by the shadows cast from the lamps.

Shallum squeezed her hand when they entered the inner court. Tikvah was waiting for them in the doorway of one of the side rooms.

"This way, my children." Tikvah's voice echoed in the almost-empty court. He beckoned them to follow, standing aside while they entered a small room.

Hilkiah stood at the front, arrayed in his priestly robes. A small scroll was held loosely in his hands. Both mothers and Amaziah were seated on the low chairs arranged in front of the priest. Tikvah took Huldah's arm, and the three slowly moved to stand before the High Priest.

Candles flickered on the low tables on each side of them, casting shadows over the families. Their eyes gleamed with the reflection of tiny flames. In the dim light, the white priestly robes shimmered.

Hilkiah lifted both gnarled hands over the heads of the young couple. "Blessed is the name of the Lord. Holy is He. Keeper of promises, leader of our people Israel, protector of the helpless, giver of good gifts. Blessed is His name." He lowered his hands and folded them together. "We ask your blessing on this union. May they always remain faithful to their God. May they be prosperous and bear many children. Hold them close to You. Amen."

Shallum stood very straight before the priest. His eyes didn't move from Hilkiah's face as he invoked the blessing. Huldah trembled by his side until Hilkiah reached out and clasped both of their hands in his.

"My children, remember the teachings of your youth, the things you learned at your mothers' knee, the lessons taught to you by your fathers. The fate of Judah rests on the heads of the young. Be an example to others who are starting their journeys. Teach your children what you have been taught. Teach them when you sit down to eat, when you walk along the paths of the city, when you lie down to sleep. Keep the name of the Lord your God ever on your lips."

Hilkiah paused and raised his eyes to the ceiling. With his eyes closed, he moved his lips without sound. When he opened his eyes and looked at them again, his wrinkled face took on a glow.

"You are now husband and wife. Be kind to each other, be strong in your faith, keep away from idols, and fail not to worship in the temple, observing all the feasts and holy days."

Tikvah stood. "Blessed is God who has brought these two together." He approached Shallum and greeted him with a kiss on both cheeks, then welcomed Huldah in the same way.

The others now gathered around, expressing joy in the union. Hilkiah soon ushered them from the room and they left the temple to continue their celebration at the home of Tikvah and Esther. When Amaziah and Salome left, Tikvah and Esther moved to their quarters, leaving Shallum and Huldah standing together.

The night closed around them, their future uncertain.

part two
One year later

sixteen

"The king is dead. The king is dead." The shout echoed through the streets of Jerusalem. It circled along the byways. It whispered around the stalls in the market. It seeped into the houses of the people, and hearts turned cold.

Tiny sprays of dirt from the path swirled from Amaziah's sandals. He knew that Hilkiah and the other priests were waiting for him in the dim coolness of the temple. They would be discussing recent events in Jerusalem, especially the death of the king. More importantly, they would discuss the rise of the next king. Who would it be?

I certainly hope it isn't Amon, with his cruel streak. It will be a sorry day for Jerusalem if he ascends to the throne.

Amaziah remembered the antics of the prince when he had been growing up in the palace. He had been indulged by his father, doted on by his mother, and feared by the servants. No one seemed able to control him.

Time and again, Amon had demonstrated his temperament. Amaziah remembered one incident when a servant had accidently spilled wine while serving the king's table. Before anyone knew what was happening, Amon jumped up, slapped the servant in the face, and spit in his eye. Raising his fists, he threatened the poor man, who dropped the pitcher and fled the room. In the silence that followed, Amon stood very still until he heard a loud guffaw coming from his father's lips. He joined the laughter around the table and moved to another spot where it was dry. Only the eyes of his mother, Meshullemeth, closed sharply; her tight lips perhaps told another story.

When Amaziah neared the temple, he could see the mass of people that thronged the outer courtyard. Their shouts rose in an angry cry. Individual faces were twisted, teeth were bared, and fists began to connect with each other. One man fell to the ground, which incited others to join the disturbance. Several others leaned over the fallen man and punched him until his blood soaked the ground. Amaziah threw himself into the midst of the fight, shoving some aside to reach the fallen man. The sight of the priest helping the injured seemed to calm the mob, and they moved back to give room. Others from inside the temple came to Amaziah's assistance. The guards soon had the riot under control and sent the people to their homes.

"We want justice," a lone voice called above the noise.

An older priest, Talmar, climbed on a nearby rock. He spread his hands toward the people. "What do you mean by justice?"

"We've heard that Amon will be the next king. That cannot be. He's evil."

Talmar dropped his hands to his sides, his eyes roving over the crowd. "The decision of kingship is not ours. Manasseh will have chosen the next king before he died. His wishes will be upheld. The palace will make an announcement later today. Go home and pray to our God for a good king. Go. There is nothing you can do here."

Slowly the people turned, whispering to each other. Some shook fingers in the air, others walked with heads bowed. They all moved off toward their homes.

Amaziah helped Talmar down from the rock.

"Thank you, Amaziah. It's so good to have you back where you belong." Talmar took the offered hand and stepped down to level ground.

"I never should have been where I was."

"Our God forgives, and we must move on." Talmar touched him lightly on the shoulder and the two moved into the outer court.

When they reached the inner room where Hilkiah and the other priests were waiting, Amaziah held the curtain back and allowed Talmar to precede him. There was little talk. The priests' faces were solemn, with downturned lips and brows drawn close together.

Hilkiah alone greeted them with a smile. "Come in, fellow priests."

Today, Hilkiah's turban was ornate, signifying his high and holy office. Amaziah recognized that this turban was the one only worn on significant occasions—particularly holy days, days of feasting, and waiting on the Lord God.

Despite the High Priest's smile, his knuckles were white from tension. *Hilkiah is upset. It must be Amon.*

"I'll not waste time," Hilkiah said. "A message has come from a reliable palace source. Amon will be king."

Gasps met his pronouncement and the priests' heads swung around to stare at each other.

"What can we do?" asked a black-bearded priest named Zephon. As the youngest, he was still learning and asked many questions.

Hilkiah turned his head. "Unfortunately, there is not much we can do. That is, except pray." A smile tugged at his lips. "I don't mean that prayer is ineffective, but I know how each of us likes to have the appearance of doing something to help."

Heads nodded while he spoke.

"Along with two other priests, I plan to approach the king's advisors and express our concern." Hilkiah shrugged. "It won't change anything, but it may calm the people to know that we have spoken with the palace."

Amaziah stood. "I would like to be one of the two to accompany you, master." He swallowed twice and coughed quietly into his hand. "I know I don't deserve this honour, but I feel I need to redeem myself in your eyes and the eyes of all present in this room."

"Amaziah, you have confessed your sin and asked our forgiveness and the forgiveness of God," Hilkiah said. "This we have freely granted to you. It is now time you forgave yourself and became useful once again. If you don't forgive yourself, you will not be whole and thus carry a heavy burden which will keep you from being the priest God wants you to be." He paused to nod, then curled his lips. "But, enough of that. I would be pleased to have you accompany me."

Jamin, the oldest priest, struggled to his feet, leaning on the shoulder of Hoshea, who sat beside him. His face was red from the effort and he breathed deeply. "I would like to be the other one. I will not have many more opportunities to be of service to our God. This task would please me greatly."

The others rose to their feet around him, clapping in approval.

"Then it's settled," Hilkiah said. "The rest of you remain here and lift your voices to our God. He may yet decide to save us."

H

The palace was in an uproar. Servants scurried along lighted hallways, carrying food and drink which was quickly seized by greedy subjects drawn to the palace by the unsettling events of the morning.

The many torches ensconced along the walls emitted writhing spirals of dark smoke, causing eyes to water and nostrils to flare. Along one such hall, Hilkiah, Amaziah, and Jamin moved slowly with the river of people all shuffling to the common room of the palace.

A guard stepped from his post at the end of the hall and raised his arm with precision. Amaziah was amazed that he could spot such trivial details at a time like this.

"Halt. All who move in this hall, halt." The guard worked his way into the centre of the mass of people, now with both hands outstretched, palms raised. "Halt!"

The mass of people flowed toward him. He withdrew a short sword from its leather sheath and slashed it from side to side. A cry from a man at the front brought the mass to a standstill, causing some to fall.

"Silence!" This time, the crowd listened and became silent. "Only those on palace business may proceed. Form a line, and we'll check each of you."

The guard turned and beckoned two other guards to join him.

"Move to the wall," a second guard bellowed, pulling his sword from its sheath.

The three priests were halfway down the hall. Amaziah watched the guards closely in an attempt to discern what they considered palace business. He was sure he and the other priests would be allowed to pass. Surely the guards couldn't keep the High Priest away, especially at a time like this.

Soon a long line formed, curving in the opposite direction, back toward to the entrance. More guards appeared to hurry them along. The purple of their robes stood in striking contrast to the dull colours of the common people.

"I hope we're soon cleared to continue," Amaziah said after a coughing spell. "We're going to choke with all this smoke."

Hilkiah nodded. "I think it won't be long. Most of those in front of us are being sent back. We just have to be patient."

"State your business." The first guard confronted Hilkiah, then stepped back with his head lowered. "Begging your pardon, High Priest. In the dim light, I did not at first recognize you. Please proceed along with your two companions. The king's advisors are expecting you."

Once out of the entrance hall, the smoke cleared. The way to the advisors' room was wide. Jamin breathed heavily and the other two slowed their pace to match his.

The curtain giving privacy to the meeting room was closed, allowing no light to seep into the hall. The room was heavily guarded. Discipline was tight. Amaziah felt sure they had been seen and approved, or they would not have made it this far.

The curtain parted when they reached the entrance, and in the opening appeared the familiar face of Amon. Dark bushy brows met in the middle and his chin jutted into the air.

"And that is my final word on the matter," he called over his shoulder into the meeting room. "I'll not have it mentioned again in my presence."

Amon whipped around and stormed from the meeting room without even a glance at the three priests. A covey of his young peers swarmed out behind him, intent on keeping up with the fast-disappearing Amon. Guards fell into place behind the retreating figures.

Once they were out of sight, the priests looked at each other, then slipped into the room just vacated by the prince. Amaziah hadn't been in this room before and his eyes roved over the lavish space. Tall gilded urns stood at intervals around the edges of the room. Linen panels in hues of purple, red, and white draped the walls; some depicted figures of men armed for battle and angels riding chariots.

In the centre of the room was a long table of dark wood, polished to a high gleam. Incense burned in vessels set in the wall. It smothered the lungs and irritated the nostrils.

Four men glanced up from their scrolls when they entered.

"Hilkiah, you are welcome," Ethan said as he jumped to his feet. He, along with the others, wore the palace garb—a white robe with bands of purple trimmed with gold thread. Fine embroidery ran down the front of their tunics. On their heads were turbans of white linen.

The four advisers—Ethan, Joel, Moshe, and Jotham—quickly made room for the priests. Together, they sank onto the ornate cushions surrounding the table.

A servant appeared with goblets of wine. Amaziah gratefully sipped his. It was mild and sweet, just what he needed. Events had moved so rapidly over the last few days that he was having trouble adjusting.

When he brought his focus back to the group, Ethan was pointing to writing on one of the open scrolls.

Joel leaned over from the other side of the table, tracing the words with one finger. "There, it is the law. The king can appoint his own choice for successor. There is nothing we can do to change the law."

Jamin wiped his forehead with the back of his hand and bowed his head over the scroll. "But there must be some provision for poor choices. We all know Amon is evil. He'll destroy the kingdom."

"You may be correct, Jamin, but the law is clear. Amon will be king." Moshe emphasized each word. "I don't like it any better than you, but our hands are tied."

"What about the ones who left the room with Amon just now?" Hilkiah asked.

"Irresponsible friends, that's all." Jotham put his head to one side. "They're no better than he is. In fact, they're worse, if that is possible. But we're his advisors, and like it or not, we'll support the law as it stands."

Hilkiah folded his hands together. "Friends, we're forgetting the most important thing we can do. We need to pray. We need to pray now and every day of this reign. God is not through with Judah yet."

The advisors all nodded.

Hilkiah lifted his hands and his eyes, offering up their petitions to God. When he finished, the others remained silent.

"For now, we must plan a funeral for a king," Hilkiah said. "And a coronation for a king's son."

H

Snapping flames burned along the walkway that led from the palace to the common area. Guards marched in precision in rows of three abreast. Wave upon wave of them left the palace gate. Behind the guards, a stretcher was lifted high in the air on the shoulders of slaves. The body of King Manasseh was wrapped in simple white linen.

The priests stood within the circle of guards, waiting for the arrival of the body. Scores of common people pressed in behind the guards, crushing against each other, craning their necks to see the procession.

Behind the body walked the king's sons—tall, rigid, eyes straight ahead. Amon led them, and there was no fighting amongst them while their father's body was born to its final resting place. When the litter reached Hilkiah, the guards halted and eased it down onto a platform built to hold it.

The crowd became restless. Robes and sandals rustled. Soft calls murmured which increased in volume when Amon appeared. Shouts of "Down with Amon" rippled across the mass of people. Guards turned with short, leather goads in hand, ready to use them. Silence, although an uneasy one, fell once more.

Night had long since made its appearance; the sky was black with a low covering of clouds. Torches appeared in the crowd, held high by brawny arms. Grotesque shadows moved in their swaying light. The princes stood with arms behind their backs as the tonal sound of priests' voices opened the burial ceremony.

Amaziah pulled his robe tightly around him. The night air was cooler than he had expected, but he shivered more from fear than from the cold. He felt uneasy, knowing that something could go wrong with the king's sons in attendance. The undulating crowd was ready to make a move if the right words were shouted.

The cloying scent of spices wrapped in layers of linen reached his nose, adding to the surreal quality of the scene.

"People of Judah," Hilkiah intoned. Amaziah was surprised at the strength in his voice. "People of Judah, listen to me."

The restlessness quieted and they strained to hear what the High Priest had to say.

"Our king is dead. We are on the cusp of a new reign."

A woman in the crowd cried as though in pain, but was quickly silenced.

"We have the opportunity to get back to our God. Leave your idols, leave your high places, and turn your hearts back to your God." Hilkiah bowed his head over the covered body of the king. "King Manasseh, you will return to the dust from whence you were taken. You will meet our God and give an account of yourself. God rest your soul."

He stepped back from the pallet and raised his hands. "God our Father, God our Creator, into Your hands I offer King Manasseh."

The priests gathered around the body. Each one placed a coin on it, symbolic of needs for the journey. When they stepped back, the slaves once more shouldered the king, and the procession moved into the palace garden.

The people tried to swarm in, but the gates clanged shut behind the procession. Only the priests and royal family followed.

They wound their way along the paths, through trees shedding their fragrances, and stopped when they reached a small cave at the back of the garden. The body was carried inside and laid carefully on the rocky floor. The king's bearers then backed out of the cave, keeping their faces pointed toward the body.

Once outside, slaves and servants alike gathered small rocks and stones, filling in the cave's opening until there was no way for an animal to gain entrance.

It was a quiet group that returned to the palace.

The priests watched when Amon and his friends hurried to the new king's suite of rooms, talking and laughing as they went.

Amaziah sighed when they turned to walk back to the temple. "What will the future hold for the Kingdom of Judah, with cruel Amon at its head?"

seventeen

"*W*hat is it, Huldah?" Shallum leaned over and shook his wife's shoulder. "Huldah, wake up."

When Huldah continued to moan, flinging her arms about, Shallum sat up and wrapped his arms around her. He smoothed her hair back with his fingers. "Huldah."

This time, she responded. Her hands stopped and she opened her eyes. "What happened? Shallum, why are you holding me so tight?"

He released her. "I think you were having a bad dream."

Suddenly sitting up, she gasped and grabbed her hair in both hands. "It's coming back. I did have a bad dream."

She swung her feet over the edge of the bed, shivering.

"Here, let me wrap this around you." Shallum grabbed a cover from the bed, draping it around her shoulders. "Do you want to tell me about it?"

"Oh yes, I'm so frightened."

Moonlight filtered through the small window outlining her face. Taking a deep breath, she snuggled into the blanket, pulling it close around her. Shallum held her hand while they sat there together.

"I love holding your hand and resting my head on your shoulder," she murmured.

"Huldah, tell me your dream."

"I don't think it was a dream. It was a vision, or at least a dream sent from God." She breathed deeply. "I'll try to relate it exactly as I saw it."

He planted a kiss on her forehead and then rested his head against hers. "Take your time. We've got all night."

"Amon will be king. It was plain that no one will take his place. I saw the throne, and he was sitting on it. But it wasn't the throne at the palace, although I'm sure that's where I was. It was a huge throne, towering to the ceiling." She paused and cleared her throat. "It was black, shiny black stone, and it rose in a twisted fashion. Eyes shone from the sheen of the stone. Knife-like projections rose from the arms of the chair, threatening anyone who came close. Upon the throne sat the king."

A shudder ran through her body and she trembled against Shallum.

"Tell me about Amon," Shallum whispered into her hair.

"He was awful. I cringed when I saw him. He, too, was all in black, dressed from head to toe. But that wasn't the worst of it. His face was terrible. He had allowed his beard to grow, so it was long and tangled, and filled with food and other disgusting things. Long stringy hair fell from beneath his black hood, and it, too, was dirty and unkempt. Bushy brows met in the middle and were drawn tight, causing his face to have a sinister look."

She glanced up at her husband and he hugged her closely.

"Go on, my love."

"His eyes seemed to have grown large, dominating his face. How do you describe evil? Evil and cruelty emanated from them. The whites were no longer white, but had a yellow, almost brown sheen. It seemed like the irises were larger than normal, and his lips were curled back in a snarl, showing all his teeth, which were stained red."

Tears began to flow at this point in her story. Shallum wiped them away.

"Try to tell me all, Huldah. You'll feel better once it's out."

"Yes, I know." Once again, she sighed. "Frightening things were happening in the throne room. I only got a glimpse, but common people were being beaten by guards, beaten until they were either unconscious or dead. Then the followers of Amon, and Amon himself, laughed at the spectacle. They took bets on how long a person could withstand the beatings. It was awful, terrible, frightening, and bloody."

Another shudder ran down her body, and she rested her head on Shallum's chest. He pushed her hair back from her forehead.

"The floor was slick with blood. Then I awoke." She twisted in his arms, looking him full in the face. "What does it all mean?"

"I'm not sure, but visions and dreams like this are often prophetic."

"Yes, I agree. Go on."

"Amon will be king, and a cruel king. Whether the actual events you saw will come true, I cannot say. But it will not be a happy time for the people of Judah."

Her breathing was steady now. She blinked, wiping the remaining tears from her cheeks. "That makes sense. It's a warning from God then, do you think?"

"Definitely from God." Shallum watched her carefully, watched her eyes for any signs of panic or fear.

Huldah rested her chin in one hand. Her eyes were partly closed and Shallum knew she was thinking. He waited quietly until she was ready to continue.

"If it's from God, and we believe it is, then we have to do something about it," Huldah said. "He expects action when He sends a vision."

"This is the difficult part. If we confront Amon, we'll lose our heads." A dry, helpless laugh escaped Shallum's lips. "We can't tell the priests, because they already know he'll be a tough one to deal with. They have no power over him at present."

Gently, he removed his arms from Huldah and stood. With arms folded, he walked a few paces around their room, arriving back before her with his jaw set and lips tight.

"I don't think we have enough to go on," he said, sitting back down beside her. "What does God want us to do? We can't know without further word from Him. I hate to say this, Huldah, but I think we need to ask God for another vision." He wrapped her in his arms again. "I know it's hard, but we've got to know what He wants, how He wants to use you. Can you handle that?"

"Oh Shallum, what a wonderful day it was when God chose you for me." She reached up and ran her fingers through his hair. "If God wants to use me, then I want to be ready. I know our lives will be in danger, but I would rather be in danger by man than disobey the living God. What will be has already been written."

eighteen

"Hurry, get this robe draped right. Not those sandals; the gold ones. I don't need my hair trimmed."

Amon flung himself around his room while a bevy of servants and slaves bowed to his bidding. He threw his arms to the ceiling, gritted his teeth, and snarled at a young servant girl. She shrank back into a dark corner holding a pitcher in her hand.

"Where did that cloak come from?" He swatted at the cloak, knocking it from a servant's arm.

A swish of the curtain caused Amon to swing around. Moshe strode into the room.

"Amon, Amon, Amon. What's all the fuss about?" Moshe grabbed Amon's arm. The servants stood back. "I could hear you all the way down the hall."

Breathing heavily, Amon stopped, put his hands on his stomach, and slapped his thigh. "That's a good one. Could you really hear me that far away?"

"Oh, believe me, I could hear you."

A gurgle of laughter bubbled from Moshe until the two men were howling with laughter, holding their sides.

The servants hadn't moved since Moshe entered the room. There were no smiles evident on their faces. The little maid still clutched the pitcher, her eyes squeezed shut, as though trying to keep tears from falling.

"Look, there are hundreds of people lining the walk from the palace to the temple. They're waiting for you. Let the servants get you ready so we can get this over with, and then…" He pushed at Amon's shoulder, his lips stretching back in a grin that showed all his teeth. "…we'll party."

The two young men slapped each other on the back and turned to face the servants.

"You heard what Moshe said. Get me ready." Amon stood still while they moved back into place, draped the robe around him, and trimmed his hair.

Moshe left the room without a backward glance.

"My lord, is this the gold you wish to wear?" A servant held out a long rope of gold, a wide armband, and heavy ring.

"Yes, yes, get them on. Quickly. We need to hurry. Can't keep the common people waiting."

Amon choked back a laugh, then stood still while an ornate chain was lifted over his head. When it was in place, it reached almost to his waist and was as thick as a man's finger. He squeezed his eyes shut and gritted his teeth when the armband was forced up his muscled upper arm. The armband was made from plain beaten gold and had been in the family for many generations. All the kings had worn the band, and he wasn't going to be the first to appear without it.

The ring was his pride and joy. It had been given to him by his maternal grandmother. She'd claimed it had been forged in the fires of Egypt for her great-grandfather, who had been second-in-line to a Pharaoh. Whether or not the story was true, the ring was a work of art, engraved with the head of a lion and circled with raised palm leaves. It was flawless and beautiful, his prized possession. He would wear it with pride, the pride of a lion. He looked at it with drawn brows when it was safely on his left middle finger.

I am that lion: the lion of Judah.

He swung the embroidered white cloak over his shoulder. "I am ready. Bow to your king."

Without waiting for their response, he swept out of the room to where Moshe and his other advisors waited.

H

The path was strewn with light, and cheers rose from the crowd pushing against the closed gates. Slaves dressed in bright tunics with eagle feathers in their hair, held back the throng. Outside the gates, guards on horseback edged their way through the gathered masses. Once they reached the gates, they forced the people back to clear a way for the prince.

Ethan and Joel appeared at Amon's side, leading his favourite horse, Belthar, whose shining black coat was partly hidden beneath an ornate saddle, adorned with a ridge of silver and inset with jewels. A collar of similar precious stones circled the horse's neck. He pranced and pawed the earth when they brought him to a halt beside Amon.

Moshe draped his arm around Amon. "Mount, my friend. We have long been awaiting this moment." He lowered his head before the prince, sweeping off his turban, apparently in reverence to him, but the cruel curl to the lips bespoke another story.

Amon turned his head to stare at Moshe. "Your mockery shows, my friend. Watch yourself or I may find you no longer useful." He slipped one sandaled foot over the horse's back and leaped into the saddle. With back straight, shoulders squared, chin raised, and lips in a deep pout, he yanked on the reins and started the procession to the palace gates.

When he neared them, the guards swung open the gates and the black horse reared and neighed. Amon pulled hard with both hands until he had the beast under control. Once quieted, he pranced through the gates to the awaiting cheers.

The struggles of the guards ended when the people burst through the lines and thronged Amon. He felt the tension in the horse's back and neck when it tried to rear again. Muscles rippled and bunched in his arms and legs as he fought to gain control. At his side, men grabbed the halter and forced Belthar to walk sedately. With a grumbled whinny, the pair eased through the masses.

The wide field was ringed with brightly burning fires that lit the night sky. An altar loomed, erected from stones gathered from the four corners of the realm to represent all peoples under Amon's reign. It rose to the height of two grown men, with a wide base that covered a vast area. Beside the stone altar, a smaller altar had been constructed to burn the sacrifices that would sizzle the rest of the night. A ring of low stones kept the sheep and goats penned from the people who milled about the field.

Cheers ascended when Amon came into view. In the darkness, no one could see the scowl darkening his face. The line of his mouth stretched tautly over clenched teeth. His eyes darted from side to side. All was as he had desired, except for the priests, who he didn't dare ignore. *They can have their moment, but what happens after will be a different matter.*

He led the horse to the base of the altar. At a hand signal from Amon, two servants in dark robes began their ascent up the stairs at the side of the stone altar. In their hands they carried torches, the flames guarded by their cupped hands.

A breathless stillness fell over the people.

Bending over, the servants dropped their torches, igniting the wood. With a sharp crack and a swirl of sparks, the flames lit the night sky.

Hovering servants escorted Amon to a wooden platform facing the two altars, and he mounted the steps. Two ornate chairs rested side by side facing the fire. He slipped into one chair, leaving the other vacant. His advisors and servants gathered around him, behind the chairs. Guards with drawn swords stood at each side, their shiny armour reflecting the firelight.

With a snap of Amon's fingers, a servant was dispatched with instructions to command Hilkiah to approach the throne. The priests stood behind the lower altar, where Hilkiah was accompanied by a contingent of twenty priests, all dressed in white ceremonial robes ornamented with bells and tassels.

On the servant's appearance, Hilkiah stepped forward, eyes fastened on him.

The servant greeted him with a deep bow. "His Majesty wishes you to approach the throne. Please follow me."

Hilkiah fell in behind the servant and they proceeded to the platform. When they reached the throne, Hilkiah sank to his knees and touched the platform with his forehead.

"Get up, priest. I don't need subservience from you." Amon reached out his hand with a flick of his wrist. "You are only here because the people would revolt without your honoured presence. I must keep my voice low so I don't antagonize the masses."

Hilkiah stood without speech, without moving a muscle. "I am here to serve the living God. If He has chosen you to be king, who am I to dispute Him?"

Amon spit before the priest. "Just conduct your ceremony, then leave us to celebrate as only we know how. Sacrifice your animals, intone prayers to your God, wash your hands, do whatever it is you do and be done with it." He swung his body away from the priest and faced the nearest guard. "Escort him back to where he belongs."

H

The other priests were moving around the altar, making preparations for the sacrifices, when Hilkiah rejoined them. He did not speak, but beckoned them to carry on with the preparations. Very soon, the sheep and goats were bled, cut, and sacrificed on the low altar. Meanwhile, the high altar sent its light and heat over the heads of the gathered people.

Round and round the priests walked, reciting prayers and invoking a blessing on the new king. When the last sacrifice had burned, Hilkiah faced his priests.

"This reign will bring evil on our land. We have done our part to make it sacred, but now it is up to God." He hung his head and took a deep breath. We will leave and return to the temple, where I will pray through the night."

H

"Halt, you are not permitted entrance!" a voice cried.

The masses parted to make room for a lone figure, dressed in white, to approach. A thick veil covered the face, but the slightness of the figure suggested a woman. A hush descended while all watched her progress toward the platform.

Amon rose from his chair and watched with the others.

Slowly, the woman made her way through the press of people, intent only on the platform holding the new king. In her hands, she held aloft a lighted torch, its flickering light sending shimmering waves over her white robe. The hem of the robe swept the ground. She moved in a perfect rhythm, her shoulders thrown back and head held high.

Only the hiss of flames on the high altar broke the stillness. Hilkiah and the other priests halted their preparations for departure and watched the spectacle with interest.

Behind her walked a man covered from head to toe with a thick woven robe. His hood was pulled down, partially covering his face. His features were indistinguishable.

The woman paused at the foot of the platform, raised the torch high, and through the veil locked eyes with Amon. He hadn't moved since she had been sighted. Three of his advisors moved into position behind him, but they, too, were still.

She lowered her torch, placing it on the ground at her feet. With both hands, she removed the veil from her face. A gasp was heard from the platform.

"It's Huldah," one of the advisors exclaimed in a soft whisper. The word was whispered through the crowd, but no one moved to approach her. Her eyes were riveted on Amon. He, in turn, seemed unable to break the gaze.

In the stillness, she raised her right hand, pointing a finger at him. "Amon."

Moshe grabbed the hilt of the sword at his side. Amon reached a hand back and stayed him. He watched her with eyelids partly lowered.

"So you would be king." Huldah's outstretched arm moved in a circle to include the throng straining to catch her words.

Amon seemed unable or unwilling to speak.

"I have come with a message from the Lord." Huldah pointed to the heavens. She lowered her arm until her pointed finger was in line with his face. "God is not pleased."

Moshe pulled out his sword and lunged to the edge of the platform. The other advisers rushed to his side. The sword was pointed straight at her heart.

Amon reached out his hand to touch Moshe. "Let her speak."

The sword lowered, but Moshe remained at the edge of the platform.

"Hear the word of the Lord," Huldah said. "Hear His message, you who would be king. 'I am who I am,' declares the Lord. 'I will allow you to ascend the throne, but your evil reign will be short and troubled.' Unless you repent of your wicked ways, and turn to the Lord your God, you will be removed from the throne through treachery. You have been given two years. Two years of grace. Two years to mend your ways and turn to the Lord."

Huldah leaned down and retrieved her torch, which still smouldered. She turned, and without a backward glance, raised the torch high, retracing her steps through the masses.

Amon and his cohorts leaned close together, in consultation. While the people watched, they backed up a pace from each other and gave a loud cheer.

Amon faced his subjects, both hands raised above his head. "The lady has lost her mind." He laughed loudly, but only those close to him could see the irritation in his eyes. "We will not be cowed by offensive words. Let the party begin."

The masses of people who had remained silent while Huldah was present now gave a huge sigh of relief, lifting their voices in cheer after cheer. Beside the small altar, the priests quickly gathered their things and left.

The celebration continued long into the night, until the king and his officials were overflowing with wine and rich food. Without the presence of Huldah and the priests, the party degenerated into a scene of drunken debauchery.

When the sky lightened in the east, the first rays shone on a scene so vile and depraved that the people looked at each other with disgust in their eyes and turned their way homeward.

nineteen

When the priests left the scene of debauchery, no one spoke. The slump of Hilkiah's shoulders matched the heaviness in his chest. He led them around the mob, through the gates, and along the laneways until they entered the silent temple. The only sound that reached Hilkiah's ears was the shuffle of their feet on the smooth floors.

They came to the room reserved for priestly gatherings, pushed through the heavy curtain, and dropped to the cushions scattered around the low table. Their faces registered shock and weariness.

"This is an evil night." Hilkiah sighed deeply and made eye contact with each priest in turn. "God is not pleased."

Talmar slowly shook his head. "We'll need to watch our steps, for our lives may be in danger. The new king will not want to hear what we have to say."

"But God is mightier than Amon," Hilkiah said. The fabric of his robe rustled as he settled into a more comfortable position. "I, for one, will spend the night in prayer, asking for God's direction. Who will watch and pray with me?"

"I will count it a privilege to watch with you." Jamin's voice was raspy, but firm.

Talmar's hands trembled when he lifted them toward Hilkiah. "I'll be here, too. I'm old and can no longer do a man's work, but I can pray and do God's work which is far better."

The others quickly added their voices, until all had agreed to pray through the night.

Hilkiah suggested they pray in shifts, allowing some to rest while the prayer cycle was maintained.

Amaziah stood with bowed head, his hands clasped in front of him. "If I pray for the rest of my life, it will not be enough to praise my God, who has rescued me from the brink of disaster."

"Amaziah, your family has done the work of God tonight. We have not so quickly forgotten the bravery of Huldah in facing the forces of evil." Hilkiah stood and faced him. "You will rest when it is your turn. We will all be more effective if we take time to rest."

Murmurs and nods indicated the agreement of the others.

"I will do what you ask," Amaziah said. "Huldah was braver tonight than her father has ever been. I am very proud of her, even though I fear her life may be in danger."

"Then it behooves us to not only pray for our nation, but for Huldah and Shallum, that God will protect them." Zephon grinned at the others. "Did you see the looks on the faces of the king and his advisors when she appeared?"

A few grins met his, but the older priests maintained their composure.

"We must never lose sight of the power of God, which we saw displayed tonight," Hilkiah said, feeling it was his place to keep the others focused on the dangerous and evil days ahead. "Huldah is truly a servant of our Lord. Now, let us begin our watch. Talmar, Jamin, Amaziah, and I will pray until the midnight hour. Let us pray that the days of Amon's reign are shortened and that evil will be expelled from our land."

H

Huldah could not sleep. Every muscle and nerve in her body was on alert. Exhausted, she and Shallum had returned to their home from the palace grounds hours ago. After a long talk about the repercussions of Huldah's pronouncement, Shallum had gone to bed, but sleep eluded Huldah. She wandered through the small set of rooms that Tikvah and Shallum had built onto the back of the main house. Grateful for this private space, Huldah sank onto cushions close to the window.

The moon was full tonight and cast a silver glimmer. Huldah made out the outline of the table that Shallum had so lovingly carved for her. It served as a desk for her scrolls, since she had begun to study. At first Tikvah had been opposed to this, expressing his opinion that she should be content to sew and weave like the other women in the Second District, but he soon came to see that God had gifted her. By law, his consent wasn't needed, but both Shallum and Huldah respected the opinion of both Tikvah and Esther and wanted to live peacefully with them.

Huldah's heart was lifted to God as she sat with the light spilling around her. Peace stole into her heart as she communed with her Father. She sensed that she had followed His commands.

"It's up to You now, Lord," she whispered so as not to disturb her husband, who had to rise early for his palace duties. "Let my heart be open to Yours. Let me think like You think, and see what You see." She adjusted her body into a more comfortable position, pulling her robe around her. "I know I'm in danger, but I'm not afraid. I know You go before me."

Her body relaxed until her head slipped down to the cushions and she slept.

H

"Mama, I'm scared." Josiah's little voice penetrated the deep sleep of his mother.

"Shh, Josiah, Mother is right here," Jedidah said, leaning over and patting his head.

"I had a bad dream." He sobbed out the words, sat up in bed, and reached out for his mother.

Jedidah gathered him to her and rubbed his back while crooning soft words to him. "Tell me about your dream."

Amid the cries and sniffles, he snuggled into his mother's arms. "Bad men were shouting at me."

More sniffles, and then choking coughs were added.

"Shh. It's all right. There aren't any bad men in here." Jedidah hugged her son closer. *Only six years old and already his father frightens him. I'm sure all the noise outside is causing him to have bad dreams.*

"They had big lights and they were chasing me." His voice rose to a wail. He lifted his head from his mother's chest and screamed. "Look, Mama. There's the lights!" He pointed a little finger at the side of his room, then buried his face again.

"Don't worry. Your father and some of his friends are having a party." She leaned her head against his. "Remember, he's king now, and the people are celebrating."

"I'm afraid of him. I don't like him."

Oh, the perception of a little child. He can see what so many others can't.

"Please don't leave me, Mama."

Jedidah rocked back and forth until Josiah's body relaxed and slumber came. She sat for a long time with him, until the early rays of the sun made lines on the walls and the shouting outside subsided.

I will protect this precious child with everything in me. No harm will come to him, if I have the power to stop it. His father will need to be careful.

twenty

The red sun gradually lifted from the horizon to expose the debris left from the night's debacle. Dark clouds rushed to cover the light, as though in shame. Trampled grass, remnants of a fire, and bones picked clean were scattered over the grass, along with broken clay pitchers which had held wine. Discarded cloaks and sandals sat amidst the rubbish next to bodies deep in sleep.

Inside the palace, in the suite of rooms allotted to the new king, the mood was quiet. Heavy drapes covered the windows and small torches continued to burn. Young men littered the beds and floors, the result of dropping wherever they were in their haste to sleep. The only sounds in the room were eruptions of snores and grunts, with gasps here and there to punctuate the morning stillness. Servants opened the doors a crack and peaked in, only to softly close them again. No one was brave enough to disturb the king in his present state.

Ethan, the one closest to the draped window, eventually stirred. A beam of light slipped through a slit in the drapery. He pulled a blanket over his head, but the damage was done and consciousness began to surface. At first he was unaware of his surroundings and supposed himself to be in his own bed, but the lumpiness under his back alerted him that he was not at home.

Slowly and reluctantly, he lowered the blanket and looked around. A sly smile curved up from his chin when he surveyed the disorder.

The king sleeps on while I watch. Perhaps I'll discover something I can use to my advantage.

He watched the sleeping king and became aware of a servant girl asleep at the king's feet.

Interesting. How did she get in here without our notice? I recognize her—Aleah, from the lower kitchens. She's pledged to Ehud.

While Ethan thought about the possibilities, the king stirred. High off the floor and carved from the cedars of Lebanon, his bed was a work to behold. Vines with flowers and fruit and small animals were carved into the surface. Only the finest of linens were flung aside when the king sat up and rubbed his eyes.

Ethan grabbed his advantage, closing his eyes and pretending to be asleep.

"What are you doing here?" the king's voice asked. "Sit up and tell me this instant what you want."

Ethan risked a peek through slitted eyes. Aleah grabbed the corner of the sheet and clutched it to her breast.

"I need… to talk… to Your Majesty." Her low voice was difficult to pick up, but Ethan tuned his ears her way. "Ehud… Ehud is being sent away."

At this admission, she burst into tears and began to wail. Heads popped up all over the room, looking from the king to the girl. Titters of laughter rippled in the morning air.

Aleah covered her eyes, jumped off the bed, and fled the room. Roars of laughter followed her. Even the king joined in.

Joel rolled over on his mat and gasped for breath through his laughter. "Stop. Stop, I can't breathe."

The others only laughed harder. Moshe lifted a pillow and aimed it at Joel's head; the fight was on. Pillows flew through the air, adding further chaos to the disorderly room.

The doors of the suite pushed open and a troop of servants entered, carrying trays of hot water and towels.

"Out, out, all of you," Amon shouted, pointing a long arm at them.

They came to a halt, bumping into each other and causing the water to spill. Their towels slid to the floor.

"Out!"

They pushed and shoved each other in their haste to leave.

Once the doors were closed, the king's advisors broke into laughter again. But this was short lived.

"And you, too. This is no laughing matter." The king's long arm now pointed to each of his advisors in turn. His eyes came to rest on Moshe. "Stay with me, Moshe."

The others grabbed robes and sandals and made a hasty retreat.

H

When the last one disappeared, the king slumped to the floor, both hands gripping his hair. "My head aches. Get me some of that powder and a cup of water."

Moshe moved quickly to a side cupboard, lifted out the packet of powders, and shook some into a clean cup. He added water and stirred briskly, then handed it to Amon, who gulped it down.

"Your Majesty, you need to get a grip on yourself—"

"Don't you start on me." Amon lifted his head and glared at Moshe. The silence in the room was palpable.

In the distance, Moshe could hear footsteps in the hall and the muted voices of servants calling to each other. He stood with arms folded over his chest.

Should I speak? It could mean my head. But maybe it's now or never.

Moshe clasped his hands behind his back, threw out his chin, and took a deep breath. "Amon, listen to me."

The king raised his head. "And why should I listen to you, oh wise and noble one?"

"Because I'm the only one who dares tell you the truth."

"Maybe I don't want to hear your truth." Amon struggled to his feet and met Moshe eye to eye. "Maybe I should banish you from my kingdom, send you to Egypt or some other distant place, far away from the palace and from me."

"Then before I go, I must tell you what I see." Moshe lifted a finger and shook it in the king's face. "You are going to ruin yourself and the kingdom if you don't change your ways. People will alienate themselves from you, and that will mean trouble."

Amon pushed Moshe's shoulder, leering at him. "You are filled with wisdom. I knew it." A coarse laugh followed. "I am the king. I know how to run the kingdom, and I'll thank you to keep your opinions to yourself in the future. When I want your advice, I'll ask for it."

He reared back and spit in Moshe's face.

"Now leave me."

Moshe turned without reply and left the king standing in the middle of the shattered room.

H

Amon stood still, his face flushed as rage boiled inside him. Fire flashed in his eyes when he spun around, taking in the devastation.

"I curse you, Moshe."

Shaking one fist in the air, he screamed the words.

"I curse you, Ethan."

His voice reached shrieking level when he began to kick at the discarded clothes on the floor. Leaning over, he picked up the earlier flung pillows and tossed them in every direction.

"I curse you, Huldah. A prophetess, are you?"

Screeching each word, he lifted one of the pallets where his advisors had so recently been sleeping, swung it over his head, strode to the door, which he pushed open with his foot, and heaved it onto the marble floor of the hall. That accomplished, he returned for another one, and it followed the first.

"I curse you, Joel."

Amon picked up a cloak and added it to the rising pile outside his door. His eyes caught servants staring at him with frightened eyes.

"And I curse you, too. Be gone!" His arms flailed in the air as he took a step toward them. "Do your palace work, or you'll find yourselves outside the gates."

He laughed hysterically when they scurried to leave his presence.

When the room was cleared, he sat on the floor and began to consider his future. Muttering to himself, he rubbed his hands together and pulled at his hair until his thoughts cleared.

"I need a plan. I'm the king, and the sooner everyone realizes that I hold the power, the better."

He folded his arms over his chest and took deep breaths, releasing the pent-up air through his nostrils.

"The people thought my father was cruel," he whispered. His fist pounded into his palm over and over. "They haven't seen anything yet. I'll show them what real power is."

A knock came on his door. He ignored it. It came again, a little louder.

"Go away."

"But Your Majesty…"

"Go away!"

The knock was not repeated.

Amon stood and began to pace. He breathed deeply and faces of his people appeared in his mind. "I need strong people around me. That's a given. If they're going to be any use to me, they must be as hungry for power as I am."

He stopped his pacing and bared his teeth.

"Moshe. He's the strongest of them all. But is he willing to set aside his own ideas and follow mine? He lusts after power. I'm sure of that." A coarse laugh bubbled up in his throat. "Ha. I think he'll do."

Flinging open the door, he bellowed for a servant. A young man named Akiva promptly appeared with a low bow.

"Get up, you fool, and get Moshe immediately."

The door slammed as Amon retreated into his room.

$\mathcal{H}$

When Akiva entered the kitchens, a swarm of servants buzzed around him.

"Is he still in a foul mood?" asked a young servant boy named Dor. His eyes danced under a thick fringe of dark hair. Uneven teeth protruded from his parted lips, which seemed unable to hide a grin. "You're a brave one, that's for sure."

Metra, one of the cooks, turned her snapping dark eyes on Dor and shook her dough-covered hands in his face. "We could all be hanged before this is over. Mark my words, this king is trouble."

"Oh, don't talk like that Metra." Shira, a young woman in servants' garb, slid over to Metra with streaks of tears on her face. "If anyone should hear you, we really would be in trouble."

"Quiet, all of you." Akiva's voice sliced through their conversation. "He's sent for Moshe. I've just been to Moshe's room, and he's not there. Do any of you know where he is?"

Akiva planted his hands on his hips and waited for their answer. Head shakes convinced him that they knew nothing.

He turned to leave the room when Oded, another palace servant, rushed in, skidding to a halt next to Shira. Oded came from a northern territory and bore a striking resemblance to the men of that area. Dark skin seemed stretched over his bony frame.

"What's going on in here?" Oded asked. "Why such glum looks, everyone? Did I miss something?"

Akiva turned to him. "Have you seen Moshe?"

"Yes, I have." Oded folded his skinny arms over his bulky cloak and nodded.

Akiva watched him through hooded eyes. "Would you care to share that information with me?" *This man is insufferable. The palace could do without him, in my opinion.* "Well, I'm waiting."

A sly grin slid up Oded's cheeks. "What's it worth to you?"

Akiva's hands curled into fists. He took a deep breath before answering. "The question is what is it worth to you if you don't answer? I have the power to have you removed from the palace, or have you forgotten who's in charge?"

A breathless silence hung in the moist kitchen air. The girls kept their heads lowered.

Oded backed up with both hands in the air. "I don't want any trouble. Moshe's in the garden. Would you like me to bring him to you?"

The mockery was gone from his voice and Akiva thought he saw a flash of fear. *Good. He needs a dose of fear or he'll have us all begging for our lives.*

"Yes, tell him I need him without delay."

ℋ

Moshe knocked on the door of the king's chambers and waited for a response. The servant had seemed nervous when he insisted Moshe come immediately. He hadn't even had time to change his robe.

What will I find when Amon opens the door? The same crazed man I left an hour ago or my friend who claims to love me? These days it's hard to predict.

"You came, my friend. Enter." Amon swept the door open. "Here, take this chair by the window."

Amon grabbed the back of the chair and pulled it around, giving Moshe a small shove into it. Amon pulled up another chair and faced him.

Amon stared into Moshe's eyes. "Ah, about this morning. It's over, done, past, no more. I'll not have it mentioned again in my presence."

Moshe read the hidden message in those dark, mysterious eyes. "It shall be as you wish."

Moshe smoothed the fabric of his robe, which was in disarray from pacing through the garden. He knew Amon would speak his mind when he was ready.

Why am I suspicious? What evil plan has he devised this time? He's clever, but I must be more clever.

Moshe let none of this show on his face. He composed his facial muscles in a relaxed fashion.

Amon leaned forward, eyes hooded. "Moshe, my friend, these are tough days for the palace. The people are restless, the priests are disgruntled, the prophetess errs in her ways, the servants think they're in charge, the army is listless, and my friends have left me."

"What would you have me do, my lord?" Moshe inclined his head and watched Amon's response carefully. Much would depend on his reply.

Amon rested his hand on Moshe's arm. "Can I count on your loyalty?"

"Of course, my lord. Has it ever been in doubt?"

"I don't know who I can trust these days. I need to be very careful." Amon leaned back and crossed one leg over the other. "I felt quite certain I could count on you, but it never hurts to ask."

Amon jumped up from his seat with a grin on his face. With a hand he motioned Moshe.

"Come over to the table. We have plans to make."

The two heads leaned over the opened scrolls before them, a plan taking place in their minds and appearing on the scroll. Moshe held the pen, but Amon dictated the ideas.

Amon leaned over Moshe's shoulder reading the letters inscribed there and pointing to different words. "Who should we deal with first? Where's a good place to start?"

"Are you asking my opinion?" Moshe asked.

"Yes, yes, of course." The reply was brisk and accompanied with a wave of the hand.

"Then I would deal with the servants first."

The king lowered himself into the chair beside Moshe. "And what would your reasons be for that approach? Not that I don't agree with you. I just want us to be clear."

"Here's my thinking," Moshe said. "You can't deal with the people until the army is in shape. You can't deal with the army if you're having issues in the palace. You can't deal with your friends, because you're going to need every last one of them, and I would advise that you not touch the priests before the people are under control."

Evil intent seemed to gleam from the king's eyes. "And what about the prophetess? Should we not eliminate her first?"

"No. Absolutely not. Do not touch the prophetess."

The king sat back, his eyes widening. "Why not?"

"Think about it, Amon. The people believe she hears from God directly. Whatever she says is believed. She's revered. She's loved. Her words are feared. If you touch her, someone will make sure her prophecy comes true."

Amon pounded Moshe on the back. "You're right. I never thought about it that way. That's why I keep you around. You keep me thinking straight." He followed his words with a deep laugh.

Moshe laughed in return. "If we think carefully, we can use her for our own purposes."

They bent their heads over the desk and looked again at their growing lists. "Then it's the servants first. Let's get this underway."

The king nodded and the two began to discuss their plans. Quiet laughter interspersed with snarls marked the passage of time in the chamber.

"No, no, cross that out," Moshe said. "We can't do that."

"I'll not cross it out. I'm the king. I can do whatever I please."

"But Amon—"

"Are you afraid, Moshe? Are you turning into a woman or a slave, no backbone?" Amon slammed the quill down on the scroll. "Well, what will it be? Declare yourself now. Either you're with me, or I'll need to replace you. Maybe even eliminate you. Which will it be? Be quick about it. Decide."

"Calm yourself, Amon." Moshe rose. "You know I'm with you, but just because something is possible doesn't mean you should do it."

"There you go, sounding like an old woman again. I really should replace you."

Finally the scroll was rolled up, sealed, and Moshe left the king's presence to start the chain of cruel events awaiting the Kingdom of Judah. A dark mist circled the palace as he pulled his cloak around him and entered the damp air, breathing deeply and contemplating the carnage to come.

twenty-one

*H*uldah sat up quickly. Morning light seeped through the cracks in the shutters, surprising her. She had actually managed to sleep. She knew it was early, yet she felt compelled to rise.

"God is prompting me," she said to herself. "I know the feeling."

Huldah reached for her shawl and wrapped it around her shoulders before moving into the next room so as not to wake Shallum. She knelt in front of the window with her hands folded on the sill before her. Light filtered over her face when she lifted her heart to God in prayer.

"God, I know you are in this. Please reveal your thoughts to me."

She waited quietly for God's response. When it came, her eyes widened in surprise.

"If that's what you want me to do, I will do it."

H

Huldah neared the palace gates as the temple horns signalled morning. With the hood of her robe in place and her eyes lowered, she worked her way past the guards who were busy checking a caravan that had just arrived. Once inside, she approached a maid in the midst of her duties.

Huldah spoke softly, leaning in close to Hadar so not to be observed by the other servants, especially the guards. "Pardon me, Hadar, but could you direct me to Jedidah's rooms?"

With startled eyes, the servant stared at her. A cleaning rag shook in her hands. "How... how did you know my name? I know who you are. You're the prophetess."

"I know your name because God revealed it to me. You are favoured by him, and if you ever need anything, you are to come to me." Huldah gently touched the young girl's face. "Do you understand, Hadar?"

Her hand continued to stroke the girl's face until she could see the anxiety leave her eyes.

"Yes, I understand… and thank you." Hadar's lips lifted ever so slightly, showing teeth that were small and even. "I will take you to Jedidah. Come, follow me."

The two figures slipped from the open foyer into a long narrow hall. Few people were about at this hour, so they passed undetected. At the end of the hall, they turned left into an even smaller hall until they reached a small, plain door. On this door, Hadar knocked.

After a short interval, the door was pulled open by a servant woman who appeared to have just risen from her bed. Her hair was tied up in a dull brown scarf, but stray pieces hung limply from beneath the scarf. A worn, faded wrapper and bare feet completed her outfit.

The servant wiped her hand over her eyes, peering at the two visitors. "What do you want at this hour, Hadar?" she asked with a strong accent.

"The prophetess, Huldah, wishes to see your mistress."

Hadar moved aside to let Huldah stand before the servant. Huldah lifted her hand and removed the scarf from her face so the servant could see that it was indeed she.

The change was visible as the old servant woman fell to her knees before Huldah, wringing her hands.

"What do you want with us?" she wailed, her face touching Huldah's feet. "We have done nothing wrong. We aren't part of the evil in this palace. My mistress isn't wicked."

"Johanna, I command you to stop and listen to what I have to say." Huldah's voice held a ring of authority. "Stand up, or you will be of no use to me."

The servant named Johanna did what she was told. Although her hands trembled, she faced Huldah with her shoulders back and her chin firm.

"I can be of use to you?" Johanna's voice held a tone of wonder.

"Yes. I will need your help, but right now I need to see your mistress. Please, take me to her."

Johanna moved aside.

Huldah turned to Hadar and thanked her. "And remember what I told you. You have only to call on me."

With a nod, Hadar bowed and backed down the hall.

When Huldah entered the small room, the door closed behind her. They moved from the entrance into a larger room. Huldah was surprised at how plain and under-furnished the space was that housed the king's son. Low couches lined one wall without the adornment of cushions or blankets. A rough table stood in the middle of the space, under the room's only window. The plain wooden floorboards contrasted the marble and carpets of the rest of the palace.

A child's voice could be heard in the quiet of early morning.

Johanna pushed open a door at the far end of the room and asked Huldah to wait. She returned quickly and beckoned Huldah to enter.

Huldah's first view was of a young woman holding a small child. Both showed signs of weeping. Lifting her face in a smile, Huldah approached.

"Jedidah, may I speak to you in private?" Huldah stopped a few paces in front of the woman.

Without a word being spoken, Jedidah handed the child to the servant, who wrapped him in her arms and disappeared into an inner room, closing the heavy curtain behind her.

"Please sit." Jedidah held out her hands and pointed to a seat across from her.

Huldah settled herself before addressing the gracious young woman. "Jedidah, I'm sorry to disturb you so early in the day, but you are in danger. Time may be critical."

Jedidah's eyes grew wide as she spoke. Her hand covered her mouth.

"God has spoken to me this morning," Huldah continued. "I've been instructed to help you flee the palace."

"How could we do that? The king watches our every move."

"Do not fear. When God speaks, His words are true. If He wants you to flee, you will do so successfully. You have my word."

"But—"

"I will be going with you, along with your son. He is also in danger."

Tears now ran down Jedidah's face. "My husband will never let him go."

"Jedidah, not only will you escape without harm or detection, but your son will be king." Huldah rose and knelt in front of Jedidah. "I have been shown the future."

"Can this be possible?" Jedidah's hand grasped Huldah's.

"Yes, it is true. I've been given the promise that he will be a good king." Huldah smiled gently at the mother. "It will be up to you and me to make sure he is taught properly."

"This is all so sudden, so overwhelming." Jedidah's arm shook. "When do we need to go, and where are we going? Oh, I have nowhere to go. We're not safe anywhere."

"We are leaving within the hour. Have no fear; your father will welcome us in his home for the present."

"But how do you know this?"

"God has shown me. He has promised that although your father will fear, he will protect you." Huldah reached up and dried the tears on Jedidah's face. "Come, we have much work to do."

Jedidah rose. "What about Johanna?"

"She will come with us. Never fear. We will be safe."

The two women pushed through the curtain, where they found Johanna and the boy already throwing belongings into bundles. Jedidah stopped and stared.

"My mistress, we couldn't help but overhear." Johanna's mouth stretched in a wide smile. She nodded several times, the brown scarf dancing on her head. "We're ready to go with you. We'll be happy to leave the palace behind."

"What about you, Josiah?" His mother reached out her arms to him and he ran into them. She nestled her face in his dark hair.

"Mama, I'm scared." His little face disappeared in the folds of her robe.

Jedidah brushed the hair back from his face with a gentle hand. "Then you don't mind leaving?"

"I don't mind, really I don't."

Planting a kiss on her face, Josiah wiggled out of her arms and ran back to Johanna to add more things to the bundles.

H

Huldah tugged on the shutters until she had an opening wide enough for them to squeeze through. She lifted the first bundle and shoved it over the ledge until she heard a soft plop on the other side.

"I'm going first, so I can help each of you over," she said. Her eyes roved over the three before her and took note of their wide eyes and tense shoulders. "Show no fear. God has told me we will arrive safely at our destination."

Huldah pushed herself out the window and landed beside the first bundle. She righted herself quickly and scanned the area. No one was in sight, so she turned back to the window in time to catch the next package.

When the last of their belongings were stacked on the ground, Josiah's head appeared. Huldah could see excitement on his face and rejoiced that they would not have a frightened child to contend with. Once he was safely on the ground, his mother quickly followed. Johanna then bravely jumped and was caught by Huldah and Jedidah.

Once free, they all looked at each other with tentative smiles on their faces.

"The first part is over. You handled that very well, all of you." Huldah touched each one on the shoulder. "We'll help each other lift our packs and then be off."

Huldah took Josiah's hand and waved the others into place behind her.

The sun was now fully up, casting a brilliant glow over the smooth walls of the palace. Huldah marvelled at the beauty. *So beautiful without, and so corrupt within.*

She led them toward a path that skirted the temple and avoided the main part of town. Morning song fell from branches, the birds welcoming the day. The chitchat of small animals rose from the grasses on either side of the path.

Oh Lord, it seems like all of creation except man rises to sing your praises at the beginning of a new day.

When they passed behind the temple, the aroma of roasting meat and baking bread wafted out to them, signifying morning sacrifices. Huldah knew the priests were as appalled and disgusted as she over the events of last night.

Hilkiah is getting old, but he has never wavered in his worship of the one true God. There's been no hint of idol worship from him. His life will be in danger if he stands up to the king, but what else can he do? She lifted her face into the breeze. *We are all in danger, but God is in control.*

Once past the temple, the next challenge was the city gate. Huldah gathered the others around her.

"We're all dressed simply, so if we keep our hoods up and our eyes down, this shouldn't be difficult. Don't make eye contact with anyone, and don't get separated. Johanna, take Jedidah's arm. I'll hold Josiah's hand."

She curled her fingers around Josiah's small hand.

"We'll pause once we're past the gates," Huldah said. "If we get separated, wait by the grove of trees on the right until we're together again." She looked over the scene before her. "There's a group approaching the gates now. We'll join them. Keep your eyes down and don't talk to anyone unless you have to."

Huldah moved quickly into place at the back of the large group. She kept Josiah close by her side, his hand gripped tightly in hers.

At the gate, there was much confusion. A caravan was entering through the gate and all had to stand aside while they passed. Guards ran back and forth. Orders were yelled which no one seemed to follow. Anyone who came within sword distance of the guards was threatened.

Huldah was thrilled with the sight of the caravan and almost forgot that she needed to keep her eyes down. When a caravaner leaned over, tweaked her hood, and made a rude comment, she remembered in time to slide back into the embrace of the crowd. A raucous laugh escaped his throat, and with a gesture he moved on.

Oh Lord, I need to pay attention.

Massive camels snorted and moaned their way past them, lifting weighty feet and plodding on. Whips slashed the air and uncouth language spurted out, but at last they were through the gate and exited the city. The press of people only grew stronger, however, and Huldah and Josiah were swept away. Huldah didn't dare look behind her to see if Jedidah and Johanna were with them.

Once clear of the gate traffic, Huldah moved swiftly toward the grove of trees. She pulled Josiah under the spreading branches, glad of a cool breath of air, for the sun and the crowd had cut off the breeze. Once under the trees, she turned back toward the gates and was dismayed to see no sign of the women.

But Lord, I know they're safe. You showed me that we would be. I will not fear, but wait and trust You.

Several minutes passed before the women came into view, moving with a flock of sheep headed to pasture. They leaned on each other, but kept up with the flock. At the trees, they turned right and fell into Huldah's arms. Jedidah was crying, and Johanna's face was a tight mask of fear.

Huldah patted Jedidah's back. "Everything's all right now. You're safe."

"We… we were almost recognized," Jedidah said. "A palace guard went by on horseback, then turned and came back. He stared at us and shouted to another guard. We moved back into the crowd, pulled our hoods low, and stayed still. We could hear him talking to the other guard, who told him he was crazy. They went off together."

Johanna lowered her bundles and collapsed on the grass.

"We're by the worst of it," Huldah said. "Up ahead, we'll take a side path and stay off the main route. The chances of us being recognized now are slim. God has already gone before us."

Huldah hugged each woman, then lifted her bundles, took Josiah by the hand, and moved into the road. The others followed.

None of them saw the dark shadow slip behind a tree and watch their progress along the main thoroughfare.

twenty-two

*H*ilkiah shifted his position on the narrow cot once again. He was restless in his sleep—face the wall, roll over, face the door, roll over again. Voices and visions troubled him, sometimes bringing him almost to the surface, only to plunge him into deeper sleep again.

"Darkness covered the face of the earth." His knees buckled under him and he sank to the ground, parched and broken. "Everything is empty. You are empty. Darkness is everything; everything is darkness."

With face to the empty ground, he wept, long and violently, until the emptiness stole inside him and slowly took over his body, squeezing life and breath from him.

"No, no, you can't have my soul." He beat the ground with his fists. "No, no, no."

A tremble started deep in the earth until he feared the ground would open up and swallow him. A voice called his name, a voice that rose in intensity while the earth shook.

"Hilkiah. Please, master, wake up."

The darkness gathered into itself and slipped away toward the barren horizon, leaving Hilkiah spent and prostrate on the hard-packed earth.

"Master, please."

The voice again. Hilkiah looked around, seeing no one.

Wait. I know that voice. It's coming from another world.

Light began to penetrate his conscious mind and the barren earth receded. Squinting at the bright light, he opened his eyes and looked directly into the startled eyes of Benjamin, his faithful servant.

"Benjamin?" He struggled to sit up, but weakness swept over him and he fell back on the cot. "What are you doing here?"

"Master, why wouldn't I be here? It's where I live." The old scribe shook his head, keeping his eyes on Hilkiah's face.

The present slowly came into focus, the dream slipping away. Hilkiah sat on the edge of the cot, rubbing his hands over his face. "Benjamin, I've had a dream. No, I think it was a vision. No dream could be that awful. It was a vision, I'm sure."

"What did you see, master?" Benjamin pulled a stool beside the bed and lowered himself onto it.

"Strange and frightening. Emptiness and darkness everywhere. And the voice… it was empty, too. Never have I heard or seen the likes of it. It's a message, or a warning, or a threat." His face paled when he reviewed the scenes from the dream. "Quick, write this down or I'll forget."

Benjamin pulled a parchment scroll from a nearby table, unrolling it with one hand while he searched for a quill with the other. He dropped the scroll when his fingers closed over the quill.

"Sorry, sorry," he mumbled toward Hilkiah.

Rising from his cot, Hilkiah stroked his beard. "Write this: 'Darkness covered the face of the land.' No, that's not quite right." He ran a hand through his hair and his eyebrows pulled together. "No, not land. Earth."

The scratching pen distracted him for a moment, but Hilkiah regained his focus and shook his hand at Benjamin.

"Write again: 'Everything is empty. You are empty. Darkness is everything; everything is darkness.'"

Benjamin formed each letter and word as Hilkiah dictated it. When he was finished, he sprinkled fine sand over the writing, then shook the sand into a container.

"Master, what does it mean?"

"That's what I'm going to figure out. Leave the scroll for me to study, and see if you can bring us a meal. I prefer to eat here this morning, so I'll be undisturbed."

Hilkiah dismissed the scribe and leaned over the scroll.

This cannot be from God. He shook his head and considered the implications. *But if not God, who? I don't like the conclusion. But maybe God allowed it for a warning of things to come.*

Hilkiah stood and walked to the small window in his sleeping room. The bright orange sun tipped the horizon. As he watched, the long rays stretched across the distance and touched his face. He lifted his hands and face to embrace the light.

"All is not darkness," he whispered. His lips curved into a broad smile. "Darkness is not everything, no matter what the day brings. Thank you, God, for revealing Yourself to me through Your creation, which is good, not empty."

Benjamin returned with a tray loaded with two bowls of porridge and fresh bread. The two men ate sparingly, with little talk; Hilkiah was deep in thought about the vision, and Benjamin knew not to disturb his silence.

When the meal was complete, Hilkiah placed his bowl back on the tray and wiped his fingers on a damp cloth the scribe had brought in with him.

"Ask Talmar and Jamin to meet me in my study room as soon as they are able. Maybe three old minds will be able to solve the mystery." Hilkiah handed the cloth back to Benjamin. "Of one thing I'm sure: it has something to do with the reign of the new king, and it does not bode well for the future."

H

Hilkiah waited in his study room until the shuffle of sandals alerted him to the arrival of the other two priests. Talmar pushed aside the heavy curtain and entered, followed by Jamin.

"Master, what troubles you so early in the day?" Talmar wheezed. He leaned heavily on his stick. His pale watery eyes glanced up at Hilkiah's face.

"Here, Talmar, sit here." Hilkiah pushed a low chair toward him, close to the central table. "Jamin, sit where you can both see the scroll I've brought."

Hilkiah sat across from them and waited for them to settle comfortably.

Both men were short of breath. They leaned their elbows on the table and watched while Hilkiah arranged the scroll and quill.

Hilkiah looked at each priest closely and noticed how feeble they were, especially Talmar. *But I know their minds are sharp, and that's what I need today.*

"I've brought you here because I need your help." Hilkiah paused to expel air from his lungs and gather his thoughts. "I was disturbed by a vision in the night. I think it contained a message for us, but I need your help getting to the truth of the matter."

"Show us what's on the scroll and we'll help you arrive at an answer," Jamin said. His eyes had a glint in them, as though he could hardly wait to tackle the mystery.

Hilkiah's stiff fingers trembled while they opened the scroll, spread out the parchment, and turned it for the others to read. He watched their faces closely for their response to the written words.

Talmar lifted his eyes to Hilkiah, his lips forming a circle. "This is a distressing message. Have you come to any conclusions?"

"No, no, of course he hasn't. That's why he sent for us." Jamin drew the scroll closer to himself and read the message again. "And you say this came to you in a dream?"

Hilkiah nodded.

"I say it doesn't mean anything and you should forget about it." Jamin thrust the scroll from him and sent it across the table to Hilkiah.

Talmar's hand reached out to grasp Jamin's sleeve. "Not so fast, brother. If Hilkiah believes it was a vision, it was a vision."

Jamin leaned away from the table. "You're right, Talmar. I forgot myself for a moment. Hilkiah, I'm sorry. Forgive an old man his impetuosity."

"There is nothing to forgive, Jamin." Hilkiah dismissed the comment with a wave of his hand. "Let's discuss the message."

The three ancient heads bent over the scroll. Talmar traced the words with a bent finger and whispered each one softly. Slowly he straightened his back and looked at the other two. "The message is in three parts. I think we should consider each part separately."

The others nodded.

"'Darkness covered the face of the earth,'" Hilkiah said, sitting back and letting a deep sigh escape his lips. "Why does that sound familiar?"

Talmar's eyes opened wide. "Remember when we were young boys and studied under Rabbi Aviel?"

"Yes, of course. He was hoary with age and passed on to his rest soon after." Hilkiah leaned in on his elbows and furrowed his brow while he stared at Talmar. "What does he have to do with this?"

"I remember that he talked about the beginning of time. He told us that before everything was, God was, and that darkness was upon the face of the deep."

"I think you're right," Jamin said.

"That sounds right, but why was I shown it in a vision?" Hilkiah rubbed a hand over his beard and softly murmured to himself. "What if I'm being told that this new reign will be like the darkness before the world began?"

"I would say that's quite likely." Talmar nodded several times. "What do we know about that time?"

"Well, if darkness covered the earth, God had not yet moved to create us." Jamin held up a hand. "Let's not go too deep into every word. We'll get bogged down trying to figure it all out. If darkness covered the earth, I think we can assume that the darkness of evil will spread over our land."

"I can accept that." The lines on Hilkiah's forehead eased as he nodded his agreement. "What about you, Talmar? Do you agree?"

"Yes, that makes sense. I think we can agree that evil is already spreading over our land."

"So part one is a true statement and one we can all agree upon. But part two, to me, is not true." Hilkiah tapped the scroll with one finger and moved it around again so the others could read with him.

"Certainly not at first reading, but look a little deeper." Jamin rubbed his hands together. He clearly enjoyed the challenge. "What if we take 'empty' to mean 'without power'?"

Hilkiah pulled the scroll back to himself again. "That changes everything. Empty of power. Hmmm. Could that be it? We are without power in this new reign?"

"It would appear so." Talmar stroked one side of his face with a gnarled hand.

Jamin dropped his fist on the table. "But remember, God is never without power."

"Then we need to make sure we spend more time in prayer, asking for God's power." Hilkiah looked up at the other two. "Only God can defeat the evil one, and only God can deliver us from this evil king."

A sound of clapping hands preceded old Benjamin sticking his head in through the heavy curtain. "Master, you're wanted at the palace."

With an annoyed look on his face, Hilkiah shook his hand at Benjamin. "You know I didn't want to be disturbed."

"Master, there's a guard here to take you, and he won't be refused. You'd better come."

Hilkiah shoved the scroll toward the other two. "I'd better answer the summons. Continue to work on the last section while I'm gone, and you'd better pray for that power we need."

125

With hands balanced on the table, Hilkiah pushed his frame upward until he was standing. Benjamin pulled back the curtain, and Hilkiah slipped through.

twenty-three

"Huldah, may we pause for a few minutes? Josiah's legs are tiring," Johanna said, her weary voice reaching Huldah's ears.

Huldah stopped on the roadside and turned to watch Johanna as she tried to lift Josiah. Jedidah wiped moisture from her forehead with her headscarf. Compassion filled Huldah as she observed her fellow travellers.

"I'm so sorry," Huldah said. I was thinking about our journey and almost forgot you were here with me."

She reached out to Johanna and scooped up Josiah in her arms. His little arms surrounded her neck, his head leaning against her shoulder. She snuggled him against her, thinking how wonderful it felt to hold a child.

"Let's pause under that tree up ahead." Huldah pointed down the road to where a lone tree jutted into the sky.

Jedidah nodded and moved forward. Johanna grabbed her arm and walked with her. Shifting Josiah's weight to one hip, Huldah followed.

"I can't believe how tired I am." Jedidah slid down against the trunk of the tree and closed her eyes. The others sank to the ground around her.

The shade felt wonderful after the heat from the sun on the open road. Crickets chirped from the roadside, invisible to the eye but pleasant to the ear. Huldah let her eyes roam over the road, which stretched in both directions as far as the eye could see. She leaned back and slid Josiah to her side, keeping her arm around the little boy. His eyes soon closed and sleep overtook him. Soft snores came from Johanna, who had collapsed in a huddle beside Jedidah.

Huldah fought off sleep, ever alert to possible danger. No one walked the road, however. No cloud darkened the sky, and soon her body relaxed and her mind drifted.

"Huldah, my child…" She stirred but couldn't quite rouse herself. The voice was gentle, caressing, caring. "Huldah…"

Her eyes refused to open.

"You must leave quickly," the voice said. "Danger lies ahead... hurry... hurry... hurry..."

Her eyes flew open and roved back and forth. No one was in sight. Nothing moved in any direction.

But I heard the voice. I know it to be a true voice, for I've heard it before.

She shook Johanna's shoulder. The older woman sputtered and moaned, but gradually her eyes opened and focused on Huldah.

"What... is something wrong?" When Johanna sat up, she rubbed her eyes with both hands.

"So sorry to wake you, but we must move. It's urgent that we do so without delay."

Worry lines appeared on Johanna's forehead. "We'll do what you say, Huldah." She struggled to a standing position and gathered their belongings.

Jedidah was also awake, her eyebrows rising.

"We must move, Jedidah. Can you rouse Josiah?" Huldah held out the container of water for each of the others to drink from before they resumed their trek.

Within minutes, they were on the road again, somewhat rested even though the time had been short. Johanna held a bun of bread she had extracted from her bundle. She broke the bread into four parts and handed a piece to each of them. They munched without talk while they progressed along the dusty road.

The heat shimmered ahead, casting a hazy sheen across the roadway. Huldah was ever alert to danger.

I must move forward with haste. The message was clear. I'll not fear, for I've been assured we'll arrive safely at our destination. But only if I'm vigilant.

Josiah scuffed his sandals in the dust. He paused, let go of his mother's hand, and whimpered. This was so unlike him that he soon had their attention.

"I am brave, really I am," he said. Tears hung from the ends of his long, dark lashes, threatening to fall. "It's just that I'm so hungry and thirsty and tired."

Huldah was the first to respond. "Of course you are. Here, I'll take you on my back for a while. We'll stop when the sun is right over us. Soon, very soon."

She bent down and his mother helped him climb on. Josiah clutched her neck and wrapped his arms and legs around her.

"Does that feel better?" Huldah asked.

"Hmm, much better, thank you."

"I'll take your bundle, Huldah." Jedidah reached for it and added it to her own.

"We'll stop soon for our midday meal and a short rest," Huldah said. "But not for long. We must reach the gates of Bozkath before dusk."

When the sun reached its midway point in the journey across the open sky, the four figures found a secluded grove of trees. They reclined under the shade and succumbed to sleep. As they slept, an unnoticed shadow flitted over them.

H

Amon circled the room, agitated and restless. Sweat beaded on his forehead, seeped down his back, and dampened the back of his robe.

Can I trust him? That's the question. He ground his teeth until his jaw ached. *Can I trust anyone?*

He paused beside the window, staring out. He saw nothing but the images in his mind.

What choice do I have? I can't do this alone.

Amon stretched his hands behind his back and took another turn around the room, kicking aside a small rug that was in his way. His bare feet slapped the stone beneath.

But I have a plan that none of them know. Someone is watching each one who's charged with doing my hidding. Brilliant plan, if I do say so myself.

He reached the door and flung it open. Akiva hovered within sight of the door.

Amon fixed his eye on him. "I am going out. Make the preparations." He snapped his fingers and turned back to his room.

"May I ask where you wish to go?" Akiva asked.

The words reached Amon just before he closed the door. "No."

And then the door slammed.

A tap on the door followed. Amon ignored the knock. Nonetheless, it opened slowly, and the face of Oded appeared. Amon ignored this, too. Oded slipped into the room and began to lay out clothes.

"Slip out of your robe and I'll help you dress." Oded stretched out his arms and Amon handed him the damp robe.

He stood quietly while Oded dressed him. *This one I'll keep. He's useful to me.*

Oded stood back when he had finished. Without even a thank you, Amon strode from the room. Akiva had obviously been busy, for a contingent of soldiers waited to escort him.

Bowing low, Akiva met him. "Your chariot awaits. Is there anything else I can do?"

"Where are Ethan, Joel, and Jotham? I expected them to be here."

"They're on their way, master."

The sound of voices raised in laughter caught Amon's ear. His eyebrows drew together as he saw three of his advisors approach. With his jaw clamped, he faced them.

"That's enough," Amon snapped. "We have work to do."

He gestured for them to fall into place beside him, and the entire group headed for the palace doors. His progress through the halls was rapid, causing servants to fall in obeisance to him. A few female servants cowered in dark corners. Amon ignored all of them.

The soldiers moved with military precision on either side of the king. They made an interesting spectacle with their dark, red-belted robes contrasting his deep blue and gold attire. His kingly robe was intricately worked with stitching along each seam in matching blue and gold threads. A belt made from the skin of a jackal held the robe in place. Golden tassels hung down from the belt, touching the hem of the robe. His sandals were of the finest leather, worked until they were soft enough to meet with his approval. An ornate headdress of beaten gold completed his outfit, circling his forehead.

Amon and his three friends jumped into the chariot. At a wave of the king's hand, the horses charged ahead, causing the soldiers to move briskly to keep up.

Word spread quickly that the king rode through the city. Soon the streets were thronged with crowds, some yelling words of cheer to the new monarch while others fell to the ground before him.

It appeared that he didn't watch the people, but in truth he watched carefully, on the lookout for potential scapegoats for his plans. He noted anyone who didn't seem to pay him proper respect. His friends chatted and waved, encouraging the people in their response to the king, but Amon showed no facial expression.

When he tired of the journey, he gave orders to return to the palace, his head filled with ways to elicit fear and obedience from the people.

Sleep well tonight, Judah, for tomorrow will bring surprises for you to ponder.

H

The guard marched at such a pace toward the palace that Hilkiah panted to keep up. His robe swished around his ankles, its tiny bells tinkling. With deep breaths, he tried to focus on the beauty around him and not the coming interview. Pleasant it would not be, unlike the gardens they passed, redolent with flowers and fruit-laden trees.

I long to sit among the flowers, but that will not be. This reign will tax every fibre of my being.

"Am I too quick for you, old man?" The guard glanced sideways at Hilkiah, his wide mouth stretched in a grimace.

No respect. It's gone from the land. The new king has already made his mark on the people. Father, show Your power.

The palace gates loomed before them, etched with the glow of morning sun, but accompanying shadows on the walkway gave a sinister appearance.

Is it my imagination or is evil rampant in the palace?

They didn't pause at the entrance, although Hilkiah could see the gatekeeper step forward to challenge them. The guard swept past without a glance in the gatekeeper's direction.

Hilkiah was ushered into an audience room and told to wait until the king was ready to meet him. With that, the guard left Hilkiah to ponder the coming interview.

Give me the words to say…

Before he could finish his prayer, the king swept into the room.

"Hilkiah, how nice to see you." Amon sported a smile that didn't reach his eyes.

Hilkiah inclined his head to the king but did not speak.

"We have much to discuss, you and I. Please sit." Amon indicated a low seat in front of the window.

Hilkiah obeyed, well aware that the king had so placed him that the light would fall on the king, leaving Hilkiah in shadow. The king did not sit.

He has this all planned. It's a strategy to put me at a disadvantage. Clever. I must be cautious.

With feet planted slightly apart and arms folded over his chest, Amon stared at the High Priest. "First things first. I am the king; you are at my command. Do I make myself clear?"

"Very clear, my lord, but you forget yourself. I am not under your jurisdiction. I am in the employ of Almighty God, who bows to no earthly king."

Hilkiah watched the King's eyes closely to determine his reaction.

Red seeped up the King's neck. Amon puffed out his cheeks and huffed, expelling air forcefully. "You misunderstand, oh High Priest. God plays no part in this. I am the king, and the sooner you recognize that, the sooner you'll be safe."

"It is you who misunderstand, if I may be so bold." Hilkiah stiffly rose from his chair. "I issue a caution to you. Do not touch the chosen of the Lord. It will not go well. The prophetess has spoken a warning to you. I add to her warning. God will not be mocked."

Amon threw his head back and roared a great laugh. He looked toward the entrance to the room. "Guards, come here."

Instantly, two guards materialized.

"Throw him out."

Amon was lifted by strong arms, then carried through the corridors and escorted from the palace.

"Next time, we will literally throw you," one of the guards said before striding back into the palace.

Hilkiah stood for a moment to calm his heart and offer a prayer to God. He began his walk back to the temple with small, slow steps.

When he passed the gatekeeper, the man cleared his throat.

"Do not turn to look at me, for we are no doubt observed from the palace," the gatekeeper said. "I would like to speak with you at your convenience."

"Come to the temple, after darkness has fallen." Hilkiah spoke without moving his head or slowing his pace.

Tears gathered in his eyes and filled the hollows in his cheeks as he approached the temple.

"Oh Lord, I weep for Israel. Only Your hand can save us."

twenty-four

The palace was in an uproar. A banquet was set for sundown, a mere two hours distant. Long tables were covered with royal cloths, white with embroidered vines, flowers, and fruit of all description. Beaten gold plates rested at regular intervals, accompanied by silver goblets worked with pomegranates and leaves. Large platters were set in groupings in the middle of each table, laden with honeyed dates, olives soaked in oil, and grapes in shades of purple and green. From the kitchen, the fragrance of baking bread wafted into the room, along with the aroma of roasting goat, lamb, and fish caught fresh from the river that morning. It would be a feast to long be remembered.

Servants scurried from the banquet hall to the kitchen and back again. Shira and Metra worked the kitchen, supervising the young girls hired for the day. Fear hung over all, for the king had threatened Akiva that there would be dire consequences if all did not go according to plan—*his* plan.

In other corners of the palace, servants washed and polished floors, lifted rugs and shook them out of doors, and dusted the ornate carvings on walls and pedestals.

Amon was in his room, sequestered with Moshe. Both men reclined at a small table while they sipped wine and studied an open scroll.

"I've checked these names thoroughly. They've all been heard making derogatory comments about you. You'll do well to have them removed." Moshe pointed out three in particular. "I would start with these. I know we mentioned starting with the servants, but that might cause too much upset in the palace. You need things to run smoothly here."

"I agree. We'll leave the servants for now, unless one of them needs correction, but what about the men who gave you the information?" Amon rubbed his chin, letting his fingers draw down through his thick beard. "We wouldn't want them talking, now would we?"

A laugh gurgled from Moshe's throat. "I like the way you think. Keep them on their toes so they don't know who to trust or what will happen next." He crossed his arms over his chest and leaned back on the low seat. "They'll learn to obey and respect."

Amon slapped him on the back. "Of course. The people must be brought to obedience before anything else."

Rising from his seat, Amon strode to the window.

"Have you hired men capable to doing the work?" Amon asked, looking back over his shoulder.

"Yes, indeed. While we dine, events will transpire in the city. You will be revered as the best king to ever hold the throne." Moshe lifted his goblet. "Here's to you, King Amon."

Amon returned to the table, grabbed his goblet, touched it to Moshe's, and drank deeply from the contents.

"To me, King Amon."

ℋ

After a short rest and a meagre lunch, Huldah hurried her charges along. "Come, friends. We're almost at the crossroads, where we can take the shorter path."

While they struggled to gather their things, Huldah shaded her eyes and watched the road. All was quiet, as it had been all day. Encouraged, she lifted her bundle, took Josiah by the hand, and continued walking.

Small dark clouds were visible in the east, but they caused Huldah no worry. They should be in Bozkath before the rain arrived. In fact, just ahead she could see the turn toward the city.

"See, Josiah, that's where we'll turn," Huldah said, pointing.

Hope danced in the boy's eyes. "Is it close after that?"

"Well, we're certainly more than halfway." She squeezed his hand in encouragement.

At the turnoff, they stopped and waited for the others to catch up with them.

"This is it," Huldah exclaimed, indicating the grassy trail.

"It looks so refreshing after the dust on this road." Jedidah wiped her damp brow with the corner of her headdress. "How much farther, Huldah?"

"We should make good time. Four more hours should put us in sight of the gates of Bozkath."

"It'll be so good to see those gates again," Jedidah said, a vulnerable look on her face. "I haven't seen my home since I was taken from it and brought to the palace."

At first, all seemed well. Birdsong trilled in the low bushes and tiny lizards basked on the sun-drenched rocks strewn along the edges of the path. Josiah chased the lizards and laughed with abandon when they fled, flashing intriguing colours on their backs.

Huldah delighted in watching him. He was just a boy, finally enjoying himself away from the fear and protocol of the palace.

Without warning, a shiver passed through her shoulders. Huldah glanced in all directions but saw no sign of anyone. But she felt sure danger was close.

"We must go back." Huldah laid her hand on Jedidah's arm. "Now."

"But why?" Jedidah asked, confused. "We've made such excellent progress."

"No time for questions. Come, quickly, there's danger ahead." Huldah pulled Josiah close and set off at a fast pace, followed closely by Jedidah and Johanna. Both the women wept openly, but Huldah didn't slacken her pace until they were on the main road again.

"Please, don't ask me to explain." Huldah adjusted her robe, retying the belt and beckoning for the others to follow. "Only know that the danger is real. We must make haste."

"Won't this route take longer?" Josiah's face was scrunched up, as though he wanted to cry.

"Yes, but we'll move faster in order to still make the city gates by dusk."

H

The shadow of Ehud, the man pledged to Aleah the servant girl, slipped from his place of hiding once he realized Jedidah and Josiah were no longer headed his way.

My life is over. Without their bodies to prove I found them, Aleah will be pledged to someone else, and I… who knows what will happen to me? Maybe I'll just disappear.

H

Amon sat on his chair by the window, pondering the future he had planned for himself. In a reflective mood, he stared into the garden without seeing. *At the banquet tonight, my wife and son must be present. They need to see how powerful I've become. It will be a good lesson for the boy, and a warning to my complaining wife.*

He strode to the door, opened it, and spoke to a nearby servant. "Tell my wife and son that I require their presence in my room. Immediately."

The servant scurried off and Amon went back to his pondering. After some time had passed, he wondered why they hadn't arrived. A soft knock on the door assured him they were here now.

"Come in," he called.

To his surprise, it was Akiva who entered and bowed.

"Where are my wife and son?" demanded Amon.

"There is a slight problem, my Lord.

Amon stood and waited for Akiva to continue. The servant simply stared at the ground.

"Well, what is this slight problem? Speak."

"We haven't been able to locate them." Akiva kept his eyes lowered. "Yet," he added.

"Are they not in their rooms, or in the garden, or on the paths?" Amon kept his voice under control.

"No, my Lord. We've looked all those places and more. They are not in the palace or on the grounds."

Amon took a deep breath and felt anger rise in his chest. "If they're not in the palace, has anyone thought to look in the city? Maybe they went on a little excursion." He couldn't keep the sarcasm from his voice. *Sometimes I wonder if I only have fools running the palace.*

"There are people searching the city now, my Lord."

"Find them and bring them to me immediately," he shouted.

Akiva bowed his way from the room and softly closed the door.

I don't know who I'm angrier at, my wife or the bumbling servants. They'd better find her, and fast.

The next knock on the door brought Akiva again.

"Well? Have you found them?" Amon said.

"No, my Lord, and there is more bad news. It appears there is clothing missing from their rooms. It looks like someone went out the window."

"What makes you think that?" The king was so angry at this point that he could barely breathe. His fists clenched tightly at his sides.

"One of the guards found footprints in the soil beneath the window."

Amon turned from Akiva and paced to the window. *They've escaped. She's run away.*

"And where is Elah? Is he not supposed to be watching them?" Amon snarled.

"He's missing, too."

A flush crept up Amon's neck and he lashed out at Akiva with his fists, his voice rising to a shriek. "Find them! Find them all, or someone will pay for this with his life!"

H

"Look, Huldah." Josiah pointed ahead to where the gates of Bozkath caught the late afternoon sun. He danced around the women, his arms high in the air. "We did it!"

Huldah caught his arm. "We're almost there, Josiah. Can your little legs manage the rest of the distance? You've walked a long way."

"I'm strong, Huldah." He flexed his small arms, showing his muscles.

Johanna felt his arm with a big grin on her face. "You're right, Josiah, you have strong muscles."

Jedidah slanted her eyes at her son, pride shining in the dark recesses of her face. She shaded her eyes and looked toward the gate.

Huldah wondered what she was thinking. She was probably trying to picture the scene when she would be reunited with her parents, whom she hadn't seen for several years.

Will her father be happy that we've come? Lord, you promised me he would take them in, but gave me no indication if it would be willingly. Please, give Jedidah the strength to face whatever waits for us within the gates of the city.

"Let's have a sip of water before we walk the final league." Huldah reached for the goatskin bag that held their precious water. When she opened the top, she beckoned Josiah to take the first sip. When they had each slaked their thirst, she hurried them along, hoping to reach the gates before darkness fell.

They were stopped at the gates.

"You are strangers," the gatekeeper said. It was a statement, not a question. "Where are you going?"

The gatekeeper looked right into Huldah's eyes, then folded his arms over his chest and planted his feet on the road.

"We seek Adaiah, priest of the Lord." Huldah stood tall and looked directly into his eyes. *I will not be intimidated by this man. Grant me the words to say.* "I am Huldah, prophetess of Judah. You have a crippled child who is about to die."

The gatekeeper's shoulders slumped and he licked his lips. "How... how did you know that? I have told no one."

Her eyes never wavered from his face. "Direct me to Adaiah and I will consider your son."

He fell to his knees before her. "Honourable lady, the priest is in the temple. If you can help my son, I'll be your slave forever." With that, his forehead hit the dust of the road.

"Arise, Aniel. Your child will live." Huldah reached out and touched his shoulder. "I do not need a slave, and you are needed here to raise your son to honour the Lord Almighty."

H

Darkness was fast approaching when they neared the small temple. Light from an oil lamp spilled from the doorway. In its rays, a shadow could be seen moving inside.

"It's my father." Jedidah's voice trembled as she reached the entrance. "Please, may I go in first, alone?"

Huldah nodded and put her arms around Josiah's shoulders. "Go, Jedidah. We'll wait here."

H

Adaiah looked up as the form of a woman stepped into the doorway. His eyes widened and his hands shook until he dropped the vessel he was carrying. It hit the floor with the sound of cymbals crashing together.

"Father..."

"Why are you here, child? You should be in the palace with your husband." Adaiah reached out a shaking hand and ran his fingers across his daughter's face. His eyes never left hers, but she thought she could see fear in them.

"Father, I am not alone." She turned to beckon the others to enter. Josiah ran to his mother's side. "This is your grandson."

Adaiah's eyes left his daughter and fastened on her son. "My grandson?"

"Yes, Father. This is Josiah, a prince of Judah, the king's own son." She lifted her chin high, a hint of pride in her voice.

"This is indeed a miracle, that I have seen my grandson." He caressed the boy's head. "But why are you here?"

Huldah stepped forward, nodding at Jedidah. "May I speak with you, Priest Adaiah?"

The priest's eyes now shifted to her. His brows furrowed. "Please speak if you have an answer to my question."

"I do, indeed, have an answer. I am Huldah, the prophetess of Judah..."

At her statement, Adaiah's entire body began to shake. He grabbed the edge of the table to steady himself. "The prophetess? The one who challenged the king?"

"I am she."

Adaiah hugged the boy to him. "I fear this does not bode well. Why are you here?"

"We are here because your daughter and grandson are in danger. The king is evil and has plans for the land that will set people's teeth on edge for many days."

Jedidah pulled her robe around her and shivered. *Huldah says it so much better than I could have. Oh my father, you are afraid. I can see it in your eyes.*

"We come asking that you take in your daughter, her son, and her servant. Keep them safe until the kingdom is secure and the people are ready to claim Josiah for their king."

A light began to glow around Huldah as she spoke. Jedidah saw it and smiled to herself. *What a great friend I have.*

"Take them in? Danger?" Adaiah's eyes darted between the two women. "What danger?"

"The king is unstable," Huldah said. "He has made threats to Jedidah and Josiah. God gave me a vision to remove them from Jerusalem and to bring them to you."

Adaiah's shoulders slumped. "Who am I to argue with God?" His hands left the child's head and he stretched them out before him. "When

God speaks, his priests must respond. Come, my children. Enough questions from an old man. Dine with me and my wife. We will do what the Lord commands."

He led them from the temple and along a rough path that brought them to a humble home beneath a grove of trees. Jedidah felt her heart beat faster as she neared the home where she had grown up. Tears hung behind her eyelids, threatening to escape down her cheeks.

I thought I would never see this place again, this place so dear to my heart. Oh Lord, thank You for this. I know we're in danger, but this is a blessing. A dream come true.

"Chava, wife, come quickly, we have guests." Adaiah moved stiffly as he hastened toward the house door.

A woman's face appeared in the doorway, wrinkled and heavy, with grey hair poking out from beneath her headscarf.

"What is it, Adaiah?" she asked. Chava drew a sharp breath, clasping a hand over her mouth. "Jedidah?"

Chava lifted her skirts, ran, and gathered her daughter in her arms.

Tears fell as the two women hugged each other. They rocked back and forth, murmuring softly. Josiah wrapped his arms around his mother's waist and buried his face in the folds of her robe.

The women parted and Jedidah reached down an arm to circle Josiah's shoulders. "Mother, this is Josiah, your grandson. Josiah, this is your bubbe."

Chava fell on her knees in front of Josiah. "My grandson... oh my dear grandson."

Josiah stared at her, then broke into a wide grin and fell into her arms.

Jedidah looked toward the house. Her nose detected a familiar aroma. "Mother, is that red lentil stew I smell?" She could feel the tension in her shoulders relax.

Chava looked up from hugging Josiah and nodded. "Yes, indeed. Red lentil stew. Very plain fare for one used to the palace, I daresay." Her apron was put to work to wipe her eyes.

"Plain fare, perhaps, but I have never smelled anything more appealing." A laugh escaped Jedidah's lips as she looked around at the others. "Shall we go in and join these two for their evening meal?"

Another laugh bubbled up as she walked toward the house.

H

Oil lamps gleamed along the walls and table surfaces as Amon strode through the palace halls accompanied by his advisors, all dressed in splendour. Over his shoulders was slung a mantle made from the skin of a mountain lion, skinned and tanned right there in the palace. Wide bracelets of gold and silver hugged his upper arms. Leather sandals, held in place with leather thongs, completed the outfit. In his hands, he carried a sceptre.

He beckoned Moshe to take the place beside him while they walked.

"Are you sure everything is ready?" Amon hissed into his advisor's ear.

"My lord, I'm sure. Don't fret. It will be done." Moshe gave a low chuckle and slapped him on the back.

"And is there still no word on my wife and son?"

"I'm afraid not, but you must put that from your mind tonight. We have big plans."

"Never fear," Amon said. "I know how to be king."

When they neared the banquet hall, guests in the hallway lowered themselves to the floor. The king passed them without a glance.

At the ornately carved double doors, Amon paused. Two servants swung the doors open.

One of the servants stepped into the room, lifting his hands before him. "Arise for the king. All arise."

There was a shuffle of benches as the people hastened to obey.

Amon swept into the room, led by the announcing servant, and moved to the head table, which was laden with food. Amon sat behind the table, his seat covered with embroidered pillows. The others found their places on either side of him.

There was more shuffling as latecomers found places.

Akiva materialized by Amon's side with a goblet of wine. He placed it on the table at the king's right hand.

Amon lifted it to his nose, then studied the contents. "Has it been tasted?"

"Yes, my lord," Akiva said with a low bow. "But I can do so again, if you're unsure."

"Yes, indeed." The reply was surly, but Amon didn't care. All that mattered was that his not be poisoned.

Akiva lifted the goblet, took a sip, then handed it back to Amon.

Amon drank deeply and called for more.

While he waited for the food to be brought to him, his eyes wandered over the room. Colours swirled in the smoky light of the torches. Servants filled goblets with the palace's finest wines, while others placed platters of steaming food before the guests. It was truly a feast for the eyes.

At a table near the back of the room, Amon spied the priests. He narrowed his eyes and counted them.

"Moshe." He said the name without taking his eyes off the priests.

Moshe turned to him, eyebrows raised. "Yes, master."

"Look at the back table. The priests are here. I didn't think they'd come." A slow smile began to stretch his lips. "They're in for a surprise tonight."

"Indeed they are." Moshe leaned over the table and plucked a ripe olive from a bowl, dropping it into his mouth with a sigh. "No one has better olives than you do. I could dine just on them." He wiped his hands on his robe and reached for another.

"Moshe, be serious. Why are they here?" Amon hadn't taken his eyes off the priests. "I had the High Priest thrown out of the palace this morning. How dare he come again?"

"He knows you won't throw him out with all these people present, and he feels he has a right to be here as the spiritual head of Judah." Another olive followed the first one. "The priests like a good feast. It sure beats what they're forced to eat the rest of the time—bread and sacrifices. Not to my taste."

Moshe's hand reached for the bowl again, only to be slapped away by the king's arm.

"Moshe, you've already had too much wine, I fear. This had better not interfere with the plans."

"No, my friend, nothing will interfere."

This time, when Moshe reached out his hand, the king ignored it.

From the kitchens came platters with thick slabs of venison, whole river fish, lamb roasted over hot coals, and ground goat meat seasoned with spices and wrapped in grape leaves. This was truly a feast for a king. Dish after dish was offered to the guests, and consumed at a remarkable speed. Wine flowed freely and noise grew proportionately until the room was filled with aromas and satiated guests.

When the meal was almost complete, slave girls drifted into the room, moving among the tables playing light tunes on small kinnors and singing in high, sweet voices. Behind them came dancers wrapped in veils, carrying long strands of silk which linked them together. The room was soon filled with their voices as they weaved their way between the tables. Cheers followed them from table to table, erupting from wine-filled guests.

During this distraction, Moshe disappeared from the room. In the dim light, even the king was unaware of his departure until he felt him return. The glint in Moshe's eye and the lifting of the goblet to his lips told Amon all he needed to know.

There would be a surprise awaiting the departing guests, a surprise like they had never experienced before.

H

The dark of the night crowded in on Huldah while she slept on a mat close to the door of the open room. She insisted on placing her mat here, even though Adaiah had protested. Now she moved restlessly in her sleep, first to one side, then the other. Her hands, too, were in constant movement. Deep furrows lined her forehead. She struggled against the pictures stalking her mind.

"No, no, no..." she mumbled in that space between waking and sleeping. "This cannot be. No, no."

With a deep intake of breath, she abruptly sat up and became aware of the darkness pressing in on her while the dream faded.

"I must remember it."

She grabbed handfuls of her hair and pulled them in an attempt to recall the awful scenes. They tumbled back into her mind, and her mouth opened in a silent scream.

"No, Lord, please tell me this isn't true."

But the voice of God was mute.

Huldah came to her feet and approached the door. Hesitatingly, she lifted the bar, slid it open, and stepped into the early morning air. A faint lightening in the east heralded the coming day. She drew in several breaths of fresh air, appreciating the earthy smells of the house garden; mint and sage filled her nostrils.

I must be on my way before sunup.

A shiver ran down her spine as she pulled her robe closer. Taking one last look at the peaceful scene, she slipped back into the warm interior. She tiptoed across the earthen floor until she felt Johanna's mat with her toe.

Leaning over, she touched the servant's shoulder.

"Johanna. Shh, no one else is awake." Huldah held her back when she tried to sit up. "You don't have to get up. I just want to give you a message for Jedidah."

Huldah knelt beside Johanna, who had opened her eyes.

"I must be on my way. Please tell Jedidah where I've gone." She kneaded Johanna's shoulder while she spoke. "Tell her I'll be back for her when I think it's safe. Before then, I'll try to get word to you."

Johanna mutely nodded her head.

Convinced her message would be delivered, Huldah lifted her bag, pushed open the door again, and slipped out. She shivered, knowing what she would face at the end of the day.

twenty-five

The dark palace halls were filled with smoke as Aleah moved through them, carrying trays of food for the banquet. She was uncomfortable with the darkness and the loneliness she felt, for no other servant was in sight. Shapes seemed to materialize on all sides, slowly forming into statues and pedestals when she neared them. With shaking hands, she tightened her grip on the platter of lamb she carried. Her thoughts whirled, imagining every possible thing that could go wrong.

The worst thing is not knowing where Ehud is and when he'll get back. He said the king was sending him on a mission, but he'd be back before the gates closed. Well, I haven't seen him. She sniffed and lifted her chin. *Maybe I'll pretend I don't see him when he decides to show himself.* Another sniff and a humph. *But maybe something happened to him.*

Tears hung on her lashes, but she couldn't reach up and wipe them away; the tray was too heavy for one hand.

A form brushed by her, moving in the opposite direction. She almost dropped the tray and a scream caught in her throat.

"You're wanted outside as soon as you can get there," a voice whispered.

And then the form was gone.

Aleah paused, but could see no one. *Ehud must be back!*

Her heart began to sing. She picked up her steps, delivering the tray safely to the head table. She thought the king winked at her, but she could have been mistaken in the shadowy light. Once out of the banquet room, her feet danced through the once-dreaded halls, her mind filled with thoughts of Ehud. She managed to slip through the kitchen without being yelled at to carry another platter.

It was very dark outside, with cloud cover obscuring the stars and moon. Her eyes took a few minutes to adjust.

Where is Ehud? Surely he saw me come out the door. He'd better not be playing games with me. I won't be amused.

"Aleah…" It was a whisper, a thread of a sound, but she swung her head in the direction of the voice.

She couldn't see anyone.

"Over here…"

When she moved away from the wall, a hand clamped over her mouth. Two arms circled her, twisting what felt like a rope around her. A scream died in her throat as sweaty fingers bit into her lips. Her struggle ended when she was lifted off her feet by strong arms. A heavy material had been draped over her head, completely covering her mouth and nose but leaving her eyes. She stilled, focusing on each breath.

Obviously, it wasn't Ehud.

With eyes wide open, she was carried down the path away from the palace. In the distance, she saw the flames of a large fire burning in the clearing behind the palace.

A few minutes later, they arrived at the foot of the pyre, where a hooded figure awaited. The strong arms released her, letting her sink to the ground.

The hooded figure wavered before her, his shape undulating in the reflection of the fire.

"Aleah, you have been judged and found guilty. Ehud has failed in his quest for the king, and you must pay the price for his disobedience."

Her mouth opened to protest, but the same large hand clamped over her face.

"The penalty is death." The figure moved away from the fire and disappeared into the night.

A knife slid into her back, taking her breath and sight while she sank to the ground.

H

Figures in black robes with long scarves wound around their faces moved through the streets of Jerusalem under cover of the darkness. They moved imperceptibly and stealthily, unseen by careless eyes. The knives concealed deep within their robes covered hearts even darker than the night.

A soft command from the foremost figure brought the group to a halt at the end of an alleyway. Hand signals delivered orders, causing the group to divide and disappear into the heart of the city.

Cries of anguish split the night air when a woman fell on the body of a man, slaughtered in the street. Rough hands lifted her, flung her aside, and hoisted the body onto powerful shoulders. The slap of sandals reinforced with iron sounded on the roadway. The cries became hysterical, forcing neighbours into the street to face the carnage.

As they watched in horror, the scene was repeated throughout the city.

H

In the palace banquet hall, the noise of celebration had been reduced to guttural snores and discordant gasps. The king prepared to leave the hall accompanied by Moshe, they being the only two to refrain from drunkenness. Amon's eyes were sharp and roving when he called for his servants.

"Awaken these repulsive sleepers and send them on their way." With a flick of his wrist, Amon indicated the ones still in the room. He and Moshe then picked their way through the wreckage of the room, leaving the hall.

"Moshe, we need to be in place to watch the others leave." Amon's lips hovered inches from Moshe's ear. "Let's go to the rooftop garden. We should have a good view from there."

The two men swept through the almost empty halls, ignoring or not seeing the servants who dropped to the floor beside them.

They climbed to the roof, arriving just as the sun began to peek over the horizon. The morning was glorious, with red streaks stretching out across the eastern skyline.

Amon didn't notice the sunrise; he leaned over the railing to watch the palace gates. Two guards stood on either side of them, keeping watch.

"Why are they waiting?" Moshe asked. With his hands cupped to his lips, he shouted to the guards: "Open the gates."

"Moshe, settle down." Amon grabbed his arm. "They're waiting for the shofar to sound."

"The shofar?" Moshe laughed deep in his chest. "They'll have a long wait until the next holy day."

"Oh, they won't have to wait that long." Amon's lips curled back in a grin. "Remember, I'm the king."

Clear, powerful notes blasted from the palace wall and echoed through the streets of Jerusalem. The clear sounds reached the most secret places of the city, alerting the population that something was wrong. People poured from their homes, questioned neighbours and strangers alike, and turned toward the palace. Presently, they began their trek to follow the clarion call. They arrived at the palace gates only to be pushed back by the guards.

The late-night revellers left the palace, moving toward the gates on unsteady feet. Some leaned on each other, stumbling. When the rising sun hit the gates, the light revealed seventeen corpses with severed heads mounted to the wall. The heads were strewn about the lawn. Wailing began when the shock sank in. Women covered their faces with their scarves, bent low to the ground, and searched the corpses for familiar traits, hoping they were not found. Wives whose husbands were not in their beds at sunup approached with dread. Lamentation sprang from the throats of men.

The horror-stricken carousers from the party stopped when they realized that all this had taken place while they partook of forbidden pleasures within the palace walls.

Amon and Moshe lowered themselves to their knees, peering over the edge of the wall.

"This has gone well, Moshe." Amon put his arm around his friend. "You have served me well and will be rewarded for your efforts."

"The people will soon recognize that you are not only king, but Supreme Being. What will the useless priests think of this?" Moshe rubbed his hands in glee. "Yes, wail. You will have many opportunities to perfect the sound in the days to come."

While they watched, the people parted and Hilkiah and his priests moved toward the wall. They looked closely at the corpses, conversing with each other and with some of the men nearby. Hilkiah looked up to the roof, his eyes shaded with one hand. He turned to the priest beside him, gestured, and pointed. The priests, led by Hilkiah, nodded to themselves, then walked through the gates onto the palace grounds.

"Uh-oh, I think it's time we left the roof. I prophesy that you will have visitors." Moshe pushed Amon lightly on the shoulder and the two, bent low, backed away.

"There's no way he could have seen us." Amon stood up when they were too far from the edge to be seen. They made it down the back steps in record time, retreating to Amon's rooms before the priests arrived at the door to the palace.

H

Huldah wiped her brow as she leaned against a small tree in a hollow close to the road. Dust swirled in the brisk wind that had arisen in the last hour, slowing her progress. Deep breaths stilled her swiftly beating heart. Her weary body slid down the trunk of the tree and hugged the bark, scratching her back through her robe.

Just a few minutes. That's all I can afford to take.

Through closed eyelids she was aware of the blaze of the sun and the shadows lengthening on the roadway. The sweet call of an unseen bird stirred her senses; insects chirped in the still air.

It's not far to Jerusalem. I must get there with all speed. Lord, I need help. Speed me on my way. Strengthen my slow legs so I may make good time. God, you're incredible and I'm merely your servant. I know something awaits me, so I ask for the grace to accept whatever comes.

Her eyes opened when she stirred from her position. Once upright, she grasped her bundle and renewed her journey. She lowered her head into the force of the wind while it billowed her robe. The countryside did seem to disappear faster than before. Sooner than she expected, the walls of Jerusalem appeared, reflecting the light of the sun.

Thank You, God, for Your immeasurable mercy.

Before long, she stood before the northern gate. Guards stood stiffly at each side.

The guard on the right stepped into her path, blocking her way. "State your business."

"I am returning to the city after a one-day absence," she answered calmly.

"Your name, please." He threw out his chest and lifted his chin, adjusting his headgear.

She stood tall. "Huldah, wife of Shallum."

"Hey, Gaius, come see who we have here." The guard chuckled as the other guard approached.

The new guard held his head erect, deep lines stretched across a wide forehead. "Control yourself, or we'll both be in trouble." He shook a finger in the first guard's face. "Stop it."

"But Gaius, it's her!"

Gaius peered at her, but made no other movement. He lifted his eyes to the first guard again. "I fail to see the humour. Please enlighten me."

"It's the prophetess. The one who told old Amon off."

"Watch your mouth, my friend. There are spies everywhere." Gaius leaned toward Huldah, looking deep into her eyes. "Is it so, my lady?"

She was lulled by the voice, surprised at its gentle tone. "Yes, it's true."

"Then, my lady, you need to hurry," Gaius said. "You're needed at the palace, I think."

A play of emotions raged through her, but she managed to keep her face stoic. "Then if you'll grant me entry, I'll be on my way."

"Of course." Gaius stood aside, allowing her to pass.

Once inside the gates, Huldah was amazed by the crowds of people, all seeming to be headed in the direction of the palace. Her feet fled over the stones until the palace rose in front of her. With pounding heart, she ran the last distance. She stopped abruptly when her eyes focused on the bodies. Dread filled her.

"What has he done?" Huldah whispered.

Forcing herself to be calm, she began to walk along the wall, searching for the victims' identities. Without heads, it was almost impossible to identify them.

Rounding the edge of the wall, she moved through the gates onto the grassy lawn. The odour of decay hit her nostrils. She forced herself to continue until she stood next to the head of a young woman; she recognized Aleah. Kneeling down, Huldah pushed the girl's damp, bloody hair back from her forehead.

God, this is why you had me return. Direct my steps and my thoughts.

Huldah secured the head in her arms. A shudder ran down her back when she did so, but she felt compelled. Aleah's hair streamed down the front of Huldah's robe. With the head clutched to her breast, she followed the path back through the gate and began to search the bodies for Aleah's.

Oh Lord God, the horror is more than I can bear. Her tears fell on Aleah's dark hair. *This is evil at its worst. Show me the way. What would You have me do?*

Ultimately, Aleah's body was easy to identify, being the only female mounted to the wall. Her servant's robe was filthy and torn, but recognizable. Huldah leaned against the wall beside the body, but did not touch it.

Still holding the head, she turned and walked away from the palace, down through the main street toward the temple. People scampered out of her way. Mothers pulled their children against their clothing and covered their eyes; men turned their heads. Huldah was oblivious to all, her eyes fixed on the temple.

At the entrance, the guard turned toward her, his eyes wide and body stiff. Instead of questioning her, he backed away and allowed her to enter unchallenged.

Inside, the halls were cool and dark. With practiced steps, she turned toward Hilkiah's room.

When she neared, she heard voices in deep discussion—voices of anger and fear. She swept aside the curtain and marched into the room, still holding Aleah's head.

The priests gasped when they saw her, then fell silent.

Only Hilkiah seemed to accept her entrance without shock. He moved toward her, reaching out his hands and accepting the head from her.

"This is Aleah, a palace servant." Huldah stepped back and drew her hands down over her dusty robe. Her knees gave way and she sank to the floor.

"Zephon, look after Huldah, please," said Hilkiah.

Zephon leaned over and lifted her up in his arms, carrying her to a couch against the wall.

Her eyes closed and she sighed deeply. "Water, please."

"Here, Prophetess, drink this." Zephon held a cup to her lips, allowing her to drink her fill.

She sat up once she finished, lifting tear-filled eyes to Hilkiah, who still held Aleah's head.

"We need to bring her body here." Huldah's body shook, but she quickly regained control of herself. "It's the fourth one down from the gate, and the only female. Please, one of you, get it."

The shock seemed to be wearing off, because Zephon and a priest named Beriah jumped to their feet.

"We'll go if we have your permission, High Priest," Beriah said.

With a wave of his hand, Hilkiah dismissed them.

H

The small procession wound its way through the pathways behind the temple. Four priests carried a long box on their shoulders, chanting along with the others in the procession. Hilkiah led with Huldah at his side. Aleah would have a proper burial, unlike the others, who would remain on the walls until Amon gave the order for their removal.

A grassy spot was eventually reached and Hilkiah gave the signal to lower the girl's remains. When the box was set on the ground, Huldah reached in and adjusted the embroidered shift wrapped around the body.

Huldah had insisted on going home to bring back one of her personal pieces of clothing. It had been lovingly stitched by her long-dead grandmother and worn by her and her mother on special occasions. Hilkiah had questioned her choice of garment, but Huldah had insisted; God had moved her to use it.

They had placed her head in such a way that it was impossible to tell at first glance what had happened to her. Her beautiful face was pale and still, never to laugh again and enjoy the life so soon taken from her.

"Why Aleah?" Hoshea turned to face Huldah. "It seems an odd choice amidst the others who were slain."

"I believe it had something to do with her betrothed, Ehud, who's missing." Huldah didn't take her eyes off Aleah. "Somewhere in Amon's twisted, evil mind, there must be a connection."

"Let's begin the ceremony," Hilkiah said, standing at one end of the box while the others gathered around it. He raised both hands high, palms open, and intoned his prayer to God. "Merciful God, we commit Aleah to You. Accept her into Your rest."

The priests, too, raised their hands when they took part in the ceremony. "Merciful God, creator of the universe, creator of man's heart and mind, hear our pleas on her behalf."

Only Huldah remained with head bowed in silent prayer.

When the ceremony was over, the same four priests lifted the box to their shoulders and walked to an outcrop of rocks off the path. A depression had earlier been hollowed into the ground by servants, and now the priests lowered the box into the shallow grave. One by one, the priests lifted rocks from the surrounding area and covered her. When the body was completely covered, Hilkiah prayed once more.

Back in the temple, Huldah and the priests sat in silence.

Finally, Hilkiah looked up. "The last part of the vision has come true. We now know the meaning. 'Darkness is everything; everything is darkness.' Darkness has overtaken the land of the Israelites and God will not be mocked. I fear for the days ahead." His hand trembled. "I hear the wailing of the people in the streets, weeping for their husbands, fathers, sons. But there is no comfort, for it will only get worse."

Huldah stood and leaned against the table to keep her balance. "You're right, Hilkiah. We may be the only ones who are aware of what awaits us, and our awareness is only surface. What lies below that surface, only time will reveal." Her chest heaved with a deep breath. "I must leave you and return to my home."

No one said a word as she slowly walked from the room without a backward glance.

twenty-six

Two heads were bent over an open scroll in a large room off the king's audience chamber. Moshe held the quill while Amon dictated instructions.

"List their names." Amon pointed to the side of the scroll with a long finger. "Yes, just like that."

The king strolled to the window and gazed out into the garden.

"We need to find out what's happening on the streets," Amon said. "Send for the others, and tell them to make haste. I won't be made to wait on their account."

Moshe jumped from his seat, swept the curtain back, and stepped into the audience room.

"Akiva!" he bellowed.

Amon paced the floor while he waited. *Surely now they know who's in control of this kingdom. My power is ultimate.*

"They'll be here quickly, or Akiva will pay," Moshe said, reentering the room.

"Good, good. We will make plans once they get here." He paused at Moshe's shoulder. "Keep writing."

Moshe used a small knife to trim the quill. It had been lying on the table when they started, its blade sharpened to a fine edge. He dipped it in the ink once more and began to write.

The room was silent except for the scratch of the quill.

Amon looked up as Ethan's face appeared inside the curtain.

"We're all here," Ethan said, smiling. "We're at your command, my king."

"Come in, all of you." Amon waved a jerky hand at them. "What's the word in the city?"

Joel and Jotham followed closely on Ethan's heels. They each found a large pillow, then hauled it up to the table next to Moshe.

"You wouldn't believe the distress you've caused." Ethan's laugh bubbled over. "Women are weeping, men lamenting, children wailing. It looks like half the city is standing outside your walls, just gazing on the bodies."

"Have they tried to touch the bodies?" Amon leaned in for their answer, head tilted to one side.

"They tried," Joel spoke up. "The guards were faster than them, and some slashing took place. But they're under control now."

Jotham rubbed one hand over his mouth and beard. "I heard a strange tale."

Moshe swung around to face him. "And what would that be?"

"Apparently Aleah's body and head are missing—"

Amon gritted his teeth. "Go on. Tell me what you heard."

"No one seems to know when it went missing. The guards claim they've been there all the time and haven't seen anyone touch the bodies, but she's gone."

"Huldah." Amon muttered the name, then took a deep breath and held it. He knocked the ink from the table. "What fools! Can those guards not watch the bodies?"

Joel grabbed a cloth and began to clean up the spilled ink. Moshe looked on while righting the bottle and retaining what little ink was left.

"Send for Huldah. I'll have her head in place of Aleah's." Amon grabbed the scroll, threw it atop the spilled ink, then grabbed the table and tossed it to the other side of the room. "Go, one of you. No, *two* of you. Bring her at once. I will not be mocked."

Joel and Jotham ran from the room while Moshe and Ethan jumped to their feet, draped their arms around Amon's shoulders and urged him to be calm. He refused their help.

Amon spat on the floor and wiped his mouth with his hand. "I will not rest until her head is on the gate, and her body on the wall."

H

Bright orange flames lit the night sky over Jerusalem. A stench filled the air, leaving the inhabitants frightened. Rumours shifted through the streets and alleyways in nervous whispers. People moved slowly toward the palace grounds, where the flames seemed to originate. Intense heat and crackling wood assaulted their eyes and ears.

"He's burning the bodies!"

The cry reached the ears of those pushing their way to the front of the crowd. The press of people saw that the wall was barren of the bodies so recently hung there.

The sight was one they would never forget, the horror forever forged in their minds. Soldiers threw logs on the blazing inferno while servants tossed bodies and accompanying heads into the flames.

The priests smelled the smoke and hurried to the scene, aghast at the picture before them.

Talmar leaned on his stick, swaying back and forth as he gazed at the pyre.

"He's desecrating the bodies," Talmar said. Tears streamed into the crevices of his ancient face and disappeared into his white beard. "How can he be so steeped in evil?"

"Darkness is everything; everything is darkness." Hilkiah clutched his chest. "Truly, darkness covers the face of our land this night."

"I think I see Amon approaching from the palace door." Jamin squinted his eyes at the back wall of the palace. "It's him. How does he dare show his face?"

"Because he holds the power." Hilkiah's mind reeled from the sight. "What will happen next? What fresh evil will sweep our land?"

He desired to stride forth and face the king, but he felt held back. His gaze swept the mass of bodies, then moved on to the distraught and frightened people. They fell prostrate before the fire, the sounds of which were dwarfed by the keening of the masses.

Amon chose that moment to appear on a raised platform that had been hastily assembled.

"My people, tonight you have witnessed justice being carried out in our land. These people had to die. Had to die the death of evildoers because they defied their king." Amon paused to adjust his robe. "They shall not have died in vain, because you, my subjects, will learn from their wrongdoing. You will know that your king must be obeyed." A long pause followed. "Must be obeyed on penalty of death. We must rid our land of those who do not practice loyalty to their king."

With hands folded in front of his chest, and head pointed straight ahead, he waited.

"Long live the king." The words rang out from somewhere in the crowd. Others took up the cry until the night was filled with the sound.

Hilkiah tried to see who had started the cry. He suspected it was one of Amon's cohorts.

The king bowed his head, accepting the tribute from his loyal subjects. He stepped forward and raised his arms out over the crowd. Silence fell again.

"Go home, my people. Go home and obey your king."

The crowd turned and moved out through the gates, much slower than they had entered; their slumped shoulders indicated their defeat. Amon and his advisors re-entered the palace once the people had all turned to go.

At last, only the priests were left. They stood before the waning flames, not much more than a pile of ash by now, and bowed their heads.

"Merciful God," Hilkiah prayed, "we commit these, Your children, into Your hands. We know that You can raise them again in the last days and take them unto yourself." He lifted his eyes to the heavens. "And God, forgive the offense of Your people against You."

The priests then turned toward the gate and followed the last of the mourners into the darkness.

H

"Where is Huldah?"

The king's scream appeared to freeze the blood of the small group crowded into his bedchamber.

Joel sank to the floor in front of Amon. "We were not able to find her, oh king."

Amon snapped his body around to face Jotham. "And...?"

"We've looked everywhere." Jotham stood his ground and stared into the eyes of the king. "If she were in Jerusalem, I promise we would have found her."

"First my wife and son disappear, and now the prophetess is gone. Have I only incompetent fools in my service?" Amon's body swung around again, this time to find Ethan. "Lock them up."

"But Amon..." Ethan began.

"Now."

Ethan and Moshe quickly escorted Joel and Jotham from the room, leaving the king with saliva dripping from his open mouth.

H

Moonlight fell over the grass while a dark, hooded figure glided along the path to the burial site. Jagged edges of stones were visible in the reflected light. The figure headed for the largest group of rocks and slipped behind them, then bent to peer into a depression in the side of a low hill.

"Our God is good," the figure whispered.

A woman crawled out from the rock and embraced the dark figure. "Shallum, you've come."

"Of course I've come." Shallum hugged his wife; he never wanted to let her go. "Oh Huldah, circumstances are not good."

He reached up and pushed her hair back from her face.

"I know, Shallum. God has visited me, and I know I must go away for a while." Huldah bent into his embrace, laying her head on his chest. The two stayed in that position while in the distance small animals scampered about their nightly rituals.

"I know you need to go, but I'll miss you so." Shallum buried his head in her hair, kissing the top of her head. His fingers lingered on her face. "Where will you go?"

"I'll go back to Bozkath. I think I'll be safe there."

He stiffened, trying to still his beating heart. "You may be right, but it's such a long distance away."

"I know, but you can come and visit."

"I'll come as often as I can. I will have to be discreet, so as not to give away your location."

Oh Lord, how can I let her go? he wondered. *Only through Your power.*

He struggled to his feet and lifted her with him. He clung to her. As they embraced, a cloud passed before the moon.

"I need to tell you something before I go," Huldah whispered.

Shallum leaned in to catch every syllable. "What is it, Huldah? What's wrong?"

She caressed his face. "It's not something wrong. It's something very right."

He thought he detected a smile in her words.

"Shallum, I am with child."

He gasped, gripping her arms. "Truly, Huldah? Truly?"

"Truly, my love. That's why it's even more important that I go somewhere safe, to protect our baby."

He kissed her gently, then leaned back with his arms still around her. "We should leave. Let's waste no time putting the city behind us."

"We?"

"Yes, we. And that's an order from one very happy, yet sad husband."

Hand in hand, they slipped through the night, leaving Jerusalem behind them.

H

Early morning light filtered through the slats on the window behind Hilkiah's back. Slumped over the low table in an exhausted sleep, dreams troubled him. Emotions flicked over his face, muscles twitching and eyes fluttering. Soft moans accompanied the twitches. The other priests had gone to their beds well past midnight and had not yet appeared this morning.

The heavy drapery covering the doorway slid back, revealing the face of Benjamin, his eyebrows drawn together. In his hand, he carried a steaming cup and a small bun of fresh bread. He allowed the curtain to close behind him.

Lingering near the door, Benjamin cleared his throat.

Hilkiah sat up abruptly and shook his head to clear the remnants of sleep. His half-closed eyes struggled to focus.

"Benjamin, is that you?" The High Priest's voice was still thick with sleep.

The servant shifted the cup to his other hand and moved to the table, setting the two items before Hilkiah. "Yes, master, it's old Benjamin. Here, I've brought you warmed wine and fresh bread to break your fast."

Hilkiah glanced at the offering and felt a pang hit his stomach. "I don't think I can eat, Benjamin, but I appreciate the gesture."

"You must eat something. Take a sip of the wine." Benjamin held the cup to the priest's lips.

Hilkiah took the cup in both hands and sipped the warm liquid. "You're right. I'll need the sustenance for the problems of the day."

The priest picked up the bread, broke off a small piece, placed it on his tongue, and chewed thoughtfully.

"It's good, Benjamin. After last night, I wasn't sure I'd be able to eat again." He bowed his head in remembrance of the awful night, with the fire and burnt corpses. And the arrogance of the king. "Would you summon the other priests for me?"

"Indeed. I'll rouse them right away." Benjamin's feet shuffled across the floor and out through the curtain.

Hilkiah chewed slowly, not tasting the food as his mind circled around the events of the last few days.

Lord, what am I to do? I'm your chosen one, but I feel helpless in the face of so much evil. How can I, an old man, fight against the might of the king?

With a cloth from the table, Hilkiah wiped his lips and fingertips, then set the cloth back on the table when he finished.

Remember Huldah's words.

The thought filtered through his reverie. What had Huldah said? That the king's time would be cut short.

Voices from the hallway told him that the other priests had arrived. He stood on shaky legs to greet them. Once they were seated and quiet, he reached for a small scroll, unrolled it, and looked over the contents.

"I made some notes last night after you left. We need a plan, and this is what I propose." Hilkiah's hand shook as he glanced at the writing before him. A sandal rustled, a throat cleared, but not a word was spoken. "We have been amiss in our duties. Since it is the month of Tishri, and we are near the Day of Atonement, we should rally the people and bring them before God for forgiveness."

Beriah began, "But the king—"

With watery eyes, Talmar turned his gaze on Beriah. "Will even the king dare stop this most important of festivals?"

"We have to try," Zephon said. "The king may want to stop us, but we'll have the element of surprise." The young priest leaned forward, his eyes bright and clear. He reached out and touched the scroll. "Let's go ahead and make our plans. I, for one, am tired of the king's arrogance."

A priest named Nimrah jumped from his seat. "I'm with Zephon."

"Quiet," Hilkiah cautioned. "If we're going to do this, secrecy will be important. What do the rest of you say? Talmar?"

"Yes, yes, of course. We have to try." Talmar's hands fluttered, but his voice was strong.

"Jamin?"

"If the rest of you are willing to put your lives on the line, I'm with you."

"Beriah?"

"How could I say no? Yes, I'll be with you."

"Then listen closely to my plans."

Dark young heads bent with elderly white ones while Hilkiah outlined his thoughts.

When at last they were satisfied, Hilkiah rose and faced them once more. "We have one week to put our plans into action. Then we put our lives on the line, in a public place, where the king will have easy access to us. Like Queen Esther, we say, 'If I perish, I perish.'"

twenty-seven

After the bonfire, Amon kept to his rooms, meeting with Moshe from time to time and playing a game he had developed using pebbles and boxes with Oded, one of the servants. The game was complicated and well beyond what the servant could comprehend, but Amon kept at it, poking him with a stick when he wasn't able to follow the play.

Food from the previous meal still lay on gold trays scattered on small tables. Amon hadn't allowed Dor to clear the room; instead he had threatened the boy with death if he didn't leave at once. A very frightened looking Dor left the room and hadn't been seen since. Amon smiled to himself when he thought about it.

Footsteps in the outer room alerted Amon that Moshe had returned. The king gathered up the game and gave Oded a good push. "Get out, but be ready when I call you to come back. Be quick about it."

Without a backward glance, Oded scurried through the entrance, almost colliding with Moshe, who was on his way in.

"Take it easy there, slave. The house isn't on fire, is it?" Moshe grinned, showing all his teeth, and allowed a deep guttural laugh to escape his lips.

"Enough of that, Moshe." Amon shoved a cushion toward Moshe with his foot. "Sit."

Moshe let his body collapse on the pillow and drew up his knees in front of him. He blinked a few times, taking deep breaths. "You should have been there."

"You know I couldn't. That's why I sent you."

"I know, I know. It was just such a pleasure to see their fright." Moshe hugged his knees to his chest. "Everyone is talking about you and how you have so much power. I sense a new respect for you, perhaps born out of fear, but there nonetheless."

"Do you think they're aware that this is only the beginning?" Amon asked.

"Actually, I don't think so."

"Good." Amon relaxed his muscles and leaned back against the wall. "They'll not be expecting tonight's onslaught. We are ready for tonight, I presume."

"Oh yes, we're ready." Moshe snapped his fingers. "The crew can barely contain their glee to unleash more destruction on the populace—and, of course, to feel the gold in their hands."

"You have the list with you?"

Moshe reached inside his robe and flourished the small scroll. "All here and accounted for. Everyone knows their part. When the day is spent and night is at its deepest, they'll strike."

"Well done, Moshe. Together, we're formidable." Amon stood, stretching his arms and back. "Bring the others and we'll have an early celebration."

"Have you forgotten that you have Joel and Jotham locked up?"

"Let them out," Amon said. "Huldah is probably a witch, anyway. She'll turn up. They always do."

Moshe left the room, leaving Amon to brood by the window.

Something tells me I need to watch Moshe, to be on my guard. For now, I still need him, but that may not always be so. Everyone is dispensable.

H

The High Priest sat alone in his room, head in his hands, deep in thought. The others had long since left him to begin their preparations for the Day of Atonement. A troubled spirit moved inside his chest while he turned the plans over and over in his mind.

Will the people respond and turn from their wicked ways? Or is the power of the evil King too much for them? Is it too risky to openly defy him?

Intense heat sifted in through the window. A buzzing fly circled the room, finally settling on a dusty scroll on a shelf high above the priest's head.

Even the shuffling of Benjamin's feet was lost on Hilkiah until the curtain moved aside. Hilkiah's shadowed eyes lifted when Benjamin leaned into the room. He cleared his throat.

"Master, you have a visitor." Benjamin's gnarled hand gripped the curtain, exposing wrinkled skin stretched over swollen knuckles.

Hilkiah shook his head to clear his thoughts. "Who is it, Benjamin?"

"His name I know not, but he guards the palace gate and seems friendly enough." Benjamin came the rest of the way in, dressed in a dishevelled robe and muddy sandals. A streak of mud stretched from hem to waist.

Hilkiah couldn't stop the amusement that showed on his face. "Where have you been, Benjamin?"

"Ah, master, it's been a hard morning. The palace shepherd lost control of his flock and I… well, let's just say I was in the path."

As Benjamin wiped a hand over his face, another gob of mud clung to his cheek.

"Show the guard in and get cleaned up," Hilkiah said, fighting the urge to laugh. "I'll need you this afternoon."

He gestured for Benjamin to leave and welcomed the guest, who entered on Benjamin's departure with his head and knees bent low.

"Rise, please," Hilkiah greeted his guest. He indicated a bench for the guard to sit. "I recognize you from the gate. I believe you spoke to me the other day. Am I correct?"

The guard slumped down on the bench, his head in his hands. "You're right. I did speak to you." His voice was muffled and came through his fingers. When he lifted his head, his eyes were drawn together tightly as though in great pain.

"What troubles you?" Hilkiah asked.

"I hear things. Things at the palace. Things I'm not supposed to hear, but sometimes I can't avoid it."

Hilkiah waited, letting the guard take his time. Taking the seat across from the guard, Hilkiah leaned on his elbows, supporting his chin with his folded hands.

So much trouble. So much hurt. Where will it end?

"The massacre…" The guard sighed deeply. "I heard rumours about a killing, but didn't believe them. There wasn't anything I could do about it."

The guard's eyes wandered the room, seemingly looking for answers on the shelves of scrolls. They ended up back on Hilkiah's face.

"But it's not over," the guard said. A tremor ran across his shoulders.

"Tell me what you've heard." Hilkiah kept his voice calm, not wanting to upset the man more than he already was. "Did you hear more rumours?"

"Yes, yes. The servants are agitated, and there is much unease in the palace." Another deep breath. "Some say Ehud is dead, and that's why he hasn't returned. More frightening are the whispers that this isn't over."

Hilkiah leaned forward and gripped the guard's arms. "Does anyone know you've come to me?"

"I don't think so, but it's hard to trust anyone. Hard to know who's the enemy."

The two men sat quietly while the everyday noises of the temple seeped in through the closed curtain. Voices conversed, a lyre played softly, and sheep bleated. All were unaware of their impending doom.

"What is your name?"

"Noach."

"You've been very courageous to come to me," Hilkiah said. "I'm not sure what you hoped I could do, but I appreciate the information. Are you willing to come to me with any rumours you hear? It will be dangerous, but it may save someone's life."

Hilkiah waited, watching Noach's reaction. Satisfied with what he saw, the priest leaned closer, lowering his voice. "Is there anyone else who can be trusted?"

"Yes, one other guard," Noach said. "I'm not certain about the others. Some seem trustworthy, but these are troubling times and loyalties are easily compromised."

"Then go, my son. Trust no one other than the one person you're sure of. Keep your ears open and come to me when you can."

Hilkiah kept his eyes on Noach as the guard rose from his place and left the room.

The curtain fell back into place, but still Hilkiah did not move. His eyes closed, but every pore in his being was aware of his surroundings. He sensed the evil pressing in on the kingdom.

Dark days are ahead. My vision was true. Darkness is everything... He gasped when it hit him, his eyes flicking open. *The vision wasn't true! It appears that everything is darkness, but God is light.*

Hilkiah rose from his bench and walked to the window, staring out at the brightness of the day. He let his lips stretch in a smile.

Yes, the days are evil. The king is evil and will do much damage to our land and its peoples, but God is sovereign—always was and always will be. I cannot forget that.

H

The noonday sun glared down on the weary travellers. Shimmers of heat radiated from the rocks along the roadway while Huldah and Shallum passed. Birds were silent, having long since fled to the distant trees, seeking respite. Wave after wave of wildflower fragrances swept over the road, causing the two to inhale deeply.

"I love the smell of the flowers." Huldah paused in the middle of the dusty road and lifted her nose, taking deep breaths. Until she stopped, she hadn't realized how tired she was getting. She shrugged her shoulders to ease the muscles.

"Let's stop in the shade over there." Shallum pointed to where a cluster of tall bushes threw shadows on the ground.

Once they were seated side by side, Shallum opened the pack he had carried on his back and lifted out the meagre food portions he had put in the sack before going out in search of Huldah.

"I'm sorry, my love," he said. "There's not much here."

"There'll be enough, I'm sure. It won't hurt us to have a bit less while we walk. We have water, and that's far more important." She unwrapped the packages and pulled out a small loaf of bread, olives and dates, and a handful of nuts. Her laughter rang out. "Shallum, there's plenty, you foolish man."

"I do believe you're mocking me."

This only made her laugh all the more. Huldah wiped her eyes on a tiny cloth she carried in her sleeve. She watched her husband closely, enjoying this special time together.

"It's good to laugh," Shallum said, pulling her close and kissing the top of her head. "This will make a happy memory we can hang on to while we're separated. Now, let's eat before it gets cold."

"Oh, you are so funny today." She reached for his hand. "I'm going to miss you so much."

"It'll be a difficult time for both of us, but God has a plan." He broke the loaf in two, held one piece in each hand, and lifted them to the sky. "Lord God, know that we're thankful for all good gifts from You. Keep us safe until we are together again."

He handed one piece to Huldah and took large bites from the other.

When they resumed their quiet walk, they walked close together, arms touching as though to absorb strength from each other.

Before the sun was low in the sky, they arrived in Bozkath. Jedidah was overjoyed to see them and welcomed them into the family home.

Shallum stayed the night, leaving when the sky was turning pink. It was hard to say goodbye, but Shallum promised to visit as often as he could until it was safe for all of them to return to Jerusalem.

H

Music floated from an inner room of the palace when Amon and his advisors drew near. The court musicians had been summoned to play while the king dined with his friends. It was a small room, perfect for an intimate celebration. Ornate designs worked in gold decorated the walls, and scattered through the room were screens of gold and silver, with decorations of lilies. Palm trees fashioned from bronze and copper stood in the corners. Light from the candles reflected off the screens, creating a burnished glow.

Servants quickly set platters of steaming food before the king and his four friends, then filled the goblets with red wine.

"I see we are dining on your favourite meal, Amon," Moshe said, bending over a platter and taking a long sniff. "Ah, I detect lamb."

"And onions and garlic and leeks, I would guess." Ethan leaned in for a closer look. "Are those pomegranates?"

"They had certainly better be." Amon scanned the platter. "And it must have dill, too, of course."

Not bothering to give thanks for the meal, the king was the first to scoop food for himself. The others followed, their plates heaped not only with lamb but also the cucumbers bathed in olive oil, cumin, and mint.

Joel laughed and popped a piece of lamb into his mouth. "This is a feast fit for a king!"

The five young men celebrated while the sun slowly receded and darkness came to the streets of Jerusalem, a darkness deeper than the night and wider than the imaginations of men could comprehend.

H

Shadows crouched against brick walls in alleyways. A watchman called from the palace wall that all was well. Street noises diminished until even the slightest cough could be heard—but still the shadows remained motionless.

Sharon Dow

At the sound of a soft whistle, the alleyway became alive and bodies shuffled along the wall toward the door of a house. With a terrifying cry, the door was broken down and intruders poured into the home.

All over the city, the scene was repeated until the streets ran with the blood of innocent men. While they lay dying, the perpetrators of the evil slipped away into the dark reaches where no one would find them.

ℋ

Once again, the sun rose on a scene of carnage which could not be explained. Mothers, wives, sisters, daughters, and grandmothers all wailed in mourning while they kneeled beside their slain loved ones.

The party in the palace had long since disbanded, and four of the five were sleeping off its effects. Moshe alone was alert, having not slept. He'd gone out of the palace in the dead of night to witness the slaughter. He now entered the palace gates.

He slipped through the quiet hallways to Amon's door, which he pushed gently, entering the room. Snores and heavy breathing greeted him. He curled his upper lip in distain.

I don't know why I put up with this brood of snakes. They disgust me, especially the so-called king. I could easily dispense with him, but the time is not yet right.

Moshe moved through the room, stepping over sleeping forms until he stood beside the king's bed. Amon was sprawled on his back, his mouth open, with drool slipping from one side. He was still arrayed in the clothes from the party, now wrinkled and dirty.

And this is the king? God help us all.

"Amon, wake up." Moshe's voice was insistent. He placed a hand to the king's shoulder, shaking him vigorously.

That got a response.

"Leave me. Leave me if you want to keep your head." The king's words were muttered, but their intent was clear.

Moshe shook his shoulder again. "And I tell you to wake up."

Amon's eyes snapped open. "Who dares... oh, Moshe, I didn't know it was you." He scrambled to sit up. "Well, is it finished?"

"Of course." Moshe shrugged his shoulders. "What did you expect?"

"True. You wouldn't dare come back if it didn't happen." Amon swung his feet over the edge of the bed. "Ah, parties are great while they're happening, but they leave a bad taste in your mouth the next day."

"Only if you eat and drink too much."

A laugh escaped the king. "You're a wise one this day, Moshe."

The others stirred and soon the room was filled with talk as they discussed the results of the night's raids.

"What will happen with the bodies this time?" Ethan asked.

Moshe snorted. "Even as we speak, military men are loading them onto flat carts for dumping outside the gates."

"Outside the gates?" Joel's eyes grew round. "Really?"

"I'm not in the habit of lying." The words seemed to be ground out through Moshe's teeth.

"Me thinks the man needs his sleep," Amon chided. With a slap to the shoulder, Amon pushed Moshe toward the door. "Go, and come back when you've had some rest and you're in a better frame of mind."

Moshe heard the laughter when he thankfully left the presence of the King. *I need to be more careful. He's right about one thing: I do need sleep.*

On his way home, Moshe paused to watch carts pass through the city gates, followed by a throng of street dogs, tongues hanging out and barking wildly. When the bodies were dumped, the dogs were all over them. Moshe could watch no more.

twenty-eight

The priests moved among the people, comforting where they could, supplying food where needed, binding self-inflicted wounds that some of the women had suffered, and praying for all. Hilkiah was sick at heart, but he tried to minister to the needs of the people. He had been awakened at dawn with the news of this latest massacre and been on his feet ever since.

At one point, he found himself working beside Amaziah. The two men hadn't seen each other for some time, for Amaziah had been out of the country visiting relatives and making arrangements for his youngest son to move in with them. They nodded to each other and walked off to the side of the road, where they could speak quietly.

"Amaziah, it's good to see you back." Hilkiah patted the younger man's shoulder. "The other priests and I have missed you at our meetings. Your input has been sorely needed."

"Thank you, Hilkiah. I am glad to be back. My wife is ill again and the household has fallen into disarray." Amaziah wiped his forehead with the edge of his sleeve. "The situation in the city has really heated up since I've been gone."

"It's a sad time for Jerusalem, and I fear it's only begun. There is evil afoot in our city, corruptions greater than what we experienced under Manasseh." Hilkiah shook his head sadly. "But tell me about Jairus and the plans you've made for him."

"Ah, how I've wronged him over the years." Amaziah's lips pinched together in a frown. "He's not like me at all, and I took that for weakness. He's a strong man, though he has different ideas and interests than I do. My sister's husband is a worker in gold and silver and has agreed to have Jairus work with him. It's a good fit for both. The couple has no children and welcomed him with open arms."

"We will pray that all goes well for Jairus."

"Yes, please do." Amaziah paused to take another deep breath. "But as for my daughter, do you know where she is? My wife tells me she is not in Jerusalem."

"I wasn't aware that she had left, but I'm not surprised." Hilkiah put his hand on Amaziah's shoulder. "Don't worry, God has her in His hand. I believe He has great plans for her. She'll appear when He's ready for her."

"Shallum appears to be missing, too. His father seems to have some idea of where they are, but he's not talking." Amaziah turned his face away from the High Priest, lowering his head to his chest. "I know God has her in his hands, but being her father, I feel like I've lost her."

Hilkiah gripped his shoulder. "Amaziah, in one sense you have lost her, but in another you've released her to do an important work for God among His people. We're going to hear more from her. I've sensed that she's going to do something remarkable that will become part of our heritage."

Amaziah's eyes opened wide. "What makes you think that?"

"Let's just say it's an old man's musing, but I keep tuned in to God. I believe He's going to use her in ways we can't even imagine."

"Thank you." Amaziah's voice was soft and low. "You've made this separation easier for me. I'm proud of her. Unfortunately, I can't take any credit. All I did was put her down and try to instill fear in her."

"But God used that to meld her into the person He needed her to be." Hilkiah stared into the distance, praising God for Huldah, and for her father's redemption. "Now it's time to get back to work and help where we can."

The two men joined the group of mourners, bringing comfort and promises of proper burials at sundown.

Hilkiah shuddered on the inside when he made the promises, for fear Amon would burn these bodies like he had before.

H

Flashes of light caught Shallum's eyes and he knew he was nearing Jerusalem. He quickened his pace, anxious to see what had transpired in his absence.

The king scares me. Peace has left Jerusalem. Working in the palace is no longer a pleasure. I don't have to see the king most days, but the possibility is always there.

Movement caught his eye at the same time he heard the sound of barking dogs. He craned his neck to see what was happening, but only the usual gate activity was discernible—camels laden with bulging saddle bags, a young shepherd boy leading his flock, merchants hurrying out to do business elsewhere, a farmer's empty cart returning from a distant market.

But that wasn't what had caught his attention. Dogs were an ever-present part of the gate scene, but not such frantic howls as these. When the camels passed him, Shallum could see guards hovering to one side of the gate, keeping onlookers from approaching that which they guarded. One soldier drew his sword and slashed a cloak from one man's shoulders, causing the others to draw back, heads together with arms and hands gesturing rapidly.

"Something's wrong," Shallum told himself. He gathered his robe in one hand and began to run.

Within a few paces of the gate, the smell hit him. It was like a physical blow. Blood; it was the smell of blood. That would account for the frantic activity of the dogs, which now ran in circles just beyond the soldiers. Shallum slipped to the side while the soldiers looked the other way, dealing with a group of angry men.

When Shallum saw what was on the grass, he stopped. His stomach lurched in its haste to dispose of the lunch he had consumed on the way. He staggered, then backed away from the awful sight. He slipped into the city unseen by the guards.

As he neared the palace, planning to pass by quickly, a servant ran toward him, holding up a hand to stop him.

"Shallum, the king has been asking for you." The servant stopped in front of Shallum and panted for breath. "Come with me. Come quickly, for the king is in a foul mood."

With reluctant steps, Shallum fell in beside the servant.

The two entered the cool interior of the palace, their sandals treading lightly on the smooth marble floor.

The splendour of the halls belies the rot within.

Shallum could hear loud voices coming from the king's chambers. His heart constricted when he thought of the coming meeting. He had hoped to avoid it until he was in a better frame of mind, but the king had to be obeyed.

The doors into the foyer of the king's suite flew open and Joel and Jotham fled from the room, a pillow following their progress along with angry shouts.

172

"…and be grateful you're not chained in the holding cells again!" The two didn't pause in their flight. "If I see you again today, I'll not be responsible for what happens to you."

When Shallum's escort entered the room, he bowed low before Amon. "I have brought Shallum, my lord."

"Shallum… ah, then you have done a good thing." Amon's eyes grew round, his voice coming out in a purr. His eyes flicked to Shallum. "Come in, Shallum. Just the person I wished to see."

The king extended a welcoming arm.

"The rest of you, leave me!" Amon shouted. "Except Ethan."

The others scurried away through the open doors.

Once the door had closed, Amon swung his body around to face Shallum. "Where is she?" His eyebrows drew together as he folded his arms.

"I presume you are referring to my wife." Shallum kept his voice calm, knowing that riling the king wouldn't be in anyone's best interest.

Spit flew from Amon's mouth. "Who else would I refer to?" He took one step closer to Shallum. "Where is she?"

Forcing his shoulders back, Shallum lifted his chin and looked the king directly in the eyes. "Begging pardon, Your Majesty, but I'm not at liberty to say."

Red spread up Amon's neck and his nostrils flared. "Ethan, me thinks the man wants to lose his head. What think you?"

"My lord, that would not be wise." Ethan moved to stand beside Amon, putting his hand on the king's arm.

"What has wisdom to do with this, I ask you?" Amon asked. The only sound in the room was the grinding of his teeth.

As the silence stretched between them, Shallum breathed slowly and prayed rapidly, not for himself, but for Huldah. He was willing to give his life to protect her and his unborn child, should that be necessary.

Amon stepped back and let his arms fall to his side. "Oh, keeper of the wardrobe, your life is spared for now, but know that I'll be watching you with a hundred eyes, in a hundred ways." His narrowed eyes seemed to bore holes into Shallum's face. "Go, before I change my mind."

Shallum bowed low before the king, and with great dignity walked from the room.

H

Two heads were bent over a scroll resting on a flat rock in front of Huldah. Next to her sat Josiah, his dark curls uncovered. Huldah wore a white linen headdress, bordered in blue and held in place with a twisting strip of matching blue cloth.

"Look at the letters again, Josiah." Huldah lifted his hand and placed one of his fingers on the scroll.

He bent his head and traced the letters with one finger. "א Alef, ב Bet, ג Gimel, ד Dalet." Raising his eyes to meet hers, his lips stretched wide. "I did it, didn't I?"

"Yes, you did. I'm very proud of you."

Huldah let her eyes roam over the garden. It was peaceful here, but her mind refused to leave Jerusalem for long.

"Huldah, why do we have to stay here? I like my grandparents and their house, but I want to go home." Josiah's head rested on her shoulder. He sniffed, wiping his face on his sleeve. "Why can't we go home?"

"Josiah, I'm going to tell you some things that I hope will help you understand why you must stay here." She turned to face him. "I want you to be very brave and listen carefully. Can you do that?"

"Yes, of course I can." He shoved his hair back from his face, straightened his shoulders, lifted his small chin, and looked her in the eyes. "I'm six, you know."

Her lips couldn't help but curve upward. "I know you are."

"I'm ready, Huldah."

"Josiah, you know that your father is the king."

"Everyone knows that."

She nodded, wondering how much to tell him. "Do you remember your grandfather?"

"I heard about him, and my mother says that I saw him once. But I don't remember." He ran a hand across his forehead as a frown appeared. "My mother said he was wicked. Is that true?"

"Yes. I'm afraid it is."

"Is my father wicked, too?"

She watched his face as he scrunched his nose. "What do you remember about your father?"

"I didn't see him very often. He was busy. But when he did come, he didn't say much to me. He always yelled at my mother. That made me feel sorry for her, for it made her cry." A tiny tear escaped, but he swiped it away. "Is it bad to say I was happier when he didn't come?"

"No, it's not bad," Huldah said. "Do you remember anything else about him?"

"Only what I overheard people saying."

"What did you hear?"

"A couple of the servants said he was a cruel man. What's it mean to be cruel?" He looked at her with questions in his eyes.

O Lord God, how do I answer this child?

She looked around and saw a small grasshopper sitting on the branch of a nearby bush. "Josiah, do you see that grasshopper?"

"I see him."

"What would you think if I caught him and pulled off his wings and legs one by one?"

His lower lip stuck out in a pout. "I would say you were mean. Very mean."

"You would be right. Another word for that would be cruel."

"I understand." With both hands over his mouth, he widened his eyes. "Would my father do that?"

"I'm not sure what your father would do, but because he is cruel and wicked, we must keep you here so you'll be safe."

Josiah looked into the distance, as though trying to see the future. Huldah could feel his thin shoulders shake.

Huldah brushed the curls back from his forehead. "Do you know that you will be king one day?"

"My mother told me, but she said it would be a long time, that I would be older than she is now."

Reaching her hand to his chin, she turned his head to look at her. "Listen carefully, Josiah. You will be king before you reach your mother's age, or even my age."

His large eyes stared at her, then lowered to the ground. "How do you know?"

"I know because God has revealed it to me."

"Does that mean He told you?"

"Yes, that's what it means." Would he accept that, she wondered?

175

"But… but how can I be king? I'm only six, and I don't know any-thing about being a king."

"I'm going to help you, that's how." Huldah slanted a smile his way and was rewarded with a tiny grin. "We'll talk every day that we can. But the first thing I want you to know is that you don't have to be a wicked king. Would you like to be a good king instead?"

His little chin started to tremble and he put his hand in hers. "Yes, please. I don't want to be wicked or cruel. But I don't know how to be a good king."

Huldah rubbed her hand over his silky curls. Her eyes scanned the horizon. She marvelled at the beauty of the day and wondered how God could continue to display the wondrous works of creation when man's heart had turned so cold against Him.

While she watched, a figure appeared in the distance, walking along the old road that approached the village from the north. It wasn't much more than a path these days.

The figure was bent, with a bundle on his back. Huldah speculated that he had come a long distance and was weary. He held a rough stick in his right hand and appeared to lean heavily on it. While she watched, he paused and looked around. His sleeve served for a towel with which he vigorously wiped his forehead. His bundle then slipped to the dirt and he slid down to rest on it.

She rose from her place on the bench, drawing Josiah up with her. "Tell your grandfather that I wish to speak with him in the garden."

She gave him a gentle shove.

"Why do you want to see him, Huldah?" he asked, standing his ground.

"Josiah, a good king also needs to learn obedience. Please do what I've asked."

His eyes fell. Turning quickly, he fled toward the temple where Adaiah would be at this time of day.

Very soon, Josiah returned with his head held high and holding the hand of his grandfather.

"What is it, Huldah?" Adaiah asked, walking as quickly as his stiff knees would allow.

She waited until he was close before replying, then she lifted her arm and pointed toward the traveller. "Is that someone you know from the vil-lage? It seems strange to see someone coming from that direction."

Adaiah shielded his eyes while turning to peer in the direction she pointed. "I don't recognize him as one of the villagers. We don't see many strangers."

Jedidah and Johanna entered the garden, strolling up beside them.

When Jedidah looked in the direction they indicated, her body stiffened and she clasped her hand over her heart. Her face paled. "It's Ehud. The king has found us."

twenty-nine

"Into Your hands, I commit their spirits. Almighty God, You are the giver of all good gifts. You are the protector of all Your children. We have sinned against You."

The priests circled the shallow depression where the bodies had been laid. There were seventeen bodies, all men, all innocent of wrongdoing, all guilty of expressing their dismay at the new king, and all silenced.

Outside the circle of priests, a small crowd had gathered—wives, mothers, children, and neighbours, all grieving their losses. The keening stopped once Hilkiah took his place before the grave. Only an occasional sniffle could be heard in the gathering darkness. Soon it would be night, but the glow of the setting sun touched the pile of stones ready to cover the grave.

Hilkiah was surprised these bodies hadn't been burned. Guards had collected the bodies in carts and unceremoniously dumped them outside the city gates where street dogs had been permitted to ravage them. Guards were positioned at the side of the carnage to keep people away, guards who were still standing where they had been all day. The priests and families had watched helplessly as the carts moved through the streets, falling in behind them in a procession of grief.

The people had been held back from the slain men until dusk approached. At that point, the guards took up positions at a distance, allowing Hilkiah and the others to move in to view the bodies.

Hilkiah circled the gruesome sight and sighed audibly. *God, why did this have to happen? I marvel at the resilience of these people who have spent their afternoon collecting rocks to cover their dead.*

When the last beam of light touched the graves, Hilkiah gave the signal for the mourners to cover the bodies. Rocks rained from the hands of the people as they covered their loved ones. It was a fitting monument, stones from the soil of Judah to cover the sons of Judah.

A shout was heard from the watchtower on the gate. All eyes turned to see.

"Danger approaches. Run for your lives!"

Every guard was on alert when a horde of people burst through the gates carrying torches and stout sticks. They swarmed the guards, who quickly became helpless amidst the rioters. Like a flood, they surrounded the mourners, using their sticks as clubs, striking out at everyone within their reach. Cries of pain and helplessness shattered the air while mourners fell to the ground, bleeding from open wounds. The smell of smoke blended with the odour of spilled blood. The darkness was broken by flickering torchlight.

Hilkiah tried to spirit his people away, but he was struck on the shoulder by a man whose face was hidden beneath a scarf, concealing all but his eyes. When Hilkiah went down on both knees, he was grabbed by the shoulders and hauled away. Other arms grabbed him until he was carried to safety. His rescuers lowered him on a grassy area. The sounds of the carnage were muted here, but shifting lights reflected the chaos in the distance.

Three men, each a stranger to him, sprawled on the ground beside him, eyes riveted on the scene outside the gates. From their vantage, two figures appeared on the wall, one clad in a long robe and the other completely engulfed in a hooded cloak.

"Look, it's the king," one of the strangers said. He rose to his feet, pointing toward the figures.

The other two joined him, shading their eyes and peering into the darkness.

"How can you tell from here?" one asked.

"I'm sure it's him. No one except Amon has that stoop to his shoulders. He's responsible for the mob. You can count on it."

"There is much evil afoot in our land," the third man ventured. "And I agree, the king is behind it."

Hilkiah hadn't yet regained his breath to thank the strangers for rescuing him. He watched where they pointed while they moved off for a closer look. They disappeared into the darkness without him being able to get their names.

He raised himself to a sitting position and rubbed his shoulder to check for injuries.

"I think I'll live," he muttered to himself as yet another man approached him. He was relived to see that it was Zephon.

Zephon leaned down. "My master, are you all right?"

"Yes, yes. I'll be fine." Hilkiah continued to rub his shoulder, flexing it back and forth to ease the pain. "Where are the others?"

"Beriah is helping them back to the temple. I came to find you."

"But what about the mourners? We can't just leave them." He grasped Zephon's hand and struggled to his feet, dusting off his robe.

Zephon's strong arm took him by the shoulders and they began to move. "Most of them have fled back into the city. I think the guards have the situation under control. They've chased the mob away. There's nothing else we can do tonight."

Hilkiah stopped short, fear flashing in his eyes. "The gates… they'll be closed."

"No, no, it's fine. The guards have kept the gates open until everyone gets back in safely. But come, we must make haste. They'll only keep them open so long."

Without further talk, the two stumbled through the grass and along the stony path. When they neared the gates, only the guards' torches could be seen, throwing long shadows on shallow graves only partially covered with stones. Victims lay close to the graves, still alive but bruised and broken. When Hilkiah and Zephon passed, they saw friends lifting the fallen and assisting them through the gates.

$\mathcal{H}$

Several heads bent over the table in Hilkiah's study room at the temple. Talmar held the quill and looked around at his peers, his eyebrows raised.

"How will we go about getting the message to the people that we're planning a day of national repentance?" Talmar asked.

"We must be very careful. If the king finds out, he'll put a stop to it." Hoshea breathed deeply, his shoulders lifted.

All the priests were present, with Amaziah having joined them for the first time since returning from his journey. The tightly drawn curtain covered the entrance, and Benjamin had been posted on the other side, cautioned to alert them if anyone came near.

"Fellow priests, you are right," Hilkiah said. "No word of this must reach the palace. After the second massacre, we know that no one is safe from the wrath of King Amon."

Hilkiah's gaze lingered on each of his priests, weighing their faithfulness and courage. His restless hands were clasped together in front of his robe.

"I need to ask each of you a question. We're putting our lives on the line by planning this day, and I would have you search your hearts and decide whether you want to be a part of this. I know you all agreed to this, but that was before the second massacre. I won't hold it against any of you should you decide not to participate. Make the decision now and we'll excuse any who feel they can't proceed. It will be better for you if you don't know the details."

In the silence, Beriah and Nimrah looked down into their laps, considering Hilkiah's words.

Zephon threw his shoulders back and raised his chin. "I'm in."

Amaziah shifted his position on the bench. "Will it really matter? Won't we all be accused, even if we're not involved?" He shrugged, lifted his hands, and looked at Hilkiah. "I'm in, too."

"I'll be a part of this, of course," Talmar's whispered in a raspy voice.

Jamin nodded. "And I, too."

Hoshea gave a little laugh. "Me too."

This left Beriah and Nimrah. The silence stretched as Hilkiah gave the two some time to make their decision. Sandals scuffed the floor and distant voices filtered in from the rest of the temple.

Beriah lifted his head, took a deep breath, and put his arm around Nimrah's shoulders. "I think I can speak for both of us. I admit I'm afraid, but I want to be a part of this. I believe Nimrah does, too."

Nimrah raised his head. His face, though pale, looked calm and at peace. "Yes, I want to be involved."

Hilkiah felt the tension leave his shoulders and back. They were all in, every one of them. It was more than he had expected.

H

Huldah turned to face the others who were staring at the approaching man. "Please, all of you go inside and bar the door. I will go out and meet him."

Adaiah started to protest, but she silenced him by shooing him away. "God will protect me. And if He doesn't, it will be His will for me. Now, go."

Jedidah grasped Josiah's shoulder as they all moved toward the door of the house.

"Lord, my life is in Your hands, as it always is," Huldah said. "Your will be done."

Clasping her hands loosely in front of her, Huldah took the first step onto the path where Ehud walked slowly toward the village.

Ehud's head was lowered, but after several minutes he lifted his eyes and met hers. He stopped when she had almost reached him.

"Ehud, what brings you here?" Huldah called. "I'm hoping you have come in peace."

Upon hearing her voice, Ehud slipped to the ground on his hands and knees and put his forehead in the dirt. His shoulders shook and Huldah wondered if he wept.

She knelt beside him. "Ehud, please sit up. I'm not here to harm you." She gently shook his shoulder. "Please, tell me why you're here."

The commanding tone in her voice roused him and he sat back on his legs. His tear-streaked face looked at her, covered in grime from the journey.

"Ehud, speak to me," Huldah said, growing alarmed. "Nothing is so bad that you can't share it with a friend."

"I'm no friend…" His words came out in a gasp. "You don't know; you don't understand." His face fell to the earth once again.

She rested her hand on his shoulder and felt the tenseness there. "I know more than you would think, Ehud. Please, sit up and tell me everything."

He rose and Huldah took his arm to lead him to a nearby rock. He sat with shoulders slumped and took a deep, ragged breath.

"I have sinned, Huldah, sinned against you and God and others." He finally looked her in the eye. Gripping her hand, he sobbed. "I'm a broken man."

"Ehud, try to tell me the story from the beginning."

"Aleah…" He steadied himself with an intake of breath. "I was pledged to marry Aleah, but the king planned to send me on a long mission with the army. Aleah asked him to let me stay. I didn't want her to do that, but she insisted."

"Go on, Ehud. What happened?"

"It didn't go well, and he sent her from the room before she could even voice her request. He must have known what she wanted, because he sought me out later that day. He's a cruel man." Ehud faced Huldah. "He told me to watch you day and night. If you left Jerusalem, I was to follow and kill you."

Huldah let no emotion show on her face, even though the words were a shock.

"When you left the palace with the others, I was overcome with glee. Not only would I get you, I'd get the royal family, too. The king would be pleased also, since it is common knowledge that he hates his wife and wants another heir." Ehud sniffed, wiping his nose with his sleeve. "I thought it would bring me happiness and a swift marriage to Aleah. Oh, how wrong I was. When you turned back from the path, I knew my life was over." He rubbed his hands over his eyes. "You must hate me."

"That's not true."

"At first I was just going to disappear, but then I thought I could sneak back into Jerusalem and convince Aleah to run away with me. I soon found out that Aleah had been murdered, and there was a price on my head. I ran. I've had many days to run, many days to contemplate my part in all this, and many days to ask God to forgive my sins. I didn't know where to go, but somehow your face wouldn't leave me. I thought maybe God was directing me to you, and here I am."

Huldah sat deep in thought. Why hadn't God revealed to her that Ehud was coming?

Can I believe his story? Is he still working for the king? If I take him in, will I put Josiah and his family in further danger? The thoughts tumbled over each other. *What should I do, God?*

But God was silent today.

She stood and walked away from him. Lifting her face to the sky, she searched for an answer in air above her. Nothing.

God, You must want me to make this decision myself. I trust that You won't let me walk into danger and bring the others with me. I'm going to offer forgiveness, just as You offered it to me.

She turned back to Ehud, who was sitting with his head in his hands. "Ehud, please look at me."

Slowly, he raised his eyes to hers.

"I'm going to offer you my forgiveness, since I know God has already given you His."

Ehud struggled to his feet, his dirty hands gripping the top of his walking stick. "That's more than I deserve. I'll do whatever you want me to do." He bowed his head.

"Then you will come to the house with me and we'll tell your story to the others."

Ehud's eyes widened as though in disbelief.

"They must make up their own minds. I cannot decide for them." She reached out her hand to him. "Come. I'll be right by your side. I'll tell them that I have forgiven you and that you have my complete trust."

Side by side, they trekked to the house.

$\mathcal{H}$

Amon and Moshe walked atop the palace roof. Nearing the edge, they leaned on the low wall and looked out over the city. It was midnight and they heard the guard's clear call. Stars overhead spread a carpet of sparkling jewels through the blackness of night. A soft breeze ruffled their robes, releasing the fragrance of tree blossoms. All this beauty was lost on the pair.

Amon turned his gaze on Moshe. "The next event must be even more shocking."

"That would make sense. Do you have a plan?"

"I have several. This next plan will set me apart from all those who came before me. I must be the ultimate king." He slapped his hands on his chest, his eyes glittering in the pale light.

"If you have the courage, we can shock this city into a weeping mass of horror," Moshe said. "You will be supreme. No one will be able to turn from you. You will be all-powerful, a god come to earth."

Their laughter floated out over an unsuspecting city, over people asleep in their beds.

thirty

*M*oshe sat hunched over a dark wooden desk, positioned before a window overlooking a busy thoroughfare. The quiet of the night was broken only by the occasional bark of a dog or the shuffle of a late partier as he headed home after an evening of dissipation. Light from the oil lamp shed a feeble beam over the surface of the desk, which threw the planes of his face in stark relief.

Moshe stirred. His furrowed brow, beads of sweat, and worried forehead betrayed that all was not well with the king's closest advisor.

After a time, he arose from his seat and paced the small room, seven steps along each side of the room, six across the ends. With his hands behind his back and shoulders bunched forward, he made several circuits of the room before seating himself at the desk again.

My life is like the view from my window, he thought. *Dark and empty.*

A deep sigh accompanied his thoughts. "There's danger afoot in this city, and I'm in the centre of it," he said to himself. "Moshe, be careful."

A discreet knock sounded on the door. He quickly snuffed the lamp and rose from his seat. Placing his ear on the door, he waited.

The faint knock sounded again. This time, he heard a voice, almost a whisper: "Freedom."

Moshe silently drew back the bar on the door and allowed it to open wide enough to let his visitor enter the room. The two gripped shoulders, greeting each other.

"Close the shutters," his visitor commanded.

Moshe hurried to the window and drew them closed. Once secure, he lit the lamp and opened his mouth to speak.

"No names, my friend," the visitor said. "Names have a way of finding the wrong ears."

"Yes, you're right. Please, sit while we talk." Moshe indicated a stool drawn up beside his seat at the desk.

The visitor sat and removed his headscarf, revealing a weathered although still young face crowned with a dark, unruly beard with curly locks. When he smiled, large discoloured teeth filled his mouth with the exception of two noticeable gaps.

He leaned forward on the stool and looked at Moshe from deep-set eyes. "I hear rumours."

"What is being said on the street?"

"Ah, you don't want to know."

"I *need* to know." Moshe reached out one hand and tapped the visitor on the chest. "You are my ears and eyes outside the palace. Speak."

The visitor gave a low chuckle. "There will be a price to pay. Information is not free."

"I'm well aware!"

"Lower your voice or I'll be gone before you can rise from your bench."

Moshe took a deep breath, ground his teeth, then let out the breath in a sigh. "You will be paid. Gold pieces, I know."

"Now we're talking a language I understand." The visitor folded his arms over his chest. "The talk on the street. Yes, interesting. Rumour has it that the king is evil. No surprise there." He shifted his body, leaned forward, and looked directly into Moshe's eyes. "Rumor has it that he has to die."

The words hung in the air between them. "Are there any plans or plots?"

"No, not yet, but it's only a matter of time."

Moshe rubbed his hands together, over and over. "Then we must be certain to be first. It must be done right, or not at all."

The visitor's eyes widened. "You have a plan?"

"Not yet, but the time has come to contemplate one." Moshe drew in his shoulders and glanced around the room. Shadows bothered him. He knew no one else was in the room, but darkness made him uneasy when he spoke of treason. "The assassination of a reigning monarch is not to be taken lightly. Our lives will be on the line."

"Not my life. Yours. I'll be gone long before anyone knows what has happened." His lips stretched in a wide grin that showed all his yellow teeth. "But you, my friend, are a different matter."

Moshe swallowed. He knew the visitor was right, though he didn't like to think about that. "There's much work to be done before the day arrives. The timing must be right, the heavens must give their blessing…"

"The heavens? You believe in God now? You shock me."

"No, not God. There are other sources."

"You're going to consult a witch, aren't you?"

"My plans are my own, until I need to include you." Moshe stood abruptly. "I'll pay you the first installment, and then you must be gone from my house."

Moshe reached into the desk and withdrew a small leather pouch. He extracted five gold pieces, thrust them into the visitor's hand, and ushered him to the door. Once it was barred and the light extinguished again, he felt at peace.

H

Following Huldah into the house was the hardest thing Ehud had ever done. He remembered all the times his life had been in danger on the battlefield or in hand-to-hand combat. Nothing compared to this, a confrontation with these people he had so blatantly wronged. What would they think? How would they react to him?

He kept his head down and his hands loosely clasped in front of him. His heart raced so fast, he could feel the beat in his chest. His dry mouth made it difficult to swallow, and a lump seemed lodged in this throat. Sweat trickled down his back under his dusty robe, making the fabric stick to his body, a very uncomfortable feeling, he decided.

Adaiah looked up from the table where he was sorting through an assortment of small coins. "Hello, Huldah. Come in and introduce your friend." His voice was low and even, betraying no hint of fear or anger.

"I would like the others to join us." Huldah moved further into the room, approaching Adaiah.

Ehud saw what he thought was the first flick of fear in Adaiah's eyes. He couldn't blame him. Jedidah knew who he was and had likely shared that information with her father. At last, he rose, brushed the curtain aside, and entered a side room.

The silence stretched long while Ehud hovered near the door, wondering if he should bolt or face the condemnation he knew was coming.

A soft gasp from the other room riveted him to the floor. He lifted his eyes when the curtain parted and Jedidah slipped through.

"Huldah, is this necessary?" Jedidah asked, her voice trembling.

"Please, Jedidah, trust me." Huldah stretched out her hand, palm up. "Tell the others to come."

Jedidah faltered, then turned and waved her hand into the other room. Soon her mother and father joined them, followed by Johanna and Josiah. When they had found seats, Josiah sitting on the floor beside his grandfather, Huldah backed up to stand beside Ehud.

They all stared at Ehud.

"As you know, this is Ehud, from the king's palace in Jerusalem." Huldah rested her hand on his arm in a comforting gesture. "He has a story which you need to hear. I want you to know that I have forgiven him, but each of you must listen and decide for yourself whether you can believe, and more importantly, whether you can forgive."

Ehud's feet felt like quarry rocks. Both hands were wet with sweat. For a moment, he could not speak, but then he felt the breath of God on his face and lifted his eyes to those he had wronged.

"I... I must tell you my story. It is tragic and violent, threads of an empty life were it not for the ministrations of our God."

He proceeded to tell them the tale he had told to Huldah.

Chava kept her head down throughout, weeping quietly, wiping her face on a square of cloth crumpled in her hand. Her husband patted her hand, as though he needed to not only comfort her, but also keep himself calm. Joanna wailed at the beginning, until Jedidah wrapped her arm around her and whispered in her ear.

Josiah never took his eyes off him. Ehud was aware of the boy's bright gaze. It unnerved him at first, but then it seemed to give him courage.

When Ehud finished, he dropped his hands to his sides and lowered his head. Whatever would come, would come. He had no more control, nothing more to say; he could only wait for their decision.

The group seemed to be stunned by his revelations and unhappy story. No one moved, until Josiah stood and walked toward him. His eyes were wide as he gazed at Ehud.

"I believe you and I forgive you." The words hit Ehud with the impact of a fist to the gut. "I'm only a boy, but I know I want to be a good king, and I think a good King would forgive."

Then Josiah did something unexpected: he knelt before Ehud and lowered his face until his forehead touched the ground in front of Ehud's feet.

The gesture completely undid Ehud. His face tightened as he tried to stop the tears he knew were coming, but they came anyway, forging deep rivers down his cheeks and disappearing into his unkempt beard.

Jedidah rose from her place beside Johanna and came to her son. "My son has a wisdom far beyond his years. He has recognized a good man, and I stand with him. You are believed and forgiven."

Ehud's shoulders shook with emotion. This was far more than he deserved, but oh so refreshing to his troubled spirit.

Adaiah cleared his throat and stood. His eyes rested on his wife for a moment, then shifted to his daughter and grandson. He, too, came forward, stopping beside Ehud and placing his hands on the man's shoulders.

"God has truly been at work in your life," Adaiah said. "Far be it from me not to recognize the hand of God and welcome you into the fold." He wrapped both his arms around Ehud in a welcoming embrace.

While Ehud wept, Chava and Johanna knelt beside Jedidah and Josiah. Huldah lifted her hands over the heads of all of them, closed her eyes, and began to speak:

"Praise the Lord, O my soul; all my inmost being, praise his holy name. Praise the Lord, O my soul, and forget not all his benefits—who forgives all your sins and heals all your diseases, who redeems your life from the pit and crowns you with love and compassion, who satisfies your desires with good things so that your youth is renewed like the eagle's."

Psalm 103:1–5

Ehud's knees began to give way and Huldah led him to a chair. Food and drink were placed before him and he slaked his thirst and filled his belly, which had been empty for so long. The others gathered around and conversation flowed.

"We will need to make plans for the future," Jedidah said, broaching the topic that had been in his mind for many days. "You will not be able to go back to Jerusalem while Amon is king."

"Yes, but you aren't responsible for me. I'll move on and find work somewhere." Ehud knew sadness permeated his voice, but he couldn't seem to speak without it.

"I think it *is* my responsibility. Besides, I want to help you." Jedidah tilted her head and put her finger on her chin. "In fact, I think you can be of service to us."

Ehud's hand paused, still holding the wedge of bread he was about to consume. "You would let me be of service to you? Mother, I would count it the highest privilege to serve you and your son."

"Then it's settled." Jedidah sat back. "Father, do you have a place where Ehud can stay? There is no room here."

Adaiah rose from the table, nodding his head. "I know just the place. At the back of the temple is a little room we've used for storage, but it's almost empty. I'm sure we can make a comfortable room for him there." He made eye contact with his wife. "Wife, can you supply bedding, a basin to refresh himself, and cloths for drying?"

"Of course, my husband. Johanna and I will find what's needed and bring them to the temple." Chava rose, placed her hand on Johanna's shoulder, and left the room with the servant.

"Come, Ehud," Adaiah said. He moved toward the door while Ehud stared at his back. "We'll find wood for a bedframe."

"You're among friends now," Huldah said. "No need to fear anymore. Once this family accepts you, they will pour out their hospitality on you. I also think you may be more help to them in the coming days than any of us can foresee. Go, my friend. You are in good hands."

H

"Not a whisper of this to anyone," Amon said.

Amon and Moshe's robes swished around their ankles, their cloaks fluttering in the strong wind. The two men traversed the path that led from the palace to the gates of the city.

A new moon hovered near the horizon, spreading its pale ray of light along their way. Dark clouds scudded just above it, occasionally covering its feeble beam with inky darkness. The silhouettes of trees and shrubs crowded beside them in eerie silence.

"It is the only way to get her back into the city," Amon said, keeping his voice low. "Then we seize her."

"It will be done as you suggest."

"Suggest?"

"Sorry. Command."

At the divide in the path, Moshe turned to the left and Amon swung back in the direction of the palace.

H

Singing reached Amaziah's ears before he opened the door of his home. What a change had taken place here in the last few months. Salome was happy for the first time in many years; he knew her previous sadness had been his doing. But no more. God was good and was allowing him to regain her love and trust.

She turned her head toward her husband when he opened the door. "Greetings, Amaziah."

Salome stirred the pot of vegetables and meat as she slanted a smile in his direction.

He walked to her, wrapped her in his arms, and leaned his head against her. "You are such a joy to me. I can't believe I wasted so many years."

She put a finger over his lips. "Hush, husband. That is over and forgotten." She ran her hand through his beard and snuggled closer to him. "Let's just rejoice in the future and in the anticipation of our grandchild's arrival."

"I can't believe we're going to be grandparents again." He rubbed her back while she stayed in his arms. "What's in the pot? It smells good and I'm hungry."

Laughing, she turned to stir the contents once more. "Leave it to a man to always think about his stomach."

Lot and Malachi came in while Salome dished up the fragrant stew. Bread still warm from the oven rested in a basket on the table. The two older sons pulled their benches close to the table and reached for the bread at the same time. Malachi laughed and let Lot have the basket first.

"What news is there in the city today?" Amaziah asked, addressing his sons.

"Rumours are flying again. I've never seen so much unrest in the city." Lot dipped his bread in the juice from the stew and stuffed the whole thing in his mouth at once.

"And it's so quiet on the streets," Malachi said. "People are afraid to express their displeasure, even afraid to talk to friends, because no one knows who will tell the king and chop goes their head." He hit his hands together in a chopping motion.

Salome turned pale. "Is it really that bad?" She pushed her bowl away, apparently having lost her appetite.

Amaziah pushed it back in front of her. "Eat, Salome. You don't want to get sick again. And don't worry about the rumours. That's all they are at the moment."

"I heard that the king has planned more killings," Lot said without looking up from his bowl. "That last one was gruesome. I watched them load the bodies on the wagons. Sick."

Amaziah gestured at them to stop their stories; he could see that Salome was shaken by them. "Enough about the killings. There must be more pleasant topics."

"Did you hear about the fight my friend Amos had with one of the guards?" Malachi asked. "Amos actually drew blood and—"

"Enough. If you can't find a better topic, we'll eat in silence."

Once darkness settled in and the house fell silent, Salome slipped under the blanket of their bed.

"I'm scared, Amaziah," she said. "I don't know where Huldah is, and our sons are so vocal I'm afraid they'll get into trouble."

"Rest, Salome. We can't change what is happening. We can only hope it doesn't touch our family."

While the rest of the household slept, Amaziah stared at the wall, wondering what would happen to their family when the Day of Atonement ceremony came. The king wouldn't be pleased, and there would be trouble.

I pray to God that we'll escape the horror that follows the sacrifices.

His last thought before he fell into a troubled sleep was to wonder if he would survive the slaughter.

part three

Three months later

thirty-one

The house was quiet while Salome rested on the couch beside the hearth. Her mind lingered on her daughter and the baby to come.

How wonderful it will be to hold a little one in my arms again. It doesn't matter if it's a boy or a girl, as long as it's healthy.

She recalled the babies she had helped bring into the world. The male babies were guaranteed special attention from the fathers, but a girl often had to struggle on her own, except for the ministrations of her mother.

Maybe Huldah will stay with me for a while after the baby comes, or even next door at Tikvah's, his other grandmother's. At least I'd be able to see and hold him. Why do I keep thinking it will be a boy? Her mind wandered as she drifted closer to sleep.

She didn't hear the door open or see the figures slip into her home.

Rough hands covered her mouth and others grabbed her, wrapping what seemed to be a large piece of cloth around her body.

Alert and terrified, she was unable to make a sound. A smaller piece of cloth was stuffed into her mouth and tied behind her head. When they finished, she could neither move nor speak. Her heart pounded beneath her robe.

What is happening? I can't breathe. I'm going to pass out. No, no, I'm going to stay awake and fight while I can.

No words had been spoken between the intruders, but they didn't seem to need to communicate. One of them looked out the door through a narrow opening and beckoned to someone outside. It was the last thing she saw. A hood was pulled down over her head.

Strong arms lifted her body, and they moved her toward the door. After a sharp rap on her head, she knew nothing more until she felt her body being thrown to the ground. She landed on what felt like a straw pallet. A door clanged shut, and then all was quiet.

She wasn't sure how long she lay there before she heard the rattle of a chain and the door opened again. Hands grabbed her, pulled the hood from her head, and she looked into the eyes of one of the king's advisers, Moshe. Another face came into view and she drew in her breath sharply.

It was the king!

She hadn't anticipated the slap that hit her face with a stinging intensity. The king leaned over her. She felt evil emanating from him.

"Where is she?"

The words struck with almost the same force as the slap. She was so startled that she couldn't speak.

Moshe stepped forward and slapped her again. This time, she felt her neck twist.

Again the king leaned over her. "Where is she?"

"Who, my lord?" she asked, managing a feeble gasp. She wanted to look away, but his gaze was so intense.

The king grabbed her arm and twisted it until she cried out in pain.

"Your daughter! I said, where is she?" he demanded.

Tears escaped her eyes and ran down her neck. "I... I... don't know... I really don't know." She sobbed, gasping for breath.

"I don't believe that," Amon said. "However, we do know where two of your sons are. We can easily rid you and the world of one of them. Perhaps that will help your memory." He leaned even closer, until his nose almost touched hers. "Where is she?"

"I don't know, I don't know. Oh please, don't hurt my sons. They don't know, either! Please believe me. We don't know where she is."

Amon spit in her face.

From somewhere deep inside her, a spirit of defiance rose up. She lifted her head as far as she was able. "And even if I did, I wouldn't tell you."

The two men looked at each other when she sank back down on the pallet.

"It's time," the king said.

Moshe nodded and left the cell, followed by the king.

When two guards entered, she knew her life was over.

195

H

Ehud and Huldah sat in the garden, heads together and deep in conversation. Behind them, Jedidah and Josiah entered the garden, hand in hand. Although a brisk breeze blew in from the east, the garden felt warm from the strength of the rising sun. Birds warbled in the bushes. Doves cooed mournfully from their perches along the wooden fence lining one side of the garden. A hawk circled overhead on spread wings, looking for his morning meal.

Josiah pulled his hand from his mother's and twirled, eyes on the drifting hawk. While he watched, the hawk hovered, then plunged to the earth in the adjoining field. It rose majestically in the air with a small creature in its claws.

Josiah clutched his chest, his jaw dropping open. "Mother, did you see that?"

Jedidah shaded her eyes with one hand and looked where he pointed. "Yes, my son, I see it. What does it have in its claws?"

"I couldn't tell, but it was small." He stood rooted to the spot, watching the sky until the hawk disappeared. "I love watching the birds. I wish I could fly."

Josiah raised his arms and ran along the garden path. The three adults laughed at his antics until he came back and sat at their feet.

Huldah reached down and ruffled his hair. Josiah loved her and the attention she gave him. He knew he could trust her. He pulled his lips back in a wide grin and beamed at her.

Their conversation floated over his head, but he was not paying attention until he heard the word *Jerusalem*.

He turned to face them, eyes wide and eyebrows raised. "Jerusalem? Did you say Jerusalem?"

Their talk stopped.

"Yes, we're talking about the events in Jerusalem," Huldah said.

"You don't need to be concerned. We're safe here." His mother leaned over and squeezed his shoulder. Her smile seemed forced; he could tell she was afraid.

He blinked at her trying to assure her that he was fine. "Mother, I'm not afraid."

"You're very brave, Josiah." Huldah took his hand in hers and drew him nearer. "Do you have any questions, Josiah? Asking questions is how you'll learn to be a good king."

Light sparkled in his eyes. "I may ask any question I want?" he asked, for he had discovered that adults sometimes didn't mean what they said.

"Of course. Anything."

He took a deep breath. "Then I want to know if my father is still alive."

"Yes, your father is still alive. Why do you ask?" Huldah ran her fingers over his chin. "Are you afraid something has happened to him?"

"No, not afraid. I remember that you said he would only be king for a short time."

Josiah watched their faces. He knew they often thought he was playing when he was really listening. His mother looked like she was going to faint.

He stood and walked to her side, throwing his arms around her neck. "It will be fine, mother, you'll see."

Her arms tightened around him, and he wished he could go back to snuggling in her arms. He was too big for that now. That was the problem with growing up; you had to give up so many special things. Not that he was old, but some days he felt old.

He stood again. "May I ask another question?"

"Ask as many as you like," Huldah said.

"Then this question is for Ehud." Josiah watched a red flush begin at Ehud's neck and disappear into his hairline. "Will you help me when it's time to go back as king."

He knew he had shocked Ehud, and he was sorry if he caused him pain, but he needed to know the answer.

Ehud slipped off the stool and bent down beside Josiah. "I would count it a privilege to go to Jerusalem with you. I'll help in any way I can."

"That's all I needed to know. Thank you." Josiah jumped up from his place and spun off to the end of the garden path, watching doves scatter as he approached the fence.

H

Huldah's face paled once the boy had gone. She rested her hand on Ehud's shoulder. "Do you know the position you've put yourself in?"

He bowed his head and then shook it. "I know I've put my life on the line, but it gives me great pleasure to do anything I can. I'll even sacrifice myself to make amends for my past wrongs."

She kept her eyes on him. "You will not see Jerusalem again."

H

The stone altar to a long-forgotten foreign god rose skyward on the outskirts of the market. After a long night of searching for his wife, Amaziah and Zephon arrived at the altar.

Before Amaziah closed the distance between himself and the altar, he knew the bulge jutting from the top was what remained of his wife. Throwing himself to the ground, he shrieked in agony, beating the ground with his fists.

Zephon approached the altar. A sign over the battered body read "Don't lie to the king." The letters were bold and appeared to have been written in blood. He stood before the body, head bowed and hands behind his back.

The keening behind him stopped when Amaziah pulled himself to his feet.

"I will weep no more, Zephon, until this king comes down from the throne of our Fathers." He stared vacantly at the body. "I will devote my life to bringing down this traitor, this imposter, this pretender. He is no son of David."

Amaziah lifted one hand toward his wife.

"You, my love, will understand. You have always seen the troubles of our nation. I will find our daughter, and together we will defeat this murderous beast."

He turned from the grisly sight and walked away.

H

The buzz of voices drowned out the priests' prayers as Hilkiah led them toward the stone altar. Amaziah could not be found, so the priests set off without him to pay their respects to the dead and commit her into the hands of God. Guards had surrounded the altar, hands gripping swords ready for any attempt to remove her.

When the priests were nose to nose with the guards, a shout went up from the crowd and they surged forward, pinning the priests against the guards. When the first guard raised his sword, a knife materialized in the hands of a hooded stranger, who plunged it deep into the guard's exposed neck. Blood spurted and the guard fell, only to be trampled and hauled through the press of people.

The crowd cheered when they sensed a break in the line of defence, armed with clubs, knives, rocks, and improvised weapons. Hands grabbed Hilkiah and the other priests, hurrying them off to the side, out of the range of the rioting mob.

High-pitched screams split the air while wave after wave of angry citizens swept toward the fallen guards. Flashes of red, blue, white, and purple bobbed in and out of the crowd. Their turbans and headdresses toppled, fabric ripping as hand-to-hand fighting broke out.

At last the guards were annihilated and the crowd's anger subsided. Gradually the mob dispersed, rushing through the streets of the city while their cries drifted in the early morning air.

Hilkiah lay facedown on the rough ground, moaning a prayer to God. The other priests huddled nearby, their faces pale with horror after witnessing the senseless slaughter.

Talmar and Jamin leaned against each other.

"That I should have lived long enough to see this wanton evil and destruction." Talmar wiped tears from his eyes and looked toward the heavens. "Oh, Lord God, where are You? Your heart must be broken upon seeing the sin of Your chosen people."

"They've left their God and chosen evil, like so many before them." Jamin was dry-eyed as his eyes lifted to Salome's undisturbed body.

Hoshea knelt beside Hilkiah. "My lord, will you rise with me?"

Hilkiah allowed Hoshea to help him to a standing position and leaned on him to cover the shaking in his hands and shoulders. He faced the carnage before him, cringing when he saw the broken bodies.

"The guards were obeying orders," Hilkiah said. "I know they serve an evil king, but they are not all in agreement with him. They obey to protect their families, and their own lives."

Hilkiah moved toward the altar, the others following behind him.

Zephon shook his head and turned to Beriah. "I fear this will incite the king to greater wrath. The city will suffer for the deeds of this day, no matter how justified the people were in their actions. What can we do?"

"We must wait for Hilkiah's direction in this." Beriah's eyes remained fixed on the splayed guards. "We want to gather Salome's body, but I'm not sure how."

When they reached the altar, Hilkiah stopped to assess the scene. "Come, my priests, gather around me and we'll do what we can."

When they were all in place, the High Priest raised his hands toward the sky.

"Merciful God and Father of all mankind, forgive us our sins this day. Lift the evil from our land in Your time and show us the way."

Hilkiah lowered his hands and pointed to the four youngest priests. "You four, check the guards to see if any still live. We'll wait for you here."

They scattered to do his bidding, bending over bodies to check for signs of life. When they completed their assessment, they returned, shaking their heads.

"No survivors," Beriah reported.

"Then gather around me and we'll commit Salome's body to God," Hilkiah said. "We cannot remove it from the altar and give her a proper burial, but God can do all things."

They stretched out on either side of Hilkiah, raising their arms in prayer. The stench from the bodies was almost overwhelming, but a burial commitment had to be completed according to their traditions.

"You are all brave men," Hilkiah said once they were finished. "God will honour you for your faithfulness. We don't understand what is happening, but we serve the living God and must trust Him to make all things plain and fulfill His purposes. But we must leave, for word of this will soon reach the palace. The repercussions of the deeds of this day will reverberate through the city in waves of evil intent, the like of which we have not yet seen."

Hilkiah turned and led the way from the altar. Even then, shouts could be heard approaching from the direction of the palace.

thirty-two

Amon paced the length of his throne room while his advisors reclined on embroidered silk couches, their eyes on him. He paused before them, eyes wide with anticipation.

"We've got her." The king clapped his hands together. "She'll come now, and when she does, we'll be ready. No prophetess will be allowed to get away with what she has done. And I believe that when we find Huldah, we'll find my wife and son. I'm sure she's the key to their disappearance."

Ethan let out a peel of laughter and punched Joel in the shoulder. "Did you hear that? She'll not get away with it. No, she won't."

Amon started intently at Moshe, almost afraid that his luck was too good. "Moshe, are the plans in place?"

"Yes, Your Majesty. I have spies on every gate. She'll not get in the city without my knowledge."

The king pressed for details. "And once she is sighted? What then?"

Moshe rose from the couch, his brows pulling together in a tight knot. "She will be brought to you immediately. Never fear, my lord. All is in order and will be done as you have commanded." He bowed before the king.

"I'm not liking your attitude, Moshe. Is there a problem?" Amon stroked his chin whiskers.

"My apologies, oh king. I have not been sleeping well."

"I will accept your explanation. For now." The last was muttered under Amon's breath, but was heard by all.

Moshe hunched his shoulders and turned to the window overlooking the garden.

Amon rolled his eyes, but kept his thoughts to himself. *I'll need to keep a sharp eye on Moshe. For now, no one can accomplish what he can. These others are a bunch of fools.*

The room became very quiet, allowing them to hear two guards push through the door into the king's presence. Amon noticed that their faces were pale and their eyes had a wild look.

"What gives you the right to come in here?" Amon's voice was edged with scorn.

Both guards fell prostrate before their king.

Amon scowled at them and in a thunderous voice commanded them to rise. "State your business."

"There's been a massacre in the city," one guard managed to say between breaths.

"A massacre? I didn't order a massacre." Amon snapped his finger in their faces. "Explain yourself."

While the story was told, Amon sank onto this throne and breathed deeply. He let nothing show on his face.

When the guards finished, the king stood and pointed to the door. "Leave my presence."

The two guards backed out of the room. Once the door closed, Amon faced his advisors.

"This cannot and will not go unpunished." He began to pace again. Moshe left the window and joined the others on the couch. "We must regain control of the city. The people cannot treat their king this way!"

His voice rose several notches until he was screaming. When he began to pull at his hair, Moshe ran to his side and led him from the room. The others followed, and they walked through the marble corridors of the palace, scattering servants and slaves.

When they gained the private suite of the king, they put their heads together and planned their retribution. The people would pay.

H

Although guards were posted throughout the city, the people were restless. Groups of angry men swarmed the streets, defying the guards to attack. Surprisingly, the guards ignored them. The people's numbers swelled until the streets were choked with sweaty bodies, everyone shouting obscenities to the king.

Women and children huddled in their homes, fearful to venture into the streets and go about their daily business. The marketplace stayed open, though the odour from the fallen guards had spread through the laneways, causing many to cover their mouths and noses.

A lone woman pushed her way through the crowds and entered the marketplace. Her robe was long and a nondescript colour. She pulled her hood down over her forehead. A dark scarf covered her mouth and nose, obscuring her features. Over her arm she carried a basket, the contents covered with a clean cloth. She paused at one stall and leaned in to speak to the owner.

"I need to purchase some thyme."

"Yes, of course. How much would you like?" The man kept his eye on her, squinting in the hot sun to see her better.

"Two gerahs, please." She fumbled inside her basket and withdrew a small coin.

He took the coin in his rough hands and held it up to the sun. Satisfied that it was genuine, he lifted a clay jar from beneath the table and scooped a small amount on his scale. After adding another scoop, he wrapped the spice in a torn piece of cloth and handed it to the woman.

She shoved it into her basket, and without a word of thanks left the booth and moved through the marketplace, emerging close to the stone altar. The sight that met her eyes almost deterred her from her purpose, but she took a deep breath, gritted her teeth, and proceeded to the base. She ignored the death all around her, having eyes only for the body still atop the altar.

Setting her basket down, she removed the cover to reveal a small jar of cinnamon mixed with cloves, another jar which contained a small portion of myrrh, and a long piece of white fabric. She removed the top from the jar of cinnamon and cloves, opened the package from the merchant, and shook the thyme leaves into the mixture, gently mingling them with her fingers.

Esther bowed her head and prayed for God to receive her neighbour, Salome, the mother of her daughter-in-law Huldah. It had taken great courage for her to come, but her heart had told her she must do what she could.

But how will I gain access to her body?

While pondering the problem, she heard military sandals approach.

"Woman, what are you doing here?" The soldier's voice was gruff but contained a degree of respect.

She kept her head down, her hands gripping the handle of the basket. "She was my friend, and I must honour her body."

He turned from her, exchanged a few words with a fellow soldier, and both quickly approached. They scaled the rocky side of the altar, then lifted the body between them. Others saw what they were doing and ran to assist in lifting Salome down.

Once they regained the ground, the first two soldiers laid the body close to where Esther was standing.

"Do what you wish to do, but quickly. We have our orders and must obey." The soldiers moved away, watching while she knelt beside her friend.

Tenderly, Esther shook the contents of the jar over Salome, praying while she worked. When she was finished, she shook out the fabric and covered what was left of her friend. Stepping back, she looked up at the soldiers to indicate she was finished.

They swept to the altar in military precision, causing Esther to fall back. A fire was soon lit and the bodies, including Salome's, were consumed in the flames.

Even after the soldiers left, Esther remained. She stayed until the fire went out, then turned and walked slowly through the crowded streets, mourning the loss of her friend, and the loss of the city's innocence.

H

The dusty road stretched out before Amaziah as far as he could see. Few people moved under the blistering heat. Amaziah paused to wipe his forehead and pull the damp robe from his sweaty skin. He had been walking for hours. Shallum hadn't wanted to tell him where Huldah was, but he had asserted himself. He had been walking toward Bozkath ever since.

Somehow he had missed the path that would shorten the journey, but he had no desire to turn back. He trudged on, each step a necessary agony. He wouldn't allow his thoughts to go to Salome; there would be enough time for that when he faced his daughter. Huldah would have to do something now; surely she would see that she had powers to stop this insanity.

Would she agree to come back with him? He didn't know. He barely knew his daughter anymore.

H

A heavy mist settled over the desolate valley, dampening the rocks and making them slick and dangerous. The stunted trees were bleak and barren of leaves, pushing grotesque branches into the gathering gloom. Huldah picked her way carefully between the rocks, her sandals slipping on the damp ground. The hem of her robe clung to her ankles, impeding her progress.

Moans stunned her ears when she pushed toward the lower reaches of the steep hill. She felt compelled to go on. The voice had told her to come; she obeyed.

The hiss of a snake startled her. She paused, holding her breath as the creature slithered past her, twisting and turning between the rocks.

Lord, why have you brought me to this desolate place?

"Carry on, Huldah," the Lord said. "All will be made clear."

I believe, Lord, but I am afraid.

"Do not be afraid. I walk beside you."

During a break in the gloom, she saw people huddled together on the shore of a river. The water gleamed red with blood. Huldah gasped as the people, one by one, entered the river and floated away amidst shrieks from those who remained on shore. Her hands covered her mouth, helpless to do anything for them.

"Rescue them, Huldah. Rescue them."

But Lord, how can I rescue them? I am but one person.

"You have Me on your side. We will fight together. Go. Rescue them."

The mist began to fade, the trees disappeared, and the people vanished. She opened her eyes in the darkness, still in the house of Adaiah of Bozkath. Her body trembled as she recalled the dream. She recognized it was a vision from God. She had to return to Jerusalem. God had work for her there.

Rising, she quickly donned her clothes, gathered a meagre lunch, and slipped out into the darkness.

$\mathcal{H}$

The heat was intense, but Amaziah laboured on.

In the distance, he thought he saw a woman walking toward him. *I must be hallucinating. A woman would not be walking this road unaccompanied.*

He rubbed his hands over his eyes, but the vision remained. Definitely a woman, and definitely alone, coming his way. The distance between them narrowed, and he began to think it looked like his daughter.

Lord, have you sent her to me? That would be a miracle in a day devoid of miracles or joy.

He became convinced it was her and increased his speed until he was running toward her. She must have recognized him, for she, too, began to run.

They fell into each other's arms on the deserted road, under the midday heat. He broke down, sobbing on her shoulder.

"Father, what has happened?" Huldah asked. "I know things are troubling in Jerusalem, but this is more than that, isn't it? Please tell me." She leaned back and looked into his eyes. "Please, Father."

"Your mother... they've taken your mother."

Between sobs, he poured out the story, clinging closely to her for comfort. When he finished the tale, she led him to the side of the road and together they sat.

"Why were you on the road, Huldah? You shouldn't be traveling alone." He wiped her forehead with his sleeve, letting his hand caress her cheek.

"I had a vision in the night. God told me to go back to Jerusalem and rescue the people." Huldah leaned back and closed her eyes. "I was on my way."

"Then we will go back together. That's why I was coming—to convince you that we need you in Jerusalem." Grief overcame Amaziah again and he rested his head in his hands.

Huldah put her hand on his shoulder and gripped it tightly. "How did you know where to find me?"

"I made Shallum tell me. I had to know. He'll be waiting for you when you get home." He shook his head, the face of Salome crowding into his mind. "He wanted to come with me, but I persuaded him that I needed to do this alone. He reluctantly agreed." The first hint of a smile lifted the corners of his mouth. "You have a fine husband."

"Yes, I know. I'm not sure why God allowed me to have him." She lowered her head. "It's not easy being married to a prophetess, especially one who keeps disappearing."

"Are you ready to start walking again?"

At her nod, Amaziah stood, brushed the dust from his robe, and gave her his hand to help her.

His eyes opened wide. "Huldah, I almost forgot you are with child. Will this be too much for you?"

"No, Father, it will not be too much." She placed her hand over her abdomen in a protective gesture. "If God has called me to go to Jerusalem, he will look after the child in my womb."

She reached out and grabbed her father's arm.

"Come," she said. "We have a long distance to go before nightfall."

H

Dusk had fallen by the time Huldah and Amaziah neared the gates of the city. Guards lined the walls and the gates remained open, even though it was well past sunset. Torches hung in brackets along the walls and along the main street into the city. Smoke fanned out in long tendrils, blotting out the faces of the guards and giving the city a sinister look. The acrid smell of smoke reached the two travellers, irritating their throats. Huldah coughed into the white cloth she pulled from beneath her robe.

She reached out and stopped Amaziah before they came into view of the gates.

"Father, we need to pause here for a moment."

He looked at her, his eyebrows raised in question. "Are you too tired to go on, daughter?"

"Not too tired. But something is wrong. The gates are never open at this time, and notice we're the only ones on the road." She looked over her shoulder, peering through the gathering darkness. "It's a trap, Father. They're waiting for us."

Amaziah gasped and put a hand over his heart. "A trap? Maybe they're waiting for a dignitary to arrive, or a needed shipment of goods that has been delayed."

"That's hopeful thinking, Father, but I tell you, it's a trap." She put her hand over his. "Let's move off the road until we have a plan."

H

Huldah shoved her father toward the side of the road. He seemed in a daze, and she realized that she had to take control.

"There must be another way into the city," she said. "Think, Father. Some obscure gate or opening you know about that won't be watched."

He breathed deeply. "There is an opening, but we'll have to make a wide circle around the city to get to it."

"Then let's get started. You lead the way, and I'll be right behind you. The main thing is to make sure we stay out of sight of the wall."

A wooded area afforded them cover. Soft moss under their feet allowed no noise to penetrate the distance. It was easy walking and Huldah began to enjoy the path, though her pleasure soon ended when they emerged into a rocky field. Now the going was harder, and their pace slowed. Amaziah helped her over the larger boulders.

Huldah could see the next gate, up ahead and to her right. This gate, too, was open despite the late hour. More guards, more torches, more smoke... all for her capture, she was sure.

"One more gate and then we'll be close," Amaziah said. "It's behind the temple. Hilkiah has been neglecting repairs to it because of the turmoil."

Huldah felt her lips curve upward at her father's words. "I think God kept the repairs from being made, for He knew we needed entry to the city. Isn't God amazing? He went before us and planned this whole thing."

The scene was the same at the third gate. They moved by as quickly as the rocky path would allow. Once past the lights and smoke, Amaziah moved in closer to the wall.

"Stay close to the wall, Huldah. The opening is hidden and I don't want to miss it."

She stayed close, running her hand along the rough stonework. It was now so dark that she couldn't see her father, thought she sensed his presence.

"Here, Huldah. Bend your head. The opening is low."

His hand found hers and he led her through the opening into the wide space behind the temple.

She brushed beside him, holding onto his hand. "Father, we need to enter the temple and find Hilkiah."

"Stay close to me, child."

She thought she detected a note of triumph in his voice.

ℋ

"Every gate is being watched, oh king." Moshe bowed low before Amon, the disgust on his face hidden. "She will arrive soon. She was spotted on the road an hour ago. It's just a matter of time."

"An hour ago?" Amon's mouth twisted downward and he thrust his hands onto his hips. "She should have been in your grasp by now. You are a fool, man. Find her! Don't let any space in the city escape your search. Lock the gates."

The king's feet stomped on the marble floor.

"She's in the city, I know she is," Amon shrieked. "Find her!"

Moshe fled.

The king continued to stomp through the halls. "She's a dead woman. When we find her, Moshe will join her."

thirty-three

oft light filtered under the edge of the small door situated in an alcove at the back of the temple. Huldah and Amaziah crouched just inside the wall and watched the door for activity. A temple servant emerged carrying a basin, which he emptied into the large receptacle to the side of the door. He wiped the inside of the basin with a towel. While he wiped, he gazed around the yard and looked in their direction.

"Don't move, Huldah." Amaziah's whisper was so quiet, but she felt his breath on her ear. "Keep your head lowered so he can't see your eyes."

Huldah did as instructed, but glanced now and then to see if the servant had moved. He seemed to be enjoying the night air. *Probably a relief from his duties in the temple. Hopefully he soon goes back inside.*

The servant took one last look in all directions, pulled the door open, and entered the temple.

After a short pause, Huldah rose to her feet, rubbing her cramped legs. Amaziah stood beside her. She gripped his arm and steadied herself.

"It's time," Amaziah said. "Keep your head low and we'll walk slowly to the door. Don't make any quick movements. We don't want to attract any attention."

Amaziah took her hand and led her toward the door. It was unlocked, and the two entered without delay.

Inside, it was very dark. The hall where they entered was narrow, but ahead they could see the flickering of candles.

"Follow me."

Huldah let her father go ahead. The soft swish of her sandals on the marble sounded loud and intrusive to her ears.

They paused at the end of the hall and Amaziah looked both ways before moving out into the wider room. He seemed to know where he was going.

Around the next turn, a maze of rooms stretched out before them. A light burned, visible behind a heavy curtain covering the entrance to a side room. When they drew closer, a figure emerged from a recess in the wall, watching their approach.

"Benjamin, don't be alarmed. It's me, Amaziah."

Amaziah held out his hand toward the servant.

Benjamin's bright eyes fell on Huldah. "The master will want to see you right away. Go on in."

Huldah had pulled her headdress low on her forehead and wrapped her scarf over the lower part of her face. She held her breath and wondered if Benjamin would challenge her. He appeared about to speak, then closed his mouth, obviously thinking better of it.

When Huldah eased through the break in the curtain, Hilkiah looked up from his table, where he had been bent over a scroll. He struggled to his feet, setting the scroll aside. His face was pale, but he looked at them with clear eyes.

"Amaziah, my friend, you have returned." Hilkiah moved around the table to greet him. The two men exchanged greetings. "And who do you bring with you, Amaziah?"

Her father turned, reached out his arm, and pulled her beside him. "I've brought my daughter."

Huldah lowered the scarf and shoved her headdress back from her forehead. "Greetings, my lord."

The High Priest placed his hand over his chest and took a deep breath. "It is not safe for you to be here, Prophetess. Your life is in great danger."

"Wherever God calls me to be, I am safe, and God has told me to return to Jerusalem." She inclined her head to him. "Have no fear for my safety. I will live as long as God allows. No more, no less."

"But the king wants to kill you." Hilkiah's words came out in a gasp.

"Remember, High Priest: the king is not in control. God is."

"I know, I know," Hilkiah said. "But you have no idea what it is like in Jerusalem these days. The people no longer believe God is in control. The king is all-powerful."

"Then it is certainly time I returned." She spoke with great confidence, being filled with the power of God. Her face shone.

H

Shallum rubbed Huldah's back. She had been talking for what seemed like hours, her experiences pouring out in a stream.

"Shallum, I know it seems strange, but I'm not afraid." Huldah rested her head on his chest. "It was the right time for me to come back. For Jerusalem, but also for us." Her hand caressed his face, tracing the outline of his features. "We need to be together when this baby arrives. You must not miss this great event."

He raised himself on one elbow. "I always want to be in God's will for our lives, but how wonderful it is when God decides that we can be in the same place!"

"It's so good to be home," she said. "Home with you."

"What will you do, Huldah? The King is certainly looking for you. I'm surprised we haven't been disturbed tonight."

In the silence, she wrapped her arms around him, breathing in his clean scent. How she loved this man. *Oh Lord, you have been so good to me. This man you've given to me is more than I could ever have asked for or imagined.*

"What will I do?" Huldah said. "I'm not sure yet. I plan to spend all day tomorrow talking and listening to our God. We know he brought me back for a reason. Will you pray with me?"

Shallum nodded. "I, too, will spend the day in prayer, but I need to be at the palace for part of the day. At those times, I'll pray in the spirit. Oh Huldah, God will need to fill us with peace. I sense it's going to be a dramatic time. God doesn't do things in a small way."

The last thing Huldah heard before she drifted into sleep was her husband's even breathing.

Lord, why do I feel this is the lull before the coming violence?

H

The evening shadows deepened as Huldah wove her way through the crowds gathered outside the palace. Word had gone out today that King Amon would address the people as the last rays of sun disappeared from Jerusalem. The rim of the sun hovered on the horizon. It appeared to stand still, reluctant to sink and bring on the night.

Noises wafted from the crowd assembled before the gates. From this distance, it sounded like a celebration, but Huldah knew that was deceptive. When she topped the hill above the palace, she heard individual voices raised in protest and complaint. Amon hadn't yet made an appearance.

Palace servants moved from the safety of the palace doors to light the torches. The smoky reek soon reached Huldah's eyes and nose.

A swell of light behind her silhouetted her against the backdrop of the night sky, but she wasn't afraid to be seen; she was where God had told her to be. She watched with intense interest as the doors of the palace were flung wide. Trumpets echoed their mournful sound while palace officials poured from the doors. Behind them came Amon, arrayed in purple garments trimmed with white, and on his head rested a crown of gold. He paused on the threshold of the palace, lifted his arms, and stepped onto the platform assembled for his use.

Huldah, too, raised her arms. The breeze billowed her white robe, tossing her long hair in tendrils behind her.

Amon lifted his eyes to his people and became aware of Huldah. She knew when he recognized her presence by the tightness in his shoulders.

The crowd followed Amon's eyes and shouts rose from their lips.

"The prophetess!"

"It's her!"

"She's back."

"Huldah has returned!"

"We're safe now!"

She sensed rather than saw the look of hatred that swept over Amon's face. He beckoned to his advisors, who were instantly at his side. A quick conversation took place and they moved off, supposedly to do his bidding. While she watched, soldiers separated themselves from the wall where they waited at attention, and stood beside their king.

Amon lifted one arm and pointed toward Huldah. "Seize her!"

They swarmed toward the hill, but the light behind her dimmed, plunging the hill into darkness. She slipped away.

H

Amon watched while his soldiers combed the hillside for Huldah. He stood still, every muscle in his body held tight. *She can't escape this time. I just saw*

213

her! Why can't they find her, and what happened to the light behind her? What was the light? Fear shuddered through his body when he realized the light hadn't been earthly. *She's a witch, a sorceress. How else can the light be accounted for?*

"Moshe, stand beside me," Amon whispered.

Moshe moved closer to stand at his side. "I'm right here, Master."

There will soon come a day when Moshe is no longer needed. Amon ground his teeth as he thought about Moshe's demise.

"They're not going to find her, are they?" Amon breathed in Moshe's ear.

"I think you're right. I'd call them back."

"When I want your opinion, I'll ask for it."

Moshe bowed. "Yes, my lord. I am in error."

"Watch yourself, Moshe. No one is indispensable." With that final word, Amon spun on his heels and marched back toward the palace doors. "Get the others and meet me in my rooms."

With a swirl of his cloak and a stamp of his foot, he disappeared into the palace.

Let the soldiers keep looking. It'll do them good. And maybe, just maybe, they'll get lucky and find her. I await the day when I can watch her hanging from the palace wall.

H

Huldah disappeared from the hillside while the sudden darkness confused the soldiers. She slipped past them and took a path that would lead home. Far behind, she could hear their voices raised in their search.

Scurrying noises in the bushes alerted her to small animals in their nightly quest for food. It was very dark along the path, but she knew it so well that she was able to travel it without benefit of light. A branch scratched at her arm as she passed, but she ignored the slight pain.

When she emerged from the path, there was no sight or sound of followers, so she walked the rest of the way in peace.

Once inside the house, she removed her sandals. A dull pain grabbed her side. *I must have moved too fast at the beginning.*

She placed her sandals beside the others lined up along one wall and hung her shawl on a hook.

"Huldah, I'm in our bedroom," Shallum called.

Huldah moved toward their room and met him halfway. He wrapped his arms around her and held her close.

"I'm so glad you're home," he said.

"So am I."

"Come, sit with me and tell me everything that happened. I've been praying constantly for you." He led her to a comfortable seat and slid down beside her.

"Oh Shallum, it was wonderful and horrible." Huldah rested her head on his shoulder and told him the details of the evening. She trembled when she told him about the soldiers chasing her, and his arm tightened around her.

"God was certainly at work," Shallum said. "What's the matter?"

Huldah held her side and moaned.

"Huldah, what's wrong?" Shallum cupped her face in his hand.

She put her hand over her waist and gasped. "There's a pain, right here."

"I'm getting Mother." Shallum jumped from his seat and ran to the other section of the house. He called Esther's name as he ran.

When he returned with Esther, Huldah was lying on the bed with her eyes closed.

"Huldah, can you hear me?" Esther asked.

"Yes, yes, I can." Her eyes were still closed, but her voice was strong.

"When do you think your baby is due?" Esther wrung out a cloth in the water basin and placed it over her forehead and eyes.

"My baby? Not for a while yet. Why?"

"Because I think this baby is planning to be born tonight," said Esther.

Huldah struggled to a sitting position. Her eyes were wide. "How can that be? I'm sure my baby's not due yet. It can't be."

"I may be wrong, but it sounds to me like the time is close. I'll send Tikvah for the midwife. You remember Dena? She sometimes helped your mother. She can tell us when the baby will come."

"Yes. Yes, I remember. Please send for her." Huldah moaned softly and dropped back on the pillows.

When Esther left the room, Shallum sat on the edge of the bed and held Huldah's hand. It was very quiet and night shadows from the oil lamps danced on the wall. A light breeze ruffled the bed covers and brought in the fragrance of flowers from their garden. Somewhere, a night bird hooted.

In this interlude of peace, Huldah silently spoke to God. *Father, I didn't expect to become a mother so soon, but your timing is perfect. Prepare my heart for nurturing this child still in my womb. And Father, look after Jerusalem.*

$\mathcal{H}$

A baby's cry broke with the dawn of a new day, and Huldah sighed with joy and relief. It had been a long night of travail and anguish, but through it all she had been sure her baby would live. God had told her so, but her mind returned to the little babe who had died when she'd stood in for her mother as midwife. God had other plans for that baby boy.

She gazed in wonder at the tiny babe snuggled at her breast, and planted a kiss on his curly dark hair.

"Yaacov Benyamin, son of Shallum," she whispered into his small ear. "You are my son and I promise to love you unconditionally."

The only answer was a soft sigh, expelled from lips gone slack. The baby's eyelids fluttered in sleep. She wanted to hold him forever.

The curtain was pushed aside and Esther entered. Huldah lifted her eyes to her mother-in-law, who was such a big part of her life. Her dry lips stretched into a smile of welcome.

Suddenly tired, Huldah held out her son to Esther.

"How would I have managed without you?" Huldah's eyes drooped from the aftermath of a night of birthing.

"You couldn't have kept me away, Huldah." Esther grinned at her. "I don't have the skill that your mother had, but I helped her several times and learned her secrets. Besides, with Dena here, it was easy. She really knows what she's doing, and I just followed her directions."

Esther sat in the bedside chair and held her grandson. She pushed the blanket back from the boy's face and gazed at him. "Have you ever seen a more beautiful baby? Just look at that dark hair and those eyelids with long lashes. And his nose has the nicest shape." She traced his nose with one finger, then rested her hand on his head. "I've certainly never seen a baby like him. We are fortunate to have such a wonderful boy."

"You make me so happy," Huldah said. "I think he's beautiful, but I'm his mother. If you say he's beautiful, he must be."

That was the last thing Huldah remembered until she awoke several hours later.

Her eyes opened slowly and she stretched her arms. In the first moments of wakefulness, she didn't remember her baby, but then the memories came in a whirl of happiness.

The room had been tidied, nothing left to indicate that a baby had entered the world a few hours prior.

My mother-in-law has done a great job. And I didn't even hear her working around me! Where is my baby?

With that thought, she abruptly sat up in bed.

The curtain parted again, and this time Shallum entered with a small bundle in his arms—and a large smile on his face. His eyes danced with pleasure as he held the bundle close to his heart. Her eyes locked with his, and she knew she loved him far beyond what her words could convey.

"Huldah, my love, are you rested?" Shallum knelt by her side and slid the baby into her arms. His gentle hands cupped her face and his lips sought hers. "You have made me a very happy man."

She giggled as he rubbed his nose against hers. "I'm glad you approve of our son."

"Of course I approve of our son. He's far superior to any baby in Jerusalem."

Shallum pulled the blanket back from the baby's face and gazed on him.

"Look at how he clings to my finger," Shallum said.

Huldah nodded. "I love the names you have chosen. Yaacov—completion and harmony. Benyamin—strength."

"Don't forget that Yaacov also means 'held by the heel.'"

She laughed. "Yes, I know the story, but I like the other meaning."

"I like that Benyamin also means 'son of my right hand,'" Shallum said. "That is such a beautiful picture of what I imagine our father-son relationship to be."

"Son of my right hand. Yes, I can see that's what he'll be to you."

She paused, her eyes focused on the future. Was another vision coming on?

"Huldah, what do you see?" Shallum asked, his voice urgent and harsh.

"Everything is fine, Shallum. I only see good things in your future together."

A stringent cry ended the conversation. Yaacov demanded his next feeding.

H

"Why have you not arrested her?" Amon snarled. He paced the length of his room, his long dark hair streaming out behind him. "I will not be patient much longer. Your lives are on the line.

Fools, all of them are fools. Why do I keep them around me?

Moshe pulled himself up from the deep seat where Amon had directed him to sit. He crossed his arms and faced the king.

Amon watched him through eyelids partly lowered and waited for him to speak, if he dared.

"Your soldiers could not find her," Moshe said. "We have searched the city. She will be found when she wants to be found."

"Oh, you're a bold one, Moshe. Let me tell you something. If Huldah is not soon delivered to me, blood will run in the streets of Jerusalem, and this time it will be your blood."

Amon's eyes swept to the others in the room—Ethan, who stood with his chin elevated and lips downturned; Joel, who cowered in the corner; Jotham, with eyes averted.

"What a sight you are, all of you! My advisors, you say? My cowards." He glared at each in turn. "I'm giving you one more chance. Have her here by sundown, or one of you will not live to see the morning."

thirty-four

*B*enjamin leaned over Hilkiah's table to light the clay lamp. Long shadows blurred the contents of the scrolls, but Hilkiah seemed unaware. The flame wavered under Benjamin's touch, causing Hilkiah to raise his eyes.

"Is it evening already?" Hilkiah's voice held a note of doubt.

"Yes, my lord."

Benjamin seemed to hover over Hilkiah, making the priest uneasy.

"Benjamin, I have a task for you. I must speak to the other priests tonight. Please take the message to them and bring me a light meal." He dismissed Benjamin with a wave. "Wait, no meat. Just bread and water and a bit of wine."

The shuffle of Benjamin's feet disturbed Hilkiah, and he didn't resume reading until the footsteps could no longer be heard.

Once again, he bent his white head over the scrolls.

Everything must be just right for the Day of Atonement. These scrolls are useless. One would think there must be better records somewhere, but where?

He rolled the scrolls and secured them with a piece of leather, set them aside, and cleared the table.

Amaziah was the first to arrive.

"Am I too early?" Dark circles etched Amaziah's eyes and exhaustion showed in the slump of his shoulders. Losing his wife had taken its toll, but a strong, determined light shone from his eyes.

"No, not early. I'm glad for a private moment to talk with you. Please, sit and tell me about Huldah and your new grandson."

Hilkiah indicated the chair across the table from his and Amaziah settled there.

"Huldah is doing well and the baby has brought great joy to all of us. It's the first glimmer of hope in our fractured family."

"I had hoped she could participate in the Day of Atonement, but now with the baby..." Hilkiah's voice trailed off and he averted his eyes.

Amaziah reached across the table and put his hand on Hilkiah's arm. "She plans to be there. She goes where God sends her, speaks what He says to her, and nothing, not even the birth of a baby, will stop her."

The two men smiled at the picture of Huldah so ably painted by her father.

"I should never have doubted it," Hilkiah said.

They laughed together—a pleasant sound which Hilkiah had not heard often of late.

Quiet voices beyond the curtain alerted Hilkiah that the others had arrived. Tamar and Jamin entered first, both frail and bent but with determined looks in their eyes. They were followed closely by Hoshea, Zephon, and Beriah. They all found places around the table.

Hilkiah tightened his shoulders when Talmar sat, the creak of his bones audible to the group. *We're all getting older, but Talmar seems to be struggling the most. I should send him back to his room, but I know he wouldn't appreciate it.*

"Welcome, priests, but where is Nimrah?" Hilkiah looked toward the curtain again.

Hoshea cleared his throat, but glanced at Zephon before he spoke. "My lord, we've been taking turns watching Huldah's house."

"Who's been taking turns?" Hilkiah turned bright eyes on Hoshea.

"The younger priests, Master. Zephon, Beriah, Nimrah, and I. It seemed a good idea to have an extra pair of eyes to watch over her."

Amaziah turned away from the others in silence. Hilkiah was sure he saw a tear slide down his face.

"And you're right," Hilkiah said. "It is a good idea. I would have preferred that you keep me informed of your movements, but all the same, I'm proud of each of you for taking on this task."

He took a deep breath, spread his hands on the table and sent up a quick prayer for guidance.

"And now we must make our final plans for the Day of Atonement," Hilkiah said. "The time is approaching quickly and we want to be totally prepared, no detail left undone."

Hilkiah called Benjamin to the table to scribe, and soon the servant had his quills ready and a fresh scroll unrolled.

"Let's begin with a list of things we need to find or purchase."

The list soon contained:

holy linen tunic
linen underwear
linen sash
one young bull
two male goats
coals for the altar
finely ground aromatic incense
knives
one man appointed to take the scapegoat
one man appointed to burn the offerings outside camp

"Does that cover everything?" Hilkiah leaned over Benjamin's shoulder and read the list aloud. He looked around the table and saw that all were nodding agreement. "Then we just need to divide the list and discuss how we'll get the word out to the people."

"I'd like to get the incense," Talmar said, his voice weak. "I remember where we used to get it, before the land turned away from God. I think the merchant still carries it."

"A good plan, Talmar," Hilkiah said. "I'll look after making sure the linen garments are ceremonially washed and ready for me to wear."

"I can get the bull." Beriah stood, his voice warm and enthusiastic. "Nimrah and I will get it together."

"Thank you Beriah, but you would do well to remember that we are placing our lives on the line, perhaps putting the people in danger from the king." Deep frown lines creased Hilkiah's brow, but the younger generation needed to be curbed now and then. "Now, who will take responsibility to purchase two male goats?"

"I will," Hoshea said, his full lips stretching in a wide smile.

"I'll look after the coals," said Zephon.

Hilkiah nodded. "The knives are already in my possession, so no one need concern themselves about them."

Jamin raised his eyes to Hilkiah. "I know this is fraught with danger, but it is the right thing to do. We must let the people know that God is still right where they left Him. I will speak to my nephews regarding the scapegoat and the burnt offering."

"Then that's everything," Hilkiah said, "except getting the message out."

"I will work day and night spreading the message and encouraging people to come," Amaziah said.

Hilkiah was well-pleased with their willingness to spread the word to men they felt they could trust.

"We have seven days to prepare. I would like us to devote that time to prayer. Pray wherever you are, and pray long and earnestly. I will pray here. Join me when you can." Hilkiah stretched out his hands over their heads. "May God bless you. May God bring our plans to fruition. May His name be glorified."

They rose and left the room until only Hilkiah and Benjamin were left.

"Benjamin, please send word to Huldah to join me at her pleasure."

ℋ

"Mother, it's my birthday, isn't it?"

"Yes, Josiah, it is."

"And I'm eight today, right?"

"Yes, son."

"And that means I'll soon be king, right?"

Jedidah pulled herself from under the covers of the big bed and pushed her feet into cold house slippers. She touched her hand to her forehead, ran it through her unruly hair, and rubbed the back of her neck. She slipped from the bed and hurried to sit beside her son, his eyes still mellow from the night's sleep.

His hair lay in curling circles. Big, dark eyes looked questioningly and trustingly into hers.

She placed a small kiss on his forehead. "Why are you thinking about that on your birthday, Josiah?"

He rolled onto his side and stretched under the blanket.

"Because I have so little time to get ready." He yawned loudly and rubbed the sleep from his eyes. "A king needs time to work out his battle plans, and his plans for how to run his kingdom. And don't forget, I have to train Ehud, too."

Oh my son, my son. You have been robbed of your childhood. Someone will have to answer for this loss someday.

"But today's your birthday." She grabbed both his hands and pulled him to his feet. "Let's put your plans aside and celebrate. What do you say to that?"

"You're the best mother I could ever ask for." His hand smoothed her cheek. "And you will come to Jerusalem with me, won't you?"

She sighed, her heart heavy as she hugged his little body to her. "I'll never leave you, my son. Not if I can help it."

Hand in hand, they entered the living area of the house, where Chava was already cooking Josiah's favourite breakfast—hot bread from the oven, quail eggs cooked in their own shells, honeyed figs which had been soaking since yesterday, and a clay cup filled with fresh goat milk.

He ran to his grandmother and wrapped his arms around her in a tight hug. "Thank you, Bubbe. My very favourite food, and you make it the best."

Jedidah watched through tear-filled eyes. *My child, so child-like in some ways, yet so mature in others. What does the future hold for you? For all of us?*

ℋ

Long tendrils of fog curled around the base of trees and hugged the rose blossoms. Amon surveyed the early morning scene from his bedroom window. Deep in thought, he almost missed the movement of a walker on the path below. Amon leaned closer to the window, pushing the heavy curtain all the way to the side.

Hmm, I do believe it's Moshe. Now, why would he be walking in the garden this morning? He should be here giving me a report, explaining why my advisors didn't appear with Huldah by sundown last night. No one could find them, not even my best soldiers. Another failure. One of those advisors must die!

"Akiva, come here."

The door opened silently and Akiva bowed his way into the room. "What is your wish, Master? You only need to make it known and it will be done."

"Oh, stop with all that talk." He shook his fist in Akiva's face, causing the servant to back up.

"Get out on that path," Amon said, pointing through the window, "and bring Moshe to me immediately."

Akiva bowed again and fled from the room. The door closed softly behind him.

At least someone gives me the proper respect, the proper fear. He's necessary, at least for now.

Amon returned to the window to watch the servant approach Moshe. Akiva had to run to catch him. Moshe turned as Akiva approached and a conversation took place between them. Amon could see Akiva point at the palace. Moshe turned and began walking away.

Amon felt rage sweep through him. It began as a tightening of his stomach muscles and then gripped his chest. *He's trying to get away. I can't believe it.*

"Dor!"

Amon ran for the door and threw it open. Dor was there almost instantly. "Get some of the servants and help Akiva, out on the garden path. Moshe must be brought to me at once."

Dor asked no questions and Amon stormed back to the window. By now, Akiva had grabbed Moshe's cloak and the two men argued more strenuously. While Amon watched, Dor and three other servants ran toward the two, surrounding them. Moshe was overpowered.

Even from this distance, Amon could tell that Moshe was angry. He fought the group all the way.

It's too bad I need him, or he'd be the one to die.

Amon massaged his hands. His feet were set apart, shoulders back, chin elevated, and lips pressed together when Moshe unceremoniously burst through the door.

"What is the meaning of this… this seizing of an innocent person who was simply out for a morning stroll?" Moshe demanded. "Please tell me there is some mistake, that you didn't order these servants"—the word was pronounced with disgust—"to accost me and strong arm me into the palace."

Amon gave a tight laugh. "Who are you to burst into my room posturing all this innocence?"

The two stood a distance apart, but their eyes were riveted to each other.

"Sit down, Moshe. We have much to discuss."

"No apology for the treatment I just experienced?"

"None, and you'd be wise to drop the subject." Amon indicated a seat and waited until Moshe was seated before he, too, sat.

They faced each other without smiles. Birdsong drifted in from the open window, along with the fragrance of the roses. Amon's heart pounded deep in his chest, and he controlled his voice only with great effort.

The king leaned forward, a lock of dark hair draped over his forehead. "Perhaps you could explain why Huldah wasn't brought to me by sundown last night, and why I have neither seen nor heard from even one of my so-called advisors."

Moshe's shoulders seemed to relax. "My lord, we could not return last night because we were still pursuing the elusive Huldah. You must remember that she is a prophetess, and thus able to stay out of our sight and reach."

"And you must remember that I am the king." Amon pushed a long finger into Moshe's chest. "The sooner everyone remembers this, the longer will be their lives." He sat back and stared at Moshe for a moment. "Which one do you suggest should die?"

"Die? Are you suggesting you would have one of your royal advisors killed? Have you considered the consequences?"

"Consequences?" There was no laughter in Amon's voice.

"My lord, the people would lose confidence in a king who cannot keep his advisors under control. You would be advised to seek another form of discipline."

Amon jumped from his seat and paced to the window. His mind was a flurry of thoughts. *Is he right? It has a ring of truth, but can I trust him? Do I have a choice?*

He turned quickly from the window and strode back. "You're right, I can't have them killed *at this point*. Put Joel in the darkest prison without bread and water for twenty-four hours." He wiped his hands together. "That should settle him and the others."

"Wise decision, my lord. Now, we have more pressing matters to discuss. According to my spies, the priests are up to something."

"Oh, the priests," Amon said. "They're a weak and powerless group of fools. What could they possibly be up to?"

"I don't know, but there's something in the air. It bears watching. If they gain control of the masses, we're in trouble."

Amon snapped his fingers. "The solution is simple. We kill one of the priests!"

thirty-five

"Shallum, Shallum."

Huldah shook his shoulder repeatedly, keeping her voice low to keep from waking Yaacov—not to mention Shallum's parents, asleep in another section of the house.

Lord, why is he such a sound sleeper? I know it is a blessing, but I need him to wake up.

"What is it, Huldah?" Shallum rolled over to face her. "Is something wrong? Can't you sleep?"

She kissed his warm cheek and wrapped her arms around him. "Yes, there's something wrong."

He sat up quickly, a look of panic on his face. "Tell me."

"Shallum, I've had another vision. Amon is going to kill Talmar! I can't let him kill that holy man."

"Talmar is truly a man of God," Shallum said. "But what can you do?"

"I don't know yet, but I need to get to the temple as fast as possible. I need you to be awake to look after Yaacov."

"You're talking foolish, my wife. There's no way I'm letting you go to the temple alone in the middle of the night." Shallum was already on his feet, slipping his robe over his head. "I'll get my mother. She'll be delighted to look after Yaacov."

As he left the room, Huldah smiled a secret smile. *Lord, you knew what you were doing when you put Shallum in my life.*

She hummed a little tune while she dressed, then laid out the supplies Esther would need for Yaacov. The baby didn't move when she placed a kiss on his curly head.

Shallum soon returned with Esther. Soon after, husband and wife entered the night air.

ℋ

Talmar left the courts of the temple at the end of the middle watch, having spent hours with Hilkiah in prayer. The sentinels left their posts, and their replacements took over. By the time he reached the path behind the temple, the changes had been made and all was quiet again.

He walked with his head bent, deep in thought and leaning on his stout staff.

Oh Lord God, we have seen nothing but trouble in our land for many long years. Is there no end to the evil? Forgive me, Lord. I do not lay the blame on You; it is ours to bear. We turn from You and then are surprised when wickedness invades our home-land. Forgive us, Lord, and shorten the time of evil.

Talmar was aroused from his prayer by an alien yet familiar sound. His brain was slow to focus on it, but when he did, he knew it was a knife being withdrawn from its sheath.

Lord, is this to be the end for me? I can only rejoice that I will soon see Your face, but it tells me that evil has not abated.

Talmar decided to keep walking and not turn to confront his pursuer.

Let him make the moves. I will not assist him. The evil deed will be on his head. May God forgive him.

It was the darkest hour of the night. No moon shone, and no stars were visible. Talmar was able to keep to the path only with the aid of his staff. The swish of a wing and the hoot of an owl were the only sounds. Although his heart beat faster, Talmar sensed no other signs of fear.

I'm in your hands, God, and there's nowhere else I would ever want to be.

A tiny point of light up ahead told him he was close to the end of the path, where it joined the main road through the city, just inside the sheep gate. In a few hours, this area would be alive with people and animals and overwhelming noise. Tonight, it was silent. Talmar walked across it, wondering if this was where his pursuer would attack. But he continued on to the street that would lead him home. His pace did not change, nor did he look back, but he was aware of a follower.

There were houses now on either side of him, houses of the poor of the city—small, mean, ill-kept, and emitting the harsh odour of discarded refuse, unwashed bodies, and dead animals. It was an appalling assault on the nostrils. Talmar knew he could knock on one of these doors and be admitted to safety; he knew that the head of the household would offer hospitality; but he also knew that he would be putting the family in danger.

When he neared his home, in a small court off the main road, the pursuer struck. He felt the knife touch his back and knew that his life was over.

Into your hands, Lord, into your hands.

But the knife went no farther and a commanding voice split the night air.

"Stay your hand."

Talmar stood perfectly still. The knife left his back and clattered to the stony ground.

"Release your hood so I may see your face," the voice said.

Talmar made the decision not to turn. He didn't want to know who was behind him.

"Yes, I recognize you. Return to the palace and the evil man you serve. Tell him there will be no slaughter of priests. God has spoken through his servant. Now, go!"

When Talmar turned around, there was no one in sight.

ow-hanging clouds scudded over a sky already laden with clouds, but a thin red line on the horizon gave hope to Hilkiah's heart.

Today's the Day of Atonement. We live or die today—at the whim of the king, but really by the hand of God.

He shaded his eyes with one hand and scanned the heavens. No rain yet. The land needed rain, but it would be more welcome tomorrow. *Lord, I know you can withhold the rain. Let it be dry so the people will come.*

Hilkiah was aware that the priests had worked diligently to spread the word, leaving a message here, a whispered direction there, until they felt the people knew. So far, there was no indication that the palace knew.

He re-entered the temple, walked slowly to his room, and shoved aside the curtain. Benjamin was there before him.

"Master, you've come. All things are ready, just as you asked." Benjamin swept his arm to where the clothes were laid out for him. "But first, come eat. I managed to get some fresh dates to add to your daily bread. Sit."

Benjamin tugged on his arm and led him to the table. He then helped him sit and poured the thin wine in a clay cup.

"Benjamin, you must join me this morning."

"No, no, there's work to do."

"I insist. I don't wish to break my fast alone. Please, the work can wait."

Benjamin sat on the bench on the other side of the table. Hilkiah lifted the warm loaf and broke off a piece for Benjamin, then another for himself. He wasn't hungry, but it did taste good. He would need his strength today. The wine was weak, but it began to restore him.

When they finished their meal, Benjamin cleared the table and left.

Hilkiah removed the ornate clothes befitting the High Priest. He set aside the blue robe trimmed with pomegranates and bells, the ephod with the two sardonyx stones, the breastplate with twelve precious stones, and the turban with a gold plate in front. Today, he would wear the simple garments of fine linen, more appropriate for the Day of Atonement. He then bathed himself, using clean cloths to dry himself.

Hilkiah donned the white linen underwear and the holy linen tunic, tied the linen sash around himself, and put on the white turban.

Just like Aaron did so many years ago. All by God's design.

He lifted his eyes to the doorway when Benjamin pushed back the curtain and entered.

"The other priests are ready, Master."

"Then it's time to begin. My staff, please."

Hilkiah moved through the inner court to stand with the other priests. The great doors were thrown open and he led them into the outer court, which was already filled with people. Silent people, heads raised to watch their entrance, crowded together in the outer court until there was no more room, yet still they came.

Hilkiah stood before them, tears of joy rolling down his aged cheeks. *They came, Lord. They came. They want to find their way back to You. If not today, then in Your time.*

He lifted his hands over them and prayed. His weak voice gained strength until it was the voice of a young man, a man filled with promise and confidence.

At the conclusion of his prayer, Hilkiah turned and entered the inner court with the other priests. Beriah and Nimrah, with a bull on a chain, approached. While they held the bull, Hilkiah slaughtered it, catching the blood in a basin.

"Lord God, I offer this bull as an offering to You. I offer it to make atonement for me and my household."

With arms outstretched, Hilkiah mounted the ramp to the altar, then filled a censer with burning coals and a ladle with two handfuls of incense. He carried the two receptacles into the Holy of Holies, where he placed the censer of coals between the staves of the Ark of the Covenant before carefully throwing the incense on the burning coals. He waited for the smoke to curl from the coals and fill the holy place.

Lord, if it is Your will, I will not die here today, but the offering will be accepted in Your sight.

He emerged again to find the people waiting in silence.

Lord, they're listening. Joy fills my heart. Give me the physical strength to do Your will today.

With a trembling hand, Jamin handed him the basin filled with the blood of the bull, and Hilkiah once more walked into the Holy of Holies. The smoke still lingered in the holy place, obscuring the ark.

Hilkiah dipped his finger in the blood and sprinkled it on the front of the atonement cover. He paused and breathed deeply.

Oh Lord, what an awesome privilege to be a High Priest before You. Lord, cleanse Your holy place where You dwell. We have sinned as a nation and plead for Your forgiveness.

He again dipped his finger in the bull's blood and sprinkled it before the atonement cover seven times.

He left the Holy of Holies and moved to where the two goats were held by Hoshea. Hilkiah put a hand on the head of each goat and lifted his eyes to the heavens.

Here are the two goats, Lord. I will cast the lots, but You will make the decision, just as it should be.

Hilkiah slaughtered the chosen goat, catching its blood in a basin. This goat was for the Lord, for a sin offering for the people. He lifted the basin in both hands and returned to the Holy of Holies, sprinkling the blood of the goat the same way he had for the bull.

Lord, we are an unclean people, a rebellious people, and we offer this sacrifice to You.

Once out of the Holy of Holies, he approached the altar and sprinkled the blood there, to cleanse the altar.

Now Hoshea approached him with the live goat—the scapegoat. Hilkiah put both hands on the head of the scapegoat.

Hilkiah raised his voice. "On your head I now lay all the sins of the people, all our turning away from the Lord, all our rebellion. All our sins be on your head."

Jamin led his nephew to Hilkiah, who placed the live goat into his possession.

"You must lead this scapegoat out of the city and away from our sight," Hilkiah said. "It must not return to us but wander in a solitary place with our sins on its head."

The goat was led away under the watchful eye of the people. Once it and its keeper were out of sight, a cheer rose from the people.

Pieces of the bull and the goat were placed on the altar as burnt offerings. The searing smell of the sacrifice reached the waiting people, and a cheer again rose from their lips. Hilkiah stood back and watched the smoke curl upward from the sacrifice. He raised his arms to the heavens with uplifted eyes. The people, too, raised their arms and eyes.

ℋ

Amon walked in the palace gardens with Moshe and his other advisors. Their early morning meeting had become heated and Moshe suggested a break for tempers to cool. Moshe had been surprised that the king agreed, but here they all were, walking for exercise and settled tempers.

They rounded the corner of the palace and Moshe lifted his head in alarm. "What is that smoke rising behind the temple? Is the temple on fire?"

Amon slapped his leg and laughed. "Now, wouldn't that be fortunate."

"There is also an odour of burning flesh." He grabbed Amon's arm. "Amon, I'm sure the fragrance of incense is in the air."

"The priests, the disloyal priests! They're holding a ceremony! Forbidden by me." His face twisted into outrage. "Get the soldiers, get the servants, get everyone you can find. Kill them, every last one of them! They must be punished. The people must know that I am king."

Already Amon was headed toward the palace, issuing orders.

Ethan and Joel ran one way, Moshe and Jotham the other. Moshe breathed heavily and ran to where the soldiers were housed. Fortunately for the king, the soldiers were at their training ground and left immediately once Moshe gave them the order.

Hooves thundered through the streets and cries from the soldiers split the air. Moshe mounted and rode with them. When the temple appeared, the fragrance of incense and searing flesh overpowered his nostrils.

This day will not have a good ending for the citizens of Jerusalem, or for the priests.

ℋ

Talmar stood through the ceremony with his head lowered in prayer. His heart was attuned to God's leading and he rejoiced in this beautiful ceremony of forgiveness. When the flames began to die, a sound caught his ear. He lifted his head and gazed over the heads of the people. Suddenly, he knew. Soldiers approached!

Other heads turned toward the sound and a great shout rose above the mass of people. "Run! Run for your lives!"

Talmar moved to stand beside Hilkiah. His knees were stiff with age, but he covered the distance at a remarkable rate. "Hilkiah, we must go, too." His voice held a note of urgency.

The other priests joined them and they watched as the people poured from the temple and ran into the streets.

"God, go with them and protect them." Talmar knew tears were on his cheeks, but he made no effort to wipe them away.

Hoshea turned from the sight of the fleeing people and faced the priests. "Come, we must leave now if we hope to escape the wrath of the king." He linked his arms with Talmar and Hilkiah, leading them deeper into the temple's outer court. "We'll head for the door at the back and pray that we arrive there before the soldiers."

Zephon put his arm around Jamin, and together with Beriah they followed the others.

It was quiet in the depths of the temple. The noise of the crowd had dimmed and none of the priests spoke.

They reached the outer door in safety and Hoshea led them through. Once outside, they followed the path behind the temple and reached the city's southern gate. No one was in sight when they passed through—not even the usual guards.

Talmar looked back at the gate. *Why do I feel we'll not see the inside of Jerusalem for a long time? But the timing is yours, Lord; we are merely your servants.*

When they reached a small grove of trees, they paused to confer with each other.

"I think the Lord has led us in this direction," Hilkiah said. "We aren't far from the home of our brother, Asher. I know we will find shelter there."

Talmar leaned on this staff and made eye contact with him. "That's a good plan. It won't be safe for us to return to the city for now, and I know Asher will welcome us. Mayhap we will be able to minister to him and his household."

"Then are we all in agreement?" Hilkiah shaded his eyes. "Let's proceed."

H

From a hillside overlooking the temple, Huldah watched the mass of people flee before the soldiers. She had been in constant prayer since sunrise, just as she and Hilkiah had planned. The day had gone well until the soldiers appeared, but she was confident every person present arrived home safely. God had given her the assurance that no lives would be lost today.

The priests are safely out of the city and the soldiers have turned toward the palace, empty-handed. Amon will not be pleased. Evil plans will be afoot in the palace this night.

While she stood, Huldah became aware of God speaking to her. Slowly she sank to her knees on the warm earth, lifting her hands to the morning sky. "God, You are my master, and I Your humble servant. Speak and I will listen."

The voice of the Father wrapped itself around her, and she drew comfort from the embrace. She closed her eyes and the voice whispered, "Go to Bozkath. Josiah needs you. You must teach him how to become a good king; it will not be long now."

Yes, Lord, your servant will do as you have commanded.

"There will be evil times while you are absent. But do not fear, for the end is coming."

When she opened her eyes, she was surprised to see that the sun had moved to the midday position. *How long have I been kneeling here? Oh Lord, I feel such peace from Your presence. Now I must arise and make plans.*

H

Moshe took a deep breath and smoothed his tunic before knocking on the door to Amon's room. His heart pounded uncontrollably and he knew his hands shook.

I must not let the king see that I'm afraid.

The door was opened by a servant, who ushered Moshe into the presence of the king. He was surprised to see the king seated beside the window, apparently calm.

His calm demeanour may be deceptive.

The king's head swung in his direction, a smile in place. Moshe was aware that the smile did not extend to the eyes, which gleamed with hardness.

"Well, well, Moshe, my friend and advisor. Come, sit near me." With his foot, Amon indicated a low seat just below his elevated one. "Don't delay. We have things to discuss."

Reluctantly, Moshe sat. He had to lean back and tilt his head to meet the king's blazing eyes. The king was silent.

I will not speak first. I must know what direction he will take. His silences are more deadly than his rages.

At length, Amon leaned forward, smile gone, until his face was inches from Moshe's. "I trust there is an explanation for this morning's fiasco."

To Moshe, his voice sounded like iron scraping over iron.

"I have no explanation. Perhaps you should check with your chief soldier." Moshe knew these were dangerous words.

"Are you referring to the commander who has conveniently disappeared? Perhaps you know something about that."

The king's face changed. His eyebrows drew tight, saliva seeping from one corner of his mouth. Without warning, Amon circled Moshe's neck with a strong hand. The grip tightened and Moshe could barely breathe. He scrambled from his seat and grabbed Amon's hands. Slowly the grip loosened, but the fight was on. When Amon punched him, Moshe reciprocated, and the two fell to the floor, grunting and snarling.

The sounds alerted the guards, who burst into the room. Together, they pulled the two apart. One guard grabbed Moshe and led him from the room.

"It would be wise to disappear for a while," the guard said to Moshe.

"Take your hand off me. We haven't finished this yet."

With that, Moshe turned and rushed back into the room. By this time, the other guard had Amon sitting on a couch, wiping blood from his face.

"Guards, leave us!" Amon commanded.

They left quickly, closing the door behind them.

Moshe stared into Amon's eyes. "So, do you feel better now that you almost killed the only dependable person you have around you?"

Amon began to laugh, softly at first, then bursting into fits of raucous howls. "Moshe, you kill me."

Not yet, my most excellent master, not yet. Aloud he said, "Are you ready to discuss the situation?"

Amon wiped a cloth over his face, wearing a more sober look. "Oh yes, I'm ready. We needed that fight to get us back on track. It cleared the air, my friend."

Moshe didn't reply, but Amon didn't seem to notice.

"As I see it," Amon began, sitting back in his seat and putting his feet up, "the priests have disappeared, the captain of the guard has disappeared... anyone else I should know about?"

Moshe waited a minute before he replied. *He's too relaxed. I need to be very careful.*

"The priests should be easy to trace, especially if they went together," Moshe said. "They must have run to the back of the temple and escaped. From there, they could have gone in any direction. The gates are always guarded, though, so they must still be in the city. I would advise sending out teams of soldiers to search the homes of the people we know are still loyal to the priests. One of them must be hiding them."

Amon rose, walked to the door, opened it, and gave a message to the guards in the hall. When he came back to his seat, he had a sardonic grin on his face.

"The guards have been given instructions to bring the priests to me immediately," the king said. "I expect we'll see them before the sun passes another mark on the dial."

"What will you do with them?" Moshe asked. He then listened carefully for the king's answer. His own plan would depend on Amon's next steps.

Amon rested his chin on his hands. "I won't have them killed at this point. The masses are still divided between the priests' fantasies and my power." He jumped up and strode to the window. "I've got it! Why don't we send them away, each to a different place where they can be held under guard? That way, they can't communicate with each other. The people won't rebel because there'll be no bodies, so we can't be held responsible. Later, we can send someone to kill each one separately, and no one will know what happened. They'll be out of our way."

"A good plan, master."

"If the captain of the guards returns, he'll be sentenced to death immediately. I need the soldiers, so they're safe for now." His chin jutted out from his clamped jaws. "But where was Huldah in all of this? I can't believe she wasn't involved. Once the priests are dealt with, I want her head."

"Is that wise right now?" Moshe asked.

"Yes. Your assignment is to find her, remove her head, and deliver it to me personally. Now, leave me."

Moshe moved toward the door.

"And don't come back without her head, or your head will be next."
Moshe left without a backward glance.

thirty-seven

Shallum faced his wife. "You must have someone with you. I won't allow you to go on your own."

"But Shallum, you know I'll be fine. If God has told me to go, He'll protect me." She tried to smile, but her attempt fell short.

"I still insist that someone go with you." He placed his hands on her shoulders, leaned in until his nose touched hers, and looked directly into her eyes. "Please trust me on this. I know you plan to take our son, and there's no way I'll let you travel alone."

She attempted a smile again, this time with a hint of triumph. "And just who is this mysterious person who should accompany me?"

I've got him now, she thought. *There's no one to go with me.*

"My mother," he said simply.

"Esther? She won't want to travel to Bozkath."

"I've already spoken to her, and she's packing as we speak." Shallum kissed her nose and pulled her into a hug. "You know you'd love to have company, and who better than Yaacov's own grandmother? Mother can look after Yaacov when you take the time to rest and help others. Besides, I'll feel so much better knowing you're not alone."

Huldah wrapped her arms around his neck and kissed him. "I'm so blessed to have you, my husband. But you certainly have the more difficult role. I can't be what you hoped for."

Shallum stroked her hair. "You, my love, are even more than I hoped for. God has been so good to both of us."

H

Early morning mist hung low on the fields along the main route to Bozkath. Esther and Huldah, wearing plain head coverings with the ends covering mouths and noses, joined a noisy group of merchants on their way to distant towns. Yaacov slept in a sling tightly wrapped around Huldah's dull brown robe. Nothing distinguished them from other housewives.

About a league from the gates, Yaacov stirred and Huldah patted his back, hoping he would return to sleep. Instead, he started screaming, crying frantically. The women stopped along the side of the road and Huldah removed him from the sling. She tried to comfort him, but the crying intensified.

"Esther, hold him for a moment. See if you can comfort him."

Huldah handed him over to his grandmother, who patted his back and walked up and down the side of the road.

"I'm not helping, either," Esther said. "Why don't you try again?"

With the baby in her arms again, Huldah sang to him and rocked him back and forth. Nothing helped. His little face was very red, and soon he became sick.

"It's no use, Esther. He won't be comforted." She looked around to get her bearing on exactly where they were. "Up ahead, there's a path that leads to Asher's house. You remember him? He's stayed loyal to God through all the troubles of the past several years."

Esther nodded. "I remember. Tikvah once had business with him in the marketplace. Is it far to his place?"

"It's still a bit of a walk, but it seems the best thing to do. Yaacov won't make it to Bozkath like this."

Yaacov continued to scream as the two set off again. Huldah put him back in the sling so they could make better time.

They soon reached the path to Asher's home. A grove of trees marked the entrance. It was cooler here than on the main road, which seemed to help the baby.

At last the low roof of Asher's house came into view. It was a large home, for Asher had money and had carved out a nice property. Fragrant flower and herb gardens graced the sides of the walkways around the house.

When they approached, they were surprised to see several people walking the paths.

"Esther, isn't that Hilkiah walking with Asher?"

The two women hurried along the path and arrived breathless in front of Asher and Hilkiah.

"Huldah, what are you doing here?" Hilkiah left Asher's side and reached her. He looked from face to face, his own face wreathed in a wide smile. "I'm so happy to see you and you, too, Esther."

"We're on our way to Bozkath," Huldah said. She looked down at Yaacov and realized that he had stopped crying. In fact, he'd fallen asleep. "Yaacov was crying and sick, so we decided to come in to see if we could find help here with Asher. But he's fine now. Hilkiah, I think God used the baby to lead us to you."

Asher stepped forward and gave a low bow to Huldah and Esther. "Welcome to my humble home, ladies. I will serve you in any way I can."

"Thank you, Asher, we knew we could count on your help," Huldah said. "But it looks like it's a different kind of help than I expected. God is so good."

"That he is, Prophetess," Asher said. "Please come into my home. I'll see that you have a comfortable place to sit with Hilkiah to talk, and I'll serve you the best my house has to offer."

They followed him into the home, where it was cool and comfortable. They were soon seated in the rear of the house, overlooking the garden.

Asher bowed his way out of the room to see to the meal.

"Are the other priests here with you?" Huldah eased Yaacov from his sling and into her arms. He sighed, but continued sleeping.

"Yes, we're all here… and anxious for news."

"Then call the others to join us and we'll tell you everything we know," Huldah said. "We also need to make plans to keep in touch."

Esther left the room to look for the priests. Huldah and Hilkiah sat in comfortable silence while they waited.

Talmar and Jamin arrived first.

"Huldah, this is a pleasant surprise," Talmar said. Esther led both men to comfortable seats close to Huldah. Once they were seated, the others arrived.

A touching scene unfolded when Amaziah realized that his daughter and grandson were there. He embraced Huldah with tenderness, kissing her cheek and placing a soft kiss on Yaacov's head.

"I can't tell you much more than you already know," Huldah began, "but I can tell you that I watched the entire Atonement ceremony from the hillside. Once the soldiers arrived, I watched the crowd disperse. They all arrived home safely."

"That was my biggest worry, that lives had been lost." Hilkiah bowed his head and clasped his hands tightly in his lap. When he raised his eyes to look at Huldah, there were tears on his face.

"That's the good news." Huldah paused. "The bad news is that Amon is very angry, as you may well suppose. While I was still on the hillside, God spoke to me and told me that I must go to Josiah, that he needs to be taught how to be a good king. Esther and I were on our way when God turned us aside to find you here." She stroked her baby's head. "I'm just sorry that Yaacov had to suffer so much for me to turn from the road."

Yaacov gave another contended sigh, assuring his mother that there was no lasting damage done.

"God also told me that it wouldn't be long now," Huldah continued. "So be encouraged, dear priests. You must stay hidden for now. There are rumours in the city that if you are found, you will be dispersed throughout Judah and later killed."

Her words met with silence. She knew they were aware of the danger, but they accepted whatever God sent into their lives.

"You remember that I prophesied that Amon would reign for two years." Nods of agreement met this statement. "We are well past the first year, so I need to be sure Josiah is ready. He'll have advisors in place, and it is my hope that some of you will be part of that. I will always be in the background to listen and advise, whatever is needed."

"Some of us may not see his reign come to pass," Talmar said, "so it is comforting to know he will be a good king and turn the land back to God."

"Amen to that," Jamin said.

"It is important that all of you stay here until I bring word that it is safe to return." Huldah's voice was deep and commanding. "Please know that you won't be helping anyone if you decide to enter the city. Not only will you bring harm to yourself, you may lead the soldiers to the others. Do I have your promises?"

Hilkiah's hand shook when he reached out to her. "Huldah, I feel I can speak for all of us. We will do as you have instructed, is that not right?" He took in each of the others with his glance and was rewarded with agreement.

Asher entered the room, followed by three servants who quickly set up tables in front of them. Another servant brought drinks and still others brought platters of food. Huldah hadn't realized she was hungry until the taste of roasted lamb and fresh vegetables touched her lips. The talk around the tables was pleasant and interesting.

Huldah finally stood, wrapping Yaacov in her shawl. "I hate to leave you, but if we are to arrive at Bozkath before the gates close, we must be on our way."

The last view Huldah had was of Hilkiah and Talmar waving to her. She and Esther then turned their eyes to the road ahead.

H

"More nails. I don't want those boards coming loose," Amon bellowed from his horse as it pranced before the temple gates. He pulled the reigns tightly with one hand, squeezing his horse's sides with his heels. "No one must be able to enter."

He grimaced, watching each worker carefully. *Are there no competent people in all of Jerusalem?*

"Not like that, you fool!" His whip whistled through the air and a young worker cried out in pain and surprise. "Waste no time moaning. There's a job to be done."

Do they realize I could have their heads decorating the palace walls before dark?

Back and forth he paced on his black horse, which became more agitated as the day progressed. Sweat beaded the horse's flanks and Amon's face. He swiped at his face with the back of his hand, cursing under his breath.

"Where is Moshe?" Amon demanded, flinging the words at the temple gates.

A head popped into view from the gates.

"I'm here, my lord. What is it?" Moshe lifted a soiled towel from the ground and wiped his hands on it while moving toward the king. "What is it? What's wrong?"

Amon slipped off the horse to face Moshe eye to eye. "Nothing's wrong that a few severed heads wouldn't help. Why are these workers so lazy? Was there no one else available? Is this what this kingdom has come to—inefficient workers, dishonest dealers, thieves, cheats, and Moshe, who pretends to be so loyal?"

Moshe stepped back.

"What?" Amon said, swinging down from his horse. "Even you, my loyal advisor, can't take some advice from your leader?"

Moshe pushed Amon's chest and moved them out of earshot of the workers who were staring at them; they had probably heard every word.

"Are you out of your mind, Amon? You can't come out here and throw your weight around," Moshe said, pushing his finger into Amon's chest. "Go back to the palace, unless you want this to end badly. I'll come as soon as we've finished the job. It will be finished and finished properly. You have my word."

"Now that's rich. Your word, is it? And just how good is that word, Moshe? Can it be trusted? I have my doubts." Amon swung back up on his horse. "But for now, I'll be the good king and go back to my palace."

Amon pulled the reigns and turned the horse's head in the direction of the gates.

"I will expect a full report before sundown," the king said. "I want this place sealed so tight that not even the cleverest thief can gain entry, to say nothing of the priesthood. I'll wait for your report. Oh, you can be sure I'll be waiting."

He flung his final words over his shoulder just before the horse galloped away.

H

Deep in the hills outside Jerusalem, the darkness was intense, so close that it wrapped itself around the lone traveller who walked along it, shivering with dread. Moshe picked his way over the rock-strewn path, pausing to sense, rather than see, directions to the cave he sought.

I must be mad to have come here, but there's no turning back now. No one knows where I am, not that I want anyone to know… but if I don't arrive back, no one will look for me here.

A tiny pinprick of light flickered momentarily in the distance. *Probably a fire within the cave entrance.*

The speck of fire grew in intensity and he knew he had found the right place. Wild laughter poured from the cave. Wave after wave of it assaulted his ears. The sound stopped as quickly as it had started, and the night was once again quiet—an eerie quiet, a quiet that throbbed with dread and suspicion.

"Moshe… Moshe…"

Did I really hear my name? My imagination has gone wild.

"Moshe… Moshe… come closer…"

The light from the cave grew brighter and he knew he was close to the entrance. He walked on, until a woman appeared before the fire and cut off most of the light. The shape of her silhouette rose and fell with the movement of the flames. A misshapen form materialized by her side.

Maksim! So it's true. She does keep company with a hyena.

A shudder slid down his back as he pulled his cloak tighter around him as protection against the evil he sensed.

Only a fool would come here, so I guess that makes me a fool. Steady now, Moshe. Don't forget you're here for a reason.

The stench was overwhelming. Between the unwashed body of the witch and the odour of the hyena, he clamped his mouth shut so not to gag. He straightened his shoulders, lifted his chin, and took the last steps to the cave entrance, where the pair awaited him.

A low growl sent a chill through him. The firelight glanced off the witch's eyes and the hyena's bared fangs.

Maksim glared at him in silence, until a quick movement of her hand sent the hyena his way. Its wicked jaws clamped onto his leg with a powerful force.

"Maksim, call off your creature," Moshe said.

Maksim remained silent, watching him with folded arms and narrowed eyes. The hyena's fangs deepened their hold and Moshe cried out in pain.

"Maksim, now. Call it off." He shook his leg in the hopes of disengaging the jaws, to no avail.

The witch lowered her arms and stepped closer. "Lilith, cease."

Immediately the hyena released him and slunk to Maksim's side, still grumbling in its throat. It then threw its head back and a series of laughing calls filled the night air.

"There are rules to be followed, if you seek my wisdom." Maksim swayed before him, horrible in appearance and voice.

Fear crowded the corners of his mind. "Tell me. I'll do anything you say."

"Nothing I say here is ever to be repeated."

"Agreed."

"If you want results, my instructions must be followed exactly."

"Yes, of course."

"Any deviation from them will result in instant death."

"I understand."

"I must be paid for my trouble."

"I've come prepared to pay."

"Ha, gold coin? And what would I do with that?"

"Please, just tell me what you want, and it shall be done."

"I think we may be able to make a deal."

"Anything you want."

"I need supplies, food, comforts…"

"I will get you whatever you desire."

"Then enter my cave, if you dare."

I am in deep. There's no turning back now.

Maksim stood aside and allowed him to enter. Lilith followed closely on his heels, nipping at them.

If I don't kick Lilith, it will be a miracle. Get away from me, you brute. Maybe the beast can read minds… I'd better be careful.

"Sit here." Maksim indicated a heap of rags along one side of the cave, on the side where the smoke from the fire drifted.

He sat and wiped his eyes in an attempt to stop the sting from the smoke. She sat on a low stool where he could only see her through a haze. Lilith sat at her side, beady eyes focused on Moshe.

"You want to kill the king," she said. Her words seemed to be spit through the murk.

Moshe jumped from his seat, eyes wide with terror. Lilith stood and the low growl intensified.

"Sit, Moshe, advisor to the king. We have not finished our business."

He sat.

The silence stretched out between them. Only the crackle of the fire and the swirl of smoke broke the stillness.

When Lilith edged toward him, displaying powerful teeth, he decided it was time to speak.

"I keep my reasons to myself. I come with inquiries for auspicious times—"

"To commit murder, you mean."

"I told you, my reasons are my own."

"And I told you that I already know what you're after." Lilith gave a sharp yip when Maksim finished speaking.

Almost like a warning. I'd better be careful. I'm in way over my head.

"All right," Moshe said, "supposing I am going to commit murder, which I'm not."

"Double speak. You're correct that you're not going to commit the murder, but you are definitely orchestrating it." She pointed one long, crooked finger at him while her ragged sleeves hung in tatters from a scrawny arm. "Deviser of murder, oh yes, that is what you are. How soon the lofty fall. But I am anxious to hear what other lies you wish to tell. Sit, Lilith."

Moshe tried to ignore the hyena and focus on Maksim's withered face. This didn't help, as her face was repulsive, forcing all rational thought from his mind. He swallowed twice, then determined to get through this.

"It may be as you say," Moshe continued. "Nevertheless, I must know the optimal time to commit this imaginary crime. My sources tell me you are able to foresee signs and times."

"Does that surprise you, advisor to the king?"

"Not in the least. Your reputation is well-known on the streets of Jerusalem."

She put her hand under her chin and stared into the fire.

What is she doing? I wish there was some way I could get out of here, but that hyena has its eyes fixed on me. What a mess I'm in.

With a deep breath, she eased herself back from the fire. "Give me details and I can help you."

Once he had completed outlining his crude plan, she rose from her place by the fire and disappeared into the back of the cave. At length she returned, carrying an array of items which she set down beside her stool. She pulled a small table to her side and placed her items on it.

The heavy haze of smoke made it difficult to see what she had brought. He watched her lift a small pot and place it in the fire on a low grate he hadn't noticed before. Into the pot she began to place items. He was sure he saw herbs being torn into small pieces and dropped in. Water was added, as well as another indistinguishable liquid. Tiny rocks were added next. A broken stick was used to stir the concoction, and soon the mixture came to a boil.

Steam rose from the pot, overpowering the smoke momentarily. This new irritant was potent and harsh. Moshe found himself gulping great breaths. His vision blurred and he heard her voice as though from a great distance.

"Powers of darkness, I command you. Come." A large puff of steam escaped from the boiling pot.

The putrid stench repulsed his nostrils. Unable to prevent it, he felt himself passing from wakefulness to trance. The last thing he saw were oddly shaped moving creatures—evil spirits, he supposed. They carried with them foul odours. He knew he should flee, but darkness overcame him.

When he awoke, he was alone in the cave. He sat up, rubbing his head in an attempt to clear his thoughts. The fire was reduced to embers and all signs of the pot and contents were gone. It was still dark outside the cave, and a chill crept in.

He heard snarls and then saw Lilith peering around the cave entrance at him, fangs exposed and a fearsome glint in her eyes. Lilith opened her mouth wide and emitted a series of hollow sounds resembling crazed laughter. Moshe froze.

"Lilith, be still."

Moshe couldn't believe that he was actually relieved to hear Maksim's voice. The woman ducked her head into the cave without a glance at him. Once seated again beside the glowing embers, she began to chant, softly at first, then rising in crescendo. To Moshe, she seemed to be in a trance, unaware of his presence.

"Shishi, just before Shabbat," she said in her trance. "Never kill on Shabbat. In the month Tevet, on the day Shishi, just before Shabbat. Just before the new moon. Darkness covers evil deeds. Shishi, Shabbat, Shishi, Shabbat."

She rocked back and forth before the embers, continuing to mutter softly. Moshe recognized names of demons and other evil beings.

With a soft moan and with his head held in his hands, he fled the cave. He ran until there was no more breath in his body and his legs gave out. The grassy knoll accepted his fall and the night went dark.

thirty-eight

"Where is Moshe? I ordered him to the palace hours ago. Why has he not arrived?"

Akiva stood before Amon, his face stiff except for a slight tremble of the chin.

"Answer me. I demand an explanation." Amon's eyebrows pulled tightly over angry eyes.

"He can't be located."

"What do you mean, he can't be located? If he's in Jerusalem, a messenger could find him anywhere."

"He's not in Jerusalem, my lord." Akiva bowed his head, his clasped hands whitening at the knuckles.

Amon stilled. "Not in Jerusalem, you say?" he asked in a low, threatening voice. "Then where is he?"

"No one knows, Master."

"But someone must have seen him leave the city. Send for the guards, all the ones who have been on duty for the hours he's been missing." He ground his teeth and spat at Akiva's feet. "Go!"

ℋ

Damp fog drifted over a grassy hillside outside the gates of Jerusalem. Shrill bleats and the sharp tinkle of bells pierced the morning air.

Moshe sat up and rubbed his head, which ached with a stubborn persistence. He watched a shepherd lead his goats over the top of the hillside.

Where am I? Outside the gates, it looks like. But why?

The events of the previous night invaded his conscious thought and he jumped from his place on the grass. Cautiously, he turned in a full circle, expecting to see Maksim or Lilith, but the hillside was empty.

I need to get out of here and back into the city. This could be a problem.

He stood in contemplation for a few minutes. He was dressed as a country farmer and so would be able to slip through the gates more easily than if he had donned his palace robes. And yet, someone might be watching for him. He needed to time his entrance when there was a distraction.

Swaying colours caught his eye. In the distance, a large caravan approached the gates. Without further thought, he walked swiftly toward it, mingling with the crowd. Street urchins from the city soon milled around the camels and drivers. Fortunately for Moshe, many men were on foot and some led camels and donkeys.

In the end, entry into the city was easy. He slipped down a side street, away from the crowded thoroughfares. He eased himself through a narrow divide between two buildings and continued along a crooked path that wound its way between tattered houses. Refuse covered the dirt path, and dirty children played before derelict homes. Dogs joined the fray, jostling each other among the children, who ignored them. No one paid him any attention and he was able to pass without being questioned.

At the end of the path, a rickety structure jutted over a small pond. *It's laughable that they call that a pond. It's really a puddle filled with refuse and dirty water.*

The odour reached his nostrils and he covered his nose and mouth with the end of his scarf. Without a backward glance, he slipped into the building through a door that was slightly ajar.

Inside, it was dark and musty. *A fitting scene for a nasty deed.*

"I've come." Moshe paused to allow his eyes to adjust.

A form appeared to his left. "It's about time. Where have you been?"

Moshe stiffened at the sound of the rough voice. "Where I go and what I do is my business."

"Oh, high and mighty Moshe."

"No names. We agreed on that."

"Fine, oh lord and master. No names."

"Then let's get on with it. Is there somewhere in this filthy hovel we can sit?" Moshe said.

"I'm offended you don't appreciate my fine abode. But there are benches at the back. Follow me."

Moshe was surprised to see an old woman bent over a pot balanced on a stool. She was stirring a powdery substance into the contents of the pot. She didn't speak as they passed her.

When they were seated, Moshe turned his face toward his accomplice. "Can she be trusted?" He jerked his head in the direction of the old woman.

"No worries. She's deafer than the pot in front of her."

Moshe sat back on the bench. *How much do I tell him? Not everything, for sure.*

"I have the date for you," Moshe said.

His companion appeared to study his dirty fingernails. "Perhaps the date won't suit me."

"Perhaps I'll find another who will be happy to work for the scandalous price you think you deserve."

"Tell me the date."

Moshe leaned toward his accomplice until his mouth was lined up with his hairy ear. "Tevet on Shishi, the third Shishi in Tevet."

"Just before Shabbat, clever. Wouldn't be good to kill on Shabbat." The man rubbed his chin, pondering the date. "If I'm correct, that should line up with the new moon. A good dark night."

"A very good time for what we want to do."

"We? Are you to be a part of this? That's news to me."

Moshe raised his brows. "I'm a big part of this. Without my money, where would you be?"

"Couldn't be a much worse place than this, now could it?"

"Talk sense. Are you in or out?"

"Oh, I'm in."

ℋ

"When will I be king, Huldah?" Josiah snuggled close to the prophetess's side as they sat on a flat stone beyond the garden. He could see a long way down the dusty road, empty of travellers today.

"What made you think about this today?" Huldah asked.

"I think about it every day and wonder when it will happen. I know you said I would be eight, and I've just had my eighth birthday. Besides, you've been teaching me how to be a good king. And I will be." He sat up straight. "You can depend on me, Huldah. I want to be a good king. I'm not like my father, am I?"

"No, Josiah, you're not like your father, and God has promised me that you will be a good king." She rose, lifting him from the rock. "Let's walk for a bit."

"Can we walk along the road to Jerusalem? It makes me feel the time's getting closer."

"Yes, of course. Why don't we ask your mother to come with us, and bring Yaacov with her?"

"That's a great idea." He released her hand and ran toward the house. "Mother, mother!"

Jedidah came out of the house, carrying Yaacov in her arms. "What is it, Josiah? Are you all right?"

"Oh yes, Mother, I'm fine. It's just that Huldah and I are going to walk a ways along the road to Jerusalem and we want you and Yaacov to come with us. Please say yes."

Jedidah laughed. "Of course we'll come. Yaacov will love it."

She said something to Johanna, then closed the door and joined her son.

Soon the four were on the road. Huldah had bound Yaacov in his sling before they set off, where he promptly fell asleep.

H

Josiah ran ahead, chasing flies, lizards, anything that moved. Jedidah and Huldah took a slower pace, enjoying the warm air.

"Jedidah, I know you don't like to talk about the future, but the time has come when you must," Huldah said. "God has sent me another vision which you need to know about."

Jedidah stopped and stared at Huldah. After a deep breath, Jedidah began to move again. Huldah let her have all the time she needed.

I know this is hard for her. I'll wait until she's ready.

"I'm ready to hear what you have to say," Jedidah said. "What did you see in the vision?"

Huldah nodded. "I saw you as the regent to King Josiah."

Jedidah let out a sharp gasp. "I can't do that. You know I can't. Oh, what will we do?" Her sobs came in quiet gulps.

"Jedidah, God doesn't call people and then leave them alone to face their trials. If He places you as regent, He'll be right beside you. You believe that, don't you?"

Jedidah's hands covered her eyes and damp tears ran over them. "Yes, I do," she whispered. "But how can I be sure that's what God wants me to do?"

"I saw it, Jedidah. It's true."

"But I only have your word for it. What if it was just a dream?" Her eyes peeked out between her wet fingers.

Huldah laughed softly. "You don't believe that. You know from experience that if I saw it, it's true."

"I just don't want to believe it. It frightens me. It terrifies me! Huldah, I don't think I can do it."

"Of course you can." Huldah took her arm and they strolled after Josiah, who had gotten far ahead of them.

"Huldah, what else did you see?"

"Nothing at present, but you can be sure God will reveal more when it's needed."

"Will you help me when the time comes?" Jedidah took both of Huldah's hands in hers. "Please."

"You can count on it Jedidah. I'll be in the background, ready whenever you need me."

"And Ehud. He'll help, I know."

Huldah's body stiffened as she gazed off into the distance. "It's as I said before: Ehud will not see Jerusalem again."

𝓗

Moshe strode through the palace gates and entered through the wide doors. The guards stepped aside to allow him passage. His face was set in a scowl. At the door to the king's rooms, Moshe rapped on the door with impatience, and it was quickly opened by Akiva.

"At last, Moshe. The king has been distressed by your absence." Akiva bowed low and left the room.

Moshe entered and faced the king, who stood when the door opened. The two men faced each other at a distance.

"I presume you have a reason—no, pardon me, an excuse—for your absence," Amon said. "You were summoned to the palace and I do not tolerate disobedience."

"I received no such summons."

"But where were you?"

"I was on business."

"On business? My advisors only attend to *my* business." Amon approached, his hands reaching for Moshe's neck. "Do I make myself clear, Moshe?"

Moshe gripped the king's hands and lowered them. He stared into Amon's eyes. "Very clear, my lord. It won't happen again.

And that's the truth, noble king. Soon I will not be under your command.

Amon's body visibly relaxed and he indicated two chairs for them to sit in. Moshe was sleep-deprived, but knew he must stay alert. Amon was especially dangerous today.

"It appears that our plans have met with obstacles," Amon said.

Moshe remained silent.

"The prophetess has not yet been brought to me, the priests have disappeared, my wife and son are still missing, and the masses are still not completely under my control." Amon's eyes narrowed and he sat forward. "Could it be because my advisors are disloyal? Or perhaps they are just ineffective."

Moshe knew he was on treacherous ground. "My lord, the prophetess has powers from another world, whether for good or evil I know not. The priests have been spirited away by her, and I believe the people are moving toward your cause."

Amon jumped from his seat. "You believe, you believe! What kind of answer is that? I don't care a silver shekel what you think."

Careful, Moshe. Careful.

"You're right, what I believe isn't important," Moshe said. "The plan is important. We need to get the others in here and discuss our next steps."

Moshe placed a hand on Amon's shoulder and eased him back onto his seat.

"Yes, that's what we need to do." Amon's shoulders slumped and he motioned to Moshe with a limp hand. "Find them and we'll meet here as soon as possible."

Moshe's last glimpse of Amon was of a hunched figure with his hands clutched in his hair. Low moans followed him from the room.

H

"Come closer, everyone. We must keep our voices low." Moshe waited while the others pulled their seats closer until their knees touched. The room was almost dark; only one small candle burned on a low table beside Moshe's elbow. He glanced around the group and took note of each one— Ethan, Joel, and Jotham. He had spoken to them individually after their last session with Amon, where the king had laid out a plan so evil that even the most brutal of them had shuddered.

"Friends," Moshe said, "before we begin, I must ask you again. Are you ready to be a part of this venture? Ethan?"

"I can see no other way, so yes," Ethan said, his eyes steady on Moshe's. "Joel?"

"Yes, of course. This evil violence must be stopped."

"Jotham?"

"I wasn't sure at first, but I haven't been able to sleep since our meeting. I feel I have no choice but to join you. The land and the people deserve much better than this crazed and evil king." Jotham bowed his head in his hands when he finished speaking.

"I have posted trusted men as guards at the door, but nothing is safe in this city." Moshe blew out the candle and left them in semi-darkness. He waited until his eyes adjusted before continuing. "My proposal is that each of us will only know part of the plan. The less we know, the better our chances for success. All you need to know at present is that I have sought help in choosing the optimum date. I have also hired an accomplice to execute the plan. Even I won't know exactly what form the death will take." He watched them in the dim light for any signs of disagreement; none were visible. "The date selected is the third Shishi in Tevet."

"Close enough to avoid his great plan to wipe out half the population, and far enough off for us to ensure the plan goes off without a hitch," Ethan said.

"We need to make sure that we know where he will be at all times that night. Thoughts?" Moshe made eye contact with each of them. They appeared to be deep in thought.

At last, Joel sat back with a pleased look on his face. "What about this? We plan a pre-celebration banquet, just for the four of us and the king. He loves celebrating, and we can make sure he drinks lots of wine. Between us, we'll know where he is every minute."

Ethan gripped his shoulder. "That's a great idea. What do you think, Moshe?"

"I couldn't have come up with a better plan myself," Moshe said. He leaned toward Jotham. "What do you think?"

"It's brilliant. Let's do it."

The four joined hands and pledged to keep the plan and rid the country of the brutal rule of Amon.

thirty-nine

*L*ight blazed from candles placed at intervals around Amon's private rooms. Servants scurried about, setting the table with the best the palace had to offer. Chatter among the servants was light and inconsequential, setting a festive tone.

Akiva entered bearing wine glasses and stood aghast as he listened to the light banter among the servants.

"We have a job to do," Akiva said. "Do your duty and stop the idle chatter."

He lowered the tray to a side table amidst the silence that followed his words.

"Hadar, place these wine glasses on the table. Then return to the kitchen and ask Metra when the meal will be ready."

Hadar bowed to Akiva, set the goblets in place, then hastened from the room.

"Dor, have the cushions been aired, the room cleaned, and fresh towels set out?"

"Yes, Akiva, everything has been attended to," Dor said. "Hadar, Oded, and I have been working since early morning."

"Then, if the food is ready, we only need the guests for the feast to begin," Akiva said.

After one last glance around, he left the room.

H

Wine flowed, talk swelled, and the five men partook of the banquet.

"The cooks have really outdone themselves tonight," Moshe said to Amon.

"They only do what they're commanded to do. Otherwise they wouldn't be long at the palace." The king stared at his food, then gave a deep laugh as he lifted his wine goblet. "To us, and good food, and obedient cooks."

The others echoed the words and the feast continued. Course after course was carried in by the servants and set before the king. The wine goblets were filled time after time, until Amon's words were indistinct.

The evening progressed until the final course appeared: the dates soaked in honey that Amon loved so well. He reached into the pot and withdrew the first one, popping it into his mouth whole. When his teeth sank into the date, his eyes flew open and he jumped from his seat.

With both hands over his throat, he choked out, "Someone's trying to poison me. Do something!"

He fell to the floor, taking the table with him. Moshe and the other three left him where he lay and disappeared into the night.

H

Early in the morning, the residents of Jerusalem were awakened with the noise of military voices shouting from their palace mounts. "The king is dead. Treachery!"

Quickly the streets filled with crowds, all trying to make sense of the message. Behind the soldiers walked the king's advisors, dressed in sombre colours, carrying the king's banner.

"The king is dead. Mourn for him, people of Jerusalem."

Someone in the crowd dared to cheer. Three soldiers sprang from their horses and the search was on for the culprit. When they were unable to find him, swords slashed and people scattered amidst screams and commands.

Moshe watched the scene through hooded eyes and glanced at the others with him.

We walk a treacherous path. Thankfully, the palace servants seem trustworthy and nothing has been said. But the captain of the guard is no fool. It will take everything in our power to keep the focus from us.

Moshe had been present while the servants were questioned early in the morning. Once word of the king's death reached the military encampment, the captain and a group of his finest arrived at the palace. By this time, Moshe had returned to the palace and sat in on the proceedings.

He smiled to himself. *No one knew anything. I didn't even have to lie. I knew nothing. And I'm sure my accomplice is far from Jerusalem by now. I think we're safe.*

Akiva had been marvellous. Even the story about the strange man seen milling around the back door of the palace had been brilliant. Right that moment, a small army of soldiers was combing the countryside looking for him. Of course, he wouldn't be found.

I loved the cook's story about how she had to leave the kitchen unattended for a few minutes... just enough time for someone to slip into the kitchen and poison the dates.

The night had been brutal, though it was all necessary. Now the land was free.

ℋ

Alone, Shallum stood at the edge of the crowd while the soldiers marched past. His mind was filled with turmoil, though he kept his face still and his turban low on his forehead.

This is an incredible turn of events. Not totally unexpected, but shocking nonetheless. Huldah must be informed—and who better than me?

Shallum had arrived at the palace early in the morning to be greeted by shaken guards, fearful for their lives.

"What will the future hold for us?" one of the guards asked Shallum, who didn't know how to answer. "Will we be thrown on the fire with the king?"

If I were one of the guards, I, too, would fear the military. They are certainly loyal to the king.

He turned his steps homeward and reported the evil events to his father.

"Naturally, I'll need to go to Bozkath and let Huldah know," Shallum said. "I'll also check on Mother."

Tikvah ran his hands through his beard. "Yes, I believe you're right, Shallum. But that doesn't mean I like it. You'll be in danger. Soldiers will be combing the countryside looking for the king's killer, and if you're caught on the road they'll know you're on your way to Huldah. Nothing would suit them better than to find her who prophesied the early demise of the king. They may even now be accusing her of treachery."

"Yes, Father. I know it's dangerous, but I must go to Huldah."

"Then God go with you, my son."

Shallum left the house by the back entrance and worked his way through the city by back alleys and paths. He arrived at the smallest gate just as the guards were busy with a large group of angry and vocal merchants who wanted to enter the city. The guards refused them entrance, and Shallum was able to slip through unnoticed while the guards were occupied.

When he approached the path that led to Asher's house, he heard a voice say, "Turn here, Shallum."

He stopped and looked around. There was no one in sight. He wiped his hands over his eyes and looked again. Still no one.

I must have imagined it. He took another step along the main road.

"Turn here, Shallum."

He stopped again and lifted his hands to the heavens. "Yes, Lord, I hear Your voice. I'm turning."

Asher must need a visit.

The rocky path soon turned grassy under his feet. Trees cooled the air and made the walk pleasant. Up ahead, he saw the gates to Asher's property and was surprised to see the gates closed.

Now that's strange. I wonder why the gates are closed.

When he neared the gates, a guard stepped from the side with his sword drawn. "Stop. What is your business here?"

"Is that you, Malachi?"

The sword lowered and the guard looked at him carefully. A wide grin replaced his stern look. "Shallum, is it truly you?"

"Yes, it really is, Malachi. Why all the security?"

"We've seen soldiers on the main road. Asher felt we would be safer with added protection."

Shallum nodded. "A wise move. Will I be permitted entrance?"

Malachi jumped back and released the lock on the gates. They slowly swung open. "Of course, Shallum. My master will be pleased to see you, as will his guests."

"He already has guests? Won't I be intruding?"

"No, indeed you won't. You'll be most welcome. Please, follow me."

Shallum was led to the front door of the house, on which Malachi knocked briskly. A servant opened the door, and after a whispered conversation the servant beckoned Shallum to enter.

"Come, please. The master will want to see you right away."

Shallum followed the servant through the house and into the back enclosure. His jaw dropped when his eyes took in the company.

"Shallum, welcome." Asher rose from his place. "You know the others. Come, sit with us. We'll be happy to hear your news. The world passes us by in our secluded spot."

The priests greeted him one by one. Amaziah hugged him closely, tears clinging to his eyelashes. "Ah Shallum, how good it is to see you."

Asher led him to a seat and the two sat together. "Sit beside me and tell us the news."

Shallum let his gaze touch each one before he spoke. "Friends, the news I bring is both terrible and encouraging. Please prepare your hearts for it." He swallowed and took a deep breath. "There's no easy way to tell you that the king is dead, at the hands of treacherous men who have not yet been identified, but it is supposed that his advisors were involved."

He paused to let this sink in, watching the play of emotions over their faces. Gasps filled the air.

"No one should have to die the way he did," Shallum said. "At the hands of men and far from the God who is over us all. But the land is now free."

At those words, several priests raised their eyes toward the heavens, their lips moving in silent prayer.

I will not ask if they're praising God for this deliverance, or lamenting the death of a king.

"I was on my way to Huldah with the news when God told me to turn in here." He smiled at them, with a tenderness for these men who had been so much a part of his life. "I suggest that you stay here until I return. I feel sure Huldah will have had warning from God and will know her next steps. We're all aware that she has prophesied that Josiah will be the next king."

The priests nodded, though they remained silent.

"I'm afraid that won't be an easy task, because he is so young," Shallum continued. "The king's advisors will have other ideas. We must be cunning, and careful."

Talmar rose from his seat, a frail old man, and raised his hands. "O Lord, You have allowed me to see the end of this reign of evil, and now I feel You're calling me home."

With those words, Talmar sank to the ground. The others quickly gathered around him, but the man was gone. A look of peace had settled on his still features.

Hilkiah knelt by his side. "Goodbye, my friend. I will miss you, but I know that you are in God's hands, where each of us desires to be." His head fell to Talmar's shoulder and he wept.

Asher turned to Shallum. "Go with God, Shallum. Do not delay. I'll ensure that Talmar gets an appropriate ending, but you must hasten to Huldah."

Asher embraced him, then turned him toward the door.

When Shallum left the house, hurried steps behind him caused him to turn. Amaziah reached him, breathless, and laid his hand on his arm.

"Shallum, you must let me go with you. Huldah is my daughter and I must be with her."

Shallum placed his arm around Amaziah's shoulders. "I agree. She will need both of us in the days ahead. I welcome your company."

The two headed down the path, away from Asher's house and into an unknown future.

part four

forty

*G*evira stirred in her sleep, the covers bunched in a heap over her prone body. Her eyes fluttered, then opened to the early dawn. While she stretched, her mind was already in motion.

Another day in the back lanes of Jerusalem. What a sorry mess my life has become, and with no end in sight.

She struggled to a sitting position, tangled dank hair falling over pinched, sharp features. Her two bony hands pushed the dirty hair back from her face.

And what is all this for? To raise a baseborn child who Amon promised would be king? Ha! That's a laugh. He's become so high and mighty since the crown rested on his head. He doesn't even remember that we exist.

Her feet hit the floor, her rage building. Amon was still young, which meant they could be waiting for years.

I'll grow older and more destitute, and my poor son will learn the ways of the dirty byways of the city instead of how to be a king. But I could kill Amon myself... yes, I could.

With that thought, Gevira shuffled across the room and into a tiny alcove where her son was asleep. She stared with awe at his features, so like the king.

If Amon ever dies, it'll be easy. The so-called heir is six months younger than my Itamar. They'll have to make him king.

Laughter bubbled up inside her when she thought about the looks on the faces of the king's advisors and the priests.

While she watched her son, a disturbance in the street caught her attention. She reached the single small window in the hovel where she dwelled, threw open the shutter, and watched the scene unfold before her.

"The king is dead! The king is dead!" Soldiers proclaimed the news while crowds spilled into the streets.

A smile spread over her disfigured face. *Can this be true? Really true? I need to find out for sure.*

"Itamar, get up," Gevira yelled, grabbing a robe and cloak. "Get up, I said."

The boy appeared beside her, sleep still evident in his half-opened eyes. "I'm up. Stop yelling." He rubbed his eyes and yawned.

"You must not leave the house. Your father is apparently dead."

Itamar started to whimper.

She gave him a cuff on the side of his head. "Stop that noise. What is it to you if he's dead? You didn't know him."

"But I've seen him in the streets. I'll cry if I want."

This got him another slap, on the face this time. "You'll cry when I tell you to. This is our big chance. We've got to be sure, and we've got to be ready. Eat something and obey my orders, or you'll regret it."

She banged the door behind her, looked both ways in the dirty hall, and stumbled out into the daylight. The crush of people was ahead of her now, so she quickened her pace and soon reached the back of the crowd. She pulled her hood down over her forehead and adjusted the scarf over her mouth and chin. She spoke to no one but listened intently to the talk around her.

Yes, he's indeed dead. What luck! Now I need a plan.

She drifted away from the mass of people and turned down an alley-way. Her feet moved silently and quickly until she reached a hovel at the end of the alley. Peering inside, she spied the old man she sought, seated on a low stool. He moaned softly to himself.

"What is it, old man? Why do you moan?" Without waiting for an invitation to enter, she slipped into the dismal room, seating herself on the dirt floor.

The man, Ben-Ami, lifted bleary eyes to meet hers and pulled his eyebrows together. He snarled and hissed at her.

She didn't care about his hatred. She would get what she wanted from him.

"Why I moan is my business," Ben-Ami finally said. "What is it you want? I know you want something. You only come when you do."

"You're right, old one. I do want something."

"And what do I get out of this?"

She leaned in toward him. "When my son is king, you'll be well-rewarded."

"Ha, you think that baseborn monster of yours will be king? You have quite an imagination." The dry chuckle in his throat brought on a coughing spell.

"Yes, I do believe he'll be king, and so will you, if you know what's good for you."

"Just speak your piece."

She settled herself more comfortably before him, then lay a hand on his knee. He pushed it away.

"First," she said, "I need to know if the rumours are true. Is the king truly dead, or is this a palace ploy to put the people off their guard? Can you get that information?"

"Of course. That'll be easy, but I need something for my efforts. Something before I go to all this trouble." Ben-Ami reached out his hand, palm up.

From under her cloak, she pulled a small silver brooch and placed it in his gnarled hands.

"Will that do?" Gevira asked. "It's real silver."

"Yes, this will do. Return at midday and I'll have your answer. Now go, and leave me in peace."

She hurried away, an evil gleam in her eye which couldn't be hidden save for the low hood.

forty-one

*L*urid flames lit the darkening sky in front of the palace gates. Branches and logs were piled high, higher than a man's head. The wood was consumed in the crackle and hiss of the fire raging in the centre of the space.

Etched on the hillside above was the outline of a woman. Her cloak billowed in the sharp breeze that came from the country lanes outside the gates. Huldah watched, her eyes focused on the activity below. It had now been five days since her father and husband had brought her back into the city. Behind her, she'd left a household in disorder, with everyone trying to make sense of the events of the past week.

I know they'll follow my instructions to pack up and be ready to leave at a moment's notice. Ehud and Josiah are excited, even anxious to get on the road. The women are apprehensive, and I can understand that. Everything will change for them. Everything.

Her eyes never left the scene that unfolded before her. People crowded the field, row upon row, until there wasn't a space left to stand. It was quiet. Very quiet.

Huldah watched while the palace gates opened and a large procession spilled into the field. The body of the king was borne on a pallet upon the shoulders of palace servants. Behind them followed the king's advisors, dressed in formal garments suitable for the disposal of a king.

How smug they are, Lord. I know they killed him. Tell me what should be done with them. For the moment, I will focus on getting Josiah on the throne.

The cries from the long line of mourners were drowned out by the roar of the flames, but Huldah could see people's mouths open in wailing. She shook her head at the feigned display of grief.

The bearers neared the flames and mounted the steps that had been built earlier in the day. Slaves kept up a steady stream of water over them to avoid the destructive force of the fire. Slowly the bearers tipped the pallet until the body of the king slid onto the top of the pyre. The mass of people dropped to their knees, their heads touching the ground. Wails ascended to meet the smoke.

As the flames died down and only embers remained, Huldah kept her watch. The crowd dispersed quickly, until the field was empty except for the palace servants and the king's advisors. It was time. With her cloak wrapped securely around her, she set her face toward the palace and descended the hill.

ℋ

Gevira hurried through the streets. *There is now no doubt that the king is dead. They would never have gone this far to fool the people. Now, for my plan. Ben-Ami will not be pleased, but he will like the reward.*

She moved toward Ben-Ami's dismal hovel once again. The night was dark, the moon not yet visible.

It was certainly a suitable night for an evil king to burn to ashes. I'm glad I was able to view his final destruction. It's time for revenge. A cruel man he was—yes, incredibly cruel.

She would bear the marks of his sadistic advances forever. Never would she forget him. Her only reward had been the birth of her son, but her son appeared to be as evil as his father. She only cared about what the boy could do for her.

At last, the lowly temple prostitute will rule the land. That's rich. How I love the sound of power and wealth. Mine. All mine.

By the time she reached the hovel, she was in a state of rage. Sweat clung to her body beneath the ragged and dirty robe. The opening was covered with a heavy cloth, but she pushed it aside and entered unannounced.

Ben-Ami abruptly sat up from the bed of sacking in the corner where he had been asleep.

"Who's there?" His voice was raspy, shaky, and heavy with sleep.

"Who would you expect? I can't imagine you have many willing visitors." Gevira let the cloth drop back into place and dropped onto the stool in front of the fireplace. She reached for the stick beside the stool and deliberately stirred the ashes into flame.

"No, no, you're right. Not many find their way to assist an old man."

She swung around to face him, the fire gyrating behind her. "Don't fool yourself. I don't come to assist you. You assist me."

"No, daughter, I am not fooled. Your selfishness has been evident for many years."

"My selfishness? That's a good one. Do you think I've forgotten my deprived childhood under your roof? Or that you sold me into slavery in the temple?" Her voice rose with anger and tears sprang to her eyes.

He lifted a short piece of blanket and wrapped it around his bony shoulders. "Now, now, let those things stay in the past. We can't change them."

"Oh certainly, let's forget them." Her voice was laden with sarcasm and ire. "You weren't the one who was injured and shamed. And don't look so shocked. Yes, there was shame, at least at first."

"Why have you come? You got the information you wanted." His shoulders shook under the thin wrap.

Gevira leaned over until her eyes were level with his. In a slow, deliberate whisper, she outlined her plan.

H

Ben-Ami leaned against the gate that led to the outer reaches of the city. From under his turban, he watched each traveller entering and leaving the city, his eyes seemingly cast to the ground, but alert to each passing creature.

At last his eyes alighted upon the person he awaited. He moved off from the wall and into the path of Ethan, who was just leaving the city, alone.

"Out of my way, old man," Ethan said. He lifted his hand to push him, but when Ben-Ami lifted his eyes, Ethan showed signs of recognition. He stepped back, his hands out as though to ward off evil. "How dare you accost me, Ben-Ami. It is Ben-Ami, isn't it?"

"As though you need to ask, Ethan." Ben-Ami bowed to him with a sweep of his hand. "I'll walk with you for a ways."

"And why would I want to walk with you?" Ethan started to move away from the gate, but Ben-Ami kept up.

The old man rubbed his hands together, enjoying the discomfort shown in Ethan's stiff posture. "Why? Because I'll make it worth your while."

H

"Get up, you lazy, good for nothing, so-called son." Gevira pulled the tattered blanket that covered her son.

Itamar tightened his grip on the worn edge and pulled it from her fingers. This only enraged her more and she began to beat him on his back.

"Ouch, stop! You're going to kill me."

He rolled over and shot out his feet at her flailing hands.

She moved out of his way, a cloud of ugliness settling between her drawn brows. "And wouldn't the world be a better place if I did."

A small smile tried to curve her unresponsive lips.

"Come, let's stop this," she said. "We must work together if you're to be king." She had his attention now, and she risked sitting beside him on the narrow cot. "Once you're king, I'll be Queen Mother and we'll rule this God-forsaken land together."

"What if I don't want to be king?" His voice now held an irritating whine. He sat up and rubbed his eyes.

When he was like this, she remembered that he was still only a child. *I'll have to move more carefully if I'm going to be successful.*

She leaned forward and pushed a lock of hair back from his forehead. "Sure you want to be king. Just think: a nice soft bed in the palace, always enough food to eat, servants to do everything you ask, nice clothes, money, horses..."

At the mention of horses, his eyes widened and his lips broadened in a wide grin. "I can have my own horse?"

"You can have as many horses as you want."

"And can I ride them?"

"You can ride them every day, as often as you want."

He lifted both thin arms in the air and cheered. "Okay, then I'll be king."

Gevira rose and rummaged in a small container at the foot of his cot. She pulled a robe and sandals from the bottom and handed them to him. "Put these on. We have work to do."

Mother and son soon left the upper room and proceeded down the worn steps outside the small structure. The alley was rank with the odour of rotting food. They stepped carefully through the debris and soon exited onto the street outside their home.

She hustled him along the busy thoroughfare and into another section of the city. The streets were wider here and the houses farther apart. At last they reached the wall and turned in along a side path which skirted the wall. Along the path were several hovels, crowded together.

Gevira paused in front of the last one in the row. It was certainly the smallest, crudely built and in a state of disrepair. An unpleasant smell seeped from the entrance, turning her stomach even as she bent low to enter. She took Itamar by one hand, dragging him behind her.

It took a minute for her eyes to adjust, but soon she was able to see an old woman hovering over a large pot. Smoke swirled. The woman's watery eyes stared at Gevira and she was sure she saw fear. *And she should be afraid; I could snap those thin wrists in a flash.*

"Dorlas, we meet again." Gevira pulled up the only other seat in the room, a small stool, and sat.

"What do you want?"

"Ha, not another of those temple costumes you so happily made when I was in my prime. You remember... the ones you coveted, keeping the money I made rather than reporting the cruel treatment I received. Oh yes, I owe you much."

The sarcasm was not lost on the old woman. Her hand trembled and she raised it in protest. "I had no choice. You know I had no choice. It was either obey or die."

"Well, you certainly had no plans to die." Gevira settled her robe around her. "You can make up for it now. I need a favour."

"Anything. Anything you need."

Dorlas clutched her hands together in her lap—probably, Gevira decided, to hide the increased trembling.

Gevira beckoned Itamar to come closer. "This is my son. Oh, that surprised you, didn't it? Yes, out of all this mess, I conceived and delivered a son, and now he's going to be king. What do you think of that?"

The old woman made no comment.

"You're going to make him a robe and matching cloak that's fit for a new king." Gevira sat back and waited with enjoyment for Dorlas's reaction.

The woman's shaking now reached the thin shoulders. "How would I get material to make this? Besides, see how shaky my hands have become? Life has not been easy."

"Spare me the story. I know you have ways and means." Gevira stood from the stool. "I'll be back tomorrow to see what you've been able to pull together."

She pushed Itamar from the hovel and turned to face Dorlas once more.

"I know you'll find what we need," he said. "The alternative would not be to your liking."

H

"Huldah… Huldah…"

Huldah rolled over in bed and threw her arm over her husband. He didn't stir.

"Huldah…Huldah…"

This time, her eyes opened and she propped herself up on one arm. Shallum remained still. Her feet slid over the edge of the bed and she sat up. The air in the room was cool, so she wrapped a night robe around her shoulders.

I must have been dreaming. Shallum hasn't moved. I'll sit here and wait; maybe God is speaking.

A shiver shook her shoulders and she drew the robe tighter. Moonlight filtered in through the partly opened shutters and bathed the room in a soft glow. She loved this room, which was filled with treasures from her childhood and possessions she and Shallum had collected.

As she waited, the outer wall in front of her appeared to crumble until she could see the area outside their bedroom window. With a whoosh and a hiss, the city street disappeared and the countryside slid by. Huldah watched with fascination as the road to Bozkath materialized. Soon the gates were visible—closed, for the day had not yet broken.

Huldah became aware that the eastern sky showed streaks of pale pink, heralding the new day. She remained seated on her bed in anticipation.

"Arise, Huldah. The time has come."

She needed no further command or explanation. *I've been awaiting God's direction, and this is it. Josiah must come to Jerusalem. I still see the dark shadow hovering in the background. There is danger for the new king. Someone else will try to claim the throne. But we'll be ready.*

She rose, dressed, and stepped into the countryside outside the closed gates of Bozkath. The first curve of the morning sun pushed above the horizon. With a shout and great clanking of chains, the gates swung open.

Huldah swept through the gates to the stares of the guards. She felt their eyes on her, but did not stop to explain her early entrance. Through the awakening streets she walked, until she stopped before the door to Adaiah's home.

A pleasant aroma drifted through the open door. Huldah hesitated on the threshold, until the door swung open and she was face to face with Adaiah.

"Huldah, you startled me." His hand went to his chest. "Come in, come in. You are a very welcome sight. We have been anxious for your return." He turned his face into the room behind him. "Good news, everyone, Huldah has returned."

Esther reached her first, carrying Yaacov. The baby was quickly settled into Huldah's arms and his face covered with kisses. He gurgled and snuggled into her shoulder.

"Oh my baby, how I have missed you," she said. "But you look big and healthy. I don't think you missed your mother at all."

The baby giggled at her words. She cuddled him under her arm and turned to embrace Esther.

"Huldah, I certainly have missed you," Esther said. "You bring news from home, I know. Sit by the fire and we'll soon have food ready for you to break your fast."

Her mother-in-law hustled her onto a low stool by the fire.

Jedidah approached, kneeling beside her. "I, too, have missed you. I'm frightened for your news, however, as I expect we'll be on our way to Jerusalem. I'm willing to do whatever you say needs to be done."

Jedidah rested her head in Huldah's lap until the sound of running feet and a young voice roused her.

"Huldah, Huldah." Josiah threw himself at her, hugging her closely. "You're back. Does that mean we'll soon be going to Jerusalem? I can't wait. Ehud and I are ready. We've been practicing every day. I've watched the road for you every day, too, and yet you surprised me. How did you get here so early? Did you walk? Did you come by yourself? Are we leaving today? Right now?"

When he stopped for another breath, his mother lifted him from the floor and laughed with him. "Josiah, let Huldah have a few minutes to catch her breath and eat. She'll tell us everything we need to know. Go get dressed and you'll hear everything."

H

Shallum struggled to sit up. Cool air spilled over his body from the open side of the room. At first his brain refused to believe what he saw: the wall of their bedroom had been replaced with a view of the Bozkath gates. Sleep faded as he saw Huldah standing before the vista. He watched with wonder as Huldah stepped from their room.

Thank you, Lord, for allowing me to be part of this vision, for this glimpse into Huldah's life. I know she'll be safe; she's in your hands.

As Shallum watched, Huldah entered the city and walked the distance to Adaiah's house. When he saw his own mother holding Yaacov, tears of joy wet Shallum's cheeks.

Oh Lord, keep them safe and bring them back to Jerusalem. There are hard times ahead and evil forces grasp for the throne. We are at their mercy. Lord, bring us peace.

H

Dorlas spread out the rich material before Gevira, who ran her hand over the soft fabric. It was fine linen, embroidered with gold threads in intricate designs. Birds, flowers, crowns… all had been devised by a clever hand. It was truly fit for a king.

The old woman's shaky hand reached for another fabric, this one even more intricate than the first. It was deep purple with gold and white designs. Together, the garments would make a stunning pair.

"White for the robe and turban, purple for the cloak," Dorlas said.

"What about sandals?" Gevira kept her amazement to herself. *If I let her know how pleased I am, she'll want more money. But wherever did she get these things?*

"Sandals? Of course I have sandals." Dorlas held up a pair of soft leather sandals of the finest workmanship.

"Then I am satisfied. When can you have them finished?"

"Bring the boy in today, and I'll begin."

Gevira left the hovel with her scarf wrapped around her lower face. She didn't want anyone to see the wide grin she was unable to control.

It's all falling into place. I shall be queen. If people thought Amon was cruel, they should just wait and see what I will do.

forty-two

"I'm worried. We're losing control." Joel laid both hands on the table and pushed himself back from the group.

"Rumours are running wild on the streets. I even heard today that Amon has been seen alive at the market." Jotham adjusted his turban and ran his hands down his beard. "What are we going to do? What's going to happen in Jerusalem?"

"Relax, both of you. The situation is well under control," Ethan said. "I happen to know that a prince will soon come forward to accept the crown."

Moshe raised his eyes at this remark. *I don't trust Ethan since Amon was killed. I must proceed cautiously.* "Are you referring to the king's son?"

"Well, a prince could only be a king's son, couldn't he?" Ethan's voice held more than a hint of sarcasm.

Moshe examined his fingernails absently. "Where did you hear this rumour?"

"Well, you know how it is. You just hear things. I can't remember where I heard it. I just know it's around on the streets." Ethan rubbed his hands together.

Moshe noticed his hands and thought he detected nervousness. *He knows more than he's saying. He needs to be watched.*

"But where is the king's son, Josiah? Isn't he the rightful heir?" Joel leaned toward the others. "Does anyone know what happened to him after he left the palace?"

"I heard he died along with his mother. Good riddance, I say." Ethan spit on the floor and wiped his mouth on his sleeve.

Jotham's face was wrinkled into a frown. "And what about the priests? Where are they?"

"This is foolish talk," Ethan said. He stumbled to his feet and glared at the others. "They're all gone and it's time for a new age. I, for one, plan to back the prince I heard about. Do what you like."

Ethan whipped his robe around him and swept from the room.

In the silence that followed, Moshe carefully observed the others. *I think I can trust them. What choice do I have?*

"I believe Josiah is still alive," Moshe said, studying their faces. "If you two are still with me, I suggest we find out what we can and try to bring him to the throne."

"I'd rather back you than Ethan," Joel said, rising from his chair. "You can count on my help."

"Then I'm in, too." Jotham joined the other two. "What do you want us to do?"

"Meet me at my place tonight," Moshe said. "I have some ideas. In the meantime, I'd like you to follow Ethan and find out what's he's up to. I don't think we can trust him."

They left the alcove outside the former king's rooms and went their separate ways until the coming of night.

H

Moshe paced across the living space of his home while he waited for Joel and Jotham to arrive. It had been a busy day. After leaving the others at the palace, he had roamed the streets and spoken to anyone who might know something.

Rumours are interesting. They seem to take on a life of their own and grow to massive proportions. But there has to be some truth in the midst of all the fantasy.

He paused at the partially closed shutters and scanned the street before his house. No sign of them yet. His pace slowed and he bent his head in thought.

The soldiers. What did they say? They have a better pulse on what's happening in the land. I like the idea that Jedidah returned to her home. Where was that? Yes, Bozkath.

He began to pace again when he heard movement at his door. He pulled it open swiftly and Joel and Jotham slipped into the darkened room. Moshe closed and bolted the door, then moved to the window and fastened the shutters.

"Sit," Moshe said, indicating the small table. "There's no one home and the doors and windows are bolted. But keep your voices down anyway."

He sat with them. In the dim light that came from a small oil lamp, he could just make out their faces.

"Tell me what you two were able to discover about Ethan," Moshe said to Joel. "What about the rumour he heard?"

"That's just the thing," Joel said. "We weren't able to find out anything.'

"Nothing? Didn't you follow him?"

Jotham shifted his weight on the low stool. "See, the problem is, we never saw him again. Once we left the palace, he disappeared."

"We asked the guards and anyone we could find," Joel added, "but no one knew where he was, or even which way he had gone."

"Well, that can't be helped at this point," Moshe said. "Did you hear any rumours around the city?"

Joel and Jotham glanced at each other. Moshe thought he detected a look of fear pass between them, but it was too dark to be sure.

"What we heard is frightening." Joel wiped his mouth and took a deep breath. "Lean closer, Moshe. This is important, and someone may be at the door or windows."

Moshe and Jotham both leaned in, until their three foreheads almost touched.

"It's rumoured that a temple prostitute had a baby eight years ago," Joel said. "She claims that it is Amon's son. We weren't able to find out her name, or the name of the child, just that it is possible they exist." He paused. "My guess is that's the prince Ethan is backing."

Moshe pressed his lips together, deep in thought. "It makes sense. We aren't naïve enough to think Josiah was the king's only son. Yes, his only lawful son, but there may be others with mothers wanting power and revenge. Ethan has powerful friends and is capable of pushing forward a potential heir, especially if it means gaining power. We'll need to watch him and find out everything we can. But let's set that aside for a moment."

"You've found out something, haven't you," Joel said.

"Not so much found out as figured out. I think I know where Josiah is."

Jotham's eyes flew wide open. "Now *that* would be good to know."

"I think Jedidah took him to her parents' home in Bozkath," Moshe said.

"Of course," Joel muttered. "Why hasn't anyone else figured it out yet?"

"Well, the king sent Ehud, and you remember that he disappeared."

Joel and Jotham nodded in the dim light.

"And somehow Huldah is involved in this," Moshe continued.

Joel nodded. "Remember how she keeps disappearing and then showing up at odd moments? She's probably getting him ready to be king."

"I need to find her." Moshe gritted his teeth. "I plan to go to Bozkath."

"You want us to come, too, don't you?" Joel asked, looking hopeful.

"No. I need both of you here to find out all you can about Ethan's plans. Check out these rumours. I feel sure there'll be more."

Moshe rose from his seat. "I'll leave quickly, and I'm guessing I'll find the prophetess. We'll need her help to get Josiah on the throne." He placed a hand on each of them. "Go, my friends, find out what you can, and I'll let you know as soon as I'm back in the city. Life is about to get very interesting."

forty-three

*E*hud trembled as he donned his soldier's uniform. He was pleased it still fit, but that wasn't surprising, as he and Josiah had been training every day. *March to the gate and back. March again. The child has relentless energy, but it's been worth it. We're ready, he and I.*

When he tied the last sandal into place, he left the house and waited in the garden. He sensed Huldah would find him there. Something in her eye had told him she wanted to talk to him.

His gaze drifted toward the road they would soon take toward Jerusalem, this time in victory. *Josiah will be king, and I'll be by his side. There's nowhere else I would want to be.*

"Ehud."

The sound of his name, spoken softly by Huldah's gentle voice, brought him back to the present. He turned and faced her, afraid of what she might say.

He bent low before her. "Huldah."

"May we sit down to talk?" Huldah indicated a stone bench nearby.

"Of course," he mumbled, leading the way to the bench. He waited until she was seated, then took his place beside her.

"Ehud, this is very hard for me to say."

He watched her eyes, unhappy with how they looked at him.

"Please, Huldah, just say it. I'm a soldier and can take orders."

She turned on the bench. "Do you remember the prophecy I made concerning you?"

He swallowed twice, then lifted his chin. "Yes, I remember. You said I would not see Jerusalem again, and yet here I am, ready to return." He stretched his lips in a thin smile which wasn't returned. He feared her solemn look.

"Ehud, the vision was true. I've seen it again. You will not see Jerusalem." She folded her hands in her lap and pressed her lips in a thin line. "I want to give you the opportunity to leave now, for any place you would like to go. None of us will hold it against you." She rested a hand on his arm. "Go, Ehud. It's the only chance you have for life."

He stood quickly and looked down at her. "Huldah, I appreciate what you're saying, but I will not leave Josiah." He threw back his shoulders and set his jaw. "A soldier doesn't leave his king, even though it means death. I willingly, gladly go with Josiah. If I die, that is only a soldier's duty." He bowed to her. "I will be honoured to die for him."

Huldah stood, wiping tears from her face. "That was beautifully said, Ehud. You make me proud to know you."

H

It was an interesting company that left Bozkath that morning—Josiah in front, carrying a small sword his grandfather had made for him; Ehud, in his soldier's uniform, tall and erect, with a military dagger in his belt; Huldah, with the babe in her arms, white robe blowing in the wind; Esther beside her, eyes downcast; and Jedidah and Johanna trailing.

It doesn't look like a kingly procession, Lord, Huldah thought, *but You know what You're doing. I'm Your humble servant, and I obey Your commands. Give me the grace and courage to carry them out to the conclusion You want.*

"Halt." Ehud stopped, his hand raised. The group gathered around him in silence. Josiah had eyes only for Ehud.

Huldah stepped up beside him. "What is it, Ehud?"

"Someone is approaching."

"I don't see anyone," Josiah said.

"I'm trained to see small movements and sounds. Something isn't quite right ahead of us." Ehud turned toward the group. "I want all of you to sit on the grass just off the road. I'm going up ahead to see what it is."

Jedidah took Yaacov in her arms and led Johanna and Esther to the side of the road, as instructed. Josiah and Huldah remained next to Ehud.

"I'm going with you, Ehud," Huldah said with authority.

Josiah looked up at them. "Me, too."

Huldah leaned down until her eyes were able to look into his. "Not this time, Josiah. You must obey Ehud. Please, no argument."

He nodded with eyes lowered, then took his place beside the others.

Ehud shaded his eyes with one hand, scanning the road ahead. Heat shimmered in the distance, making vision more difficult, especially at that distance.

Why, Lord, why can't I see if there is danger? Huldah thought.

The Lord's voice spoke to her: "My daughter, you receive vision when you need it."

Yes, Lord, I understand.

She moved closer to Ehud. "Can you see anything now?"

"Yes, over there, to the right, just beyond that big tree." Ehud pointed toward the tree in question. "I'm sure I saw movement there."

Huldah watched until her eyes ached. Just when she decided that Ehud was seeing things, a quick movement caught her eye. A stranger on the road.

"I see it, Ehud!" She lowered her hand and placed it on his arm. "What should we do?"

"The only thing we can do. We carry on."

"Would it help to find a hiding place until the stranger passes?" Huldah asked, though she already knew the answer.

"It's best to keep going. If we've seen him, he's seen us." Ehud looked to the others and beckoned them to come. When they were once again united on the road, he pulled them closer. "There is someone up ahead."

Johanna gasped, but Jedidah put her arm around her shoulder.

"The only thing we can do is to keep moving and be prepared for an encounter," Ehud said. "Don't be fearful. Huldah and I will face any danger that comes our way. Josiah, you must walk behind to protect your mother and the other women. Jedidah, please carry Yaacov and try to keep him from crying."

Although she could sense fear in the other women, Huldah was pleased with how they fell into place behind Ehud. She turned with Ehud to face the road before them, knowing not the dangers ahead.

H

"This looks ridiculous. I won't wear it." Itamar stamped his sandaled foot at his mother. His teeth were small, sharp, and discoloured, which only added to the sinister look of his embroidered outfit. The turban was too large and

281

covered his ears and forehead; the white and gold robe was glaringly out of place on his small body.

"It's fine, Itamar," Gevira scolded. "Dorlas will adjust the turban. With the purple robe, you'll look like a king."

When he began to whine, a sharp slap to the side of his head stopped the noise.

"I'll not have that," she said. "Stop now or there'll be more."

Itamar sniffled. He ground his teeth together and wrinkled his face into a hideous grimace.

With one more slap, Gevira moved across the room to where Dorlas stood with the robe over her arm.

Geriva scowled at her. "Fix the turban if you want your money."

"Yes, of course." The old woman's bland tone didn't fool Gevira, who could see that Dorlas was afraid. *And so she should be. If this doesn't go well, she's one person I can and will blame. But it must go well. I will be queen!*

Her son's shouting roused her.

"What's going on?" she demanded.

"She pricked me with a pin," Itamar said. His arms were folded and he spat on Dorlas. "I'll not stand for it."

"Stop it, both of you. There's no time for this foolishness."

At last the turban was adjusted, the purple robe in place, and Gevira led him outside the hovel to where Ethan was waiting to escort them through the streets of Jerusalem.

H

Ethan paced in the narrow alleyway in front of Dorlas's home. *Why did I ever agree to this? The mother is of the lower class, to be sure, and the son is worse. Nothing but a whiner and used to having his own way.*

He glanced at the hovel entrance when he heard Itamar's raised voice.

At least the child has some spirit. Under my direction, he might make a king. But the mother, she'll have to be disposed of.

Gevira's voice preceded her from the hovel. She emerged with Itamar, sullen and hideous, and held tightly by the shoulder. If he hadn't been pressed for time, Ethan would have laughed.

What a disastrous figure. I think we're going to need a side visit before we present him to my soldier friends.

He nodded curtly to Gevira. "Follow me."

"Not so fast, kingly advisor. I refuse to move until I know where you're taking us." Geriva released Itamar, who shrugged his shoulders, apparently in relief. She planted her feet firmly. Defiantly.

Ethan sighed. *She'll have to go sooner rather than later.*

He relaxed his face muscles into a taut smile. "Of course, Gevira, I was wrong. I should have told you what is to happen next. Come, walk with me, and I'll explain as we go."

He watched the play of emotions on her face. It seemed that power and greed fought for control. She grabbed Itamar again, and together they moved beside Ethan.

"Fine," she said. "We'll come, but only if you explain."

I thought greed would win. She desperately wants him on the throne. Right now, I'm her only hope.

"If we're to be successful, we must have the army behind us," Ethan said. "I have friends in high places who are willing to talk with us. If we can convince them that your son is the dead king's son, although baseborn, they will support him."

"Then are we going to see them now?" Geriva tightened her grip on Itamar, who was having trouble keeping pace with the adults.

"Very soon," Ethan said, slanting a furtive look at her. "First we must stop at a shop beside the palace. A friend there will look over his robes and make any necessary adjustments."

Gevira stopped abruptly. "What's wrong with his robes? I just promised a fortune for them. Look at them." She grabbed the cloak from his shoulders and thrust it in Ethan's face. "Where would you get more kingly material than this? Look at the sandals! The finest of leather."

"Gevira, Gevira, let's not quarrel." He used his smoothest tone, one he hoped would soothe her. He didn't need her insecurities to get in the way of his plan. "We only want the best for Itamar. You want him to look his finest when he meets the soldiers. Not that he doesn't look great now, but we want to make sure everything is perfect."

She stood completely still, then nodded. The cloak went back on Itamar's shoulders and the trio once again began to move.

When they slipped into the seamster's shop, Ethan breathed a sigh of relief. Old Noam shuffled out from behind a curtain and peered at them through partly closed eyes.

"Eh, eh, is it Ethan?"

Ethan stood before him, bent slightly to get on his level. "Yes, it is."

"Is this the lad?" Noam pointed a shaky finger toward Itamar.

"Come here, Itamar," Ethan instructed. Itamar obeyed without protest. He'd seemed to be in a stupor since leaving Dorlas's home.

"Tsk-tsk, what have we here?" Noam busied himself with the boy's clothes. He felt the material of the cloak, pulled the robe tighter around the waist, pulled the turban from his head, all the while tsk-tsking.

Through the man's mutterings, Ethan was able to discern the general meaning: "What a pity. Not right. Need to fix."

At last, Noam stepped away from Itamar and looked at the two adults. "There's work to be done, but it can be done quickly. Leave the boy with me."

Ethan saw that Gevira was about to protest, so he quickly gave his consent and hurried her from the shop.

She sputtered obscenities at him when they reached the street. He ignored her and propelled her toward the market. By the time they reached the first stall, she pounded her fists on his arms. Ethan pulled her behind a stall and turned to face her.

"Stop. Stop now." His face was tight, with narrowed eyes and clamped jaw. "We're both after the same thing here—to get Itamar accepted as king. You can't do it on your own. You need my help. Either you cooperate with me or I'll grab Itamar and do this on my own."

That seemed to get her attention. Her shoulders slumped and her hands dropped to her sides. "I'll cooperate. Just tell me what you're doing, and I'll go along with it. It's the not knowing that gets me stirred up."

He propelled her into the stream of shoppers who swarmed the stalls, seeking bargains. "We'll take a walk through the marketplace and then return to the shop. Noam has been around for many years and is very skilled with his needle. He's done work for the king and knows what is acceptable and desirable. No doubt, you'll be pleased with what he's able to accomplish is a short space of time."

When they re-entered the shop, Noam had just finished draping the cloak around Itamar. The change was startling. The boy's turban had been replaced with a thin band of silver and his robe and cloak were altered to such a degree that they actually looked good. Even the sandals had been adjusted.

Ethan heard a slight gasp from Gevira. He was surprised when she dropped to her knees before Itamar and touched her forehead to the floor. "My son, my king."

Itamar glanced at Ethan with a look of alarm on his face.

"Stand up, Gevira. Now is not the time," Ethan said.

While she stood and fussed over Itamar, Ethan slipped a small bag of coins into Noam's open hand.

forty-four

"We won't talk unless it's necessary," Ehud spoke quietly, keeping his eyes on the way before them. Huldah kept pace with him.

Although Ehud walked with his head lifted and shoulders back, his heart raced. *I can't let them know that I'm afraid. Well, not really afraid, just apprehensive. Why can't I forget what Huldah said? We're all going to die sometime, and she could be wrong, couldn't she?*

"Ehud, I think the traveller has quickened his pace." Huldah gripped his arm and slowed her walk.

"Yes, you're right. Do you see any others?" He shaded his eyes with one hand, squinting to bring the distance into focus.

"No, I only see one."

"Same here. Perhaps there is no threat."

They walked on until Ehud was able to determine more about the person who relentlessly moved toward them.

"Huldah," Ehud whispered. "I'm convinced it's Moshe!"

Huldah peered ahead. "Moshe? Are you sure?"

"Yes, I'm sure. What should we do?" Ehud turned toward her. His eyebrows had gathered together in a deep frown.

"Ehud, trust me, if it's Moshe, he means us no harm. I would sense any harm."

"Then we need to see what he wants." He motioned to the others that they were going to move faster.

Ehud could see Moshe clearly now. Huldah stepped in front of Ehud and put her hand out to stop the group. Moshe stopped before her and bowed low to the ground. He stood and faced her.

"Prophetess," Moshe said, "please know that I come as a friend and mean you and your companions no harm."

Huldah never took her eyes from Moshe's face. "Yes, I understand. You amaze me with your presence. Have you not blood on your hands?"

Ehud knew his mouth was hanging open. What did she mean by that?

"We all have blood on our hands, in one way or another," Moshe answered. "I'm not here to discuss that."

Huldah folded her arms. "Then why, Moshe, king's advisor, are you here?"

She's challenging him. What a brave woman.

"If I may be so bold, prophetess, I've come to offer my services to Josiah, our next king." Moshe inclined his head toward Josiah.

Huldah paused, as though considering his words. Ehud was puzzled as well.

"Why would you not wait until we arrived in Jerusalem?" Huldah asked.

"Because, noble prophetess, there is a pretender preparing to assume the kingship. It is not a good thing. Josiah needs to be king. Allow me to join your group and lead you into the city, in triumph."

She hesitated, and Ehud realized there was more going on here than Moshe had revealed.

There is evil afoot. I can smell it. What does Moshe really want? And who is this pretender to the crown? Something is wrong. Very wrong.

H

"And this is the child who is to become king?" The captain of the guard stood alert before Ethan, curling his lip in distain.

"Yes, yes. This is the next king," Ethan nodded toward Itamar, who slouched by his side with his lips pushed out and his eyes wide.

"A sorry excuse for a king, if you ask me."

Ethan shoved Itamar toward his mother, who so far had not spoken a word. Ethan had warned her but hadn't expected that she would follow his instructions.

Once the boy was out of earshot, Ethan moved closer to the captain. Twenty military men stood behind the captain; they had not yet moved or spoken, but Ethan was aware that they were paying close attention.

"Now you listen to me." Ethan poked him in the chest with a finger. "We agreed that I would find and prepare this baseborn son for the throne.

You agreed to back us and present him to the elders and the people. In exchange, I might add, for an unreasonable sum of money. Are you still in, or should I find someone who appreciates the money more than you?"

"Simmer down, Ethan, we're in. I'm just surprised to see someone who's so ill-prepared to assume the kingship. If I may say so, he does not have a kingly look."

Ethan drew himself to his full height. "I can guarantee he is the king's son, however unkingly he may look. And remember, I will be reigning until he is of age. I'll train him well, and with your backing, we should be able to have a king who does our bidding. Is that not important to you?"

"Yes, of course. What is our next step?"

The two heads bent together and rehearsed their plans. A cloud passed over the sun as they spoke, throwing their faces into shadow.

$\mathcal{H}$

Huldah motioned for Moshe to accompany her to the side of the road. They moved together, leaving the others to stand in the roadway.

"Moshe, I must know what has happened in Jerusalem. God could reveal the event, but I think He has sent you to tell me."

"Prophetess, circumstances are bad in Jerusalem. Gevira, one of the temple prostitutes, claims that her son is the child of Amon. It may very well be true, but he is a baseborn son and not the legal heir to the throne. Josiah is the legitimate heir and we must hurry before the other is crowned. If we are too late, Josiah will not only miss out on the kingship, but his life will be in danger."

Huldah lowered her eyes. *Lord, what am I missing here?*

"Who is backing this pretender to the throne?" she asked. "Gevira wouldn't be able to do this on her own."

"This is the hard part, prophetess. The backer is Ethan, another of King Amon's advisors."

"Ethan? Of course." Huldah very quickly saw through the evil plan. "He plans to rule in place of the young king."

"He has powerful friends who would be able to back him financially for a bit of influence." He punched his fist into his other hand. "We must get to Jerusalem before Ethan establishes Itamar as king."

"And how old is this child?" Huldah leaned in for his answer.

"He's eight, a couple of months older than Josiah. They will claim he is the rightful king."

"I see." She nodded. "Moshe, I appreciate your concern, but I can assure you that Josiah will be king. God has made that very clear to me. But you're right that we need to get to Jerusalem as quickly as possible. We may need to fight for the kingdom."

ℋ

The people of Jerusalem swarmed into the streets to hear the message being shouted by the small army of soldiers tramping through the streets. Heads turned and looks of disbelief crossed the faces of the people. Rumours circulated that Josiah was dead.

The tall soldier, Raviv, in the lead position stopped to talk to a large group of citizens gathered before the closed temple.

"Huldah, the so-called prophetess, spirited away our lawful king and has killed him," Raviv said. "We have it on good authority that this is true."

"He's dead. Are you sure?" A voice in the crowd was raised above the others.

Raviv turned toward the speaker. "Indeed, it is true. We've had word from one of former King Amon's advisors that the events of his death are known to the palace officials."

"What will we do now?" the same voice asked.

"We are fortunate that King Amon had another son."

The message flew through the crowd of watchers. "Another son? How can this be?"

"The lovely Gevira has a son of royal lineage," Raviv said in a loud, authoritative voice. "The boy is the son of the king."

"Gevira? The temple prostitute? This cannot be."

Raviv heard the murmuring and chose to maintain a calm voice. This was very important. The people had to believe this boy was a legitimate heir.

I must choose my words carefully.

"Ah, but you are misinformed. Gevira was Amon's legal wife." Raviv paused as the shouts from the crowd made further talk impossible.

"This cannot be true. We know who she is. We've seen her many times."

On and on the comments went until the people had run out of things to say. In the quiet after the storm of words, Raviv spoke again.

"People of Jerusalem, listen carefully to my words. I have here in my possession a scroll that proves Amon was joined to her in marriage." He raised the scroll and waved it before the people. "Legal documents do not lie. Itamar is the rightful king. Josiah, if he was still alive, which he isn't, would be the baseborn son."

The crowd started to disperse, shouting threats and whispering rumours. Raviv was well-pleased.

They don't believe yet, but I've planted the idea in their minds. Seeds of doubt have been sown and will grow into support for Itamar.

The other soldiers spread out and reported back to Raviv several hours later. Rumours were fierce, but the citizens accepted that Josiah was dead and had started to believe that Itamar was their only option.

Raviv smiled inside but didn't let it show on his face. *Money and power are within my grasp.*

H

Huldah walked side by side with Moshe. Ehud and Josiah were close behind, with the three women and Yaacov farther back.

Lord, something is not quite right.

The farther they walked, the more convinced Huldah became that Moshe was after more than seeing Josiah on the throne.

Is it that he wants to be the ruling power? Help me to be alert and careful. He will certainly bear watching. And I know he was part of the plot to kill Amon.

The road stretched out before them—long, hot, and difficult. When the sun was high overhead, they stopped along the side of the road to rest and eat. Jedidah's mother had packed food which they now shared with Moshe. They had unleavened bread, a jar of honey, olives in oil, and a skin of water which had warmed in the hot sun. But they were hungry and even this small lunch gave them renewed energy.

There was no shade, so they did not linger long. Yaacov fell asleep soon after they began their journey again, this time carried by Johanna. Huldah walked beside her for a few minutes, watching her baby. His dark, curly hair was damp with sweat, but his breathing was even and the flutter of his eyelids assured his mother that all was well with her son.

Several travellers passed them during the afternoon. Moshe stopped each one to ask for news from Jerusalem. The group was dismayed by the conflicting rumours they heard, none that were pleasant. One merchant had heard that the prophetess was responsible for the king's death, and that if she ever appeared in Jerusalem again, she would be hanged. The merchant seemed to be unaware that he spoke with the prophetess herself.

Lord, I know You're in charge and I trust fully in You. This is only a rumour. A cruel rumour, but only that. I will not be afraid. I will trust in You.

When the sun slipped toward the west, they approached the entrance to Asher's property.

"Stop here for a moment." Huldah turned to face the others and waited for them to join her. "I feel God is prompting me to turn in to Asher's home. The priests must be told of these rumours, if they haven't already heard."

When they neared the closed gates, voices greeted them from the other side. The gates swung open and Hilkiah slowly made his way toward her.

"Huldah, you are a welcome sight," Hilkiah said. "We've heard the rumours and have decided to return to Jerusalem. We shall happily go with you and face the people together."

After an exchange of news, the larger group moved toward the city. On the road once again, they came in view of the gates of Jerusalem. Ever on alert, Ehud was the first to see the contingent of soldiers marching out through the gates.

"Huldah, the time has come. You must walk behind me and allow Josiah to be in the lead." Ehud straightened his shoulders when the army came into sight. "If we must fight for entrance, we'll fight."

Huldah squeezed his arm and nodded before easing back and beckoning Josiah to walk beside Ehud.

Oh, Lord, the time has come. You have prepared us for this and we will not fear, nor will we be defeated. You will fight for us.

With no more warning, the soldiers broke into a run and the battle began.

forty-five

rumpet blasts from the palace walls startled the air, swelled over the
city streets, and invaded the hearts of the people. The crowds poured
into the streets, puzzled looks on faces, voices raised in troubled query.

"What does it mean?"

"The noise hasn't stopped. Could it be a signal?"

"Maybe they've found Josiah."

"More likely, they're planning to put the baseborn child on the throne."

"But is he legitimate?"

While they speculated, people crowded the streets, moving toward
the palace in a mass. Meanwhile, the trumpets continued their harsh blasts,
penetrating every corner of the city.

H

Ethan stood on the steps of the palace and watched the people gather. He
rubbed his hands together with evil delight as the people came.

Soon I'll be the reigning king! And then we'll see what shall happen. Amon's
work will continue, with more boldness, more courage, more ripping of the old ideas
from the hearts of the people and the streets of the city. Ha! I can taste the power. Long
live Itamar!

Ethan became aware of someone by his side. He turned and came face-
to-face with Raviv.

"You must be proud, Ethan, your plan is succeeding."

Ethan didn't miss the message. "Are you in or not, Raviv? I detect a note
of doubt in your voice. It's still not too late for me to find another captain."

"Of course I'm in, Ethan. I see the need for Itamar to be king. Keep
calm. I'll do whatever is necessary."

With a quick twist of his body, Raviv strode off to join a group of soldiers who had just emerged from the palace.

He will bear watching. I don't fully trust him, but what choice do I have? He's the most corrupt of the captains, which is good and bad.

He walked toward the gates, where the guards struggled to hold the people back. With shouts and curses, they demanded to know what the summons was about. By now, Ethan estimated, several hundred angry and excited citizens thronged just beyond the gates. It was only a matter of time before they breached the wall.

He watched, stunned, as rocks were hurled with deadly accuracy over the gate and into the weakening line of guards. When blood spurted from one of the guard's forehead, it seemed to incense the people and encourage further action. A steady stream of rocks flew over and several men were seen climbing the wall and dropping into the palace grounds. The remaining guards ran for their lives, but without success. They were trampled by the mass of people who now had opened the gates and rushed in.

Ethan fled in time and watched from inside the palace. The doors had been shut and barred, and it was unlikely the crowd would gain access. Those inside were safe for the moment, but something needed to happen to calm the crowd.

"Quick, get to the roof," Ethan said.

He grabbed two male servants he felt he could trust, and together they pounded up the stairs. The sight that greeted them as they cautiously looked over the low wall surrounding the roof was frightening. Swords had appeared and men were locked in combat with each other while women and children huddled against the walls. Wails, shouts, and cries combined into a fearful sound.

"I'm going to try to talk to them, if I can be heard," Ethan said to the other two. "Stay out of sight."

At the edge, he paused to survey the scene. This was not how he had envisioned his rise to power. While he stood and waited, someone in the crowd spotted him and the cry spread.

"There's Ethan! On the roof."

"Where?"

"Ethan, Ethan, Ethan. Dare to come down."

The others took up the chant. Ethan was too far up for hurled rocks to reach him, and he was calm. So calm that gradually the noise subsided and the mass stood, expectant eyes on him.

When he was sure he had their attention, he raised his hand.

"Citizens of Jerusalem, this is a momentous time in our history." He paused to make sure the crowd was with him. No one moved. "We have lost a great king, but he has left a legacy in his son. His son, his rightful heir, his son by his marriage to Gevira."

He paused again while a ripple of sound spread through the people. When they were quiet once more, he continued.

"Some of you have doubted that Amon was married to Gevira, but you have been told the truth. For many reasons, the marriage was kept quiet. The old king was opposed to it, but because of Amon's great love for her, he defied his father and quietly married her. Their offspring is the true, legal heir to the throne."

Murmurs passed from person to person. Ethan watched while they turned to each other with looks of consternation.

They're deciding whether to believe me. It was easy for them to dismiss what the soldiers said, but now they've heard from one who was a close friend to Amon and one of his advisors. How can they not believe?

He shivered, but with excitement. It ran through his body until his heart pounded and his face flushed warm with anticipation.

A shout from the crowd brought his attention back to the scene below.

"But he's only a child! Who will reign until he's of age?" Cheers met this question and the chants began anew. "Answers, answers, we want answers."

Ethan once more lifted his hand for silence. "By the wish of Amon, I will reign in his stead until the boy is of the age to take my place."

The crowd stilled into shocked silence until one man shouted. "Prove to us that you have the authority to do this."

Angry shouts accompanied his challenge.

"Quickly, leave the roof and find Raviv," Ethan said quietly to the servants. "Bring him to me with haste."

The two men scrambled to do his bidding.

Once again, the crowd resorted to violence. Blood flowed, women wailed, and children buried their heads in their mothers' robes. Over it all, the angry shouts of the men seeking justice mingled with the blood and horror.

H

"Onward, take the foe!"

A rush of bodies descended on the little group standing their ground in the dusty road. Flashes of sunlight glanced off raised swords while shouts of triumph mingled with terrified cries.

Ehud and Josiah stood in front, with Huldah close behind them. Huldah briefly closed her eyes.

Then this is it, Lord. Your chosen moment. Your will be done.

Josiah raised his sword, small protection against the king's army. It should have been his army, but evil had penetrated their hearts and minds.

When the soldiers reached them, Ehud stepped forward and ran his sword through the first soldier, who collapsed in a gush of blood. His companions shouted in rage. Four soldiers turned on Ehud and it was over for him almost before it had begun.

Josiah cried out and fell upon his friend's body, weeping bitter tears.

The size of the boy, the presence of the prophetess, and the horror on the faces of the priests seemed to rob the victory from the soldiers. The soldier in the lead lowered his sword and bowed his head. When he fell to the ground on one knee, the others quickly followed.

Huldah stepped forward, the light catching on her white robe, giving her the appearance of an angel. With both arms raised and a firm set to her jaw, she was a formidable presence. The priests gathered around her and placed their hands on her shoulders. Moshe hung back with the women.

She lowered her arms and stared at the soldiers. "Are you the king's army?"

The silence was complete. Not a movement or sound, not even a breath of wind stirred the air.

Her arms slowly lowered and she pointed a finger at the lead soldier. "Please rise."

The lead soldier struggled to his feet and stood before her with lowered head, hands at his sides.

"Answer my question. Are you the king's army?" Her voice held a hard edge.

"Yes." The reply was brief, but the voice was firm.

Without turning her head, Huldah said, "Josiah, please stand beside me."

Josiah looked up from where he still lay next to the dead body of his hero. Without comment, he stood and joined her. Huldah put her arm around him and drew him in front of her.

"If you are the king's army, here is your king. Josiah, take your place beside your loyal soldiers."

The child moved forward and once again the soldier fell to one knee, this time at Josiah's feet.

Josiah reached out and placed his hand on the man's shoulder. "Rise, my captain. We have work to do."

In a moment, the scene changed. Tears of relief and joy covered the faces of the priests, women, and soldiers. Only Josiah and Huldah remained dry-eyed.

Moshe chose this moment to appear and approached the new captain. "Will you lead us into Jerusalem and help us proclaim Josiah, the rightful heir?"

"Moshe, my lord, I did not expect to see you. Yes, we are prepared to lead Josiah to the throne."

The procession had swelled from the small group that left Bozkath. They were now led by an army, accompanied by the priests of the land, and one mighty prophetess who held the small hand of the salvation of Israel.

forty-six

*S*hadows gathered in the corners and behind the low wall of the palace roof. The outline of the palace stretched across the writhing mass of bodies below, seeming to incite them into a greater frenzy.

"I must say, you have managed to rile the people into a state of rebellion." Raviv spoke without a glance at his companion. His arms were folded over his firm chest, his shoulders rigid with military precision.

"You mistake their acceptance as rebellion."

"That's a good one, Ethan. We'll do well to control the violence, not to mention gaining acceptance from them." He shrugged his shoulders and continued to look over the scene below. "My men are now among them, and you'd better hope they can restore order."

Anger swelled in Ethan's chest. *Once I am king, Raviv is dead. Until then, I need him and his army of incompetent fools.*

"I believe it is their duty to restore order. That's why the king has an army. I'm running out of patience, Raviv." He forced his voice to an even tone. "What's happening now? Can you see your men?"

The two leaned as far over the wall as was safe and watched as the soldiers clubbed, struck, and slashed the people into death or silence.

Ethan turned to the two servants. "Bring Gevira and Itamar, and be quick about it."

They fled.

H

At the door to the roof, Itamar halted.

Gevira pushed on his back. "Go on, Itamar. Why did you stop?"

"I don't want to be king." The words were forced through clenched teeth. His voice trembled.

Another push, this time with more force, got him moving again, although slowly.

"What you want really has nothing to do with it." Gevira's voice was brittle and high. She gave one last shove and the boy emerged onto the roof.

Ethan turned and held out his hand to Itamar. "Come, take your rightful place beside me."

Gevira grabbed Itamar's shoulder and marched him to Ethan's side. A shiver ran the length of his body when he stood beside him. With dismay, he tried to still the agitation in his heart. Cold sweat coated his palms.

Why can't they understand? I'm just a little boy, not a king. Please let me go home.

He knew better than to say the words aloud. His mother would beat him.

"Come closer, so the people can see you." Ethan drew him to the edge, the would-be king dressed in his inappropriate robes.

The drop from the palace roof was greater than Itamar had imagined. He felt dizzy, but the dizziness soon turned to horror when he saw the violent scene. He gagged and put both hands over his mouth.

"Gevira, do something with this poor excuse for a boy!" Ethan called.

Itamar cringed, then took his hands from his face and straightened his shoulders. Ethan's words seemed to do something inside him. *I will not gag again. If I am to be king, I will do it.*

Someone in the crowd looked up and gave a great shout. "The boy is on the roof."

Heads turned and Itamar lifted his chin and faced them. The shouts increased until one voice gave a feeble cheer, which was taken up by the crowd until the air rang with their sound. Itamar saw soldiers among the crowd, swords drawn, faces fixed. But the crowd cheered on.

Are they really cheering for me? Am I really to be their king? I'm not ready for this, I don't even want to be king… but I will not cry. I will not run away.

"It's time to take your place before them," Ethan said to him. "Come, we'll descend and greet them on the palace steps. They need to be near you."

Ethan put his hand on Itamar's shoulder and led him to the stairs. The others quickly followed.

Itamar's last thought before he left the roof was that the hand on his shoulder burned against his skin, seeping into his shoulder until he wanted to cry out in pain.

H

"What is all that noise?" Moshe whispered into Huldah's ear. His heart raced.

"I'm seeing clearly now, Moshe. The noise is coming from the palace gates."

Her eyes were fixed straight ahead. Although she continued to walk with Josiah by her side, Moshe knew she wasn't with them in spirit.

He touched her shoulder. "What do you see?"

She turned her gaze on Moshe, reacting as though she was seeing him for the first time. She blinked twice. "Moshe, we will need to fight for the throne. I've seen Ethan on the roof of the palace with the baseborn child beside him. The crowd cheers, but I can see the presence of the soldiers forcing the cheers.

"So Ethan has part of the army with him, and we have part of it with us." Moshe ran his hand over his face. "What will happen, Huldah? What do you see now?"

"Don't worry, Moshe. We will win in the end." She turned her eyes back to the city, and the cheering rolled toward them in ever-increasing waves. "No more questions. You must trust me, and trust the God who has given me the vision."

She stepped away from him and headed to the front of the line of soldiers until she was in the lead. Moshe watched her go before slipping in beside the women.

What if she's wrong? What does God care about us? I've seen no evidence of Him. If she's right and Josiah becomes king, I'll need to be clever to become the ruler in his place. Huldah must go. Amon knew that, but couldn't catch her. I've always been more astute, more competent that he ever was. I'm shrewd where he was just cruel. I'll succeed where he failed.

H

"Itamar, Itamar, Itamar. We want Itamar." The chants hit Ethan when they reached the palace steps. The servants had opened the huge doors and Ethan and Itamar emerged from the palace.

Ethan's heart swelled when he faced the masses. *I've done it. I've made him king. No longer will I be under Moshe's thumb. If he shows his face, that will be his last act. He can go to the demons, for all I care. They deserve him.*

His head moved from side to side, surveying the crowd. By now darkness had fallen on the land and the soldiers had lit torches. In their flickering light, the faces of the people seemed to shrink and swell in a macabre dance; their mouths opened, their bodies swayed, their arms waved. Ethan and Itamar stood silent as they watched the writhing bodies.

"Off to the right, can you see a light advancing?" Raviv asked.

Ethan swung his head in that direction, his eyes squinting into the darkness. What he saw caused his knees to weaken.

H

The gates to the city were wide open. Torchlight glanced off the walls and drawn swords.

"Who approaches?" A tall guard separated himself from his companions and blocked their entrance.

Huldah's robe glowed with unearthly light. Long hair streamed from her scarf, framing her face. Upon sight of her, the guard fell back with eyes wide and mouth open.

"I am Huldah and I present your king, to take his rightful place on the throne." Her voice had the quality of a trumpet blast.

The guards all raised their eyes. When they beheld the soldiers and Moshe, who had stepped up to stand beside the army, they moved closer.

The tall guard bowed to her. "Prophetess, we did not realize it was you. We were told you had slain the prince and had yourself died." He swallowed and took a deep breath. "You must hurry. Make all speed to the palace. One of the former king's advisors has brought forth an imposter to assume the kingship. The people are being forced into accepting him. You must hurry."

Moshe put his hand on the guard's arm. "Is it Ethan?"

All the guards nodded their agreement.

"Are Joel and Jotham with him?" Moshe stared intently at them, almost threateningly.

"We have heard no word of any others," the guard said. "Except, of course, for a portion of the army."

The new captain stepped in front of Huldah, making his presence known. "Who is leading the army?"

"I've heard it is Raviv."

"The traitor! He will pay for this." The captain turned to his soldiers. "Come, we must make haste."

The guards joined the growing group. With Huldah in the lead, and Josiah by her side, they entered the city.

H

Ethan clutched his chest when he saw the glow from the direction of the city gates. He knew there could only be one source for that unearthly glow. He had seen it before and the results had been disastrous.

"Huldah." The word came out in a strangled whisper. "I thought she was dead."

Raviv shaded his eyes. "Well, if she was, she isn't now."

The light grew closer and brighter until its yellow haze hung low on the horizon. Ethan could see that she was not alone.

She has soldiers with her. How can that be? Raviv sent a squad to the gates to ensure no one would enter and interfere with our plans. But I'm sure there are soldiers with her; I can see the light reflecting off their swords.

He glanced back at the crowd, who by now had turned toward the light. He sensed restlessness in them, but felt sure they didn't yet know what was happening. The soldiers in the crowd gathered with heads bent in what appeared to be whispered conversations.

Ethan turned back to the light and at that moment realized that Raviv had left his side. Raviv's tall form appeared amidst the crowd, moving toward his fellow soldiers grouped by the wall. When he reached them, he began to gesture.

He's giving them orders. We can still win. Once the soldiers with Huldah realize Raviv is on my side, they won't be long in this world. Huldah will be defeated.

He felt a surge of joy and allowed his lips to stretch in a grim smile.

We'll defeat her and put Itamar on the throne, all in the same evening. The fates are with me tonight. Yes! Yes, I'll be the reigning ruler in Jerusalem.

He gave a shout of joy, which turned the heads of the crowd back to him. He seized the moment by stepping forward, Itamar by his side.

"It's time, people of Jerusalem." Ethan swung his arms high. "It's time to crown a new king."

Dismay covered his face when he watched the heads turn back to the light.

"People, content yourself with your new king. Ignore the distractions. See your king!" With a thrust of his hand, he pushed Itamar to the front of the top step. "Here is your king."

He was unprepared for the response to his plea. Loud voices raised in protest. The people hurled shouts of derision at him.

"Liar! Thief!"

"Deceiver!"

"Treacherous fool!"

An angry group of men headed for the steps. Ethan bounded back to the doors and rushed through them, clanging them shut behind him. He stood in the hall, panting and clutching his chest.

This can't be happening. The soldiers will soon deal with Huldah and we'll get Itamar on the throne.

"Itamar? Where is Itamar?" Ethan looked around wildly, but Itamar was nowhere to be seen. He grabbed the nearest doorkeeper and demanded to know where he was.

"Begging your pardon," the doorkeeper said, "but he did not come through the door with you."

"He's outside?" Ethan's mouth hung open in disbelief. He pulled at his hair and beard, desperation in his face. "Then get him. Get him!"

Angry shouts and hands pounding on the door seeped into his brain.

"He's out there," he said to himself. "My way to the kingdom is out there, in that angry mob." A handful of hair came out. "I'm done for. It's over."

Ethan collapsed in a heap, the noise and light fading together until he knew no more.

H

Outside, the noise grew to a wild crescendo. As the angry mob stormed the steps, Gevira stepped forward, grabbed her son, and disappeared into the crowd. She snatched the silver band from his head, dropped it to the ground, and wrapped her shawl around him.

No one will recognize me. Without his fancy robes, he's just a normal little boy.

She heard him crying, but she was used to ignoring his outbursts. She elbowed her way clear of the mob and slipped into a deserted alley.

I'll sort it out later. Right now, I must find safety. Where can I go? I can't go home, and I can't go to my father's hovel, not that he would take me in.

Whether it was divine intervention or a brilliant idea, she would never know, but Huldah came to her mind. Perhaps Itamar would be safe in her home.

Gevira slowed her pace in the dark alley, trying to think of where to go. Huldah's name would not leave her mind.

When they reached the end of the alley, it opened onto a main street, but no one was in sight. With a firm hand on her son's shoulder, she led him away from the palace. Itamar's sobs had subsided to a soft whimper.

They walked through the quiet streets until she realized she had entered the Second District. Would she dare go to Huldah's home? Her options were limited.

Deep resolve spread through her. It was a physical sensation, something she could feel pour through her body, though she knew not where it came from.

I'll do it. Yes, I'll do it. The worst they can do is turn me away.

The house loomed before her. From inside, light spilled onto the street, as though in invitation. Itamar had stopped whimpering; not a word had he spoken since they'd left the palace. She was oblivious to him as she stared at the closed door. The light from the window encouraged her.

With a deep breath, she stepped forward and knocked, softly at first, and then with vigour. *I have nothing to lose. Nothing at all. God, if You are real, open this door for me.*

The door swung open and she looked into the kindest eyes she had ever encountered. It was too much; kindness seldom came her way, and she responded with tears—jerking, wrenching, scalding tears. Her hands came to her eyes as Tikvah reached out and gently pulled her into the house. Itamar followed.

The older man led her to a seat beside the fire and eased her down, all the while speaking in a quiet voice.

"You don't know who I am, or you wouldn't let me in." Her words stumbled out between the gasping sobs. "You wouldn't be so kind."

He knelt in front of her and removed her hands from her face. "It doesn't matter who you are. You are in need and I'll help in any way I can."

Her story poured out. Tikvah's eyes widened at parts, but he didn't interrupt her.

When she finished, he put his hand on her shoulder. "Gevira, I want to leave you for a minute and bring my son in. I'll be right back. I think I can help you."

When he left, she wiped her eyes on a cloth she pulled from beneath her robe. Itamar had squeezed in beside her and now slipped his hand into hers.

"Mother, I know I'm a useless son, but you're all I have. I'd like to hug you."

The words penetrated deep into her heart. "Oh Itamar, what have I done to you? You deserve more than what you've ever gotten from me. But you're right. We only have each other now, and yes, I would like a hug."

When he wrapped his child arms around her, something broke in her heart and her tears flowed once more. This time, they were refreshing and healing.

The two were still wrapped in a tight hug when Tikvah and Shallum entered the room.

"Gevira, I've told Shallum your story," Tikvah said. "He has agreed to help you."

Her thin lips spread in a seldom-seem smile. "All I can say is thank you. That doesn't seem enough, but it's all I have right now."

"It's more than enough," Shallum said, returning the smile.

Tikvah stepped forward and handed her a tray with water and bread. "Shallum and I must go to the palace and help where we can. Our wives are in danger, though they are in God's care. Please, eat and rest while we're gone."

Tikvah put the tray down and motioned for Itamar to help himself.

"When we return, we'll make plans for the future," Tikvah said. "For now, you'll be safe here."

When the men left, Gevira leaned back and closed her eyes. Itamar snuggled beside her.

Maybe there is a God. Today has been incredibly awful… and now incredibly good. I feel like I've come home.

forty-seven

$\mathcal{T}$ime held its breath, hovering over the rushing armies, headed for destruction. To Huldah's ears, the silence was profound, unexpected—an eerie tableau of evil unfolding before her.

She headed to the knoll off to her left, Josiah's hand firmly clasped in hers. The other women slipped in beside her, and they huddled together as the scene released its evil.

"Jedidah, take Josiah and the women," Huldah said, indicating behind her. "Move down behind that grove of trees. I'll come back for you when this is over."

"Oh Huldah, I'm so afraid. I can't do this." Jedidah's voice quavered. Fear glistened in her eyes.

"Jedidah, you must." Huldah thrust Josiah's hand into hers and gave her a gentle push. Huldah watched as Jedidah straightened her shoulders, moved toward the other women, and led them away from the battle.

The silence was shattered when the two opposing armies drew near each other. Shouts of anger and defiance mingled with the clash of swords. The battle commenced, and blood flowed. The cries of anger soon changed to cries of agony as men fell, wounded and beaten.

From Huldah's position, it was impossible to tell which side had the advantage. She gazed steadily at the height of the battle, hands at her sides, a look of grief and acceptance on her face.

Lord God, I know You are fulfilling Your plans for the peace of Israel. I don't understand, but I trust You and know that You will bring out of this Your perfect will.

The battle was fierce and brutal. Clangs of swords, shouts of victory, and cries of despair rung in the air until the way was strewn with bodies.

How long, oh Lord? I'm listening for Your voice, for your direction in the part I am to play. I'm ready, Lord, I'm ready.

A tremble deep in the earth shook her. "Now, my child," she heard the Lord's voice say. "Now you must do your part. I am with you."

The words rang in her ears and her feet began to move toward the battle. She was aware of the light encompassing her, lighting her way, and making her visible to those below.

She paused and lifted her arms high.

"Enough!" Her voice reverberated over the heads of those engaged in the fight. "Enough! Cease!"

Swords dropped to the ground and soldiers stumbled to regain their balance. As one, they turned to her.

"Today, God has spoken. He has seen the treachery devised by man and has exacted His punishment. The battle is over. I am Huldah, the prophetess of the Lord. These words are not mine, but God's words to you. He is tired of your disobedience, tired of your unbelief, tired of your evil ways. He will tolerate you no longer."

A range of emotions crossed the faces of the soldiers. She saw disbelief and rebellion, but on some she read acknowledgement and acceptance.

"It is time to bow before your God and turn your hearts to him," Huldah declared. "As a nation, we have sinned."

Restlessness broke out in the crowd, which had now swelled to include the multitude from the palace gates. A lone soldier began his solitary walk to the place where Huldah stood. When he approached, he fell face-down before her, weeping.

It was only the beginning. The floodgates opened. People fell to their knees.

"This has been a vile day in the city of Jerusalem," Huldah continued. "An imposter has almost claimed the throne because of the deceit of a greedy man. The army has been divided, and many have been slain because of your disobedience. God has been forgotten in the land for many long years. An evil king has been given to the flames for turning away from his heritage. But there is hope. God has not forgotten you."

She paused while the crowd continued its lament, voices raised in agony. While they wept, she motioned for Jedidah to bring Josiah. Jedidah had gained control of herself and walked toward Huldah with her head held high, leading an expectant child.

Josiah's face shone with goodness and acceptance of what God had in store for him.

Jedidah stopped a distance behind Huldah and let Josiah walk alone to take his place by her side. He was dressed simply, but his head was held high. The face of a king looked out at the repentant people.

"The time for tears is over." Huldah's voice again penetrated the discordant din. Her hands lowered to her sides and the lamentation settled.

All eyes turned to her. She reached out and settled her arm around Josiah's shoulders, drawing him close.

"Here is your king! Here is Josiah, the true son of Amon, kept safe for you until the moment was right."

Huldah took Josiah's hands in hers and raised them above his head. She moved behind him so he could be seen against the backdrop of her glowing robes.

The lamentations turned to songs of praise and they welcomed their future king. Cheer after cheer rippled through the people until the earth shook with their celebration.

From the rear of the crowd, Moshe led the priests in a single file to stand on either side of Josiah and Huldah. When they faced the people, the crowd let out a collective gasp; they had been told that the priests were dead, or that they had deserted them.

One by one, the people who had strayed far from God bent their knees and touched their faces to the ground before their rightful king, and before their long-neglected God. Tears streamed down faces, mingling with the dirt.

The sky over Jerusalem took on a golden hue that spread from horizon to horizon, a sign of God's blessing on their nation. Huldah lifted her eyes and hands to the heavens in worship of the Almighty God who had restored His kingdom.

Other books by Sharon Dow:

Antipas: Martyr

Young Antipas is steeped in the religion of Zeus but his belief that there must be more to life finds him rejected and driven away from his own family and home.

Antipas finds a new friend in Epaphras, who teaches him about Christ. Laying his life on the line, he grapples with the forces of good and evil in an epic battle for his soul.

Pergamum: Satan's Throne

With the Roman Emperor's grip tightening, evil forces behind the scenes aim to root out the growing followers of *The Way* and destroy the Church. In this sequel to *Antipas: Martyr*, Sharon Dow continues the vibrant story of persecuted Christians banding together within the sinister walls of Pergamum, the very lair of Satan.

www.ingramcontent.com/pod-product-compliance
Lightning Source LLC
Chambersburg PA
CBHW071841020726
47502CB00003B/564